Adam watched the dancers and couldn't remember how long it had been since he'd held a woman in his arms in a rhythmic embrace. He wanted that, this moment, with Sydney. He almost knew how she would fit against him. He gave her a bold stare. "Dance with me, Sydney?" His voice was as gentle as a caress.

Sydney had noticed the intensity with which he'd watched the swaying couples. She wondered if he had sad memories of a lost love and her heart felt tenderness for him. How could she tell him that she was here for him? That she longed to be in his arms, to comfort him—and for him to comfort her? At that moment, the pianist riffed through the first strains of a tune that Sydney recognized instantly, a song that had always tugged at her heart. When the vocalist sang the first line of Whitney Houston's "Run to You," Sydney gasped.

"Sydney?" His voice was an insistent whisper as he held out his hand.

"Yes," Sydney murmured. She put her hand in his big palm and allowed him to lead her onto the dance floor. In a second she was where she'd wished to be.

BOOK YOUR PLACE ON OUR WEBSITE AND MAKE THE ARABESQUE ROMANCE CONNECTION!

We've created a customized website just for our very special Arabesque readers, where you can get the inside scoop on everything that's going on with Arabesque romance novels.

When you come online, you'll have the exciting opportunity to:

- View covers of upcoming books
- Learn about our future publishing schedule (listed by publication month and author)
- Find out when your favorite authors will be visiting a city near you.
- Search for and order backlist books from our line catalog
- Check out author bios and background information
- Send e-mail to your favorite authors
- Join us in weekly chats with authors, readers and other guests
- Get writing guidelines
- AND MUCH MORE!

Visit our website at
http://www.arabesquebooks.com

To Cheryl, Evelyn, Linda, Maryam and Vicki.
Thanks for the memories.

ACKNOWLEDGMENTS

I want to thank Maria and Rochelle for my delightful armchair travel experience to various cities in Italy. The descriptions were so vivid, it was the next best thing to being there. Maria, La Signora, came alive. And Jacqueline, speaking with me and giving me an inside look into the world of wines and vineyards, was a treat. Any mistakes you may see are all mine. Thanks a bunch. To my editor, Karen Thomas, who is wise, has a keen eye and is a pleasure to work with. Keep the smile in your voice.

PROLOGUE

South Carolina

At two in the morning Adam Stone picked up the phone on the first ring, as a band of cold steel clamped around his chest. He'd barely said "hello" when his worst fears were realized with the hiss in his ear.

"I ... did it ... this ... time, man ..."

"Owen! Where are you?"

Adam's feet hit the floor and before the next words spilled from his friend's mouth, his pants were on. "Owen, are you home?" Adam barked. He swore as he pulled on a T-shirt and slipped his bare feet into leather loafers.

"Adam, didn't want it ... this ... way ..."

"Owen, are you in your apartment? Answer me, dammit!"

"Home ... Adam ..."

Cursing, Adam slammed down the phone and was out his front door, cellular phone in hand. By the time he raced to the curb and unlocked the car door, he was giving the address to the 911 operator, warning of a possible drug overdose. Fifteen minutes later, Adam was unlocking the door to his friend Owen Jeffries' apartment, praying that he was not too late.

"Owen?" Adam shouted, starting to race to the bedroom, but stopped when he saw him, sprawled, almost spread-eagle on the armchair. The phone had dropped to the floor. His legs were outstretched, his bare heels digging into the floor, as if he had tried to anchor himself to keep from sliding out of the chair. His head was thrown back and he lay unmoving.

Adam touched the pulse point in his friend's neck. The faint throb almost gave him hope that this was just another episode. But, in the military, Adam had seen death sitting on the face of too many men to give himself false hope. The grim reaper would claim his prize before another dawn. Adam eased Owen's body to the floor. He sat down beside him, cradling his head in his lap and waited. Owen opened his eyes and the two men stared at each other.

Owen tried to smile but couldn't manage, so he closed his eyes his lips twitching willfully.

Adam's dark eyes blackened with anger. "You've killed yourself!"

With a summoned strength, Owen opened his eyes, trying in vain to shake his head. *"They . . .* killed . . . me." He fell unconscious.

Adam moved to revive his friend, even as he heard the hurrying clatter of the emergency crew as they bounded up the stairs to the second-floor apartment.

Adam was sitting in the shadows of the hospital room watching and listening to the sounds of a life ebbing away. How ironic, he thought. On the eve of the Fourth of July, Independence Day, one poor soul was leaving this earth. *Dependent, no more.* He looked at the figure of a man once tall and proud, now shrunken and weak. He stared at the face, once, the rich rugged brown of a mighty oak tree, now, an ashen gray. What the man once was and now is, caused a new wave of anger to ripple through Adam. Had it really only been two years? he asked himself. Only two years since the nightmare began that was claiming his best friend's life? Two years since Owen gave up on life, filling his body with alcohol until the craving consumed and ate up his insides.

A once proud marine had sold his soul to the bottle, seeking peace in the depths of the amber-colored whiskey. After a while, color preference wasn't an option; as long as the sting and the resulting numbness was the same. And sometimes, popping a little stimulant and washing it down with deep swigs made for mighty fine feelings.

Adam swore, cursing Owen for not being strong. He cursed the weakness in any man or woman who would succumb to the false promises offered by the tantalizing liquid.

A soft sound caused Adam to look toward the bed. He remained in the chair, but watched the figure with a new intensity. Finally, Adam closed his eyes as he sought to quell the burning in his throat. The soft sigh had been Owen's last breath from his slackened mouth.

Adam opened his eyes just as a nurse rustled in and hurried to the bed. After a moment she turned to Adam.

"Sergeant, he's gone."

Adam didn't answer, but turned his head toward the window. A sliver of natural light was trying to slip inside between the mini aluminum slats of the window blinds. Adam's lips parted slightly. He had been right.

Death had claimed his prize before dawn.

CHAPTER ONE

New York, five years later

Sydney Cox hugged her knees as she sat on the lush green lawn relaxing against a great oak tree. She looked toward the sky and inhaled deeply. The constant sea breeze that blew across the North Fork, Long Island, vineyard, was welcomed. The stifling heat on the July afternoon showed no letup from the heat wave that had ensconced itself in the Northeast for the last two weeks. Looking around at the peaceful scene on the grounds of Francesca Vineyards, Sydney couldn't remember a time she had come here and hadn't felt at peace. Tourists had completed the tour of the cellars, had done some wine tasting and now sat around the grounds picnicking and enjoying their newly purchased bottles of wine. As she watched the strangers, she thought of how thirteen years ago she'd been a stranger, walking about, amazed at the fantastic grounds. Then, she had been nineteen when her friend Ferne Percival had convinced Sydney to take a summer job at her family's vineyard. It would be right in keeping with her cultural anthropology studies, Ferne had reasoned. She'd be crazy not to take advantage of the hands-on experience of studying an Italian-American family by living and working with them for eight weeks. When Ferne had reminded her of a field trip paper due the first month in the new term, Sydney had wasted no time in accepting the offer. Now, at thirty-two, Sydney believed that that decision had shaped the rest of her life. Unsuspecting, she would never have dreamed that she would give up her teaching career to live her life in the fascinating world of wines.

There were no regrets, Sydney thought as she shifted her position against the unyielding oak. After five years of teaching anthropology to New York City Community college students, she'd left to manage the fine wine shop owned by the Percival family. Five years later, only three months ago, she left *Amalia Fine Wines*. She was now the sommelier at the Restaurant Louise in Manhattan. A tiny smile parted her lips. Who knew that when an eighteen-year-old African-American student met an eighteen-year-old Italian-American student that their lives would become entwined? It all seemed such a long time ago. Vaguely, Sydney wondered what her sister, Karen, would think of this latest career move.

Alone, since the death of their mother only months before Sydney entered college, the two sisters had never been close. Their father had died years earlier. Karen, who was eight years her senior, had always left Sydney to herself as a child. Sydney was used to being alone and entertaining herself.

Born and raised in Brooklyn, when Sydney had accepted the academic scholarship to far off Sonoma University in California, her sister had scoffed at her. Sydney, who was reserved and almost shy, was told that she wasn't the California type and would transfer out the first year. Sydney had wondered what a California type was. But the climate apparently had worked wonders for shy and retiring types Sydney thought. To her amazement she had blossomed, losing her shy ways, leading class discussions and voicing her opinion. When Karen, a career soldier stationed in Hawaii, had seen her at her graduation, she had been amazed at the change in her younger sister: a summa cum laude graduate. Sydney had been proud to see the respect and admiration in Karen's eyes. That had been when she was twenty-two.

But, Sydney thought, her eyes sweeping the expansive green acres, her love affair with wines had started even before the summer she'd lived here with Ferne and her family. It had started in Sonoma, California, when Sydney had visited Casanova Cellars, the winery owned by Ferne's uncle and aunt.

"Still your favorite getaway place, huh? Where are your dreams taking you now, Sydney?"

The deep baritone voice startled her, and she looked up, squinting at the older man. Edward Percival sat down beside her, stretching out his jeans-clad legs as he rested against the tree.

"Still the best, Edward," Sydney answered. It had taken her a couple of years to get used to using his and his wife's first names, but they had insisted once she'd come to work for them. But "Hannah" and "Edward" still sounded odd rolling off her tongue.

"I was thinking about Julian and Anna and the first time we met . It's hard to believe I was only eighteen. That first weekend that Ferne took me there and we toured the vineyard, I thought I was walking through one of those old movies that my mother loved so much."

Edward Percival smiled. "I remember," he said. "After you and . . . and Ferne left, Julian called me. He asked me whether he was supposed to show you the business as well as . . . Ferne."

Sydney noticed how he faltered over his daughter's name and she became somber. Then, angry. How such a compassionate and intelligent man could charm so many others yet make an enemy of his daughter was beyond Sydney's comprehension. It saddened Sydney to see both her friends—father and daughter—hurting, but neither would take the first step in trying to heal the breach between them. No matter how much Hannah Percival called her husband pigheaded and her daughter, stubborn, neither would give in to the other. Sydney chose to stay out of the family argument and when she'd stopped calling the family once Ferne left New York, they wouldn't hear of her dropping out of their lives, just like that. She remembered Edward and Hannah driving into the city to talk to her. No matter what, she would always be dear to them, they'd said. She started at Edward's voice.

"So, how are things at the restaurant? You like it?" He cleared his voice.

Sydney guessed that he did not want her to mention his daughter, so she followed his lead in changing the subject. "I love it. It seems this is what I want." She sighed. "But it certainly keeps me busy."

"That's what I hear, young lady. In three months, this is the first real day that you've taken off to relax." His look matched his stern fatherly tone. "No one expects you to be a super-woman, Sydney. When I recommended you for the job, I knew you could do it and the owner knew I'd never send him a screwup. So lighten up." He grinned, and stood up, pulling her with him. "When do you find time to go courtin'? Don't tell me you're one of these modern day ladies who thinks nothing but career. You and your beautiful friend must be breaking a lotta hearts out there."

They started walking across the lawn toward the family quarters, a huge brick house behind the cellars.

"She called. That's why I disturbed your daydream," Edward said.

"Reva?" Sydney frowned. What was wrong, now, she asked herself.

"Yeah, she wants a callback. Sounded pretty excited. Might be her big break. Better call her back, before you head out for the city." He grinned, showing the smile that endeared him to his many friends.

Sydney looked at the good-looking man with the bright brown eyes. He was not quite five-eleven and was stockily built with the strong arms and thick chest of a man at least fifteen years his junior. In his late fifties, Edward Percival's hair had turned completely white. There was no indication that it had been the rich dark brown that matched his daughter's.

"She didn't say anything was wrong?" Sydney asked as she stared into his twinkling eyes. He thought Reva was playacting her way through life, never taking anything seriously.

"Nope," Edward answered. "Just wants you to call." He

glanced at his watch as they stood outside of the front door of the big house. "It's almost three and Charlie'll be needing some help in clearing the cellars. Don't want any visitors getting locked up overnight. Oh, almost forgot, Anne Durant called, sounding more anxious than Reva. Call her before you leave." He bent and kissed Sydney's cheek then gave her a stern look. "Stop making the time between visits so long. You know you don't need F ... you know you're one of the family. Come whenever you please." He coughed, then sniffed, as he looked at the pretty young woman. "And remember what an old man once told you. Don't go keeping yourself to yourself. Nothin' makes a hard heart like spending your life alone, Sydney."

Sydney watched him go, as his words stirred a dim memory. But she hurried inside to the phone, wondering what the new manager of *Amalia Fine Wines,* wanted. Anne was handpicked by Edward, and from what she'd heard, was an excellent replacement for Sydney.

When Sydney reached Anne, she listened to the frantic woman and moments later, Sydney hung up the phone, her heart racing, as she ran in search of Hannah. She had to get to the shop, fast, and if she rushed, she'd make the train leaving North Fork in the next twenty minutes. It was only while Hannah was speeding to the railroad station, that Sydney thought about Reva. Her crisis can't be as important as Anne's she thought. Her friend would have to wait until Sydney could call her while she was on the train. She patted her pocket, breathing thanks she'd not forgotten the lifesaver. During the two-hour ride, she prayed that she would also be able to rectify her own mistake ... which was causing stress for Anne ... and might possibly damage the reputation of the shop. Once on the train, Sydney started making her calls ... and prayed.

"Five," Sydney muttered. She continued her thoughts in silence as she prepared to lock the door of *Amalia Fine Wines* where she'd been alone for hours. The blessed solitude had been a gift, for she'd needed the quiet time to fix the embarrassing mistake she'd made three months ago. Dropping the key in her jacket pocket, making a mental note to return it to Anne, Sydney walked down Lexington Avenue toward Fifty-first Street.

The dramas of her life apparently happened in fives, Sydney thought as she hurried along, remembering her earlier daydreams. Five years after graduation, she'd made a major career change. Five years later, she'd made another momentous decision. A tiny smile touched her lips as she wondered what the next five years would bring. Then, she'd be thirty-seven and she couldn't imagine what new adventure she would be embarking on. Whatever it was, she was almost certain she'd still be a solo act. She stopped that vein of thinking, immediately. No sense in belaboring for the zillionth time why she was still single. And she wouldn't feed into Edward's fear of her living the rest of her life alone. Similar words were uttered many years ago by a friend, long deceased. Sydney shrugged off what was fast becoming a bluesy mood and hurried along the quiet street. Although the heat of the day carried into the night, there was a welcoming breeze rifling her thick, dark brown, wavy hair as she walked briskly. It was after eleven o'clock and the avenue was not nearly as crowded as she'd hoped it would be. Though she knew the neighborhood and felt non-threatened most times, still, one could never be too cautious on the sometimes mean streets.

Watchful of her surroundings, she quickened her pace, thinking about her mad dash from North Fork, and how she'd messed up, big time. Apparently, three months ago when she was tying up loose ends, preparing to turn the reins over to the new manager, Sydney had gotten a huge wedding order mixed up. Instead of the bridegroom's selection of the choice and superior 1996 Chateau De Davenay white wine, she'd erroneously ordered an average, lesser-quality wine, one usually sought at bargain centers. While on the train, Sydney had frantically called friends, and other wine merchants, seeking to fill the four-case order in time for a six-thirty reception. She'd divested the Restaurant Louise of its own stock but she was short of one case. She'd made restitution with the harried customer by giving him a huge discount and making a substitution of an equally superb product. The 1996 Vernaccia Di San Gimignano was readily agreed upon. She'd sighed with relief when she was informed that all cases had been delivered on time to the catering hall.

Sydney had promised the relieved Anne that she'd lock up, once she'd completed entering the corrected inventory. After her profuse apology to Anne, Sydney had urged her out of the shop.

Now she was hurrying to her office before she set out on yet another emergency, this time, for her friend Reva. When Sydney had called her from the train, it was all she could do to calm her. As weary as Sydney was, she had ended up promising to help her friend. Not only tonight, but tomorrow, too. But she needed to hurry because she had to be at Lexington and Forty-ninth Street before midnight. Reva was depending on this favor . . . to keep her job. She'd been warned that missing one more weekend, would eliminate her from the temporary roster. Either supply a body for her shift, or walk.

Sydney was bone-tired but she'd made a promise to a friend. Accomplishing this superhuman feat was daunting to say the least and like a kid in a fairyland, she was fervently wishing for a magic carpet ride straight to Monday morning.

Sydney reached the Hotel Margit where the Restaurant Louise was located on the mezzanine. Bypassing the short escalator ride, she rushed up the stairs, and breathlessly, walked past the restaurant to a discreetly hidden door and opened it. On each side of the carpeted corridor were doors leading to offices. Sydney headed for hers and nearly collided with a figure that suddenly blocked her path.

"Oh," Sydney gasped, frightened. She'd been in such deep thought, she hadn't heard a sound.

"Woman, when are you ever going to slow down?" the brusque voice queried as a big hand reached out to steady her. "Eleven o'clock on a Saturday night and you're rushing back to that little office of yours, for what—for God's sake? Besides, I thought you finally took a day off."

"Oh," Sydney said again. "Mason, you scared me." She peered at him. He was wearing his street clothes. "I guess it is late," she said, opening her office door. "You're through for the night?"

Mason Wingate was the chef at Restaurant Louise and was the reason for its popularity. Not for tourists only, critical New York diners were longtime patrons, and frequently asked to meet the man who'd so completely tickled their palates. Some showed their ignorance and their surprise at the African-American chef, while others saw the man who'd satisfied their appetites.

"That I am," Mason answered. "As you should be," he added, giving Sydney a look of disgust. "What in the world, I repeat, are you doing here?" With thick black brows drawn across a wide forehead, he was clearly annoyed. He watched Sydney start to pack a lightweight duffel bag with some glasses and three bottles of carefully wrapped champagne and put them inside. She opened the small fridge, pulled out a cellophane-wrapped package and added it to the bag. She picked up the duffel and stared at her friend.

"I forgot these when I left last night." She hoisted the bag. "If I don't taste them and send my findings to Andy Norton by tomorrow night, he'll think I'm nothing but a flake. He's been waiting far too long."

Mason looked at Sydney, knowing that there was something she was not telling. He waited.

Sydney sighed. "Oh, all right. I promised Reva a favor, and if I don't get over to Lex and Forty-ninth before midnight, I'm in big trouble."

Mason leaned against the door, blocking Sydney's exit, and stared at her, his dark brown eyes gleaming with understanding. The deep cleft in his chin that attracted the interested glances of many glamorous women, deepened with the sudden tightening of his strong jaw. "Let me guess," he said, "another Reva Fairchild life-or-death situation that requires the immediate healing hand of mother Sydney." Sarcasm made his normally mild voice sound ugly.

"Come on, Mason, move. Let me by."

Mason stood his ground, broad shoulders against the door. "Lex and Forty-ninth? What the devil's over there this time of night but a block full of deserted skyscrapers?" Suddenly, he pushed away from the door, his eyes widening in disbelief. "You're cleaning offices for her?"

Sydney pushed past him and opened the door. "Come on, Mason, you're making me late." She locked the door and walked down the hall.

Mason followed, catching up to her at the stairs. "Is that what you're doing?" he asked.

"Yes," answered Sydney.

"And you're going to do a little tasting in between dusting offices one and nine," he said, jerking his head toward the bag. "My God, Sydney, don't you ever say no? Are you the world's latest superwoman role model? What are you trying to prove? And to whom?"

"I'm just being a friend." Sydney started down the steps but was stopped by Mason's hand on her arm. She looked up at him.

"Come on," he said, taking the bag from her hand. He steered her to the end of the hallway and through the exit leading to the garage. "I'll drop you off. What you don't need is to get mugged on your way to play samaritan." He sucked air through the tiny gap in his front teeth. "If you do get conked over the head, I'll bet Ms. Actress Wannabe won't even miss a cue, much less pay you a sick visit."

Sydney smiled as she followed her friend to the garage. There was no love lost between Mason and Reva. He'd told Reva once that she had as much acting talent as his twin sister— and he didn't *have* a sister.

"Oh stop being Mr. Nonchalant Macho Man. You'd do the same for any friend of yours that was in need, Mason." She caught his arm to keep pace with his long stride. "I've seen you in action, remember?"

Thankfully, the silent Mason had thoughts of his own as he drove the few blocks to the huge corporate building on Lexington Avenue. Sydney could imagine the thoughts going around in his head. This wasn't the first time he'd been annoyed at some of her decisions. The least not being her refusal to date him. When she'd first been offered the job at the restaurant, she had almost considered refusing it because of him. They'd met through mutual friends, and succumbing to his persuasive tactics, she had finally accepted a date. The evening had been less than romantic and she'd refused to go out with him again. His ego had been bruised. Because of their small social circle, they'd invariably run into each other, and she could always sense his discomfort around her. Once, Sydney cornered him at an affair and spoke frankly. She'd told him that at thirty-one years of age, she'd know if there were sparks emanating between her and a man. She hated the idea of a man wining and dining her in the hopes of eventually wooing her into an intimate relationship. Mason had accepted her honesty and they'd become friends.

That had been more than a year ago and she'd already passed her thirty-second birthday. The first day on her new job, he'd welcomed her and had since become her staunchest supporter. They worked well together.

Sydney couldn't help thinking about the silly error that she'd made three months ago. A mistake that brought unnecessary anguish to an already nervous bridegroom. She was usually so careful. Earlier, when she had been left alone in the shop, she had pondered how she could have made such a blooper. She envisioned that day and she had finally come up with the reason for the fatal distraction. A voice. A male voice that she'd never heard before or since.

"Okay, Miss, here you go."

Mason's voice brought her back to the present. He was parked in front of the office building. Before he could get out to assist her, she stopped him with a hand on his arm. "No, don't get out." The duffel bag was on her lap. She pushed open the door and slid out of the car with ease.

Mason peered into the building, noting the lone security officer sitting behind a desk. "Not much activity," he said, frowning. "You know where you're going?"

"Stop worrying, Mason. Reva schooled me and I have everything I need.'' She lifted the other oversize bag she was carrying. ''Thanks a bunch and I'll see you tomorrow.''

As Sydney hurried into the building, all of a sudden a tidal wave of loneliness washed over her. Was Mason right? And Edward? Was she really one of those lonely New Yorkers who spent their lives being there for friends, and pretending that they were fulfilled, and happy?

CHAPTER TWO

One hour had passed and Sydney was completing her eleventh office. Reva's assignment encompassed every office on the twenty-ninth through thirty-first floors. Each floor had approximately twenty-four offices and cubicles and each had at least one wastepaper basket that required emptying and a desk that needed dusting. Sydney had started on the thirty-first floor as Reva had instructed. After the first six offices, Sydney had adapted a system that enabled her to methodically complete one room and move on to the next. She wheeled her cart to a point, left it stationary and retrieved plastic replacement bags as needed.

On the way to her twelfth office, her thoughts began to drift. Once again she was back to three months ago and the voice she'd heard at Amalia Fine Wines. She had been sitting in her office, keying orders into the computer. The door was ajar and she could hear voices on the sales floor, her clerks assisting the many customers with selections for various occasions. It was especially busy the Saturday before Mother's Day and from time to time, Sydney would stop her work and assist her staff when they were besieged. Over the years in the shop, she'd gotten used to the many languages and various accents and was very capable of answering questions in Spanish and Italian. Although she understood French, speaking it brought big grins from French patriots, but she hung in there, always giving it her best try. She really preferred practicing in private and had to laugh at herself when she played the tapes back.

On that day, one of her clerks had trouble understanding a customer who was speaking in rapid-fire Italian. Sydney understood and smiled to herself at the woman's question. The voice was deep and elegant and faintly stirred Sydney's memory of a faraway place, a long time ago. As she was about to go and assist, a strong male voice interceded on the flustered clerk's behalf, asking in English, whether he could be of assistance. Relief was evident in the clerk's voice as she accepted the offer. The man then proceeded to answer the customer's question in perfect Italian and then interpreted her needs.

Behind the door, Sydney hung on his every word, not so much as to what he was saying, but how the melodic inflections filled his baritone voice as he skillfully maneuvered his tongue around the beautiful language.

Longing to put a face to that voice, Sydney stayed put, not wanting to appear absurd, taking surreptitious looks from the doorway. Surely, she would only provide amusement to the surprised customers. She listened as the clerk requested that they follow her. The voices faded. Sydney knew they were headed toward the front of the store where the vintage Champagne was shelved. The delightful interruption over, she had returned to her work.

Now as Sydney moved from office to office, she shook her head wondering how she could ever have been so careless. It was then, she realized, she'd made the wrong data entry.

A faceless voice had drifted to her ears, almost inveigling her good sense. She swore the hairs on her arms had risen as the tips of her breasts had tingled against the satin of her bra. She remembered thinking that anyone with a voice like that had to have soulful eyes to match. Anything less would be sinful. Later, in her apartment, the voice was still in her head. She'd heard it as she picked over her meager salad; heard it in the shower, and heard it as she slipped her silk nightgown over her head. In bed, in the darkened room, she heard it again, and her heart thumped wildly, because this time, that distinctive voice heated Sydney's body as sweet whispers of love softly caressed her ears.

"Get a grip, girl," Sydney muttered as she pressed the elevator button, banishing the erotic thoughts to a far corner of her mind. "Oh, damn," she said. She hurried back into one of the offices and soon emerged with the chilled wine bottles that she'd placed in a compact refrigerator. Finally finished on the thirty-first floor, she was on her way down to the thirtieth. A glance at her watch brought a smile to her lips. "Don't quit your day job, Sydney," she murmured. "One floor in three hours?" It was almost three-thirty in the morning and not only were her eyelids drooping, Sydney was hungry. No wonder. Reva had said to take a lunch break around three o'clock. The only problem she'd been told, was that to get a beverage, she would have to travel down to the sublevel where there was a cafeteria and vending machines. Sydney had prepared herself when she'd snatched a sandwich from her office fridge. A turkey sandwich from Mason's kitchen would assuage her hunger pangs just fine.

Following Reva's instructions, Sydney simply occupied one of the empty offices and made herself comfortable as she ate. The glass-walled office she chose was furnished in "muck-a-muck plush," Reva's term for the executive offices. When she finished her sandwich, Sydney chewed on a few crackers, ate a bit of cheese, then drank a cup of water. She cleared her garbage, lifted her duffel bag off the cart, then returned to the office. Before closing the door, which had a frosted glass upper half, she looked up and down the deserted corridor. Satisfied that she was still alone, she closed the door. Sydney hadn't seen another soul all night, as Reva had warned. Nobody gallivanted about the building. The only bodies walking around would be the security officers, and then only briefly. Reva was right. Sydney had seen a uniformed officer walk by with a nod, and disappear down the hall without missing a step.

"Good thing I like my own company and ain't afraid of shadows," Sydney said aloud. She chuckled. The sound of her voice reminded her that she wasn't walking through some sci-fi experiment on how long one can remain alone—and sane.

Sydney opened the bag, removed some items and soon she was prepared to taste. On top of a small white cloth, she'd placed the three bottles of wine, some glasses, a large paper container, a pencil and a notepad. At last, with this chore done, she'd be able to maintain her credibility and keep a friend and a good business contact. She could sense a little distance the last time she'd spoken to Andy. He was anxious to see his product on the heralded wine list at the Restaurant Louise. Sydney meant to keep her promise that he'd hear from her before the weekend was over.

"And you shall, my friend," she said, as she opened the first bottle, a Pinot Noir. Once she tasted and jotted down her impressions, and before her head hit the pillow later on this morning, her findings would be traveling electronically to Seneca, New York.

"Just what do you think you're doing?"

The harsh voice sounded far off as if it was part of someone's dream. Surely it wasn't hers: she wasn't asleep. Or was she? She must have been because the wood of the desk felt warm against her cheek. Sydney opened her eyes and sat up, rubbing the stiffness from her neck, feeling strangely uneasy.

That voice had bounced roughly off her ears and she had shivered—the ominous ring of familiarity frightening her. She looked up and her eyes grew wide.

If Sydney hadn't been sitting, she would have fallen because she cringed at the cold, hard, almost black eyes that stared down at her. She blinked as if to reassure herself that she was awake and that indeed there was a man in the room. Never in her life had she been the recipient of such a mean and hateful look. Dozing off on the job as she'd obviously done was not reason enough for such a malevolent stare. It was almost as if she had handed him a personal affront.

"I asked you a question!"

Sydney gasped. Before she realized what she was doing, she

rose from the chair, nearly tripping over it in her haste to get away. "Oh," she whispered, clutching at her chest. Her breathing was uneven.

"What the . . ." The man looked at the woman as if she'd lost her mind. "What is wrong with you?" He extended his hand toward her, thinking that she was having some sort of an attack, but she stepped quickly away, out of his reach.

Adam Stone stood where he was, watching as the woman caught her breath. She was still looking at him warily with those big brown eyes of hers and he could see that she was trying to compose herself. He waited.

The rise and fall of Sydney's chest against the thin cotton of her uniform, was not so noticeable as she began to breathe easier. Unconsciously, she reached up and pulled the scarf from her head and her hair fell in thick, dampened waves to her shoulders. Flustered, she wondered why she'd done that, and stuffed the square piece of cloth in her dress pocket.

This is the face that belongs to my voice. Vaguely aware that she'd laid claim to it, she didn't want to believe that once she'd taken that voice to bed with her. *Why was he here . . . in this building?* Of all people! Here, at five in the morning? The small clock on the big walnut desk told her that she must have been dozing for more than thirty minutes. She remembered spitting out the last taste of the Riesling at about four-thirty.

"Who . . . are you?" Sydney managed to stammer, trying to summon the courage to meet those angry eyes. They glimmered darkly under the shapely, silkiest, black brows that she'd ever seen on a man, and were arched over his imperious-looking nose. Her question must have touched a nerve because a look of disgust tightened his lips under a thick brush of mustache. Sydney would have to be wearing blinders not to notice his dark good looks. He could continue giving her those mean stares well into the next century, but nothing could mar the strong lines of his dark brown face. The thin permanent scar that was etched along his jawline, reaching to his chin, created a strong, wise-looking face.

Sydney was calm now, and waited for the man to answer her.

Adam's eyes flickered from the woman to the desk and back to her. His glance fell on her chest where it lingered before he raised his eyes to hers.

"Who I am is not important. I know that you are 'S. Cox' who drinks then falls into a stupor on the job." Adam's voice matched the look of disgust on his face. "I'll be reporting this misconduct. My name is Adam Stone."

"Now isn't *that* appropriate," Sydney blurted. Wishing for instant recall of her words, Sydney flinched under his scathing look, but then reconsidered; her feelings couldn't be so wrong. This was a cold, unhappy man. The fibers of his heart probably felt like his name and Sydney wondered if that delicate organ was pierced with a cruel streak. She eyed him, her confidence returning as she unconsciously straightened her shoulders.

Adam's eyelashes flickered and his eyebrows tilted up a notch. That slight facial movement was the only indication of his surprise at her words. This woman had to be nuts.

"Caught sleeping off a drunk on the job and you're throwing attitude?"

"Attitude!" Sydney gasped. "Just who the . . ."

"What the . . ." Adam had caught a whiff of the wine and looked down at the bucket at his feet when he spied the duffel bag. He nudged it and it fell open. He swore at what was apparently more bottles of wine, opened and then recapped. Adam's jaw pulsed. This woman had a problem that was obviously out of control.

With disdain, he pulled a notebook and pen from his inside jacket pocket. "What is your name?" he asked. "Your full name. Who do you report to and what is your assignment?" Pen poised, he waited.

Oh my God. Sydney's brain raced, fast-forwarding to when she had to tell Reva that she had lost her job for her. After Reva had begged her for this big favor. She'd pleaded with Sydney. Filling in for the second-lead role, on the last two nights of the play, was a godsend and a chance for recognition. The off-Broadway hit show was already slated for restaging and an opening in Connecticut. These two nights would show the producers Reva's work, but if she wasn't selected for the

road company, she would still need this job. The meager cash
garnered from it supplemented a host of other survival incomes
that fed and housed her. Sydney couldn't let Reva down. Deep
within, she knew that Mason was right. Reva would be needing
this little hustle. Sydney jumped as that voice bounced off the
glass walls.

"Are you hard of hearing or hasn't the effects of your imbibing left you, yet?"

No, Sydney, stay cool, she seethed. *This is for Reva, so bite
your tongue.* She clasped her hands behind her back, tightly
clutching her fingers and prayed that her acting would be better
than Reva's.

"Sydney Cox." She forced herself to look into those dark
eyes and hoped her voice held the right amount of humility.
"My name is Sydney Cox," she repeated. "I work the twenty-
ninth to the thirty-first." *My God,* she thought, *I don't know
the supervisor's first name. Reed—what?*

Adam stopped writing. "Supervisor?" he asked, annoyed at
her slow response.

"Reed." Sydney held her breath.

Adam looked at her, his eyes unwavering as he asked, "Does
it have a gender and is that 'Reed' something or something
'Reed'?"

Stay calm. "Mrs. Reed. I . . . I'm not sure of her first name."
Then, "Mr. Stone, who . . . are you and what . . . what are you
going to do?"

Adam put away the notebook and pen. "I work with security."

"Security? Mr. Stone. I need this job. If you could only . . .
I mean, this won't happen again." She gestured feebly at her
paraphernalia and began clearing off the desk, snatching up the
cloth and capping the bottle. "This was foolish . . ." She halted,
hand in midair, at the explosive sound of his voice.

"Stop that," he barked. "Don't beg!" His hand swept the
air over the desk. "Anybody stupid enough to get caught doing
this can pay the piper when the time comes."

"I'm not . . ."

"Enough!" he said in a voice that could cut glass. "Can't

you hear? Has that stuff pickled your brain?'' Adam stopped himself before the inexplicable anger he felt toward this disturbing woman got the best of him. Whatever damage she wanted to inflict upon herself was not his concern. But when she did it under his province, it became his business. He couldn't walk away from this. Especially not with what was going on in this building. Everything and everyone was suspect. Even a beautiful cleaning woman who gave new meaning to a hip flask.

Sydney was holding her breath, watching the man war with himself. She dared not interrupt. Who knew what was going on in that methodical mind? The only thing that she wanted from him was Reva's job. His sudden movement startled her and she stared as he walked away.

Adam was at the door when he turned around, his eyes gliding over the strange woman. He stood for seconds watching her. With a stiff nod toward her cleaning supplies cart, he finally said, ''If there's air deodorizer in there, I suggest you use it. Liberally.''

Sydney didn't speak but could only stand and watch as that familiar black look shadowed his face. As before, she cringed, as Adam Stone's dark eyes bored into her, raking over her body.

Adam could feel his anger returning as he stared at Sydney Cox. When he spoke, his voice had turned harsh once again. ''For God's sake, clean yourself up!'' He turned and disappeared down the deserted corridor.

CHAPTER THREE

Adam's fine-tuned sixth sense told him that she had moved to the doorway and was watching him. He continued walking until he reached the door leading to the stairs, opened it and began walking up to the next floor. On the thirty-first floor, he walked down the quiet corridor toward the office of his objective. Trying to concentrate on what he was about, he found himself strangely distracted. He sniffed the air. The pungent smells of furniture polish and cleaning liquids were evident and he realized the source of his lack of concentration. *She* had been here.

Adam stopped and with an instinct honed over the years, ducked into the shadows cast from dimmed offices. He warily watched the deserted stretch of hall ahead of him. Had that been a figure stealthily trying to escape his keen eye? And into the very office Adam had been approaching? The rooms were similar to the glass-walled offices on the floor below and Adam cast a sharp glance to the left and the right of him as he began moving ahead quietly. Nothing stirred around him and his sharp hearing did not pick up any unusual sounds. In a matter of seconds he reached the office at the end of the corridor, but stopped and stooped low, making himself less of a target for anyone inside. The room was dark and he listened intently. Relying on his senses, Adam quickly duck-walked over the threshold and still in a crouch, flattened himself against the wall. His vision quickly became acclimated to the dark and his gaze roved the office. Swiftly studying the objects on the desk, his dark eyes narrowed and he swore softly. Something was not right. He started to rise and at that moment he was warned peripherally of the dark form coming at him.

"Damn," Adam swore as he deflected the blow to the side of his head. Still in a half-crouch, he never saw the kick coming that rammed his groin. Another attempted blow to his head landed and Adam fell. Before darkness enveloped him, his last conscious thought was that he was a fool.

"Mr. Stone, Mr. Stone, can you hear me? Mr. Stone."

"All right, all right," Adam rasped, trying to stop the do-gooder from shaking the rest of his brains out. He opened his eyes and the fluorescent light forced him to hurriedly close them, but he'd seen his rescuer. "Okay, Jorge, I'm okay. Just help me up." Adam made good use of Jorge's arm as he was helped to the swivel armchair behind the desk. He sat down heavily forgetting the throb in his head and he groaned as things began to rumble inside again. "I don't suppose you saw anything?" Adam gingerly touched his head and his hand came away wet.

"You're bleeding, Mr. Stone. He got you good." Jorge left and quickly returned with a warm damp cloth. "Compliments of the executive bathroom."

"Did you see anyone?" Adam asked, holding the cloth to his temple. There was a cut but it had stopped bleeding, which was a good sign.

"Not a soul, Mr. Stone."

"Then how do you know it was a 'he' and not a 'she'?" Adam threw the cloth on the desk and raised his eyes to the worried-looking security officer who had one hip on the desk.

Jorge Cruz stood up. Solemn-voiced, he said, "I don't."

"How did you get here so fast? I didn't signal."

"You didn't check in with me as we agreed when you reached the thirtieth floor and you never appeared on any of the monitors. Too much time elapsed, so I came straight here." His gaze wandered over the desk and he frowned.

Adam followed his look and his jaw tightened. "Yeah," he said, "apparently there was a change of plans." Adam moved his head gingerly from side to side and when he didn't see a rainbow, he stood picking up the cloth and taking it with him to the private bathroom. "This is where the intruder was hiding in the dark. I never saw the attack coming until it was too late. Whoever it was, was strong and crafty. And good." The generous-size room bore the scrutiny of Adam's critical eye before he turned out the light and joined the uniformed officer at the door. Brushing at the brown stains on his light-gray suit jacket, he swore. It was his own carelessness, so he must pay the consequences. He grimaced at the familiar thought.

"Jorge, I thought I saw someone come in here. Are you certain no one passed you?" Adam paused. "What about the workers?"

"Nothing. No one, Mr. Stone. Like I said, you never signaled me and I hurried up here. I didn't see or hear a soul. And no one was where they shouldn't be. At least from what the monitors showed." Jorge looked at the desk and his forehead wrinkled. "Guess it was called off. Wonder what changed their minds."

Adam followed Jorge's look and his eyes darkened as he looked at the silver picture frame. "I wonder," he said stiffly. "Come on, let's go. There's nothing more to do here tonight." He turned out the light and closed the door. "I want a report on all activities from the time I left you until you found me," Adam said.

Adam stopped at the door leading to the stairs while Jorge walked ahead of him toward the elevator. "You go on. I'll meet you downstairs in your office. I want to check out thirty again." Without waiting for a reply from the puzzled man, Adam opened the door and started his descent to the lower floor.

The long corridor was dim and silent and like the floor above, the pungent evidence of recent cleaning permeated the air.

Adam walked to the office where earlier he'd had a disturbing encounter. It was dark and the minute he opened the door, his nostrils were assailed by the strong cherry-scented deodorizer that pervaded the room. His lips moved in an unfamiliar twitch that resembled a smile, but instantaneously his mouth reverted to its severe line. He'd remembered the circumstances that had led to the room now smelling like a cherry orchard.

Adam turned on his heel and left the office, alert to his surroundings, as he walked to the elevator. Certain this time that he was alone, he unnecessarily jabbed the touch-sensitive button, then became annoyed at his unusual emotional display. Something had knocked him off kilter so that he had acted like an amateur out on his first night of surveillance. He was supposed to be the pro in this scenario and he'd been knocked out cold. What in the world had hit him upside his head? It certainly wasn't a flesh-and-blood fist; the blow had been too stunning. And right now he had a mounting ache that threatened to crash-land inside his skull, awarding him with his own private showing of falling stars.

Adam glanced at his watch as he stepped inside the elevator and touched the button to the sublevel. It was after six in the morning. What a fruitless night, he thought. A waste of everybody's time and effort. After weeks of planning this night, it had crumbled into one big mess. What happened? Why had the suspects set the signal for a go and then reversed their decision? Who could have done it? Adam closed his eyes against the throbbing in his head and suddenly wished to end the night, but he knew Jorge was waiting to give him a rundown on the evening's activities. Might as well get this over with quick, he thought. When he stepped off the elevator, he couldn't help bring to the fore something that had been nagging at his subconscious and had been the reason for Jorge to throw him that surprised look.

Adam knew that there had been nothing that required looking into on the thirtieth floor. There was no one there but a drunk cleaning woman. A beautiful cleaning woman with soulful brown eyes that had shimmered like a black lake on a moonlit night.

Adam was grim-faced as he headed to the security office. An old feeling of anger seethed inside his stomach as he thought of what a fool he'd been to let his feelings surface and interfere with his work. Angry feelings—triggered by the sight of a beautiful drunk named Sydney Cox. Her inert form had startled, and at once, enraged him, forcing a long-ago memory to surface. His anger then had compelled him to change his life. Berating himself, Adam walked into Jorge's office and closed the door.

Sunday, at two in the afternoon, found Adam still in bed. Coming out of his second sleep, he sat up, testing his movement, and a grunt of satisfaction escaped through his teeth. The monstrous headache was gone, but even so, Adam didn't invite the pain back by leaping out of bed like he was a nineteen-year-old jock. He tossed aside the sheet, eased his feet to the floor and sat up. Another pleased sound parted his lips. The expected waves of dizziness and nausea stayed wherever they went when they weren't trying to wreak havoc with some poor soul. He stood up and walked barefoot to the bathroom. His gait was his usual steady, long-legged stride.

Adam gave himself a critical look in the mirror. Except for the bruise extending from his temple and beyond his receding hairline, his face didn't have the look that would scare a baby. On the other hand, if a scar remained, maybe it would, he thought, feeling the ridge along his jaw. He dropped his hand abruptly and reached over to turn on the shower faucet, thinking that there was no value to dwelling on old bruises.

An hour and two cups of coffee later, Adam was clearing away the remains of his sardines and eggs brunch when the doorbell rang. Unperturbed, but cautious, he nodded after looking through the viewer. He opened the door.

"Welcome. Had coffee?" Adam asked his visitor.

Lucas Parnell followed Adam into the sitting area of the combination livingroom-diningroom-kitchenette. His ever-alert eyes shifted to the open door of the bedroom where his glance took in the rumpled bedcovers. Lucas sat down heavily in the only armchair, and from beneath thick sandy lashes, eyed Adam.

"You all right?" he asked. His voice was naturally gruff, sounding like a throat parched from too many years of cigarettes and whiskey. He had put a stop to his childhood playmates who tried to tag him with the nickname Frog. Later, he found that women were drawn to his deep-throated voice, calling it sexy. At fifty-three, Lucas thought himself anything but. His own idea of sexy didn't come close to his five-foot-nine height and a middle that was fast turning portly. But his wife, Jennifer, apparently didn't seem to mind.

Lucas stared at Adam's temple and his round, light brown eyes narrowed. "Looks like you were sapped. You didn't mention that this morning." His accusing gaze continued to assess the man sitting across from him on the small two-seat sofa.

Adam threw a look at his boss that needed no words to convey his disgust at the condition of his abused head.

Lucas persisted. "So were you?"

"Like I told you this morning, I was in no condition to analyze what knocked me cold," Adam answered. His own eyes narrowed at the corners as he snorted derisively. "Nothing like a little caffeine to turn on the light."

Adam thought about the blow to his head, remembering the unnatural feel. He was in perfect physical shape and would never have been put down by an ordinary fist. But a blow from a sap would do it . . . and did. A glove with at least eight ounces of lead imbedded in the spaces where knuckles would be, had caught him unaware.

"Yeah," Adam said, staring at the older man, "I was sapped."

Lucas studied the man who was one of his sharpest operatives in the Northeast. Adam's getting caught off guard like that should never have happened. Something had disturbed that cold exterior to the extent that it had gotten him injured. Lucas didn't have to play mind games to try and figure it out. His voice softened as much as possible beneath its natural rasp. "Owen's death was not meant to be the cause of you harboring guilt and burden for the rest of your life." His penetrating stare held Adam's. "Especially, not to the extent that you put your life in danger whenever you happen upon a drunk. That lack of concentration can get you killed." After a pause, he added, "As it nearly did."

Adam's eyes grew dark at his boss's words. He should never have told Lucas what had happened earlier this morning, but Lucas being as swift as he was, wouldn't let Adam hang up until he'd gotten an explanation of the night's activities. Adam for some inexplicable reason, had been reluctant to mention the episode with a drunken woman. Now, he didn't even want to mention her name. He strove to change the subject to prevent further delving into his odd behavior, and why this particular drunk had affected him so deeply.

"The thing I don't understand is what happened to call it off," Adam said, hoping that Lucas caught his drift.

Lucas did, his eyes flashing briefly with understanding, and he obliged. He said, "Beats the hell out of me. For months we watched until we finally figured out who and then how the drug shipments were diverted." His thin, sandy-colored brows drew down toward his broad nose, and a flush of annoyance traveled beneath his light beige skin. "There was no one around after hours to right that picture frame. At least no one visible to Jorge and his crew. What scared them off?"

Adam frowned. "McGregor worked until eight o'clock last night. When he left that office, the picture frame was face-down."

"Then apparently, something happened to send him back or to notify his accomplices to get in there to set the cancel signal."

Adam shook his head. "It wasn't McGregor. Security is positive he never returned to the building."

"Then it's someone inside. He had to have gotten a message to whomever was in the building legitimately. Have you gone over Jorge's report?"

Adam scowled at Lucas. "Skimmingly."

Lucas nodded. "Yeah, you weren't in the best of shape to scrutinize anything. You're meeting with him later?"

"In the morning. Today's a dead day and it'll give him a chance to question everybody. No one expects McGregor to return on Sunday to set things in motion again. Too suspicious. Besides, I'm certain they need time to get bodies in position again to move the stuff."

Lucas agreed with a nod. "True. Nothing will happen for at least another week or so."

"Right, whenever McGregor is informed of another shipment coming to his district."

Lucas eased his round frame from the armchair and walked toward the door. He looked around the small apartment suite with approval. "I see the company's redecorated the place. Not bad. Must have spent a little change this time." He eyed Adam. "You staying or moving on?" He added, "Hardly seems like eight months have passed already."

Adam glanced around the rooms. It did seem like he'd just moved into the company-owned suite. Garrison International spared no cost in doing over the apartment, which was used by company agents on assignment. The operatives stayed at no cost for eight months. After that, if still on assignment, the apartment was let to them for a small fee. Adam liked it the first moment he walked in the door. The Sixty-first Street location near Madison and Park Avenues was convenient to his needs and the first floor with a back and front entrance was ideal for his comings and goings.

'I'm pretty comfortable. I'm staying."

Lucas gave a look of approval at Adam's decision. "I'll put in the paperwork," he said. His hand on the doorknob, he added, "Oh, nearly forgot. The boss is flying in on Monday for a week of meetings and hiring interviews. Call my secretary to see if you're part of any agendas. I do know that before Lincoln leaves next Sunday he wants to wind down with a quiet Saturday night dinner. You're included. Call Lois for the place and time." He looked intently at his operative, who he knew was still feeling an old anger. "Adam, the pharmaceutical industry has long been beset with theft, piracy of formulas and other nefarious schemes, far longer than we've been in existence. And I'm afraid it'll be happening for decades. It's big business. We only hope to do what we can to curb it and prevent more deaths." He paused. "There will always be people

... men ... like McGregor who have legitimate beefs against drug manufacturers and the harm that some of their products can cause." Lucas opened the door. "But, there will always be people like us, who seek to make things safe. Call me after you meet with Jorge." He closed the door.

Adam walked to the window and pushed aside the lightweight cotton curtain, curious as to where Lucas had left his car. Parking was almost nil on the block unless one wished to use the underground private garage down the street. Whenever Adam rented a car, that was usually where he left it instead of riding around futilely looking for a vacant spot. He looked amused when he saw his boss get into a chauffeur-driven company car which was double-parked. He should have known Lucas wouldn't have bothered with the traffic on a Sunday afternoon in Manhattan.

Turning from the window, Adam lay down on the sofa, throwing his long legs over the rolltop arm and resting his head on the overstuffed pillows. Staring up at the ceiling, he wondered what Lincoln Yates wanted. The owner and cofounder of Garrison International was an astute businessman and usually left company business to his handpicked district directors. Something special was in the wind, Adam thought, but he didn't dwell on it, knowing he'd be informed sooner than later. He already surmised that he'd find out on Saturday night.

Adam liked Lincoln Yates, a no-nonsense black man in his late fifties. When Adam had interviewed for the job more than five years ago, Yates had revealed that they had similar backgrounds. Career marines. The difference was that Yates was a retired sergeant, while Adam had put in eleven years as a sergeant with the Military Police. He had resigned after his last tour of duty, only months after the suicide death of his best friend, Owen Jeffries. Fury rippled through him. Death? A delayed killing!

CHAPTER FOUR

"Sydney, it was fabulous! *I* was fab!" exclaimed Reva Fairchild. She was sprawled at the foot of Sydney's bed, arms crossed behind her head, swinging one foot over her crossed knees. "They *liked* me."

"In the words of Sally Field, huh?" drawled Sydney.

Reva laughed. "The very same," she said. Her foot held suspended, she asked, "You are happy for me, aren't you?"

"Oh, stop being the skeptic, Reva." Sydney propped herself up. "I'm not exactly high energy yet. Usually, my enthusiasm kicks in when I've gotten a minimum of three hours' sleep."

Reva sat up and moved to a granny rocker. "Oh, a grouch this morning, aren't we?"

"You can say that." Sydney covered a wide yawn that ended in a loud moan. "Hint, hint," she said, her voice thick with sleep—or the lack of it.

Reva eyed her friend. "You're really not kidding, are you? I figured at noon you would be ready for your first cup of caffeine. I've seen you at your best with less shut-eye. What time did you get in anyway? Didn't you hit the sack right away?"

"Reva. Reva, girl, please! I'm really not up for your fire-at-will questioning, all right?"

"Oh." Dejection was evident in her voice as well as her posture when Reva stood up. "Sorry. I wasn't thinking. You do have to work tonight. Couldn't contain myself. Just wanted to share with you, is all."

Sydney groaned as she got out of bed and went to her friend. She threw her arms around her in a big hug. "Now say you'll forgive me?"

Without a thought, Reva returned the hug. "Forgiven, forgotten," she said, her beautiful dark eyes twinkling.

Sydney smiled at the familiar words. "You're right." She put her arm around Reva's waist and pulled her out of the bedroom. "It's way past time for my first cuppa. Want some?"

The two women were sitting in the kitchen drinking the hot brewed coffee, both in the relaxed, unpretentious poses of old friends. Sydney remembered their first meeting fourteen years ago, two scared young women on a plane flying out of JFK Airport; off to school in California where neither of them knew a soul. When the plane touched down six hours later, they had formed a bond that had grown, mellowing like aged, fine wine. Within days, the two friends met another young student. Ferne Percival formed the trio that would become inseparable throughout their college years. Now adults leading separate lives, they remained steadfast friends, sharing and caring as they did when they were younger. Inevitable disagreements and arguments never festered. They were always resolved and put to rest.

Sydney was genuinely happy for Reva. "So tell me, you really were 'Miss It' last night? Upstaged the Prima Donna did you?"

Reva laughed. "I wouldn't go that far, but I knew what was happening the whole time I was out there. Don't you know the feeling when something is just right? That at last you're going to get your piece of the pie?" She sounded in awe. "That feeling was in my bones and a flying missile couldn't knock it loose."

Sydney smiled at her friend's description because she did

know the feeling. Twice in the last ten years it had happened to her.

Reva's bright eyes did not miss the sudden light in her friend's eyes. "You know exactly what I'm talking about." Before waiting for a response, she said softly, "Your career moves worked for you. I should have been so lucky."

"Don't do that!" Sydney's voice was sharp as she looked at Reva. "We promised years ago that we wouldn't compete against one another. The three of us are individuals with distinct personalities. So don't compare your career changes with mine, or even Ferne's. When you quit teaching five years ago to follow your heart to the stage, we were in your corner."

Reva smiled. "Not at first."

"No, because you were the best teacher that I.S. 166 had seen in years. Kids were willingly attending class and learning *history* because of you. You were good at it because you loved teaching."

"And you didn't?" Reva raised a brow.

Sydney flushed. She remembered giving Reva a lecture to beat all when she'd made her announcement, and Sydney had just given up her own teaching position. She had loved anthropology and loved to make the subject come alive for her college students. But she had been offered a job that she couldn't resist. She looked at Reva. "I don't regret it."

Reva stared back. "I know. The discussion we had back then is still fresh in my mind. I told you that my desire for change was not as drastic and chancy as yours. For you to give up your love of teaching and a secure career for something so unbelievable was so unlike you. You were always the most sensible one. But to chase that dream of becoming a wine merchant and respected sommelier . . . was so incredible." She smiled. "You remember what I said?"

"How could I forget?" Sydney laughed, then imitated Reva's voice. " 'You're a woman and a black one at that! What makes you think that you, as a newcomer, will be accepted in that oh, so elitist world?' "

Both women laughed at the memory.

Reva was the first to speak. "And you did it, too, didn't

you? You asked me to have faith in you because you could do it. I'm proud of you." She scrunched up her nose. "God, has it been more than five years since we were in the Hotel Belle Donne, planning our futures?" She sighed, "Ah, Italy! Beautiful Florence! We were so young then."

"Even younger, five years before that," Sydney answered.

"Ah, the senior trip. When we first stayed at the Hotel Belle Donne and you met *La Signora.*" Reva saw the shadow in her friend's eyes. "I'm sorry."

Sydney shook her head. "No, that's okay. I've been thinking of her a lot lately." Her look turned thoughtful and a little laugh escaped. "I really don't know why, but it's the oddest thing. Some words that she spoke to me in the garden that last night that I saw her, seem to play over and over in my mind at certain times."

"Disturbing ones?"

"No. Rather thought provoking, as if to remind me of something." Sydney knew of what she was to be reminded, but suddenly, for some inexplicable reason she didn't want to share her thoughts with her old friend. Because that meant trying to explain a voice in her head that wouldn't go away and which belonged to a dark stranger with equally dark and cold, penetrating eyes.

Sydney stood up and cleared the table, putting the empty mugs in the sink. "I think you had better tell me about your big night. You have a matinee and I need some more sleep. Monday morning can't get here soon enough for me." Sydney linked her arm with Reva's. "Come on. It's back to bed for me. Then if I fall asleep on you, you can let yourself out." She yelped from Reva's playful pinch on her arm.

"Sydney, you know that this favor means a lot to me," Reva said as they walked toward the bedroom. "I don't know of anyone who has a friend like you. Other than Ferne, of course." A sigh escaped. "Keeping this gig along with my other money-makers, helps to keep the wolves at bay. When they all dry up, I'll have to face reality and go back to teaching full-time, if I'm lucky enough to find a spot. Until then I'm going to live my acting dream for as long as possible."

Sydney propped herself up on the bed while her friend draped her lithe form over the armchair. Reva's dark brown hair was swept up off her swanlike neck into a carefully arranged disheveled cascade of curls.

Sydney covered a yawn. "Girl, if your excited state is any indication, last weekend was probably good-bye to your dusting desks and emptying wastepaper baskets. The next time I hear your voice, you'll be telling me you're hitting the road for Connecticut. Who knows when you'll be coming back this way?" She winked. "Just don't forget from whence you came, old friend. Now, give me some of that good feedback. Just how *fab* were you?"

In the hours that passed since Reva left, Sydney caught some more winks, ate a light lunch, dusted, showered and dressed. At five o'clock, she was ready to leave her apartment to arrive at the Restaurant Louise by six. She loved the dinner hour because she never failed to meet and talk to lively, interesting folks. Almost nightly, there would be one table filled with dignitaries from a foreign land. For the most part, when guests asked for help in selecting the perfect wine to complement their fish or meat, they were appreciative of her suggestions. Occasionally, she met the wine snob who invariably knew more than anyone else in the room. Those, she always left to make the ultimate selection.

Sydney lived in Manhattan on the eighth floor in an East Seventy-second Street apartment building. Her living room windows faced Seventy-second and it was not unusual for Sydney to make a quick assessment, then dress according to what the passing pedestrians wore. Sometimes she determined whether the weather was conducive to attempting the twenty-odd block walk to the restaurant. Today, judging from the sluggish crawl of the passersby, she guessed it was too hot and nixed the thought of walking. The subway at Third Avenue would have to suffice as it usually did.

Sydney left the apartment and walked across the hall to the elevator. When she'd first looked at the apartment seven years ago, the closeness to the elevator had been a factor in her accepting it. She'd always hated the feeling she got walking down long deserted corridors, worrying that danger lurked in every shadowy crevice.

Sydney was bone-tired and she wondered how she was going to keep her eyes open until eight o'clock tomorrow morning. "Because you love your friend, and she would do it for you," she muttered, as she got on the train. She sat, even though the short ride downtown would take less than fifteen minutes. No sooner had she sat, her eyes closed. Knowing that it was bad practice to nod on a New York City subway train, she was used to catnapping every now and then. Today, more than ever before, she knew that her tired eyes would benefit from every second of cautious shut-eye. She only hoped that she would be able to spend a good part of the four hours she planned to work, in her office, rather than chatting with patrons. She had orders to place and she wanted to begin revamping her wine list for the balance of the summer.

But during the short ride, Sydney's thoughts were on anything but the Restaurant Louise. Almost instantly, a pair of angry dark eyes assaulted her senses and her eyes flew open in surprise.

The train stopped at Sixty-eighth Street and Sydney stood up. Walking to the Hotel Margit, she was seized by a great swell of loneliness that left her chilled. She was astute enough to know that it came with the thought of never seeing Adam Stone again.

After the first two hours of the dinner rush, Sydney was finally able to shut herself in her office. The warm July evening had chased many a New Yorker inside, not only to dine sumptuously, but she was sure, to bask in the cool temperature of the inviting ambience of Restaurant Louise. Of all nights, almost every other table had a patron requiring her assistance in selecting that perfect wine accompaniment. Though she had been happy to make suggestions, she found that she'd been going nonstop since she walked in the door at five forty-five. It was nearly eight o'clock and she had just tasted Mason's lemon chicken and garden vegetable casserole braised in white wine,

when the phone rang. She took another bite before reaching
for the phone, savoring the delicious meal. Whoever it was
could call back if it was so important, she thought. It would
be a sin to let this dish grow cold. She couldn't hardly keep
this for her 3 A.M. lunch break. Sydney gulped and swallowed
when she heard Reva's voice on the answering machine.

"Sydney, when you get this message, call me. I'm at
home...."

"Reva," Sydney answered in a rush. Her brow creased with
worry. Why wasn't she at the theater? The last performance
had begun at seven-thirty! "Reva, what's wrong?"

"I was fired."

A moment passed before the words sank in. What was she
talking about? "Fired? From where?" Was one fired from a
play on the last night at the final performance? Must be the
cleaning job, Sydney decided.

"The play, Sydney! They let me go this afternoon, before
the matinee. I wasn't even allowed backstage."

"The matinee? All this time? Why didn't you call me
sooner?" Sydney was dumbstruck and angry for the hurt she
heard in her friend's voice. Fired! How ridiculous!

"I was too embarrassed to let anyone know." Reva caught
back a sob as she heard the sounds of disbelief and anger
coming from her friend.

"I'm sorry, Reva."

As if unable to bear the sounds of sympathy, a new flood
of tears started, causing Reva to cry uncontrollably. Disgusted
with herself, she took a deep breath, forcing air into her lungs.
The sobs ceased and she wiped her eyes and blew her nose.
"I'm sorry Sydney. Guess I'm still in shock."

Sydney felt miserable. "No bother. You know that, Reva.
But what happened and why didn't they let you backstage?"
She started to get warm all over again. But she kept her mouth
shut and listened to the halting explanation.

"Marlene came back."

"The same Marlene you were understudying? I thought she
had a family emergency out of town?" Sydney sounded con-

fused. The family crisis that enabled Reva to perform for two days was to keep Marlene away for at least a week.

Reva smiled through her tears as she tried to joke. "I told you that I was *that* good!"

"Make sense, Reva. My brain's not ready for this," Sydney said in exasperation.

"After Saturday's matinee, word had traveled to Marlene about my performance. After the evening show, she was on her way back to New York." Reva gave a small mirthless laugh. "At least that's what I was told by a friend."

"What else?"

"Marlene was told that the producers were excited over my performance and were considering taking me on the road. They would keep her in a lesser role because of contract obligations."

"And she flew back demanding to perform in both shows today," Sydney said in disgust.

"It was her right."

"Is that so?" Sydney was not usually given to sarcasm, or pettiness. "Sounds like so much bull to me. Obviously the time needed to resolve this so-called family emergency was miscalculated?"

Reva pushed wispy strands of hair from her damp cheek, smiling at the wisdom of her friend. "The same grapevine had it that she was tired. Her role for the Connecticut run was secure, so she decided to take a long weekend in the sun with her man."

"Why am I not surprised?" Sydney asked in a droll voice. Then, "Reva, in the universal words of one not knowing what to say, I really am sorry. You were on the money when you said you were just too *fab.*" In an effort to lighten the mood, Sydney asked, "Aging does work for you, doesn't it?"

"What?"

"Did you ever think of looking for a similar vehicle?" Sydney asked innocently. Reva played a character that aged forty-five years in the three-act play. "Maybe you can take makeup lessons from Michael Dorn, especially if the play is long-running." At the sound of her friend's chuckle, Sydney smiled, though inwardly, she sighed with relief. "You okay, now?" she asked.

"It'll take some doing, but I'll survive this," said Reva. "I'm still tutoring and with my weekend gig that you just saved for me, I can still pull my share of the load with my roommates until something else breaks." Reva paused. "By the way, I'll be going in tonight, so you can make it on home and sink into your pillows, my friend."

"I can!"

Reva laughed. "Don't sound so ecstatic. You're making me feel guilty that I even put you through this."

"You'd do it for me."

"And you're right about that, too. Call you tomorrow."

"That interruption must have been mighty important." Mason Wingate stood in the doorway, eyebrow raised at Sydney's barely touched dinner. His lemon chicken was one of her favorites. He was about to tease her further when he stopped. Something was wrong. "Anything you want to tell me?" he asked, sitting down in the only other chair in the room.

Sydney looked at Mason. She knew that he was genuinely concerned for her but would he still feel the same if he knew Reva was the cause of her mood? And she wasn't in the frame of mind to allow him to tease her about Reva's acting.

"Don't tell me, it's about Reva." He looked at his watch. "Shouldn't she be on stage?"

Sydney smiled. She liked this perceptive, and down-to-earth man and wondered how long it would be before he met the woman who would give him heartburn.

"Reva was fired from the play. She wasn't allowed to perform in either show."

"What?"

After Sydney explained, she was silent, watching Mason's reaction.

"The poor kid!" He swore. "What a rotten deal. Could they do that?"

Sydney looked at him in surprise. "Why Mason, you really do care," she said.

Mason scowled. "Be serious. I'd feel sorry for anybody who got shafted like that."

"I see," mused Sydney. "Of course you would." She laughed when he cut a deadly look her way. "Okay, I know when enough is enough."

Later, after Sydney had showered and slipped into cotton pajama shorts, sans top, she turned off the light and dropped into bed. The feel of the cool sheets against her bare skin felt heavenly. Sleeping with the air conditioner on all night tended to give her a stuffy nose, so Sydney cooled the room off as soon as she entered the apartment. By bedtime it was deliciously chilled, enough to allow instant sleep.

One of the last thoughts she had was that if not for the actions of a conniving woman, her nostrils would be filled with lemon oil and cherry-scented deodorizer.

Was that the doorbell? Sydney's eyes flew open and her heart thudded when the doorbell rang again accompanied by a bang on the door. When she heard Reva calling her name, she jumped out of bed and raced to the door. The chain was barely off when Reva barged inside.

"Reva. What . . . ?"

"Sydney Cox, how could you mess me up like that? I told you not to touch anything!"

"What are you talking about?" Sydney had never seen such fury in Reva. And it was all directed at her! "What's happened?"

"I was fired!"

"Again?" Sydney asked stupidly.

Reva's black eyes blazed with the heat of an over-stoked furnace. Her beautifully shaped mouth was twisted in an ugly slash as she yelled, "Oh, so make a joke out of me! That's what you think I am anyway. A clown! All these years calling yourself my friend and commiserating with me . . . you and Ferne were laughing to beat the band, I'll bet!" Reva felt the tears burn her eyelids then her cheeks as they rolled slowly to her chin, dripping onto her chest.

Sydney stepped back as though she'd been slapped. This couldn't be her friend talking like a crazed person. As if mes-

merized, she watched the tears drop, her gaze following each
one as it soaked into the aqua T-shirt, spreading into fantasy
shapes. Vaguely, Sydney noticed that Reva was wearing the
color that was always dynamite with her butternut shade of
skin. From a distance she heard an anguished cry that brought
her out of her trance. She took a step toward Reva who was
crying uncontrollably now, and Sydney was getting worried.
Had her friend really been under so much pressure? And she
hadn't noticed the signs?

"Don't touch me! I don't want your false hugs this time,"
Reva shouted. She backed away.

"Reva!" Sydney yelled, losing it. *False? How dare she?*
"What happened to you and why are you blaming me and
Ferne? Tell me what's going on! And for God's sake, tell me
what I touched?"

"The picture frame! The silver picture frame on Mr. Mc-
Gregor's desk. You touched it." Reva fell down into the chair,
her loud cries ebbing to a whimper as she hiccuped like a child.

Sydney was stupefied. What picture frame was she talking
about and who was Mr. McGregor? She found herself in the
kitchen, returning with a cold glass of water. She set it down
on the table next to Reva and then backed away and sat on the
sofa. She watched the distraught woman warily.

Sydney spoke as calmly as she could. "What silver picture
frame, Reva?"

Spent, Reva drank from the glass, taking big gulps until she
sputtered, nearly choking. When the fit of coughing subsided,
she clutched the glass as if it was her hold on reality.

"She embarrassed me. I was humiliated and fired in front
of everyone like I was the main attraction of the evening."

*Mrs. Reed. She has to be speaking of her supervisor. How
crude she must be,* Sydney thought. *But Reva's blaming me
for whatever happened.*

Reva watched Sydney wrinkle her brow, puzzled that she
could possibly do anything wrong. Sydney had always been
the wisest of the three young women. Though they all shared
the same birth year, at thirty-one, Reva was the younger of the
trio and would catch up to her friends in four weeks. It was

Sydney she and Ferne took their troubles to, even after college. Her reasoning always seemed so right. But, she messed up last night, trying to be perfect. Even cleaning offices, for heaven's sake!

"The thirty-first floor. Mr. McGregor keeps a picture of his daughter in a small silver frame. When you dusted the desk, it was lying facedown. You righted it." Reva watched Sydney closely and knew when her friend remembered.

Oh, what did I do? Sydney did remember. "The pretty red-haired little girl."

"Yes. What was the last thing I warned you about, Sydney?" Reva's voice was filled with anger.

"Dusting, not decorating." Sydney caught her breath. She hadn't listened. "I was curious why the picture frame was lying facedown. I picked it up and wondered who would want to hide such a pretty face. It never occurred to me to lay it facedown again." Her look was incredible. "Is that the only reason you were let go?"

"There doesn't have to be more, Sydney." Reva's voice rose. "Rules are rules."

"This Mr. McGregor came into the office on a Sunday, saw that his frame was moved, and raised such a commotion that led to the firing of a worker?"

"Bingo!"

"Unbelievable."

"Tell that to Mrs. Reed. The man threatened to cancel the company's cleaning contract. But, in lieu of that, I became the scapegoat," Reva said. Her voice turned bitter. "See how many jobs I saved?"

"Reva, I'm sorry." Sydney felt helpless.

"Universal words again." Reva set the glass on the table and stood up. "I'll let myself out."

"Reva? Don't go like this. Forgiven? Forgotten?"

Reva gave Sydney a blank look, then opened the door and pulled it shut behind her.

Sydney stood mute. Did she hear her friend say "good-bye"?

CHAPTER FIVE

Adam was wrong about Sunday being a dead night. He could attest to that by the hum of the employees who obviously hadn't seen such excitement on the graveyard shift. The crowd was thinning out as supervisors sent the workers to their various floors.

It had been past eleven o'clock when Adam answered the phone to Jorge who could hardly contain his excitement. When the security officer mentioned that McGregor had been in the building and had raised hell about his office, Adam ended the conversation.

A cab had whisked him downtown in fifteen minutes.

Now as Adam stepped off the elevator on the sublevel, he was amidst a crowd of workers who obviously had been purposely assembled. He stood still, assessing the situation, his alert gaze sweeping the faces in the crowd. Each wore an expression of disbelief and all eyes were on two women who were engaging in verbal combat. The woman with the strident voice, obviously the supervisor, was a head shorter than the employee who tried in vain to plead her case. The dressing down the shorter woman was giving caused Adam to frown on the unprofessional behavior.

Skirting the edge of the crowd until he reached the door of the security office, he saw Jorge and some of his officers watching the demeaning show.

"Is this necessary?" Adam asked curtly as he nodded to Jorge.

"Mr. Stone," Jorge greeted the unsmiling man. He shrugged. "That's Mrs. Reed, the nighttime supervisor. She's the one Mr. McGregor read the riot act to and threatened to have her job."

"The frame?"

"You got it. The owner of the cleaning company got to Mrs. Reed and in turn, she fired Reva."

"Reva?"

"Reva Fairchild. She's the regular for twenty-nine through thirty-one. Her friend did her shift last night." He looked knowingly at Adam who stared back. Both realized what had happened.

Jorge shook his head and clucked his tongue. "Reva should have known better. The workers send subs a lot, no big deal. But when you do that you're supposed to let them know what's what."

"The friend obviously didn't know any better and stood up the picture frame."

"Right again. Reva's paying for it now."

Adam looked at the tall beauty who had tears coursing down her cheeks, obviously ashamed and angry at being made a spectacle of. He watched as the supervisor stalked into her office and slammed the door. The room had emptied of her audience.

Adam watched as Reva Fairchild stood dazed in the middle of the floor. Fleetingly he thought that she could use a friend and a hug right about now. Her eyes met his and she stared at him. Suddenly she turned, and head down, walked to the elevator. Adam stared until the unhappy woman was shielded by the closing doors.

"So, it wasn't canceled, after all."

Even though they spoke over the phone, Adam nodded his head at Lucas' comment.

"At least not by McGregor," Adam said wryly.

Lucas sighed. "An unwitting fill-in cleaning woman undid weeks of surveillance. All by being so nosy! Or would you call it meticulous?"

Inebriated is the word, Adam thought in disgust. Aloud he said, "A meeting later?"

"Yeah, ten o'clock. You'll get a call. Damn," he said again. "This would have to happen with Lincoln in town. He'll have to be informed."

After agreeing, Adam hung up. It was one-thirty in the morning but he was tense and unable to sleep. Several times in the last hour, he became rankled at the image of that woman standing in the middle of the floor being ridiculed. Instead of trying to force sleep, he opened a bottle of cold beer and carried it to the sitting area of the large room. He sat in the armchair by the window, silently drinking and thinking. The window was open and the slight breeze that was stirring in the early-morning hours riffled the curtains gently. Adam sat in the dark listening to the whooshing sounds made by passing cars as their tires rolled over the asphalt. The beams from the headlamps flashed shadowy slivers of light across the room. His mind was crowded with the events of the night which was the top-off to Saturday night's fiasco.

Adam frowned. Something about that drunk woman bothered him. The whole scene was bizarre and not what he would expect to see from an employee who hit the bottle on the job. Something didn't fit and he couldn't pinpoint what was disturbing him.

The beer bottle was empty and not as cold to the touch, but Adam sat twirling it between the palms of his hands as his thoughts once again turned to a few hours ago—and the woman who'd been discharged. She'd apparently needed her job because shock and distress was evident in her body and her voice. The look of panic in her eyes had startled Adam. If she depended on her job so badly, what could have been so important that she'd required a friend to work in her place? She'd obviously abused her attendance to the exhaustion point.

And her friend? Adam grunted in disgust. That word was used loosely in this case, he thought.

Adam crossed the room to the kitchen where he set the bottle in the recycling can, then went into the bedroom and closed the door. In the dark, he started to undress and he made another sound of disgust. He thought of the blow that Reva Fairchild was dealt by a friend who was bent on ruining her own life.

Adam's voice sounded angry when it pierced the quiet. "Sydney Cox, what kind of woman are you?"

Monday morning at eleven o'clock, Sydney was still in bed, but not asleep. It was times like this when she became ecstatic over her job. Her flexible schedule required her to be at the restaurant during the noon meal, and the dinner hour, which started at five-thirty. Sydney knew that for the last three months she had been foolish and risked her health by working such long hours, taking one day off since she'd been hired. But it had been so easy to justify her dangerous actions. She had wanted to learn all about her duties and she never thought about the fifty-odd hour weeks she was putting in. She was tired, but satisfied that the wine cellar was properly stocked and her wine list was commended by Benjamin Strauss, her employer.

Depending on how much work was on her desk crying out for attention on weekdays, Sydney usually arrived at twelve-thirty. Most nights she called it quits around ten o'clock. But today belonged to her because Restaurant Louise was closed on Mondays in July and August. She was grateful for the schedule because she would not have been able to make it in, especially with the way she felt and looked. Earlier, when she'd stared at herself in the bathroom mirror, her red eyes and swollen lids had given her a fright.

Now Sydney lazily turned her head to look at the bedside clock again. It was only eleven-twenty and she wondered if it was still too early to call New Mexico. Hours ago, at 5 A.M., she'd had to draw back her hand from the phone. Edward Marsh would have sworn and refused to let his wife take a call at three in the morning. The man was as protective of Ferne as a mama bear with a den of newborn cubs. But, maybe at nine-twenty, he would have left the house for his work site. Hopeful, she reached for the phone.

"Ferne?" Sydney didn't realize her throat was swollen with hurt, or that tears lay just behind her lids. The minute she heard her friend's voice, the sobs burst through and she sucked in the salty tears as they slid to her lips. She felt as though she were eight again, shy and sad, wishing she'd had a best friend like her sister had. As an adult, she had been blessed with two true friends and now she'd lost one and couldn't understand why.

"Sydney? What's wrong?" Hearing that voice, Ferne Marsh came awake instantly. Her large brown eyes widened in fear for her best friend. "Are you hurt? Is it Reva?"

Ferne inched up in bed until she rested against the pillows. Needing another, she took her husband's, and pushed it behind her head, then sank back heavily against the sturdy pine headboard. Ferne inhaled deeply. Edward's scent clung to the soft cotton pillowcase, and she missed her husband already, wishing that the sound of the door closing moments ago, meant that he was returning, not leaving her for hours.

Sydney's tears stopped. She suddenly became alarmed at her friend's silence and the breathy grunts coming in small spurts. The last thing her friend needed was to be upset and alone. Sydney was beginning to regret making the call.

"Ferne? Are you okay?" She forced herself to be calm.

Ferne rested comfortably against the mound of pillows. Her back no longer ached. "Sydney, you're scaring me. What's wrong?" she demanded.

"It's Reva," answered Sydney. "She stormed in here like a madwoman at one in the morning, told me off and left just as crazily. She said 'good-bye' and left."

"Good-bye? What are you talking about?"

"In essence, our friendship is over."

"Just like that?" Ferne frowned.

"Just like that," Sydney repeated.

"So couldn't you fix it? Forgive? Forget?"

"Not this time, Ferne." Sydney paused. "She was so . . . so . . . final!"

"What did you do to her?"

Sydney flushed. "What? Why do you think it was something that I did?" she asked hotly.

"Because you know you're the perfectionist, Sydney. You must have hurt her badly. Tell me."

Though Ferne loved her friend dearly, she was annoyed. The practical and forceful Sydney's tongue had a way of working against her. More softly, she asked, "What happened?"

Sydney was angry that Ferne had prejudged her. "Why don't you listen, then make your assumptions?" She hesitated. "If I've caught you at a bad time, I can call back. . . ."

"Sydney Cox, don't you dare go sanctimonious on me! You were obviously upset enough to call me, so just tell me what in blue blazes is going on!"

After several minutes, Sydney stopped talking, and waited. Her friend was so slow in responding that Sydney thought Ferne may have fallen asleep. Or was she just angry?

"Ferne?"

"Reva was right. You didn't listen. She warned you about the rules." Ferne paused, then said, "Think about it, Sydney. Put yourself in her place. You know how she saves her pennies from all those jobs she has to pay her own way. She never was one to ask for a handout. Even from us who know her best. We both thought she had lost it when she announced her plan to quit teaching to follow her heart into acting. Remember our trip to Florence five years ago?" Ferne's voice softened. "It was then that you, too, made a big decision, Sydney."

Sydney felt as dismal as a cloudy day when she reflected on Ferne's words. She had been wrong in ignoring the rules of that establishment, and her thoughtlessness had hurt a friend. And forget Florence? How could she? Her adult life had started there ten years ago. Visions of that beautiful city, and an old friend still haunted her.

"I remember, Ferne." Her voice softened and the last vestiges of anger subsided and she breathed evenly. Then, "You're right. I was wrong and treated my blunder too lightly as far as Reva was concerned.''

''Have you tried reaching her yet?''

''No. I'm sure she's still feeling as raw as I am. She wouldn't listen and that would only distance us further. I'll wait until later.''

''I think that's best.'' Ferne hesitated. ''Do you want me to call, too?''

Sydney's dark brown eyes glittered and she laughed, remembering their college years. All three had taken turns playing peacemaker to one or the other. ''No, that won't be necessary. We're all grown up, now.''

Ferne's laughter joined Sydney's. ''Haven't you heard? Grown-ups ain't all that!''

A short pause lent itself to the good feelings the two women had for each other. Ferne broke the silence.

''I know you've traveled to Italy on business in the past few years. Have you ever stopped in Florence, just to relax, Sydney?'' She'd not missed the wistfulness in her friend's voice a moment ago. Though that city was precious to all of them, it had meant the most to Sydney. She'd been forced to look into her heart. But Sydney held those memories close and rarely spoke of them to her best friends.

She means have I visited the Hotel Belle Donne, Sydney thought. ''No, I was too rushed to take in the old sights of Fiesole or even Siena. I stayed in the heart of the city.'' A smile touched her lips. ''The vintner I was meeting with chose to put me up just grandly. Remember once, how we sniffed at an old-fashioned thirteenth or fourteenth century hotel—can't remember which—when we peeked inside? Well it's still called the Porta Rossa and I certainly can appreciate it now. The elegant period decoration and all the hotel's appointments were excellent. I slept soundly and even wondered whether I was in the same room once used by Byron.''

Ferne smiled as she listened. *She's sidetracking again,* she thought. ''Sydney,'' she interrupted, ''you'll have to look inside one day.''

''One day,'' Sydney agreed. ''But, enough about me and

my problems. How are you, really?'' Her voice filled with concern. ''Edward must be at the site by now. What time do you expect him back? Will you be alone all day?''

''Cluck, cluck.'' Ferne laughed and Sydney joined in. ''Don't hover like an Edward Marsh clone. He'll be home by four o'clock, he's in the classroom and not at the site today, and I won't be alone when the housekeeper arrives to cook and clean.''

''And she did it all in one breath, too,'' Sydney sighed in a mock fashion. ''Don't joke. You know that man loves you like he discovered the emotion and patented it for his sole use.''

Ferne suppressed an impatient sigh. ''I know. I just wonder if there will be any left over for the little girl when she puts in an appearance.''

''Ferne! You decided to ask? I thought you wanted to be surprised!''

''I wanted to know, in case . . . well, I changed my mind.''

''Is everything okay? You're not . . . ?''

''No, there are no complications. The delivery is still scheduled in two weeks. I just have to stay off my feet as much as possible and you know how that's killing me.''

Frustration was evident in every word. ''I hear you,'' Sydney said, feeling compassion for her friend. Ferne gave credence to the phrase, ''ants in your pants'' and Sydney sympathized with Edward, who probably was catching hell in trying to lasso his wife into a state of immobility. She knew that if anything happened to Ferne or the baby, Edward would wear his guilt like a crown of thorns whenever he faced Edward Percival.

''Ferne?'' Sydney was hesitant. The sigh that sounded in her ear warned her that her next question was coming as no surprise.

''No, Sydney,'' said Ferne, ''my father hasn't called and no, he's not coming down for the big event.'' She paused. ''Mom is coming the week after next.''

Sydney had already been privy to that bit of information. When Hannah had driven her to the railroad station a few days ago, they had spoken of Ferne's upcoming delivery date and Hannah's plans to be with her daughter prior to the birth.

"I'm glad, Ferne. You know I'm here, so call me if you need anything. Promise?"

"You know I will," answered Ferne. "And Sydney, don't forget our friend. She's going to need us once she gives up on her dream."

Sydney opened her eyes, surprised to see that it was after one-thirty. She didn't remember falling asleep after she'd hung up the phone. Obviously, her body knew better than she did and had shut down for some much-needed rest. The last thing she did remember was thoughts about dreams and why did one give up on them? Survival, Sydney, survival, she'd told herself. Why else? She realized how fortunate she'd been in being able to flit from dream to dream without faltering and she'd thanked her angels shamelessly. She prayed that Reva would not shield herself with invisible armor, preventing her friends from getting close enough to offer comfort and help. Ferne was right. Once Reva gave up her quest for an acting career and went back to teaching full-time, she would deem herself a failure. Sydney wondered if she possessed the inner strength and the wisdom to play a significant role in Reva's healthy survival and philosophically moving on to the next phase of her life.

Hunger forced Sydney out of bed into the shower and to the kitchen where she prepared a hefty meal. Continued thoughts of her conversation with Ferne crowded her mind as she ate. Sliced banana covered with orange juice and a sprinkle of coconut was an indulgence and she savored the tart with the sweet. She rarely took the time to make the treat for herself, usually settling for cornflakes and coffee and toast before she dashed from the house. She'd made a sausage-and-green-pepper omelette and toasted an English muffin and slathered it with butter and apple jelly. She poured a second mug of coffee and carried it to the living room, not overly concerned about the fat and calories she'd consumed. Her appetite had been satisfied.

She resumed her thinking and soon she let herself be carried back to Florence and her memories of Maddelina Torreano. It was her old friend's home that Ferne was referring to when she'd asked Sydney about visiting old haunts. La Signora. That's what she, Ferne and Reva had called the grand old woman. And when Ferne had said "you'll have to look inside one day," she was referring to the same words told to Sydney by the old woman.

Was she running away? After all these years, she only just now wondered if La Signora's words had come true. Her heart had indeed turned to stone, and she'd been as obtuse about what was happening as a newborn babe.

"Sydney Cox, you have a heart of stone." Those words were flung at her ten years ago by Reva in the gardens of the Hotel Belle Donne. Carefree students on their senior trip to beautiful Florence, sought romance everywhere. All but Sydney who'd rebuffed every amorous overture by one very love-struck young man. He'd claimed to have fallen in love with her on sight. It was in the garden that she'd said a firm and final good-bye to a heartbroken Jon Carleton, pulling away from his kiss and embrace that had left her cold and unresponsive. She remembered his words.

"Do you find me so offensive, Sydney?"

"Jon, please don't think that." Determined to make him understand, she continued in an unsteady voice. "I believe that people do fall in love at first sight. It happened to you and I'm not taking that lightly. You fell in love, but I didn't. I . . . don't love you. I don't *feel* you in my heart."

Jon stood up, looking thoughtfully down at Sydney, almost studying her, as if remembering every nuance of her beautiful face. When he finally spoke, his voice was as tight as his stiffly held body.

"There are no imperfections, Sydney. At least none that are visible. But, inside there's one tiny flaw: a concealed heart." He hesitated, then continued. "I wish that I could see you, ten, even fifteen years from now. You will be more beautiful than ever in your maturity. I wonder then, Sydney, if you dared to reveal the secrets of your heart . . . dared to love." He turned from her and walked away.

Sydney watched him go. Somehow, she knew that she would

never see Jon Carleton again. She sat unmoving, listening to his footsteps on the stone path.

Suddenly, Sydney realized that she was not alone in the garden. Among the gentle rustle of the silvery olive tree leaves, she heard soft shuffling steps coming toward her. She turned and watched the slow approach of the odd woman.

"Signora!" Sydney exclaimed.

"Good evening, Sydney."

Startled by the presence of Maddelina Torreano in the garden, Sydney hastened to steady her as the elderly woman appeared to falter.

"Here, let me help you. Would you like to sit for a moment before going inside? I had no idea you were out here. We never saw you."

"Ah, the young only see and hear what they wish, my dear Sydney."

Her name on the woman's tongue sounded like *S-e-e-dnay,* and always made Sydney smile at the odd pronunciation. But now, she suddenly felt embarrassed. The signora must have seen and heard everything.

As if reading the young woman's thoughts, Maddelina said, "Yes, I heard the sounds of young love. What a joy to these ancient ears, Sydney. When you reach your ninety-ninth year, you will know what I mean." Though the darkness hid the twinkle in her eyes, gaiety was in her voice.

Sydney couldn't stop the small gasp. She'd known the elegant Florentine woman was old. But she never guessed that the woman who had befriended her for two weeks was almost a century old.

Sydney voiced her thought. "I never would have guessed."

"You wouldn't have child," the older woman answered. "The young have no perception of age. To you, the world and everyone in it is forever." Her stare was penetrating. "You are on the brink of the rest of your life, Sydney. You are twenty-one, twenty-two, yes?"

"Twenty-two."

"Ah, so young to have to make such onerous decisions that will use up the rest of your youth. So many responsibilities.

So many obligations to the one who will become your life partner. Who can say what one would miss if one chooses so young? Such a big world. So much to explore. To taste. To savor. To devour. Ah, such desserts. One more delectable than the other. No time to sample them all. No perfect time to choose a favorite. So you think to try only one more. Certainly, *that* will be the one to satisfy, to bring happiness.''

The heavily accented English was melodic and hypnotizing and Sydney could listen to the eloquent voice for hours. But, her words. They were meant for Sydney and her refusal of Jon. *How could she know my thoughts, my feelings about how I want to live my life? A stranger, across oceans, has perceived this restlessness inside of me,* Sydney thought. *How could she come to know me so well?* She looked at the woman's face and saw the sadness. Then, she knew. Signora was speaking of herself.

The young American's moment of realization was not unnoticed by Maddelina. She smiled and closed her eyes briefly. Searching Sydney's eyes, she said, "Yes, I see you as I was, almost eighty years ago."

"Twenty years old," Sydney murmured.

"Yes. Only two years younger than you are now. I was betrothed. My papa chose the man who would become my husband. But I was a rebellious woman."

"You did not marry?"

"No, not then."

"But did you love him?"

"I did not think so at that time. I had known him all my life and did not look upon him as my romantic love. The love of my life. So, I put off the wedding date, always searching for my one true love. My papa died and so there was no pressure on me to marry. My betrothed waited and waited until finally he discreetly ended our engagement. I felt such relief, such freedom to spread my wings. I traveled, meeting the cream of society the world over. I was the young, beautiful, eligible heiress and I was welcomed everywhere. I knew that I would find the love of my life among the gentry.''

Sydney heard the sadness. "But you never did," she said softly.

"No. Years passed before I wearied of my carefree lifestyle. On a rainy day in Paris, I realized what was missing. My journey had taken me so far from home and it was there that my destiny lay."

"Your betrothed."

"*Si*, Sydney, the man who had always loved me."

"And did you marry him?"

"He had married another."

"Oh." Sydney felt sad and imagined the hurt that the young Maddelina must have felt. "What did you do?"

"I married another."

"Did you love him?"

"I respected my husband."

"But that isn't the only reason for marriage!" Sydney exclaimed.

"I had given up the chance for true love, Sydney. I paid for my folly."

"Paid?"

"I did not love my husband and I foolishly wondered if that was why I was barren. My husband was an important man and needed to sire children to carry his name. He had our marriage annulled."

"You never married again?"

"Never. I've lived my life alone."

"But you were still so young, barely twenty-five years old! *More than seventy years alone.*

"Many years ago." Maddelina looked around the garden. "This has been my home for more than fifty I years. I'm happy here, Sydney. Now I am at peace with myself, though it was not always so."

Sydney was awed.

When the elderly woman spoke again, her voice was firm as she looked at Sydney. "Your young man, Jon. You do not love him, si?" She answered her question. "No. I see you are not in love and I fear for you. I see something that will prevent you from giving your heart to a man. You will not accept love freely.'' She shook her head, sadly. "One day you must look inside.'' She stood up slowly, grateful for Sydney's arm as they walked toward the hotel lobby. At the end of the path, Maddelina stopped. Age had not bent her body and she stood erect, looking squarely into Sydney's eyes.

"Child, you must dare to love. When you do, you will wonder why you ever denied yourself. Dare to love, or your heart will become as stone. Do not let my fate become yours.''

Sydney watched the old woman walk slowly inside the building.

The cool night breeze turned cold and Sydney left the garden. Chilled, she walked thoughtfully up the stairs to her room. Maddelina Torreano was still full of mystery. Why had she chosen to live her life alone in this residential hotel? Sydney would find her and ask her in the morning.

Arousing herself from old memories and the couch, Sydney shook out her stiff limbs and stood up. Her knees buckled, causing her to fall back down with a thud.

"Whoa,'' Sydney said. "Let's try this thing again, old girl. And methinks you'd better hit that exercise bike, pronto.'' She rubbed warmth back into her numbed legs, then tried again. This time, able to stand without wobbling, she walked to the kitchen where she began to clear the table and stack the dishwasher.

The day was nearly gone. Sydney was propped up in bed, gazing through the window, watching as the sun faded from the sky. It was nearly eight-thirty in the evening. After cleaning the kitchen, she had showered, put on fresh cotton pajamas and had climbed back into bed. She'd read, slept, watched television and read some more, languishing as she'd never done before, all in the absence of guilty pangs. She'd needed this quiet time to reflect upon all that had happened in her life the last ten years.

She remembered that that next morning, she had never sought out La Signora. She'd gotten caught up in those last-minute activities required for an on-time check out. The college professors accompanying the group were sticklers for punctuality and did not entertain the thought of missing their connections home.

It wasn't until Christmas of that year that she had learned that Maddelina Torreano had taken ill, and had died in a nursing home, alone, and among strangers.

During her daylong soul-searching, Sydney realized that the old woman's fears for her had become a reality. She *had* become a cold and unyielding woman.

The phone rang. Sydney turned her head to look at it, but remained unmoving. Her introspective mood was not conducive to trite interruptions from acquaintances.

"Mason, here. Are you there listening to my sexy voice?" He paused. "Guess not. Just wanted to know how things went with your crazy girlfriend. Hope you're out enjoying your day off. See ya tomorrow, right?

Sydney smiled. She was right about one thing. Mason did have a soft spot somewhere for Reva. She must remember not to tease him unmercifully about that, but she knew that she was not going to let this moment slide. It was just too irresistible.

Sydney got out of bed and padded to the kitchen where she poured a glass of cold grape juice, then returned to her propped-up position on the bed—and her thoughts.

"Would you like to see me now, Jon?" she asked the empty room. Her thoughts were somber. Ten, not fifteen, years was all that was needed to make his prophecy come true. He and La Signora knew. How was it that they both could see inside so clearly? How could they both know that one day her innermost feelings would be aroused? Stirred to life in the most unusual of circumstances. How unconventional that a voice without a physical form attached to it would become her awakening! Never, in all these years had a man been a part of her night dreams. And now, how was it possible that dreams of a voice could awaken her deepest womanly emotions—and in the most bizarre circumstances. Her mystery voice belonged to a man with eyes as hard and as cold as a rock. No matter what, if their paths ever crossed again, she knew that she could never open up her heart to that man. That look of disgust and disdain he'd impaled her with, had left her devastated. Adam Stone had thought that she was a drunk.

CHAPTER SIX

Sydney placed the birthday card back on the rack and hurried from the store. Reading those sentiments pertaining to friendship had unnerved her until her eyes started to tear. For the last few days, she'd tried reaching Reva to no avail. If it wasn't Reva's machine taking messages, it was one of her two roommates until they had even tired of Sydney's calls. It being Saturday, almost a week to the day that she'd last seen her friend, Sydney decided to give up the attempt. Maybe by the time Reva's birthday rolled around in three weeks, this would all just be yesterday's news, she hoped.

Sydney walked the next two blocks to the Hotel Margit, stopping to gaze in the store windows. She'd left the house an hour early today, just for this purpose, to relax her mind and think only of frivolous things. Dinner was going to be a busy meal with two private parties booked. An anniversary and a birthday celebration. Sydney knew that by ten o'clock tonight she would be feeling wiped out and wishing for bed.

Stopping and peering into one of her favorite shops on Fifty-first Street, she stared at the jewel that had caught her eye. The store, All Over the World, was a curio shop of old. The contents always fascinated her and she never tired of looking at and fondling the quaint objects. There were stuffed pillows in exotic fabrics, covered with fancy embroidery, and sparkling baubles; hundreds of odd-shaped boxes made in different materials; chairs from countries she'd never heard of, making her wonder what kind of people sat in such odd-shaped furniture. The shop owner would always call her attention to some odd object that he thought might interest her. What she saw now, piqued her curiosity and after glancing at her watch, she went inside. It was not yet eleven-thirty, so she had time to squander before scooting next door to the hotel.

Fifteen minutes later, Sydney walked from the shop to the hotel, her new bauble pinned near her shoulder on the black linen jacket. The ruby-red glass grape cluster was a rare find. Sydney justified the expense by telling herself it would one day become a collectors' item. Gold stirred in the molten glass mixture gave the nineteenth century glass its true gemstone red color. Deep down she knew that she was only appeasing her funky mood, and that the purchase reminded her of her friends. Years ago, Reva and Ferne had celebrated her transition from educator to wine merchant with a large grape cluster of pale green jade. That had started her acquisition of clusters of all kinds, varying from table pieces to jewelry. The pin she now wore was just one of many in her jewelry collection. Her step was a little lighter as she entered the Hotel Margit and headed for her office.

Sydney didn't know where the day went. Lunch was barely finished before the dinner crowd started appearing. It was six-thirty and the bar was overrun with diners waiting for their reservations. She had barely started her meal of duck l'orange before she was called to the dining room. Her assistance was needed.

Sydney wrapped her meal and put it in her small fridge, hoping she would eat it later in the warmth of Mason's kitchen, with her friend for company. After freshening up, she dabbed herself with a wild heather scented perfume, and left her office.

She hoped that the particular patron would prove not to be difficult and ornery, balking at her suggestions.

"Well, I'll be damned," exclaimed Lucas. "Seeing is definitely believing. I thought just wine snobs did that only in the movies, Lincoln."

Lincoln Yates raised one salt-and-pepper brow, then said wryly, "We're paying to drink good wine, Lucas. Only a masochist would sit in silence drinking bad wine simply because he didn't wish to make a scene."

"You're right about that, Mr. Yates." Jeremy Gage gave his boss a boyish grin and a firm shake of his head. Even if he wasn't in total agreement with his employer, he would still have applauded. His round dark eyes glittered as he looked at his tablemates for approval. Jeremy was the new kid on the block in this company of old-timers. He'd been an employee with Garrison International for only three years and he felt like the king of the peacocks for being asked to join the boss for dinner. He was in royal company with the likes of Adam Stone and Augustus Turner, two of the heavies in the firm. He turned back to Mr. Yates with nothing short of adoration in his admiring glance.

Before Sydney entered the dining room, the maître d' appeared.

"Hi, Dominic, what's this story about bad wine?" Sydney smiled. "Another 'expert' showing off?"

Dominic Ferraro's answer was a quick frown that marred his thin face. A flush traveled beneath his olive-tone skin and he let out a sigh, which was followed by a shrug of his slight shoulders. "Afraid not this time Sydney. The gentleman is quite correct in his assessment. I want you to reassure him and make the adjustment."

Sydney's smile turned into a frown. "You're sure?"

"Positive. Smells flat, tastes weak. Positive."

Sydney sighed. "Okay. Which was it?" She was surprised, though not annoyed, knowing that it was possible for a bad bottle of wine to slip through. She'd just had a hectic day and had hoped the evening would fly by smoothly.

After noting the wine selection, Sydney had already decided

what she was going to suggest as a replacement. She only hoped that the "expert" patron would agree. She headed for the table that Dominic had pointed out to her. As she neared, she groaned inwardly. Another male group of know-it-all world travelers. They are the worst, she thought when it came to being sensible about something that was no one's fault. She steeled herself, at the same time, noting what a handsome table they made. Four of the five men faced her, the fifth was in conversation with a good-looking hunk who stared at her with shameless admiration. Sydney took a deep breath.

"We're waiting for the what?" Augustus Turner asked.

Adam answered his friend's question. "The sommelier. The wine expert who will agree with Lincoln that we got a bad bottle of burgundy. It'll be replaced and then we can continue with dinner."

"Oh, I forgot that you and Lincoln are the connoisseurs. The two of you can probably tell this expert a thing or two about wine." Augustus gave his friend a broad wink. "I bet you have some stories to tell about your tour of duty in Italy, my friend." He started to laugh then gave a low whistle as he looked past Adam. "If this is our expert, she can talk to me about wine twenty-four, seven, and then some."

"Good evening, gentleman, I'm Sydney Cox. I understand you've had the rotten luck of getting a bad bottle of French Burgundy?"

Adam had his head turned and did not see Sydney approach. When he heard her voice and her name, he stiffened. He turned slowly, and stared. *It was her.*

Lincoln Yates was tall, good-looking and broad-shouldered and didn't mind looking at the ladies. He appreciated beauty when he saw it. Right now, he was appreciating Sydney Cox and was wishing he was twenty years younger. He tapped the bottle of wine.

"Appears so," he said easily. Before she could reply, he added, with a smile, "But then, as you know, these things can happen. Not the vintage, just that oxygen somehow got inside this one bottle and ruined it." He shrugged, "Who knows how?"

Sydney raised a brow and nearly gasped. A real learned wine-lover, she thought. Unpretentious, handsome and smooth. She cleared her throat. "May I?" she asked as she reached for the bottle. When he nodded, she sniffed, then frowned. She poured a little in the wineglass, this time practically burying her nose well inside and sniffed deeply. There was really no need she thought because she'd immediately smelled the odor from the bottle, convincing her of the bad bouquet of the old wine. Next, she tasted, knowing that her tongue and palate would confirm her assessment. In a second she knew the wine was not good. There were no impressions of harmony, balance or of purity. The unpleasant taste of flatness was present. Sydney held onto the glass and picked up the bottle, and looking at the distinguished-looking and knowledgeable diner, said, "You are one hundred percent correct, sir." She nodded her admiration.

Lincoln smiled and nodded his thanks at her appraisal and her silent approval of his astute observation.

"May I suggest the . . ." She was stopped by his deep voice.

"That won't be necessary, Ms. Cox," Lincoln said. "I'm certain that there's nothing wrong with the vintage. Suppose you bring another bottle of the same white burgundy. Since we all agreed on a Chardonnay, I doubt that any of us has changed his mind." He looked down at the other end of the table. "Would you agree, Adam?"

Adam had been staring agog at the beautiful woman talking to an admiring Lincoln. When she sniffed, then tasted the wine, he all but fell out of his seat. For more than a week, the image of a beautiful drunk had pierced his brain, bringing confusing images. He'd been nagged at something that would not present itself to him clearly. Something about the scene in a deserted office. Now, he knew. *She had been wine tasting!* The different bottles of wine, the stoppers to preserve the ones she'd already tasted, the sparkling white cloth, the bucket holding the wine she'd spat out! *Sydney Cox was a wine connoisseur!*

Adam, his eyes on Sydney, answered his boss. "I would, Lincoln," he said. "No reason to change. I'm sure Ms. Cox can accommodate us."

Sydney froze at the sound of that voice. She'd placed no

importance to the name when Lincoln had said it, but the sound of that voice, mesmerized her. *Adam Stone.* How could she forget his name? And that voice? She looked at the man who now held her gaze, rendering her speechless.

All four men at the table stared from Adam to Sydney. It would take the most obtuse not to see the underlying currents, waffling between the man and the woman.

It was Lincoln's voice that broke the silence. Very smoothly, as if there had been no break in the conversation, he said, "Then it's decided, Ms. Cox. We'll be happy if you provided us with another bottle of the Corton-Charlemagne."

It was all Sydney could do to keep her back straight and her knees from shaking as she walked away. Instead of stopping at an area near the bar where an abundance of fine wines was stored, she continued out of the dining room. Leaning her back against the wall, both hands clutching her quivering stomach, she struggled to regain her composure. His presence had affected her in a way such as she would never have imagined. She didn't even *like* the man, yet looking at that face and staring into those surprised, dark eyes, she'd realized at that moment that the thought of him had always been just beneath the surface of her mind. She had wanted to meet him again. To talk to him. To know him. And now, here he was, looking as flabbergasted as she had felt.

"Sydney? Are you all right?" Dominic was staring anxiously at her, wondering what had gone wrong at the table.

Sydney pushed away from the wall, straightened her jacket and smoothed back her hair, which she wore pulled into a bun at her neck. Only occasionally did she let it fall to her shoulders while she was at work.

"I'm fine, Dominic. There's no problem. I was foolish again, going all day without eating. As soon as I eat something, my stomach will stop talking to me. Thanks for asking." She started back into the dining room. "I guess those gentlemen must be wondering what happened to me. I have to get . . ."

"No problem, Sydney. I took care of it for you. The new bottle is just fine as we all knew it would be. They're quite a happy bunch now." He smiled and gave her a conspiratorial nod, as if to say, there couldn't possibly be another such bottle in Restaurant Louise's cellars. "You'll excuse me? I think I'm needed." At the beckoning of the hostess, he walked briskly toward the reservations desk.

Sydney was not lying when she told Dominic she hadn't eaten. She was famished and the delicious smells reaching her nostrils from passing waiters, made her crave food. Before another hour passed, she had to take some nourishment. A quiet gossip session with Mason later on was out of the question. But first she must see to her gentlemen diners and offer her apologies. If she didn't, possibly jeopardizing the good name of the posh eatery, her employer, and good friend of Edward's, Benjamin Strauss, would forever lecture her on the need for impeccable public relations. Her only discomfort was meeting the eyes of Adam Stone.

Lucas stared after Sydney, then at Adam. When he caught the stunned man's attention, he said, for Adam's ears only, "McGregor's S. Cox?"

Adam looked at Lucas and nodded, his jaw stiff and unyielding. His demeanor invited no further questions.

Lucas understood and only nodded, letting out a soft snort.

Lincoln had read the report on Adam's latest assignment only two days ago. A keen mind and an excellent memory did not fail him when Sydney introduced herself. He had instant recall and was nearly disbelieving. Associating the Sydney Cox from the report with the beauty standing beside him was jolting. But his eyes didn't lie. He couldn't miss the bomb that had caught one of his best managers square in the gut. He pretended ignorance to the dynamic byplay between Adam and the astonished Ms. Cox. With the others present, he kept his questions to himself. Now was not the time to talk business. But before his plane left in the morning, he would have to meet with Adam. He watched Sydney approach their table.

"Gentlemen," Sydney said. Although her glance swept the table, she avoided looking at Adam, then directed her next remarks to Lincoln, who appeared to be the one the other men seemed to defer to. "I trust that your meal was satisfactory? And the wine?"

Lincoln smiled and said, "I believe I can speak for all of us. Your chef outdid himself with all our selections. Our compliments, please. The wine as we all knew it would be, was superb."

"Thank you sir. I'll convey your sentiments to Chef Wingate. I'm certain he would like to thank you himself before you leave." Sydney smiled when she added, "Please accept the wine with our compliments. We at Restaurant Louise appreciate your patronage and hope you choose to dine with us again."

"I'll make that a date, when I fly in again," answered Lincoln. "My colleagues here, I'm afraid, will have sampled all of Chef Wingate's dishes before I return."

Sydney laughed. "I hope so," she said, a sparkle entering her eyes. "I'll make sure that something special is added to the menu in anticipation of your next visit. Just let us know in advance."

"I certainly will," murmured Lincoln.

"Ms. Cox," Lucas said, "you can tell your chef, that I'll be bringing my wife in here next week. She won't believe that there's another body around that can make a roasted duck taste as good as hers."

"I can, Mr. . . . ?"

"Parnell. Lucas Parnell."

"Mr. Parnell, you may have the honors, yourself." She watched as Mason approached with the maître d'. She had discreetly signaled to Dominic that Mason's presence was requested. On occasion, Mason would comply when he was not swamped.

"Gentlemen, I present to you, Chef Mason Wingate." Sydney looked at Mason, her eyes twinkling. "Their compliments, Chef." She stepped back as her friend gave her a look.

Mason addressed the diners who were introducing themselves and murmuring their praise of his culinary skills. They all had spoken with the exception of one who remained silent throughout the short discussion. Mason observed the quiet man who stared at Sydney almost without blinking an eye. For that matter, the man sitting next to him and who had called himself Turner, had a hard time keeping his eyes off her. *Whew,* Mason thought to himself. *What havoc has my girl wrought here? She's going to need protection walking to the subway tonight,* he swore. As Mason said good night and turned to leave, he didn't miss the glance that passed between Sydney and the stoic one. He heard Sydney say good night to the men, then follow him out of the dining room. Turning to give her a brief look, Mason didn't stop, but kept on going toward the kitchen.

Sydney was glad that Mason had to get back to work. She wasn't ready for any explanations. She hurried to her office, wondering at her actions. Was she actually flirting? No, she answered herself, as she entered her office. Never, she thought as she warmed her food in the small microwave. Isn't it Sydney Cox who has the heart of stone? Cold and unfeeling? She couldn't be the one who was flirting to beat the band with that handsome older man! And the one called Turner? She hadn't missed his looks either. The only one who didn't catch her eye was the one with the boyish-looking face although he could pass for fortyish. She hadn't liked the way he seemed to curry favor with Mr. Lincoln Yates, the obvious biggie in the group. And Adam Stone? He'd barely spoken except to murmur his name and nod curtly at Mason.

It was after nine o'clock when Sydney returned to her office after taking her dishes to the kitchen. Avoiding Mason hadn't been a problem because he had his hands full with wet dumplings. She'd waved as she left. She was beat and decided to call it a night. If any problems arose, she was sure Dominic would handle them with his usual aplomb. She went in search of him.

Adam was sitting alone in the softly lit bar. After saying good night to the others, Lincoln had invited him to the lounge where they had a drink and talked. They'd sat for a half hour in which time, Adam confirmed the identity of Sydney as being the cleaning woman in the corporate office. Before he left, Lincoln hit Adam with some disturbing news about the past attempts on his life in Boston and in Italy. The company was investigating a new lead on the Italy attack. The man they thought responsible—an enemy of Adam's client—apparently wasn't in Italy at the time. Lincoln warned Adam to watch his back. Adam, instead of leaving with Lincoln, stayed in the lounge, waiting. Before the night was over, he had some unfinished business to take care of. As he pondered his next move, the reason for his unsettled nerves, walked by, apparently leaving for the night. He stood up, placed some bills on the bar and left. He caught up to her as she was about to step on the down escalator.

"Ms. Cox." Adam spoke low but his deep-timbered voice was audible above the low whine of the motorized stairs.

Sydney stopped and stepped back, turning to face Adam. Here he was and all she could do was stare.

"Ms. Cox. I owe you an apology. I'm sorry."

"Sorry? For what Mr. Stone?" There was no warmth in her voice and she was sure her eyes weren't sparkling. Why was she acting this way? she thought. Hours ago she'd realized that her wish was to lay eyes on this man once more; to talk to him. The opportunity had appeared and she was acting like Miss Hurt Sophisticate! People were right about her. She had no feelings.

Adam never flinched though his stomach was churning. He had to do this. He owed it to her.

"I'm sorry I misjudged you. Apparently I overreacted, allowing anger to cloud my judgment." He cleared his throat. "I should have been more observant of what was really going on. Again, I offer you my apologies."

Sydney was silent, recalling that night. All she saw clearly were those cold dark eyes and that look of disdain for a drunk. He'd been disgusted. She'd felt embarrassed and ashamed at his misguided appraisal of her. Now he wanted her forgiveness. Well, too bad, she thought. He could go bark at the moon as far as she was concerned. Her lips tightened as she stared at him.

Adam saw the decision in her eyes and was certain of it when she set her jaw. Feeling that there was nothing further to say, he took a step toward the escalator. "Then I'll say good-bye, Ms. Cox.'' Without another word, he took a step and was moving slowly downward.

Sydney watched the proud set of his head and his stiff back as distance separated them—this time forever? *Who cares?* she argued with herself. What kind of relationship could be established between them? He of the unsmiling face and she with the cold heart. All he asked for was to be forgiven, she thought, and suddenly the simple little word, *yes* was lost from her vocabulary. She'd started down the escalator and she watched as he disappeared through the revolving doors. Gone. Another person saying good-bye to her in less than a week. Reva! Sydney had asked for her friend's forgiveness and all she got was a cold farewell and not another word since. Sydney recalled her feeling of desolation and her need to share her pain with someone else.

Adam Stone had asked for forgiveness from a stranger and she'd turned a cold shoulder to his distress. The man had been on the job, protecting his employer's interests. Who was she to be so unforgiving? Why should another person suffer from more mistaken misunderstandings? What occurred a week ago was history and harboring ill against another was a waste of energy. She was certain she could reserve her frowns for more worthy wrongs.

Sydney was outside the building, looking up and down the street, hoping to spot him. Had he been driving? If so, he was probably already stuck in the Fifty-first Street traffic. The warm, muggy night was right in keeping with July, which was why the sidewalks were crowded with people moving at a snail's pace.

Sydney peered around the bobbing heads, searching for one that looked familiar. Finally giving up, she walked toward the subway, but changed her mind, thinking that the air, such as it was, would do her good if she walked a few blocks. She felt a self-pitying mood coming on, and that was the last thing she needed. Suddenly, Sydney stopped as she saw Adam walking a few steps in front of her. It had to be him. She couldn't forget the shape of that head or that distinctive walk. He held his shoulders straight and his hips appeared to roll into the next step. Besides, she thought, a smile touching her lips, he was the only male dressed in a tailored blazer. Very easy to spot amidst the pastel-colored cotton tanks and T-shirts. She noticed the plastic bag from the trademark all-night pharmacy and realized why she'd missed him. She quickened her step.

Now that she was so close, what was she going to say? She nearly gasped when he stopped, paused a second, then entered the café. Sydney was perplexed. Should she follow him in? Suppose he was meeting someone? She blinked when a waitress appeared and Adam followed her to an outdoor table. The woman said a few words then disappeared. Almost at once, Adam looked up and saw her staring at him. Sydney could do nothing but walk toward him.

By the time she reached him, he was standing.

"Ms. Cox?"

There was a little light but not enough for her to see into his eyes, but she heard the surprise in his voice. He was unsmiling.

"Mr. Stone, I . . . I hoped to catch you and . . ." She was interrupted by the waitress who set a huge dish of chocolate ice cream on the table. She asked if Sydney was having anything and appeared surprised to see the man and woman standing, just staring at each other. She waited.

Adam said, "Won't you sit, Ms. Cox?" Then, "Do you like chocolate ice cream?" When Sydney nodded, Adam said, "The same, please." When the waitress left, Adam pushed the dish toward Sydney. "Why don't you start on this before it melts?"

Sydney spooned the smooth delicacy into her mouth, unbelieving of what she was doing. The glass-enclosed candle on the table afforded light and she was able to see his face more clearly. He looked baffled. When he spoke she nearly jumped.

"You wanted to catch me to . . . ?" Adam was as surprised as she appeared to be. Curiosity at her boldness had him stumped. The cold look she had given him not ten minutes ago had told him what she thought of him. Now here she was, wanting—what? His ice cream arrived and he tasted it. He ate several spoonfuls before he spoke again.

"Ms. Cox?"

Sydney found her tongue and blurted, "I was rude back

there. I accept your apology and now I want you to accept mine.''

Adam pushed his dish away and sat with his hands clasped on the table. After a moment, he said, "Thank you. And yes, I accept yours.''

Suddenly Sydney smiled. "Oh, you make me feel like the bad guy.''

Adam shook his head. "Never," he said. His voice was solemn as he added, "A guy you could never be, Ms. Cox.''

Sydney flushed at the unexpected compliment. She didn't think that he'd noticed that she was a woman. But, all the same, she couldn't ignore what was going on inside of her when he spoke. Afraid that she would suddenly experience those explosive feelings, she hurriedly drank the cold water the waitress had brought. She relaxed against the chair as her body cooled down.

Adam had been watching her. "I agree," he said. "It is a warm night.''

Sydney gulped, then smiled. "Yes, it is," she answered. After a moment of silence, she said, "Mr. Stone, can I ask you something?''

Adam nodded.

"We're strangers, yet we've met and spoken twice. And now we're together for a third time, breaking bread over chocolate ice cream. Even though we may never see each other again, do you mind if we can be 'Sydney' and 'Adam' for the duration?''

For the first time since he met her, Adam smiled. She was a surprise. "For the duration," he replied.

"Good. And thanks for the smile. I was beginning to think that your face wasn't made that way.''

This time, the smile traveled to Adam's eyes. "It happens on occasion, I'm afraid.''

"Don't be. It looks good on you." Sydney felt warm again. What was she doing? Trying to flirt? Suddenly flustered, she said, "I'd better be going, it's getting late and tomorrow is another heavy day.''

"You work every Sunday?" Adam was surprised.

"Yes. Weekends, you know. We're very busy."

"You worked last Sunday?"

"Yes, why?"

"You worked last Saturday at the restaurant, left, filled in for your friend, and then worked Sunday?" Adam paused. "When did you sleep?"

Immediately, they both knew.

Adam swore beneath his breath. He'd been completely wrong, every which way, where this woman was concerned. She was not a drunk, but a respected wine connoisseur. She was not a failure as a friend, but one who was loyal. And he'd accepted *her* apology. He felt her stir and when he looked, she'd stood up.

"Well, I guess I'll say good-bye, Adam. Thanks for the cream. It was a delicious pick-me-up."

Adam was standing beside her. "Would you wait one second, Ms. Cox ... Sydney?" When she nodded, he signaled the waitress and seconds later he joined her on the sidewalk.

Sydney waited, wondering what he wanted to say to her. There was really nothing that they could possibly discuss. It was after ten o'clock, hardly a time to make small talk when what she needed was her bed. *There you go again,* she told herself. *No wonder you're still single. You can see the man is delaying your departure and all you can think about is sleep.*

Adam gestured toward the street. "Are you driving? Mind if I see you to your car?"

"In this mess? Not a chance," she answered. She shook her head. "Two stops on the train and I'm home. I was going to catch the number six at Sixty-eighth Street, but now I think I'll walk back to Fifty-first. My intention to cheat on exercise has disappeared." She smiled at him. "But thanks for asking." She paused. "And you? Car or iron horse?"

Adam's mouth moved in a tiny smile. "Apparently we did think alike on one thing. I needed to walk also, but got side-tracked." He nodded down at the plastic bag. "I plan to hail a cab." He eyed her. "It would be no problem to drop you off at Sixty-eighth Street. I'm at Sixty-first and Park."

Sydney was surprised. "We're practically neighbors," she said. "My place is on Seventy-second and Third."

Adam drew an inaudible breath. Was he being given a chance to know this woman? From the second he saw her tonight in the restaurant, his body had reacted in the same way that it had a week ago, causing him to retrace his steps to the thirtieth floor. He'd wanted to see that strange and beautiful woman again. And now, here she was, just as beautiful and mysterious—and he wondered if he was ready to face his emotions. Because after all these years, she had invaded a part of him that he'd thought impenetrable; she'd chipped the armor around his heart. Before Sydney left him this night, Adam thought, he would make certain that she would not be walking out of his life forever.

CHAPTER SEVEN

After exiting the cab, Adam walked along the narrow cement path beside the building. The rear door to his small apartment led into the kitchen. The backyard went unused by the building's tenants, not because they hated sitting around the small patch of grass, but because they worked all day and hadn't the energy to drag themselves back downstairs just for a minute of inhaling the gas-fumed air. Cooling off with AC was the better way to go, especially in this unrelenting heat. But Adam sometimes took advantage of the quiet place. The few park-type benches were just outside his door. There was no public light, only what illumination was afforded by some apartments above, so the area was dark and in shadow. When Adam rounded the building, he stopped, then dropped his bag, suddenly going into a crouch. Someone was sitting on the bench, closest to his apartment. Damn, he thought, he wasn't packing. Though he was licensed to carry, he usually left his gun at home when he wasn't working. He braced himself.

The voice was low and steady. "Cool out, buddy. It's Augustus."

Adam let out a curse and straightened his taut muscles. He picked up his bag and walked toward the voice. He stared at his friend, then without a word, unlocked his door and turned on the light. He heard Gus follow him inside.

Adam tossed his parcel of paper towels and dishwasher detergent on the countertop, then turned and glared at his uninvited visitor. "What is so important that you have to camp out in the dark waiting to tell me? Whatever happened to late Sunday afternoon phone calls?"

Gus had a keen ear and he didn't miss the emphasis on *late*. He moved past Adam into the sitting room and deposited himself in the easy chair, throwing one long leg over the arm.

"Too hot to sleep," he drawled. "What's cold and wet?" Gus and Adam were cut from the same mold and could almost pass for brothers. They were the same height at five-eleven. One ninety-nine was their common weight, with Gus carrying the extra four or five pounds from time to time. Both men had the same dark brown skin, were broad-chested and had strong necks. Where Adam favored facial hair, Gus was clean-shaven. Like Adam, Gus had dark brown eyes that could turn black, cold and deadly in an instant. It was his sharp, cold eye that had saved Adam's life three years ago in Boston. The bond between them was strong.

Adam handed Gus a beer then sat across from him on the sofa. "I don't believe you. What's the real reason you're here?" Lincoln and Gus had taken rooms at the Millenium Hilton, across from the World Trade Center, and Adam was ninety-nine percent positive that the air-conditioning system was working to the max.

"You never did mention your session with Lincoln this week." Gus took a sip of beer. He stared intently at his friend.

Adam returned the pointed look. Several of the security managers had private meetings with Lincoln Yates. "You never mentioned yours either," he said cautiously.

Both men were silent, each weighing how the other was going to feel about what had come out of his session with the head and cofounder of Garrison International. Would their relationship become strained based on the decision each had made?

Gus broke the silence. "I turned it down. I was pegged for Chicago."

Adam let out a breath. "So did I. Mine was Los Angeles."

The room was quiet again, as both men thought about the choice they had made. It was Adam whose voice ended the quiet self-examinations.

"Lincoln was surprised." Adam hesitated. "But he also understood. He knows about taking giant steps." A second passed. "Getting tapped for executive manager and becoming stationary is a whole other world. As security manager supervising an officer force in the field, well . . . I'm not ready just yet to go inside. Maybe after another year." He looked at Gus. "Is your reason open for discussion?"

"Sure," Gus drawled. "I want an assignment in Singapore before I pack it in." He shifted his other leg onto the arm of the chair. "Next thing you know, I'll start developing a paunch like Lucas if I'm on my rump all day."

Both men laughed.

"Besides," Gus said, "there's nobody around who can save your butt like I can."

Adam was thoughtful. "I'm glad you were there, buddy."

Gus cleared his throat, then changed the subject. "I know about the investigation. We think Reynard's about to surface." He finished the beer and as he walked to the fridge to get another, he said over his shoulder, "Jeremy and I have new assignments."

The sagacious Adam's voice was dry. "Me."

Gus saluted Adam's keen perception with the bottle as he resumed his laid-back position in the chair. "Among other loose ends that need tidying."

"How does one become a loose end, I wonder?"

"When you're the best and you get tapped for another heavy. Somebody has to stay behind to see to the cleanup."

"You and Jeremy landed that?" Adam was referring to the Olson Pharmaceutical case—and Thomas McGregor. That assignment was over for Adam. It had ended just five days after the mixed signals on last Saturday night. All because of a cleaning woman who liked things to be perfect and had foiled an attempted drug theft.

"Yeah. With you personally tapped for this special assignment, Lucas wanted a manager to supervise the other officers. I'm it, but Jeremy and some others will be doing most of the follow-up paperwork. Lucas made the suggestion and Lincoln agreed." He halted for a second. "They don't want you distracted, looking over your shoulder for Reynard. And since I watch your back so well, Lucas figured why stop now?" He turned serious. "That little girl is going to need your total attention."

Adam nodded, but they could talk about that later. Now, he wanted to know how McGregor was.

When Garrison International was first hired by the pharmaceutical firm to investigate its cargo thefts, Adam suspected an outsider-insider setup. Because of the distant schedule of deliveries, it had taken months for Adam and his officers, working with the building security force, to get a handle on the operation. When Thomas McGregor had emerged as the one suspect, Adam had felt empathy for the man. The pretty, red-haired little girl in the silver picture frame on his desk was his six-year-old daughter. She had died as the result of being given a new antipyretic drug that had killed her. The high fever-reducing drug was manufactured by his company. McGregor held his firm liable because they neglected to label the new drug for adult use only. The potent drug was too powerful for a six-year-old's heart to withstand.

"How's McGregor?"

"Distraught." Gus explained how, when confronted, the man had broken down and confessed to spearheading the cargo thefts. When asked where the drugs were, he admitted to destroying both shipments.

Adam shook his head. "Can't help feeling that it's wrong for him to be put away. His child is dead and his wife needs him."

"A crime was committed, Adam."

Adam shifted on the couch. "You're right."

"You gonna be all right with this new one?"

Adam knew that Gus was referring to a little girl whose life was threatened. He nodded his head. "The joker's not even going to get close."

"When do you start?"

"A week from today. That's when the client will return with her daughter. Until then, Lucas ordered me out of the office for a few days. Says it'll clear my head."

"He's right," Gus said. "Can't hurt and you're overdue. Where's the client coming from?"

"After the stunt this nut pulled at the camp, Mrs. King took Kyla to California. She stayed with her parents until she thought what to do. After doing her research, Garrison International was hired to protect her daughter."

"The guy's got a lot of balls," Gus said in disgust.

"Granted. But he had a lot of help from the cooperative camp counselors and from the kid herself." He waved an impatient hand. "Can't understand why people are so ready to respond to a quick grin and a pretty face. If he'd resembled Quasimodo, he would have been kicked off the grounds before he'd gotten the first word out of his mouth."

"So posing as a friend of her mother's, he was allowed to take her away for a day, bringing her back in time for the dinner bell."

"Correct. The same day, when she arrived at home, a parcel was given to her by the doorman. Inside was the note. He'd described what he'd done, adding how easy it was to kidnap, rape, then kill an unsuspecting nine-year-old."

Gus swore. "A bank president's life's not all that sweet after all. How much?"

"Half a million."

Gus whistled, then scowled. "For starters."

"Probably. But the guy's a fool. There's a composite floating all over town." Suddenly, Adam swore. "Not a fool at all."

"An accomplice," Gus said.

"No. He's the accomplice and the one showing his face. He's long into the wind by now."

"You're gonna have your hands full." Gus set the beer

bottle on the table and stretched his legs. "Taking the next few days off sounds like a good bet. What're your plans?"

Adam hesitated, as if he contemplated sharing. "Well, I, er . . . have a date on Monday." He looked defiantly at his friend.

"A what?" Gus sat upright, feet planted firmly on the floor. Stunned, he fell back in the chair, his thoughts going around like a carousel as he ran over the events of the evening. Immediately, he guessed. "The wine expert." At Adam's look, he slapped his thigh, and in awe, murmured, "Well, the iceman is finally in meltdown mode."

Adam only stared.

Still looking bewildered at his friend, Gus said, "Lincoln told me that he left you behind in the bar. Said you had business to tend to." A soft chuckle escaped. "Lincoln decided he was too old and me, well, I was just too slow."

Adam glared. "It didn't start out like that."

Gus smiled. "It never does," he said softly. "So you were tuned in to our scheming minds after all and you never said a word." Gus laughed. "I saw you eyeballing the chef. He stood a little too close and acted more familiar than you liked."

Adam's look grew darker. "They work together man. And how is it that you were hawking me?"

"Couldn't be helped. None of us missed those signals between the two of you, buddy. We were just waiting for the next utterance but you both chose to play the ignorant game." Over his initial shock, Gus asked, "Got her number?"

"How else am I to call?"

"Okay, okay, just wondered how?"

"I asked," Adam snapped.

Gus stood up, preparing to leave. "Well, if you need me, just call. Better yet, I'll be watching your back anyway and if I see you acting the fool, I'll pull your coat." He winked and walked to the front door.

"Watching my back starts next week. For now, I'm on my own," Adam growled.

It was nearly midnight before Adam finally closed the King folder that Lucas had sent to him by special messenger the day before. He turned out the light, but remained propped up on the pillows. During the hour or so that he'd been reading, his mind kept wandering to where he would be on Monday at twelve in the afternoon. He squirmed and rubbed his chest. Gus is not far wrong, he thought. Something happened inside whenever he thought of her. When she had smiled at him as she left the cab, he'd caught his breath and winced at the sudden sharp pain in his chest. It wasn't indigestion and he knew that another chip of armor had just fallen away.

Gus stopped in his tracks and spun around, staring at the near-empty street behind him. His sharp gaze caught everything that moved within thirty feet on both sides of the lamp-lit sidewalks. He walked the block back to Adam's building and stood quietly, watching, and peering into the shadows. He even crept to the back of the alleyway, to the same place he'd waited in the dark for Adam. The yard was empty. Moving with the stealth that enabled him to keep himself and his officers alive, Gus eased down the narrow walk without disturbing a pebble. Glancing once more at Adam's lighted windows, he walked away, satisfied that his friend was still awake and would not be taken by surprise. But not tonight. The danger had passed. Gus was certain of that, but he still felt uneasy. After years of surveillance on both sides of the game, he knew what the chill meant on the nape of his neck. He had been watched. He walked cautiously to Park Avenue and hailed a cab.

The large shadow, several doors away from Adam's lighted windows, became a dark form that peeled itself away from the steps leading down to a basement apartment. The masculine body climbed up the stairs, watching the spot where minutes before, Gus had stood, ready to do battle.

"His days are numbered, my friend." The whisper was quickly lost in the air as the dark-clad form disappeared down the quiet street.

Sydney entered her eighth-floor apartment on a cloud and wondered if it were she. Never in her life had she experienced such heightened senses from the nearness of a man. Now she could genuinely imagine what her women friends felt when they spoke of their bodies not being their own when they were with their man. She'd always held her tongue in check and suffered in silence until their episodic conversations ended. When Edward Marsh had walked through the door of Amalia Fine Wines, Ferne, who'd been manager, had fallen in love in an instant with the rugged-looking man. Later, she'd told Sydney and Reva that he could've carried her off on his expeditions to the wilds of anywhere. Now Sydney knew what Jon Carleton felt all those years ago; an indescribable, painful ache, but for a cold and unyielding young woman.

As Sydney undressed, she wondered if a man's body experienced the same warm sensations as a woman's. Had Jon felt his blood gurgle as if seared by the heat of a swollen volcano? When he'd touched her bare arms and caressed her face, did he feel movement in his toes, like she had when Adam touched her hand; his iron grasp steadying her as she stepped from the cab. When they had lurched together, and the static from the cloth of his pants and the friction from her nylons practically sizzled in the quiet, had she let out a sigh?

Sydney let the silk gown slide over her head and down to cover her nakedness. As it whispered over her belly, stopping at the top of her thigh, she imagined that the tactile sensations were caused by the fingers of Adam Stone. She was shameless with the erotic thoughts that followed as she slipped between the sheets. Months ago, she'd had these same thoughts and feelings—all because of a voice she'd heard. Now that she could put a body and a name to her mystery voice, her erotic dreams were dreamlike no more. What she was feeling was real. The once cool sheets were dampened from the heat of her body. Sydney closed her eyes and quickly opened them because the image of his face floated behind her closed lids.

Sydney sat up in bed and threw off the covers. Barefoot, she hurried to the kitchen, opened the freezer and grabbed a handful of ice cubes. Wrapping them in a paper towel, she rubbed her neck, her throat and her arms. She lifted her gown and massaged her belly, then her thighs. Slowly the heat wave dissipated. Tossing the towel on the sink, Sydney turned out the light but instead of going to bed, she headed for the darkened living room where she stood looking down at the street. She hugged her arms across her chest and watched the parade of cars and the pedestrians. She wondered if those hundreds of strangers had ever felt like she was feeling now. She wondered if she was feeling the first pangs of love. Who could tell her? Dumbski! she chided herself. No one can *tell* you that you're in love. One just knows. Sydney smiled as she rocked her body. *And she knew.*

The smile disappeared. Come Monday, how would she react to a rigid and distant Mr. Stone? Unsuspectingly, he'd be meeting a different Sydney Cox. Would his astuteness alert him? Sydney clasped her hands behind her back and pulled on her fingers. Her face, reflected back to her, showed worry lines around her eyes.

"I'm daring myself to love, Maddelina Torreano," she whispered. "Now, we'll just have to wait and see."

Sunday morning brought cooler temperatures without high humidity, and a slight breeze riffled at Adam's bedroom curtains. He'd been awake for the last five minutes but he balked at getting up, wishing that he could recall the dream. She was a vision that had danced in his head all night. She'd been laughing and talking, and frustrated, he couldn't remember what she'd been saying. But from the smile on his face, he knew that he'd been enjoying every word.

In all his adult life, Adam had never known himself to grin and smile like that. He actually saw himself happy! Growing up in Brooklyn, with his parents and his brother, Lawrence, he could see himself horsing around with his younger sibling. When was it then that he'd become so hard and cold? He used to be one who'd sit around with the guys, telling poor jokes. His sense of humor was not that bad.

Adam threw the sheet off and got out of bed. He knew what had happened to him. After eleven years with the military police, he knew. And after the death of his best friend, Owen, he knew. And after Adam had been beaten unmercifully, all in the name of racism, he knew. Yeah, his smiles were few and far between and why the hell not?

Adam brushed his teeth vigorously, then spat as if ridding himself of his bad thoughts. He smirked as he rinsed the sink, envisioning Ethan Reynard floating down the drain, drowning in Adam's spit.

Dressed in running shoes, shorts and T-shirt, Adam unlocked the front door, prepared to sprint to the store for a Sunday newspaper. Today would be his first lazy day in a long while. May as well go all the way, he thought. This is going to be a real do-nothing day, with newspapers spread all over the floor, a home-cooked meal from the corner deli, and no calls or visits from Lucas.

When Adam opened the door, he stepped on the long white envelope that lay at his feet. It was facedown, so he couldn't see the addressee. Military episodes flashed through his brain, making him hesitant to pick up the unorthodox mail delivery. Flashbacks showed scenes of him opening the steady doses of hate mail during the time of the court-martial. Why should the man change his style of delivery now, Adam thought. Grim-faced, he bent and picked up the envelope. He swore. It was addressed to him. Adam looked at the street that had yet to come to life at eight-twenty in the morning. A thought made him grimace. The well-heeled residents in pricey apartments and old mansions, had no idea what filth had slithered pass their doors during the night. "There goes the neighborhood," he murmured. He stepped back inside, closed the door, making certain that it was double-locked.

Adam's look was murderous and his voice steely when Lucas answered the phone. Ignoring the disgruntled, sleep-thickened tone of his boss, Adam said, "Lincoln never said he'd surfaced in New York. Literally on my front doorstep!"

Lucas was instantly awake. His feet hit the floor with a thud. "Are you all right?" he demanded. "What did . . ."

Adam stopped him. "I'm okay, Lucas. I never saw him. Came and went like the sneaky coward he is. In the dark. Or he sent a lackey like he did when he was doing his time."

"Another letter?"

"Yeah. Same kind. Same words. Same ignorant threats."

Adam hesitated. "He added a little something this time. Pictures."

"What? Of who for chrissakes?"

"Us. Everybody who was at dinner last night. Inside and outside the restaurant." Adam's mouth was dry. "There are two of Ms. Cox. One caught her leaving."

"Christ!"

"He's telling me something, Lucas."

"Maybe. Maybe not. What's she got to do with any of this? She's only an employee in the restaurant we chose to eat at. Besides she's a beautiful woman."

Adam cursed. "You don't believe that." But his stomach knotted at the possible implication of the pictures.

"Read it."

"Sure you want to hear this crap before you and Jennifer listen to the word of the Lord today?"

"I'll pray for the sick puppy. Read it!"

"Some things never change," Adam said. "He still addresses me out of my name."

BuckWheat, my old friend, what's up? Been a mighty long time. Not since Boston. No, correction. Make that Italy, sergeant. Had you laid up pretty good in Boston, didn't I? But that wasn't my intent. Wanted to put you to rest, but you got some pretty good backup in that friend of yours. You lucky bastard. Not many men can acquire best friends so easily. How does he match up to the dead drunk? Keep old Gus close at your back, B.W., exactly where he was in Italy, because it's time. Me and Frank's waited long enough.

Adam dropped the paper on the table and waited for Lucas to speak. He sat on the arm of the chair, clenching and unclenching his fist. He wanted to hit something and he finally slammed his fist onto his thigh.

"Frank?" Lucas asked.

"Frank Mulhare. The other Marine captain."

"All right, I remember. He died," said Lucas.

"Murdered. Stabbed to death in prison. The inmate he insulted took offense to the racial slurs."

"Never learned, did he?"

"He was where he belonged," answered Adam. "His hatred was ingrained. He was one who wasn't going to learn."

"Like Reynard."

"Just like Ethan Reynard."

Lucas heard the anger. "You gonna be all right today? Want some company? How about dinner tonight with me and Jennifer?"

"Thanks, I'll be okay, Lucas."

"Adam? You handled everything?"

Adam knew what Lucas was getting at.

"I did," he answered. "Taking precautions is useless. Like all the others, the handwriting is different. And why change and leave prints this time?" Adam rubbed his chin in a weary gesture. "When you test the envelope as well as the letter, as usual, the only prints you'll find will be mine."

Lucas gave an annoying snort. "What a way to start a day. Look, bring the stuff over in the morning and we'll look it over anyway."

"Not tomorrow."

Lucas was puzzled. "Why wait?"

"I have a date," said Adam. He hung up on Lucas' sputter.

Sydney turned off the TV at 11:30 P.M. She was already in bed, ready for sleep and anticipating tomorrow. An uneventful evening at the restaurant afforded her the opportunity to leave a little earlier than usual. She was grateful for the extra time to shampoo and roll her hair and check out her wardrobe.

She hadn't the smidgen of an idea where they were going to wind up tomorrow, but with a sunny day forecast, anything lightweight and casual would suffice. She hoped. What if she needed to dress up instead of down? She wished she had the nerve to call Adam and simply ask. But given her newfound feelings, she'd probably sound like an idiot with words tumbling every which way.

When the phone rang, Sydney glanced at the clock and then the Caller ID display, and frowned at the blocked name and number. She chose to listen to the message. Startled, when he called her name, she picked up the phone.

"Adam," she said a little breathlessly, "is anything wrong?" He sounded so—so, isolated, she thought.

"Are you okay?" He paused. "Last night? No problems?" *Damn,* Adam immediately swore to himself. Mistake.

Puzzled at the intensity of his voice, and the odd question, she answered, "I'm fine. Are you . . . did something happen?"

"No. Nothing." His voice was steady. "Sorry if I frightened you. Nothing to worry about."

Alert, Sydney knew that *that* wasn't true, but she said, "I'm glad you called."

"Why? What happened?" Adam asked too quickly.

"Adam. When I left you Saturday night, I said good night to the doorman, took the elevator up to the eighth floor and entered my apartment, all without meeting a soul. Today, at work, it was almost boring. Really." She could hear his softly expelled breath. There is something wrong, she thought.

"Sorry." Adam had scared her for no reason. Hoping the uneasiness was gone from his voice, he said, "You're glad I called. Is tomorrow . . . ?"

"No," Sydney said hastily. "Tomorrow's still on. I was just wondering how to dress? It'll be early afternoon and I wondered if later, well, I wonder if . . ." Her words got tangled in her throat. She knew it! What was she trying to say?

"You're wondering if we'll still be together later on in the evening, and whether your day wear will be appropriate?"

"Yes, something like that," she managed. She rolled her eyes heavenward. *The man is probably wondering what in the world he's got himself into,* she thought. Turning a simple afternoon lunch into a long day's journey into night. Would he want to spend so many hours with her? Sydney held her breath.

"Then, I'm glad I called," Adam said with a lowered voice. "You're one hundred percent correct." Seconds passed before he said, "I hoped that you might consider meeting a little earlier than noon."

Sydney was speechless until she heard him make a little sound. Disappointment? Finally, she answered. "Earlier?"

"If you're a breakfast person like me, I thought that we could get a head start on the day."

"I'd like that," Sydney murmured. "what time?"

"Eight-thirty?"

"Fine. Don't bother to come up. I'll meet you out front."

Adam hesitated. "Are you sure? It wouldn't be a problem." He wondered if the doorman's presence was constant.

"Positive," answered Sydney.

"Okay, out front at eight-thirty," Adam said with resignation.

Sydney smiled. "I think we're forgetting something." She could almost hear him thinking over his plans. She said, "Dress?" This time, she actually heard the smile in his voice when he answered.

"Do you like the water?"

"Certainly do."

"Good. Dress for the waterfront and wear comfortable shoes. Whatever you choose will be fine for evening."

"Sounds like a fun day. Good night Adam. See you in the morning."

"Sydney?"

"Yes?" Her body convulsed at the way he said her name. It was the voice in her dreams.

"I want you to know that I'm looking forward to tomorrow." The volume in his voice lowered when he added, "Sleep well, Sydney."

Sleep well. Did the man know what he was saying? She would never sleep well as long as she was here and he was there!

Sydney slid under the cool sheet, a smile forming on her lips. *Oh, how suddenly bold we are: from ice maiden to wanton.* Sleepily, she wondered if all women in love became so possessive. Why, she hadn't even tasted his kisses and she had him in her bed.

Adam was afraid. His earlier apprehensiveness when he'd seen the snapshots of her was no longer camouflaged as a mere general concern, the kind that he would normally feel for any client. After hearing her voice tonight and his overreacting to her simple statements, he knew that he was scared. The knot in his stomach was his antenna for danger and had helped him escape from some hairy situations. Even as Lucas tried sloughing it off, Adam sensed that the evil captain was warning him.

The more he thought about it, Adam wondered how wise he was in exposing Sydney to this madness. Her very nearness to him could become explosive. She could be harmed. Adam closed his eyes and ran his hand over his face, pulling on his mustache. His thoughts were driving him wild. He didn't want her to stay away from him. He wanted her close. So close that he could smell her as he had in the cab the night before.

Quietly, he'd inhaled her scent, and he'd prided himself on his acute sense of smell. In the restaurant when she'd stood by their table, he thought then that he had caught a whiff of wild heather, reminding him of the heaths he'd passed by in northern Italy. She had looked so smart and sophisticated in her short, black jacketed dress, yet she brought to his mind a hill of wildflowers.

Seeking to ease his fears, Adam picked up the phone.

"It's midnight," Gus growled.

"Wake up. It's Adam."

"I assumed." Instantly recalling last night, Gus roused himself. "He's here." Adam wouldn't be calling otherwise. "He made contact? How?" Gus shook a cigarette out of the pack, lit it and inhaled deeply. With each cigarette, he promised it would be his last. One day. "Tell me," he demanded. The cunning man had probably watched his every movement when he left Adam's last night. He listened.

"Same way. The guy hates change," said Adam. He ran down the morning's events including his conversation with Lucas. When he finished, he asked, "Everything quiet when you left last night?"

"Too quiet." Gus knew Adam would ask.

"Meaning?"

"I was watched."

"Proof?"

"Nothing tangible."

Adam knew without a doubt that Reynard had been *that* close. He trusted Gus' male intuition with his life—and had. "I believe you."

"Thanks." Gus frowned and worry crept into his voice when he said, "The two pictures. You think he'll go after her?"

"If I can't satisfy him first." Adam coughed. "She's one of the reasons I'm calling you. I want to see her. And not only tomorrow."

Gus thought before he spoke. He knew what Adam was asking. "There are no glass houses, Adam. Go on and live your life, man, and stop beating up on yourself. You can't protect the world." After a moment's thought, he said, "I think I can go there, buddy, so if you're going to gnaw on it . . ."

"Good night, friend."

Gus chuckled as he hung up, but his face soon took on the deadly calm that his adversaries feared.

He knew all about Owen Jeffries, the way he'd lived, and had died, practically in Adam's arms. He knew the whole sordid story of the court-martial of Ethan Reynard and Frank Mulhare and the joke sentences they'd received. He knew about the derogatory "BuckWheat" notes sent to Adam, spewed with hate messages.

But Gus believed that life shouldn't be put on hold until all the crazies became extinct. He believed in living and doing the unexpected as long as it made him feel good and others weren't harmed.

Gus turned out the light. His last thoughts were of Adam. It was time for that man to bring something meaningful and lasting into his life. He had no doubt that making a move on Sydney Cox would bring change to Adam's life forever.

CHAPTER EIGHT

At 8:15 A.M., Sydney was still trying to match her footwear to her outfit. "Comfortable" to her meant flat, very little heel. She'd been up since six o'clock and had finally selected a crushproof fabric pants set that would still look fresh in the evening. The casual drawstring pants had slits at the ankles and the cropped jacket had cap sleeves. Beneath it she wore a white cotton camisole with narrow straps. Delicate lace trimmed the neckline.

Now she was trying to match shoes to the melon-colored set. What did Adam mean by "Like the water?" Were they going to walk by the waterfront or go sailing? Would she need deck shoes or would leather bottoms suffice? Men can be so vague, she thought.

Sydney finally pulled out the footwear she was most comfortable wearing on her treks to wineries. A sand-colored slip on canvas shoe with a thin rubber sole was her choice for a day of activity.

At 8:25, Sydney was locking her door. By eight-thirty she was standing under the canopy outside of the building. There was no sign of Adam.

At eight-forty, she promised herself to remain cool. Anything could have happened, she reasoned. Especially on a Monday morning in the transit system. Saturday night in the cab, she'd learned he used the company vehicle when on assignment, otherwise he rented. She put herself in his place and knew that she would have been as skittish as a kitten showing up late for a first date. Getting worried that something serious had happened, she glanced at her watch. Maybe he was trying to call her. Deciding to wait another five minutes before going back to the apartment, she saw a car pull up and double-park. The door opened and Adam got out and walked toward her.

Sydney's heart raced as she flushed at his penetrating appraisal. His admiring glance made her pleased with the care she'd expended in selecting her attire. When he reached her, she knew that her face was flushed under his scrutiny. The crushable natural straw bowler-style hat that she held was her anchor as she stared into his eyes.

"Good morning, Sydney." Adam's eyes raked over her again. He was glad he'd changed their plans. Waiting until noon to be with her would have been a ridiculous waste of precious hours. "Sorry I'm late."

Sydney acknowledged his apology with a smile. "Good morning, Adam. Is everything all right?"

"Now it is." His dark eyes glittered as he continued to stare at her. She carried her jacket over one arm, leaving her shoulders bare. He was certain that his fingers would glide over that tan, smooth and creamy skin. Was he going to have to keep his hands in his pockets all day?

"You slept well," Adam stated.

Surprised, Sydney answered, "As a matter of fact, very."

"It shows." His voice was meant for her ears only. He steeled himself when he touched her elbow and guided her toward the car. "Ready? You must be starved."

"You've guessed right." Sydney walked beside him, totally aware of the pressure of his cupped fingers on her elbow. This is only the beginning, she breathed. She only hoped that the miracle cloth she wore could withstand the strong sun rays and her fast overheating skin.

Adam pulled into traffic and crossed Fifth Avenue. Once

through Central Park, the tension left his shoulders as he maneuvered downtown to the Lower West Side. He glanced at Sydney with a wry look.

"We're closer to brunch instead of breakfast. Can you hold out? We've not much farther to go."

His voice penetrated her concentration. She had given no thought to sustenance as she watched his defensive driving skills. His silence had afforded the time she needed to arrange her thoughts. For all her bold revelations of the night before, she hadn't the faintest idea of what to do with her discovery. Now's the time to share her feelings with Reva. Her face clouded.

"Something wrong, Sydney?" When she didn't answer right away, Adam looked and caught the quick frown disappearing from her face.

Sydney shook her head and smiled, "I'm sorry. Everything's fine." Her face brightened. "I can make it, but be prepared," she said in a warning tone. "Where are we headed?" She was curious.

"Chelsea Piers."

"Mmm, breakfast on the water." Her eyes sparkled. "Adam, your idea is wonderful. It's been quite a while since I've taken the time to visit the waterfront."

At Twenty-third Street, Adam veered into the parking area of Chelsea Piers. He drove a few yards then pulled into a parking bay near the sports complex.

A few minutes later, Adam took Sydney's hand as they turned and walked alongside the dock that was berth for several private luxury yachts. They stopped by a beauty, where a white-suited man greeted them.

"Welcome aboard the *Margo* and watch your step, please."

On board, after being greeted by the captain, Sydney and Adam were led to the middle deck of the huge three-level yacht and seated at a private table for two. Coffee was immediately served and minutes later they were moving from the dock.

"This is lovely," Sydney murmured. "Thanks for making the suggestion. July is nearly gone and this is my first trek out on the waters."

"You're welcome," Adam replied. "I think you'll enjoy the ride."

Sydney regarded him thoughtfully. "Somehow, I take you for an out-of-towner. Is this one of the things that a tourist must do before leaving? I know this city is full of surprises but I certainly wasn't aware of breakfast cruises on the Hudson."

Adam inclined his head toward other occupied tables and shrugged. "Probably a mix of residents and tourists. Word gets around about a good thing in New York. Lincoln Yates obviously heard."

"Mr. Yates. He's your employer?"

Adam nodded, but didn't speak until after the waiter served them, then left. Adam buttered a hot biscuit and watched Sydney do the same.

"He's cofounder of Garrison International."

"A security firm?"

"Yes." Adam didn't elaborate.

"International?"

"Yes."

"So you travel worldwide." Sydney took a breath. That explained his Italian.

"Frequently."

"At Olson's," she flushed at the memory, "you were on temporary assignment."

Adam was alert to her sudden embarrassment and he became angry at himself. He was the cause. "Yes, that's all over now. I begin a new assignment in a few days." Adam noticed the quick sad smile that she tried to hide. "Sydney, if there's anything that I can do to make . . ."

"No, Adam, it's not you." He looked so distressed that Sydney suddenly reached out and covered his hand with hers. "Please believe me. That's buried between us."

Adam flipped his wrist and captured her hand in his. He held it while staring into her dark eyes. She felt so warm and soft and when her fingers moved inside his palm, chills crept down his spine. He released her hand but held her gaze. He frowned.

"Then what is it? Your eyes are still sad. I said something."

"No, it's just that I'll never forget Olson Pharmaceutical

and that night. It was the night that I lost one of my best friends.'' Sydney couldn't stop the lump that formed in her throat and she swallowed, turning her gaze to the Hudson.

''Reva Fairchild,'' Adam said. How could he forget how she'd stared at him, disgraced and ashamed.

Sydney looked up in surprise. ''You've met?''

Adam shook his head. ''No. I was there when she was fired.'' His eyes darkened at the memory.

Sydney saw and wondered at his scowl, but Reva's face swam before her. ''That night, she came to my apartment. She blamed me. She was so angry with me . . . said it was my fault for trying to be so perfect. I should have left things alone.'' Sydney stopped, looking at the expression on Adam's face. Slowly, she said, ''The silver picture frame. You!''

Adam returned her stare but said nothing.

''The assignment you just completed. It had to do with that person's office and the frame. Reva said he was practically a madman, when he . . .'' Dismayed, she said, ''What a mess I made of things. I probably did the same for your case, too, didn't I?''

''Sydney . . .''

''No, I know you can't answer that.'' She looked at him. ''Looks like I'll never be able to stop telling you how sorry I am.''

''That too, is buried between us,'' Adam said firmly. In a lighter tone, he asked, ''Your friend? You haven't spoken?''

Sydney gave him a grateful smile. Beneath that cold look was a compassionate man. ''I've tried. She won't take my calls.'' Spreading her hands in a futile gesture, she said, ''But I won't give up. Her friendship means a lot.''

''Don't,'' Adam said, lightly patting her hand. ''You won't regret trying.''

Sydney did not remove her hand from beneath his. She loved the way his touch made her feel so comfortable inside.

Softly, Sydney said, ''You've lost a friend.''

Adam removed his hand and sat back, staring at a spot beyond her head. ''It happened a long time ago.'' His voice was brusque.

Their dishes had been cleared away and Adam took another sip of his second cup of coffee. His gaze lifted to meet her look of concern.

"Don't worry about that, Sydney," he said in a mild voice. "It happened a long time ago," he repeated. "But, you always remember," he murmured.

Sydney heard the controlled anger in the ominous whisper and guessed that his friend's passing was very fresh in Adam's mind. A sudden shiver shook her as she felt for any individual who had the bad luck to fall under those strong hands in anger.

Sydney pushed away from the table. The lightness of their mood was dissipating and she wanted to bring it back.

"I am quite stuffed, Adam. Two biscuits, a three-egg cheese omelette, ham *and* sausage, juice and two cups of coffee! If we ever do this again, *please* restrain me. I love to eat as you can see and," she shrugged, "can't help myself sometimes." Her eyes twinkled. "For a first date . . ." she stopped. "Oh," she said, feeling the flush go clear to the roots of her hair.

Adam laughed. He checked himself when she looked even more stricken at the sound. "Don't be embarrassed," he said softly. "You've verbalized what I've been thinking since the first minute I saw you this morning. So, can I say, 'when we meet again' and not 'if'?" He was satisfied when the panic left her eyes and she smiled at him.

"When we meet again," Sydney said demurely.

Seconds passed in amiable silence.

Sydney suddenly leaned toward him and whispered, "Nice sound. Is there more where that came from?"

Puzzled for only a moment, Adam studied her face. "Maybe." His voice hinted at things to come.

Sydney's toes wiggled against the soft canvas of her shoes. The unexpected sensual tone in a voice she already loved, and that one word, exuding sexuality, brought a flash of heat to her body so fierce, she wondered at the absence of flames leaping from her skin.

There was another silence. This time both felt that something special had just passed between them.

Adam spoke first. "Let's walk, Sydney."

"Great idea," answered Sydney in a rush. "I'd like to get a look at the combo. They're good."

Adam nodded in agreement as they walked down one flight. The three-piece combo played soothing music to dine by as the yacht glided up the Hudson River. Now that most diners were talking and exploring, a female vocalist appeared, and the tempo and the selections changed, encouraging some couples to dance.

Adam watched the dancers and couldn't remember how long it had been since he'd held a woman in his arms in a rhythmic embrace. He wanted that, this moment, with Sydney. He almost knew how she would fit against him. He gave her a bold stare. "Dance with me, Sydney?" His voice was as gentle as a caress.

Sydney had noticed the intensity with which he'd watched the swaying couples. She wondered if he had sad memories of a lost love and her heart felt tenderness for him. How could she tell him that she was here for him? That she longed to be in his arms, to comfort him—and for him to comfort her? At that moment, the pianist riffed through the first strains of a tune that Sydney recognized instantly, a song that had always tugged at her heart. When the vocalist sang the first line of Whitney Houston's "Run to You," Sydney gasped.

"Sydney?" Adam's voice was an insistent whisper as he held out his hand.

"Yes," Sydney murmured. She put her hand in his big palm and allowed him to lead her onto the dance floor. In a second she was where she'd wished to be. Tentatively, she reached up and put her hand on his shoulder as he enfolded her in his arms, her skin tingling at his soft touch.

Adam saw her emotional reaction to the song and wondered. Was this special to her? Her eyes had grown sad again and suddenly he longed to be the one to bring the sparkle back into them. As they swayed to the music, he really listened to the lyrics. He pulled her a little closer to him and when she didn't resist, he held her firmly. He bent his head, inhaling the gentle scent of her warm skin and soft hair. She wore it up off her neck, and the long strands dropped in wispy tendrils, grazing her nape. His hand moved up her back until his fingers touched the bare expanse of her skin. Unable to stop himself, they moved to glide gently over her smooth shoulder. As soft as he knew it would be, he thought. He felt her quiet shudder and the tightening of her arms around his neck.

All too soon, the song ended. Adam reluctantly released her and the place where she'd lain across his chest grew cold when she left his embrace. He felt deprived. He felt her hand slide into his.

"Adam?" Her voice was breathless.

He looked longingly at her. "Yes?" he breathed.

"That was nice." She looked up at him with sparkling eyes. "Let's walk?"

Adam exhaled deeply and a slight smile touched his lips. He'd succeeded. The sadness was gone. "Good idea," he said. They walked back up the steps.

Sydney and Adam stood on the top deck watching the panorama that was New York glide by. They'd passed the Statue of Liberty and Ellis Island and the yacht had turned around, making the return trip to the harbor.

Sydney and Adam had been silent since they arrived to stand at the railing. Both realized the intimacy of the dance they'd shared and both had been visibly affected.

Sydney was convinced of her feelings. She'd been in the arms of the man who had finally stolen her heart. What was she to do if he couldn't see the truth? Although his fingers were bare, she didn't know whether he belonged to another. She'd never asked. But she had to know. Otherwise, she would have to pack up her emotions and store them deep inside herself, because she felt that there could be no other for her. After all these years, she instinctively knew that. Unlike her friend, La Signora, Sydney did not have to travel far and wide to find her true love. He was standing beside her in all of his handsome glory. He wore his casual clothes as attractively as his business attire. Without his dark suit or tailored blazer, he still exuded strong masculine sex appeal. In contrast to his dark professional wear, he wore an ivory-colored boat-neck short-sleeve shirt that was tucked inside of white baggy drawstring pants. Dark brown leather sandals enclosed his bare feet. The muscles of his strong arms had rippled under her fingers when they'd danced, sending shooting flames through her body. They were standing close and even now she could feel the warmth of him.

Adam's body had yet to cool down since he'd felt her firm breasts pressed against his chest and her sweet-smelling hair had tickled his nose. His awareness of her sensuality as a woman was severely acute and such as he'd never previously experienced. Her effect on him brought feelings that had never been aroused even in his most intimate moments, which he now knew had meant nothing. How could he feel this way from the simple act of dance? No, never simple, he thought. From the dawning of time, man and woman, though ignorant of the terminology, had instinctively, through the sensuous rhythmic movement, wooed the object of their affections. The tradition was time-honored even today. Adam knew that he would never hold another woman in his arms as intimately, because she would not be Sydney. Amazement swept through him as he realized that in a scant three hours of his life, he knew the depth of his feelings. He was ready to let someone inside. But anxiously, he wondered if she would shrink away from what she would see. The dark side of him could bring fear to his worse adversary. Would he chase the sparkle from her eyes then? He felt her stare and he turned to her.

Sydney smiled and whispered. "My, we're so serious. Do you think that we should never dance together again?"

Adam laughed, then grinned as she joined him.

In a new intimacy, he covered her clasped hands with his and said in a low voice, "Don't even think that." His voice turned huskier when he asked, "What do you think?" His eyes sought and held hers.

Sydney's voice held a slight tremor. "I think that I've completely lost that thought."

Adam's arm went around her slender waist as he guided her down the steps and to their table. The yacht was nearing its berth and passengers were gathering their belongings.

Sydney stopped midway in putting on her hat to protect her head from the strong noon sun. Before putting on her sunglasses, she looked over at Adam and smiled.

''You never answered the rest of my question.''

He gave her an inquiring look. ''Which one?''

''Are you from out of town?''

Adam smiled and shook his head. ''We passed my hometown a while ago. I was born and raised in Brooklyn. My family still lives there.''

''Me, too,'' Sydney said in surprise. ''I mean, me and my sister were born there. But my parents are dead and my sister, well, I never see her. She's a career soldier, living in Hawaii.'' She said the last with a tinge of regret in her voice. ''It's just me and my best friends now.'' This, too, was said with just a hint of sadness.

Adam saw, and reached for her hand. He gave it a gentle tug but said nothing.

Sydney read the message. As in the song, he was not running away from her. She answered with a squeeze of her own and her heart soared.

Sydney regretted the arrival of evening. She couldn't remember the last time she'd spent such a glorious day. She would never think of the Japanese Garden in the Brooklyn Botanical Gardens without seeing Adam in her mind's eye. It was there they'd become friends, tentatively exploring the budding something that was happening inside of them. Her apprehension had dissipated when she learned that he was not in a relationship. But when he'd learned the same of her, Sydney's heart thudded with joy when she saw the apparent relief in his eyes.

At six-thirty, they were having cocktails in The Melting Pot, an Upper East Side restaurant.

''I'm impressed,'' she said, looking around at the rustic-styled inn and studying the menu, which touted international dishes. ''You're the globe-trotter and you're introducing me to a place that's practically in my backyard.'' Her glance was admiring. ''How *do* you know these things?'' She smiled. ''*I* should know these things.''

''It's my job,'' Adam teased. He was watching her every movement. She was as fresh and beautiful now as she was early this morning. Yesterday, he'd been wary of the outcome of this day. Now, the uncertainty was but a dim memory. Adam knew that he would keep it that way.

"Hungry?" Adam asked. His dark eyes twinkled. "I'm almost positive that that one bottle of water and a peach is long gone." He barely contained his laughter.

Sydney laughed. "Oh, you know me so well, do you? Okay, I'm starved."

"Good," Adam said, finally letting the smile break through, "because you're going to love this dinner."

"Mmm," Sydney said, after tasting the french onion soup. "Scrumptious." She eyed him after taking another spoonful. "Different. What's in this?"

"That's only the beginning," Adam said.

After finishing her meal, Sydney sat back with a look of contentment, meeting Adam's inquisitive look. "I love this place," she said. "Dishes from around the world as you desire: Andalusian soup, tempura, creole gumbo and fish stew. Fabulous idea."

"Don't forget the Southern Spoon Bread."

"Or the Italian wine." Sydney gave him a curious look. "That was a great choice by the way. One of my favorites." After a slight hesitation, she asked, "You're a connoisseur, aren't you?"

Adam looked up in surprise. "Why do you ask that?"

Again she hesitated. How could she tell him about his visit to the wine shop months ago?

"Well, it . . . it's not very well known . . ." Sydney stopped abruptly as he looked at her as if her nose suddenly grew eight inches. *You just complimented the man and now you come up with a lame excuse like that!*

"That's not the truth, Sydney," Adam said softly. "Tuscany wines, especially those from the Chianti region, produce some of the best reds and are popular worldwide."

"You're right, of course, I just . . ." *Oh, God. I messed this up, and after such a wonderful day.*

"Sydney, what's wrong?"

"You'll think me an idiot."

Adam leaned back in the comfortable armchair and cupped his chin in one hand. Probing her eyes, he said, "You're much too perfect for me to think that."

"Don't call me that, please?" Her eyes clouded. "I don't think of myself that way."

Adam remembered. "Okay." He continued to look thoughtfully at her. A memory was trying hard to surface when his dark eyes glittered. That night!

"Sydney, I'm going to mention this once and then never again." At her nod, he continued. "You were terrified of me that night. When I spoke, you nearly fell trying to get away from me. You practically leaped a foot. Why?"

"Because I'd heard your voice before," Sydney said in a rush.

Adam's intrigued look and his nod, invited her to continue.

"Months ago you acted as interpreter for a woman in Amalia Fine Wines. I was in my office and I heard your voice. I remember how beautiful it . . . er, how wonderful you spoke the language." *Does one tell a man he has a beautiful voice?* Under his scrutiny, Sydney thought her nose grew two more inches.

Sydney sighed. She could see him thinking and she took a sip of wine, then explained. When she finished, Adam nodded.

"Parla italiano?" Adam asked, fascinated by this ever-surprising woman.

"Del," Sydney answered. "Yes, I speak some, thanks to my best friend and her relatives."

"I'm intrigued," Adam replied. His voice turned curious. "Reva?"

"No." Her expression changed. "I had two best friends." Sydney explained about the Percivals.

Adam remained silent while she spoke, still mystified by this woman, such as he'd never met before. When she finished, he was deep in thought. Her words had brought to mind his own memories of Tuscany.

"Adam?"

"You're one hell of a woman and don't let anyone tell you otherwise, Sydney." He saw her flush.

"Why should that bother you?"

"Because people tend to call me perfect."

Adam nearly flinched at the quiet but sad tone.

Glancing at her watch, Sydney sighed and held out her hand. Adam took it and she squeezed. "Thanks for a wonderful day. I'll never forget it."

Adam's words came hard as he swallowed. "And I'll never forget *you*." Before she could speak, he said gruffly, "Come on, let's get out of here."

"A what?" Adam looked skeptically at Sydney and then at the building as they sat in the car.

"A day of absence." She tilted her head and raised an eyebrow. "You've never heard of that?"

"Yeah," he growled. "My parents participated, back in the sixties when it *meant* something." He stared at the doormanless doorway and his forehead wrinkled. "When was this decided?"

"Only yesterday," Sydney answered, wondering at his behavior. Mentally, he was in his professional suit, and his voice held no humor at the sudden worker absence. "There had been some talk of it for a month or so and just like that, they voted on a job action."

"This is not citywide." He'd heard nothing about any such impending strike.

"No. Just a beef with the new management company. I'm sure they'll settle their differences and everyone will be on the job tomorrow."

Adam swore beneath his breath. He couldn't let her walk inside that unsecured building. If Reynard found him, why not her?

"Adam? What's wrong? Where are you going?" Sydney was worried as he drove away slowly.

"To park. I'm going up with you."

"Adam," she protested, "that's not necessary."

"It's necessary."

Sydney was bewildered at the sudden grimness of his face

and the voice that had turned to steel. She watched as he looked for a space.

"Is there a lot nearby?"

"Yes. Around the corner on Second Avenue."

She could feel the tenseness in his hand and sensed his taut body as she walked beside him. His eyes were alert, observing passersby and darkened parked cars. Relief flooded over her when finally they were at her apartment door. His glance swept the deserted hallway and he nodded with satisfaction.

"Unlock it."

Minutes later, he stood by the closed door, his hand on the knob, ready to leave. Sydney stood by the sofa, watching him. Calm had returned to his face and his off-duty posture was evident in his voice and his stance as he looked at her.

"Sorry," Adam rasped. He brushed a hand wearily over his head and closed his eyes briefly. "I know I frightened you." A disgusted look swept his face. "What a rotten end," he muttered.

Although he had calmed down, Sydney was still I disturbed. His concern had been for *her*. But why?

Sydney walked to Adam and looked up at him steadily. "Frightened, only because I don't understand," she said quietly. "If you explain, maybe it won't be such a rotten end to a lovely day, after all."

Adam saw the fear in her eyes and the brave way she was ready to confront the unknown. Suddenly, the thought of Reynard's taunt with the photos became all too real. Would the man really try to get to him through her? The thought made him tremble with fear. How could he protect her?

"Adam, what is it?"

Cat and mouse! The terror of that dreaded game brought a dryness to Adam's mouth. He emitted a sharp harsh breath when he grasped her shoulders and pulled her into his arms. He crushed her against his chest, burying his face in her hair.

"Sydney, my God . . . Sydney . . ." he whispered. "If he touches you . . ."

"Adam . . ." Sydney was silenced as his mouth captured hers.

God forgive him, Adam thought as he crushed her lips. The fearful look she'd given him—the sound of her frightened whisper—all he wanted to do was to hold her, keep her from harm. Her sweet lips responded to his and almost uncontrollably, Adam ravished her mouth. Her moist lips were warm and inviting and when she parted them, he thrust his tongue inside. He explored the inner tenderness of her mouth with such intensity, he imagined his tongue to be a flaming torch. Instead of releasing her, the pressure of her breasts against his chest caused him to hungrily devour more of her. His hand moved down her back, across her slender waist until he found one soft breast. He groaned from the ache that sped to his groin as he released her lips only to rain kisses on her neck, her throat, her shoulders.

Sydney strained her hips against Adam's swollen manhood. She needed to feel all of him against her. On her toes, she kissed his face, his neck and when he touched her breast, the agony was sweet.

"Adam . . ." she whispered. She wanted to touch him; to feel him as his touch seared her bare shoulders. She wanted to explore the body of this man that she loved. Sydney tugged at his shirt and soon her hands were on his back, exploring the muscled ripples, when a hoarse cry burst from Adam's throat. She felt him grab her shoulders and put her from him.

"Sydney." Her fingers on his bare flesh had jolted him out of their spiraling tailspin. Adam said her name in a ragged breath as he leaned against the door, his hands still holding her tight as he stared down into her eyes.

Sydney's chest was still heaving as she looked at Adam. He was perfectly right in stopping them when he did, because she knew that she had lost control. Wherever he wanted to take her, she would have gone. And she was certain that he was aware of that fact.

"You know we had to stop, don't you?"

Sydney nodded. She was calm now and Adam's breathing had slowed. When he released her shoulders, she felt divested of the powerful female emotions that had invaded her body like an army of aliens. New, strange, delicious sensations. *She wanted more.* She must have gone somewhere else because his hand in hers, made her flinch, bringing her back.

Adam led her to the sofa where she sat without a word. He was beside her, still holding her hand. "Sydney?" He spoke softly. When she looked at him, he said, "I didn't want to stop, either. I believe you know that." His voice was a deep caress, like crushed velvet. He watched her.

Sydney smiled at him and then squeezed his hand as if to say that she knew and that she was all right. She stood up. "Would you join me in something cold to drink?"

" 'Cold' will definitely do it for me," Adam said. His voice was smooth and his look innocent.

Warmth flooded Sydney as she turned away, thinking that if he didn't control what he did with his voice, she definitely wouldn't be responsible for whatever happened next. A smile tugged at the corners of her mouth. *I wonder if he realizes what pushes my buttons.* She returned with two ice-cold colas and sat beside him again. Neither spoke until after they let the cooling beverages sooth their seared mouths and heated bodies.

Adam set his glass on the table. When he spoke, his voice matched the serious look in his eyes and he didn't mince his words.

"A man wants me dead, Sydney." His eyes flickered at her fearful concern. "He's ruthless, unscrupulous and a convicted murderer. He's taunting me now and he'll try again to kill me but before he does . . . I believe he'll come after you."

CHAPTER NINE

Adam's words paralyzed Sydney for a fraction of a second until only her lashes blinked in stupefaction. "What did you say?" A chill settled in the middle of her chest when she saw his face. He had no doubts. "Why?" she asked in a small voice. She looked bewildered.

Adam's eyes darkened. He wished to spare her, but keeping her in ignorance would be foolish and dangerous. He tried to keep the anger from his voice. "There is no sane explanation for this man's actions. Unless you want to dignify insanity as the reason for racism. No." he shook his head, "he is cunningly evil, and a trickster." Adam shifted and caught Sydney by the shoulders, forcing her to look directly at him. "I want you to be watchful at all times, no matter where you are. Promise me?"

Sydney nodded. "Yes."

Adam let her go and moved away, leaning on the rolled arm of the overstuffed sofa. His lids shuttered the darkness of his eyes, but there was no such curtain to mask the fury in his voice. "His name is Ethan Reynard and I blame him for the death of my friend."

Sydney's heart melted at the pain she saw and heard, and

all fear for herself dissipated as she listened. He had taken himself to a hated time and place inhabited by his foes and his friend Owen Jeffries.

When Adam finished relating all the sordid details of the killing of the young marine recruit, the court-martial of Reynard and Mulhare and the savage beatings of him and Owen, he stood up and walked to the window. He stared in silence as if listening to the heartbeat of the street, comparing it to his own. The pulse of the city hummed with life and Adam was glad that he was alive. The story on his lips had brought to life the vivid images of hate, anger and the suffering of his friend. Now, for the first time in many years, Adam thought consciously about the precious gift of awakening every morning, sound and healthy. He was alive! What a waste to Owen's memory, and his death, that Adam had lived so long afterward only going through the motions of surviving. That wasn't healthful living. But knowing that when he awakened each morning, and only a few miles away Sydney was doing the same, a rush of exhilaration burst through him that made him want to explode. He would die before he let anyone harm her.

Adam smelled the heather scent before he felt her warmth next to him. He didn't turn from the window as she wrapped her arms around his waist and laid her cheek against his back. He inhaled sharply.

Sydney had tears in her eyes before he had finished his story. She watched as he walked in silence toward the window, wresting with all he'd told her. Finally, she went to him.

Adam twisted until he faced her, then wrapped her in his embrace. He kissed her forehead then lay her head on his shoulder as he held her close.

Sydney looked up, studying his face. Reaching up, her fingers smoothed the ridged scar on his jawline. "The beating?" she whispered.

Adam nodded.

Sydney kissed the scar then lightly pressed her lips to his. "I'm sorry," she murmured.

Adam hugged her and then slowly led her back to the sofa. He held her hand, giving her an intense look. "I have to leave.

I didn't intend to scare you, but it was necessary that you be aware.''

"I know," agreed Sydney.

He pulled her up and they walked toward the door. Noticing the strong locks and the chain, he made a satisfied noise. Touching the strong links, he said, "This is good only if used all the time, not just at bedtime, as many people do. Put this on the minute you close the door." He unlocked the door and started to open it when she stopped him.

Sydney still had her hand in his but now removed it and put her arms around his neck, tilting back so that she could look into his eyes. She smiled. "Do you still think it was a rotten end?"

Adam's arms went around her waist and he bent his head. His kiss was soft and gentle on her yielding lips. His fleeting probe of her tongue spoke of many sweet mysteries to come as he released her.

"Not on your life," he breathed. He opened the door. "Good night, Sydney. Lock up." He closed the door behind him.

The minute he heard the locks and the chain snapping in place, Adam became instantly alert to the stillness in the hallway, wondering what was wrong.

Studying the proximity of the elevator to her door, it hit him. Unless there were others waiting for the car to stop, anyone could come and go and not be seen by any other residents on the floor. His mouth went dry when he thought about chance possibilities. Turning back, he rang the doorbell.

"It's Adam," he said in a low voice.

"Adam," Sydney breathed, when she opened the door, her forehead furrowed in a worried frown. "What happened?" She tried to peer around his broad shoulders.

"Nothing." Adam gave her a curious look. "Is your day off the only time you eat breakfast?"

Surprised, Sydney shook her head.

"Then, can we do this tomorrow and the day after that and the two days following until I start my new assignment on Saturday?"

Relief washed over Sydney. He was okay. When his words

penetrated, her face brightened at their meaning. *He wanted to be with her!* She could burst with the happiness that sent rivulets of warmth flowing through her blood. He said her name and she answered.

"Yes. That can definitely be arranged."

Adam's smile broadened. "I promise I won't be late. Eight-thirty again?"

"That's good for me. I'll have time to get back and dress for work."

Adam frowned. "Can't I drop you off afterward?"

Sydney laughed and shook her head. "No, my fifteen-hour days are over." She tilted her head, "Maybe eleven, twelve . . ."

"Uh, uh," Adam growled. "I want those extra hours this week."

Sydney glowed. "Okay, but let's make it nine o clock?"

"Nine, it is. But this time," he added, "I'm coming up if there's no doorman." His voice was firm.

Sydney was unmoving until she heard the closing of the elevator doors, then she walked to the bedroom, undressing on the way. Naked and barefoot, she padded down the hall to the bathroom and shut the door. Humming and lathering her body with hyacinth-scented soap, Sydney was lost in her dreamlike thoughts. Whatever happened between her and Adam, this day would be hers to cherish forever.

Stepping from the shower, Sydney lifted the damp shower cap over one ear. She listened, then shouted, "Just a minute, I'm coming." She'd heard the ending peal of the doorbell. She pulled on a terrycloth body wrap and hurried to the door. "Who is it?" she asked. "Adam?" Sydney looked through the door viewer but saw no one. The elevator was out of range but she heard the doors closing. Fear rose in her throat. Suppose it was Adam, she thought. If he's hurt, he could be lying on the floor. Terrifying images flashed across her brain. First, she unlocked the chain lock and then the second lock when she stopped. *"Keep this on at all times."* Adam's warning sounded in her ears. She fastened the chain lock and breathing a prayer, she opened the door. Almost immediately she slammed it shut and sagged against it. The hall was empty. "Thank God," she whispered. She secured the door and raced down the hall of her apartment. *I had to know. It was crazy, but I had to know*, she told herself. Suppose he *was* there, unconscious, needing my help.

Sydney was in bed at 10:25, when the phone rang. She jumped and then frowned when she saw the name displayed. She picked up. "Ferne?"

"No, Sydney, it's Hannah," Ferne's mother said in an excited voice.

"Hannah?" In New Mexico? Oh no, something went wrong.

"I know it's late, but Ferne insisted I call you tonight. I flew down last night. I'm at the house now but Edward's still at the hospital. They're doing just fine. Sydney, they have a beautiful baby girl!"

"What? Oh my God," she shouted. "But it wasn't time. Are you sure she's okay?" Tears sprung to her eyes. "Thank God," she whispered.

"Sydney, they're fine, I told you. The baby is healthy and weighed seven pounds on the nose. Head full of hair just like her mother had." Hannah's voice was full of pride. She added, "This is going to be one spoiled little girl with all the doting godmothers she's going to have."

Sydney was still dazed after Hannah hung up. "Well I'll be darned," she said aloud. "One week before Reva's birthday." Tickled and without another thought, Sydney dialed Reva's number. A moment later, shocked, she hung up the phone.

Reva's number had been disconnected.

Adam stood outside Sydney's building looking almost relaxed before walking to the parking lot on Second Avenue. There were few people passing and even fewer cars. The street was dark and quiet. Then, walking at an even pace, he reached the corner, stopped and looked back. Nothing moved, and Adam turned and disappeared around the corner.

* * *

The man dressed in dark clothing driving a dark-colored car, passed slowly in front of the building just as Adam opened the door and stepped outside. The driver looked straight ahead as he drove by. In his mirror he saw Adam take on a pose of nonchalance to the casual observer, but he knew better and laughed. "Gotcha," he said aloud.

At 11:45 on Tuesday morning Sydney was at her computer, checking her wine inventory to see what would complement the lunch and dinner menus.

Normally, Sydney kept the cellars stocked with excellent wines that could be paired with any foods. One of her pet peeves was to be forced to listen to the stories told by a few arrogant sommeliers at social gatherings. To them it was unthinkable and deplorable that a patron of a fine restaurant would ask for " a good red" or "a good white." Worse, was to ask for "whatever's good."

Sydney loved to experiment with matching foods and wines. But, while she was excited and enthusiastic about her profession, she realized that not every diner parked herself or himself in seventh heaven while pondering the wine that would wash down dinner best. But she also encouraged those who showed a tentative, but genuine interest in food and wine pairings, to go ahead and experiment, without making them feel gauche.

The chef has outdone himself today, she thought with an amused look at Mason's exotic selections for lunch. She accessed the file for types of white wines that would comple- ment his goat's cheese salad. Selecting a sauvignon blanc from an eastern Long Island winery, she was about to scroll for a red when she turned at a knock on the door.

Mason popped his head around the door. "Want a java break?" He came inside carrying a tray with coffee and fresh- baked croissants. He kicked the door shut and set down his burden.

Sydney raised a brow and looked from him to the menu.

"So you've taught your assistant all about making your sautéed pork tenders?"

Mason sat with coffee and pastry. "Don't be such a skeptic, she'll be fine for fifteen or twenty. I need a breather. Eat."

Sydney groaned. "Mason, I just got here, practically, and I'm still stuffed from breakfast."

Mason stopped midway taking a sip of the hot brew. He viewed her over the rim of the cup. He swallowed, then said, "You? Since when is juice, coffee and a roll on the run, 'stuffing' food?"

"Oh, I skipped my regular this morning. I ate out." Sydney squirmed under his stare. "All right," she said, "I had breakfast at The Good Food Place." Averting her eyes, she busied herself with her lists.

"You had *breakfast.*" Mason poured another cup. "I hope you complimented my man the chef."

Sydney nodded, head down. "Kevin came out to say hi." She sighed inwardly, knowing Mason wouldn't let up until he got all of the details. After all, The Place as everyone in New York called it, was special. Patterned after the famed BET Soundstage restaurant in Maryland, every meal was a stuffing, good time treat.

"Hmm," Mason fished, "special day?" He sounded smug when he exclaimed, "Reva's back!"

Sydney's eyes clouded for a moment and then she said, "All right, all right, Mason." She looked at him. "It was a date."

Mason had reared back in the small wooden chair and now the legs hit the carpet with a thud. "A what?"

"You heard me."

Mason's eyes narrowed as he stared at his friend. He would swear in front of twelve judges that his girl was not romantically engaged when she left the restaurant on Saturday night. So between Sunday and Tuesday what happened? He looked at Sydney in amazement and then admiration.

"I'm impressed, Ms. Cox." A grin spread across his handsome features. "Want to tell a friend all about it?"

"No. It's not for sharing." Sydney could have bitten her

tongue, but it was too late. Mason was not going to let that slide.

"Whoa." He whistled. "Like that, huh?"

Sydney flushed. "Mason please," she said, uncharacteristically flustered. "It . . . it's still too new . . ." Oh, what was she saying? She should be gushing her feelings to Reva and Ferne, not her best male buddy. The thought of not being able to reach Reva had jolted her. Where could her friend be?

She looked at Mason who called her name. Oh, why shouldn't she tell him? Since when did she stop sharing her good news and bad news with him, as he did with her?

Mason had guessed and patiently waited for her to tell him. Whatever happened, had to have taken place on Saturday night. With five dudes hawking her, one of them had caught her eye. He waited.

"I—we . . . met Saturday night. He had dinner here. His name is Adam Stone."

Mason thought, visualizing the table seating. He was excellent with faces and names and that little feat had been very beneficial to him in the past.

"The dark, mysterious-looking one who never smiled."

Although Sydney wasn't surprised that he'd remembered Adam's name, she was curious. She asked, "You guessed he was the one?"

Mason grinned. "The baby-faced one, you wouldn't look at twice and the beefy guy is married. Turner, the one sitting next to Stone, had a smile on his face but had cold, deadly eyes. Yates, the older guy had a yen but you'd turn him off by treating him fatherly, not romantically." His grin broadened. "How'd I do?"

Sydney was chuckling by the time he finished. She stood up. "You just know me too well, mister." She bent and kissed his cheek, then loaded the tray and handed it to him. "Now scoot, before they send out an SOS for you." Under his protests, she said, "We'll talk more later. Now go." She closed the door and went back to work, smiling at his continued grumbling until he disappeared.

Lunch was finished, and at three-thirty Sydney was back in

her office. Shoes off, wearily she rested her head against the high-backed chair and briefly closed her eyes. Since her coffee break with Mason, she'd eaten nothing except for drinking a bottle of water and nibbling on some crackers and she looked forward to tasting Mason's delicious foods later on. All day, Sydney had Reva Fairchild in the back of her mind. After Mason left her office, she'd dialed Reva's roommates. One answered, telling Sydney that Reva was out of town and there was no date given for her return.

Earlier, Sydney started to call Ferne, but decided to wait until Ferne returned home from the hospital. She knew that it hadn't been an easy birth, and Ferne didn't need another call, only to repeat for the umpteenth time the same news.

Sydney sighed and turned on the computer to update her inventory. Her thoughts were bittersweet as she worked. At such a time in her life, she should be at her happiest. Almost overnight, she'd fallen in love. Now she was feeling cheated that she had no one to share her discovery with after all these years.

She'd been there for Ferne when Edward Marsh had walked into her life. She had been there for Reva many times, because with each new man in her life, Reva thought she was in love. She was there, more so, after Ferne moved away. She and Reva had each other.

Sydney looked away from the computer screen and closed her eyes. Was she being self-centered and selfish? she wondered. Or pitying? Refusing to go that route, she banished the negative thinking and resumed working, resolving not to dive into a funk. Not now. She'd done all she could to find Reva, to apologize for her mistake. But what more could she do or say when there was no one there to listen?

Sydney decided that she would cloak herself in the happiness that she'd found in just being with Adam. Last night, she had taken the taste and the heat of his kisses to her bedroom. This morning when she had opened the door to him, all her strong feelings for him had been renewed. After breakfast, when he'd driven her to work, she knew by then and without a doubt in the world, that her heart could belong to no one else but Adam.

The phone rang, startling her, but she answered quickly. "Sydney Cox."

"It's Adam, Sydney. Can you talk?" He spoke in a low, smooth tone.

"Yes," Sydney said and smiled. "Why are you whispering?" she asked in a whisper of her own. She'd teased him this morning about all the nuances of his voice and she could have sworn that he was embarrassed.

Remembering, Adam smiled. This woman was fast getting under his skin and he didn't know what to do about it; knew he *shouldn't* do anything about it. There were safer men that she could be with who would love her company. He cringed at the thought.

"Sydney, something's come up and I won't be there in time to take you home. I'm sorry."

Sydney's jaw drooped. The thought of seeing him in a few hours had helped her through her downtime earlier. "Me, too," she said softly. "Is everything okay?" Worry crept into her voice.

"Just business," he answered crisply, then said in a milder tone, "Will you take a cab?"

Sydney started to protest, and then realized that his concern was for her.

"Sydney?"

"Yes," she answered, "I will."

"Promise?"

"I promise."

"Be watchful?"

"Yes," she answered. He was thinking of the absent doorman.

"Good. Nine o'clock tomorrow morning." He paused, but without another word, abruptly hung up.

Adam finished dressing, knotting his navy tie and shrugging into his dark gray suit. *Now why didn't I just say funeral service?* He went and looked out of the window, cloaked by the sheer curtains. *Because the killing was business.* His thoughts turned bitter when he reflected upon the officer who had been killed while on duty. The man that he had been guarding was also killed. Gunshot wounds, up close. Adam swore and wondered what Curtis could have been thinking. Getting caught out in the open like that. In a crowded outdoor parking mall! What happened to the eyes in back of his head?

Adam's lashes flickered when he remembered his own folly. He had been caught unaware, distracted by a mysterious woman whose frightened brown eyes had burned an image in his mind so clear, it was like seeing a hologram. He wondered if Curtis Johnson had been so deadly distracted.

It was past four o'clock when he spotted the company car. Jeremy Gage double-parked and lifted his hand in greeting. Gus, as passenger, did the same. Adam signaled that he would be right out.

All three men were silent while Jeremy skillfully guided the car through the heavy downtown traffic and into the Lincoln Tunnel. The New Jersey Oranges were not far and soon they would be in the company of their fellow officers and the grieving wife and family. At one point in time, all three somber men had escaped the ill-fate met by Johnson. Those situations were prominent in their minds and each remembered their own private hell as if it were now. They each breathed one prayer: Thank you, Jesus.

Gus broke the silence, speaking mildly to Adam without turning his head. "R and R okay?"

Adam was fingering his mustache and his hand hid the slight tug of his mouth. Only he could hear the real question behind that tone.

"No complaints." His tone was just as mild.

Gus acknowledged the comment with an imperceptible move of his head but said nothing more. He turned his attention to the driver.

"Not bad, Jerry." Praise laced his voice as he watched the deft maneuvering of the streets once they had turned off Route 280. "You assigned here before?"

Adam was alert to his friend's voice. He watched, interest deep in his eyes.

"Nah," answered Jeremy as if the question was absurd. After all, seniors were privy to tristate area jobs. "I used to work in Newark for years. Been up and down and all around these towns. You name it, I worked there.'' He grinned while glancing quickly at Gus to catch his eye. Trying to catch Adam's look was a waste of effort because Adam was staring at a point in the back of Gus' head. Jeremy, in an ''ah shucks'' type of gesture, shrugged and gave his full attention to the road. Nonplussed, he said, ''I haven't forgotten a thing though. We're just around the corner.''

Gus didn't answer.

Adam looked thoughtfully at the grown man and though it didn't show, irritation gnawed at him. This was the only forty-something man that he knew that gushed. When he said *thing,* it came out *thang,* like he was in the old, wild wild west. Inwardly, Adam shrugged. The world is full of self-effacing men like Jeremy, so why be judgmental he argued? The man was good and came with high recommendations from a respected Chicago-based private investigative firm. Later, he would find out what was on his friend's mind.

Adam got out of the car, looked at the crowd milling about and his attention turned to the widow and her children. *Why would you want to leave a woman behind to face this?* Ignoring his nagging conscience, he followed Jeremy and Gus into the funeral home. He glanced at his watch and breathed easy knowing that Sydney was still at work. Safe.

''Mr. Yates, good to see you, sir. Mr. Parnell.'' Jeremy pumped the hands of his two bosses then moved on to greet other acquaintances. A look passed between the two older men as they walked away to pay their respects. Both acknowledged Adam and Gus when they passed by.

Adam watched Gus as he watched Jeremy.

''What's going on?'' Adam asked. The closest person to them couldn't hear a word. ''Why the geography quiz?''

''No reason,'' answered Gus. ''Just playing, is all.'' His gaze wandered over the crowd.

Adam's eyes glinted in the low-lit room. ''You don't know how to play,'' he said dryly.

* * *

When Sydney left the cab, she hurried to the building and rushed through the door. Her mouth went dry when she looked behind at the man who followed her inside. Her knees nearly buckled in relief when she recognized a neighbor. They expressed their views about the building dispute until he got off the elevator on the sixth floor. By the time she set the locks on her door, Sydney was no good and it was all she could do to make it to the bedroom. Fully clothed, she lay on her back, chest heaving, while she stared at the ceiling. Her hands were balled into fists at her side.

Realizing she was safe in her apartment, no one chasing her, anger began to replace the fear. Where had her confidence gone in barely twenty-four hours? she asked herself. Adam! She was making his fears her own. But they were justified she reasoned. He would wear that scar every day of his life. Yes, his concern was indeed justified. But she couldn't allow herself to fear every shadow as she had earlier when she waited for a cab. Was the man standing by the curb, really waiting for someone? Or was he sneakily watching her? She'd seen her neighbor walking toward the building when she jumped from the cab. Why did she nearly freak out when he was suddenly behind her in the lobby? Sydney closed her eyes briefly and said a silent prayer, and when she sat up, her face was set with a look of grim determination. She decided that she'd exhibited her last behavior bordering on the hysterical.

Composed, Sydney began to undress. Before she started her nightly ritual, she had to call New Mexico. It was time to wish her friend well and also time to share her news. Sydney could barely contain herself. She needed to tell someone that she had fallen in love.

"Sydney Cox, where've you been? Why haven't you called before now?" Ferne's voice was accusing. "Your goddaughter will be mighty upset with you if that's all the attention she's going to get!''

Sydney laughed. "My, aren't we full of zest. Is that what giving birth does to one?" she teased. Not waiting for an answer, she said, "Ferne, I'm so glad everything's turned out good for you and Edward. Are you sure you're okay? Can you have more?"

"Oh my God, Edward, she's asking for the next one," Ferne shouted to her husband. To her friend, she answered, "We can have a half dozen, if we want. No foreseeable problems." Her voice was filled with happiness. "She has my good looks and Edward's raven hair. A beauty she is and a heart stealer, already."

"What's her name?"

"Amalia," said Ferne, softly.

"Oh, Ferne, I think that's wonderful." Sydney was happy that Ferne had named her daughter after her paternal grandmother. Edward Percival would be proud. She wondered if the baby's arrival had mended the rift between them.

"I hear you thinking friend. No, it hasn't happened," said Ferne. "Only Ma came down." She sighed. "Maybe one day he'll really see the man that I married." Then she asked, "Have you and Reva talked?"

"No."

"That's it? No? What's going on with you two? Ma called her and found her phone is disconnected. What's that all about?"

Sydney's eyes clouded. She explained to her surprised friend.

"None of this makes any sense." Ferne sounded frustrated. "So, if Reva's gone, what in heaven's name are you doing for a social life? Are you still working around the clock, Sydney? I have a good mind to call Mason and tell him to take you out on the town one night. I'll even pay for the date for heaven's sake!"

Sydney laughed, knowing that if Ferne wasn't caught up in the new world of motherhood, she would be true to her word.

"No need, Ferne," said Sydney in a soft voice, "I've been dating."

There was silence only for a second before Ferne's voice exploded over the line. ''You've been what?''

''Ferne, I've fallen in love. No, please listen. I can hear Hannah and I agree that you have to rest. Let me say this now and when I see you, we can talk. Okay?'' She nodded at Ferne's weak acknowledgement.

''There's an old saying, 'What goes around comes around,' '' she began. ''A long time ago Jon Carleton fell in love at first sight . . . with a woman who couldn't return his love. Now, it's happened to me. I've fallen for someone that I fear will reject my love. No, I can't explain now, Ferne,'' she said. ''It's just a feeling . . . something in the way he looks at me when he thinks I'm unaware of his stare. Almost as if he wants to reveal his thoughts, but something prevents him.''

''Oh Sydney, I'm so sorry,'' cried Ferne. ''First I'm happy for you and now you make me want to cry. What are you going to do?''

Sydney smiled. ''I'm a novice at this love business, Ferne. You got me.''

''When are you going to see him again?''

''Tomorrow. I'm expected at some tasting events in North Fork and he wants to drive me.''

''Sydney, don't rush to judge him. Give yourselves a chance. I know you, and in the blink of an eye, you'll shut yourself up inside again. Listen to what he has to say. Promise?''

''Promise.''

Ferne paused, then asked, ''Will you see Dad?''

''I'll be passing right by the Francesca Vineyards, so I'll probably stop for a minute.'' Sydney heard Hannah in the background again and after a quick promise to call soon, she said good-bye and hung up.

Sydney was brushing her teeth when she stopped and stared at herself in the mirror. She searched her dark eyes. Would she see fear or confidence in their depths? She hadn't known that she would reveal her unsettling discovery to Ferne. She'd barely let it rise to her own conscious level, refusing to entertain Adam's possible rejection. Was she reading something into nothing? But, by voicing her fears, she was forced to look for the meaning behind her words.

Ferne's plea weighed heavily on her mind. Would she listen? Sydney knew that she would.

But, would she be so confident in herself as to accept his crushing rejection of her and go on with her life? Or would she return to a place that she now knew had been a barren world. *Because there had been no Adam.*

CHAPTER TEN

"Sydney, wake up."

That voice would never leave her dreams, Sydney thought. But was she dreaming? She opened her eyes to find Adam staring at her.

"You're home." Adam purposely kept his voice low so as not to startle her.

"Already?" Sydney blinked the sleep away and suddenly flushed when she saw the time on the dashboard clock. Nine-twenty in the evening.

"No," he said, eyeing her steadily. "Don't be embarrassed. You were tired."

"I must have slept for more than an hour," she protested. "I could have kept you company."

Adam reached over and very gently slid the knuckles of his hand down the side of her cheek. He brushed a wayward strand of hair away. "I never felt alone," he murmured.

The heat emanating from his gentle touch was enough to ignite the tiny embers that always lay beneath her skin whenever he was near.

"Oh," she whispered as he leaned over and kissed her lips with a velvet touch. She responded spontaneously and intimately as her tongue searched for his. "Adam," she murmured throatily.

Her voice sent a sweet, sharp pain to his groin as he reluctantly released her. They were on stage for amused passersby.

"Sydney, I can't say that I'm sorry about that." He gestured at the street. "But, this is not a good idea."

Sydney saw what he meant and nodded. "You're right," she said. Her eyes twinkled. "Who's sorry?"

She saw that he had miraculously parked in front of her door. "Miracle worker Stone. Ordered special?"

"Just for you." Adam caught her hand firmly as they walked to the building. As they waited for the elevator, he gave her a probing look.

"I know exactly what you're thinking and I still say that there was nothing to be worried about." She ignored his grunt. "I left my apartment this morning, locked the door and rode down in the elevator without incident. In the absence of the doorman, I walked to the door and outside to wait for you."

"You never did say why you had to exhibit such a show of independence, Sydney." Adam's voice was not accusatory. He watched while she unlocked the door. "Was it because of me?"

His voice stopped her from going inside. She looked at him and her chin lifted slightly. "Actually, it was." Her stare was direct.

Adam nodded as if he'd known and his eyes grew almost sad. "Because you caught my fear."

"Yes. I—I . . . was not me, anymore. I felt that I was losing myself and becoming someone else. The feeling reminded me of my insecure teenage years."

Adam lifted a brow in surprise. He would never have thought that of her. She exuded confidence and carried her slight frame with the grace of royalty.

Sydney saw his look and smiled. "That's the one part of my life that I didn't touch upon today. Would you like to hear the rest over coffee? I can . . ."

"No," he interrupted, "it's late and I'd hate for you to cancel out on our date in the morning." He stared at her. "You would tell me if you were getting tired of our early-morning meetings?''

Sydney was hesitant. ''Well,'' she finally said, ''since you asked, there is one thing . . .''

Adam was taken aback. He stared at her with a dark look.

Sydney stood on her toes and whispered in his ear. ''They're entirely too short. With the exception of today, of course.'' Her smile grew wide at his expelled breath. She yelped as he firmly steered her inside the apartment and closed the door.

Adam caught her by the waist, pulled her into a tight embrace and buried his face in her hair. ''I'm not used to being teased,'' he growled. He closed his eyes as if that would help the tailspin he was in. All day, her nearness had done quixotic things to his body. More than once, he had to call on every ounce of willpower to keep his desire for her hidden. He felt her arms tighten against his waist and her breasts rub against his chest. The thin cotton of their clothes did nothing to absorb the heat coming from their bodies. The moan he heard was his as he sought her lips while his hand found one satin-covered breast. Almost immediately, the soft, pliant flesh became taut, and the delicate throb against his hand shot excruciating pleasure up his arm. He thrust his hand beneath the fabric and was emboldened when he felt her release them to his touch. The cloth fell away and he caressed the tight buds, first with his fingers and then his mouth. Relief burst through him like a geyser as he emitted a hoarse cry against the tender sweetness he tasted.

''Adam, Adam,'' moaned Sydney, as her hands explored his muscled physique. *How can he not see how I feel,* she agonized. *He must know that I want him.* Too late, the sob that caught in her throat, burst through her lips. Adam's body went still and she felt her breasts grow cold where seconds before they were enveloped in the warmth of his mouth.

Adam's heart nearly stopped. Tears? Had he hurt her? Or was she ashamed? *Oh my God, what am I doing?* He stepped away and smoothed her clothes. She refused to meet his eyes and he felt a pang of remorse. *What have I done?* He had to know what she was thinking.

''Sydney.'' His voice sounded hoarse. ''What is it?'' With

a finger, he raised her chin until her eyes met his. His gaze was unwavering and his voice frank. "I cannot apologize for my behavior. All day, I've wanted to taste you like that. No, that's not true. I've wanted that since I first laid eyes on you. I felt it beneath all my anger." He caressed her face with his eyes, keeping his hands at his sides. "Tell me that I'm not wrong, that you were feeling the same," he whispered. "Otherwise, then I apologize."

"You're not wrong."

Sydney's voice was so low that Adam strained to hear, but she repeated herself, this time in a strong voice.

"I've felt this way long before that night, Adam. I tried to tell you before but I—I . . . couldn't."

Adam listened, curious at her sudden anguish.

Sydney caught his hand and led him to the sofa. "I have to tell you this time, before I lose my nerve again." When he sat, she remained standing. "There's chilled wine in the fridge. Would you mind?" she asked. "I won't be long," she whispered and disappeared.

When Sydney returned with a freshly scrubbed face, she had changed into a silk mandarin-style lounge pants outfit. The blood-red top was sleeveless and the full pants' legs brushed her ankles with every step. She had regained her composure and smiled at Adam as she sat across from him in the big easy chair.

Adam handed her a crystal stem filled with a chilled chardonnay and then resumed his position on the sofa. He found it hard to take his eyes off her. She was ravishing. Her hair fell to her shoulders but was caught with a matching red silk ribbon. Her face and voice did not match the vibrant, playful color she wore. They were serious.

Sydney unconsciously rolled the wine around on her tongue, savoring it before she spoke. "That day that I heard your voice in the shop, well, I never forgot it. I brought it home with me and lived with it while imagining the body it belonged to." She hesitated. "You must think I'm out of my mind, revealing this to you." She flushed. "Adam, I've only known you for three days!"

He shook his head. "No," he murmured. "You're not mad. I want you to talk to me." He smiled at her. "Would three hundred make it better?"

"No. I would still feel the same. The way I felt tonight, it was the same feeling inside of me whenever I imagined your voice in my head. Only there was never anything for me to . . . to hold." Her face warmed. "But tonight, there was." Sydney stared intently at him. "Do you understand?"

The face of Johnson's widow flashed before him and an inner voice cried, *Don't say it, Sydney!* Adam steeled himself but said, "Yes."

"I once turned up my nose at such a ridiculous thing as 'love at first sight.' Not anymore. Now, I'm wearing that shoe. If I had doubts, they were left in the wake of the Margo on Monday."

Sydney shut her eyes for seconds before she said, "I believe that I've fallen in love with you, Adam."

Oh, God, Adam thought. How was he going to respond to her without hurting her? She'd bared her soul to him and he couldn't help her. The only way that he could protect her was to keep her away. If that madman thought that she was special, that would be the end. He stirred at her movement and saw that she had gone to stand at the window, her back to him.

There, I've done it. Satisfied? He doesn't feel as I do! Sydney argued with her alter ego, feeling crushed. Boy did she mess up. Does any woman do what she'd just done after only three dates? The man must want to run for his life. Reva would have known exactly what to say and do, Sydney thought miserably.

Adam stood quietly behind her, unsure of what to say. He knew that he couldn't touch her. His resolve would break and he'd put her life in danger.

"Sydney?" He could see the proud stiffness in her shoulders. "Please, listen to me. I've never been so honored in my life. Only a fool would walk away from your love." His voice dropped. "The life I live, my work . . . I can't offer that to a woman . . . to you . . ." A coldness crept into his voice. "It's touched you already," he said. "If Reynard harms you, I will kill him."

Sydney turned to him with a stifled gasp. "No. Oh, Adam, no." She flinched at the look of cold, dark hate etched on his face; a look that she'd shrunk from. She thanked God that she was not the recipient this time and prayed that he would never find Reynard. "Please, you can't," she whispered. Tears shone in her eyes.

Adam realized he'd frightened her with his threat. How easily his world could come between them. He knew that he was right in keeping her at an unemotional distance. It was the best thing to do.

"Don't worry Sydney. I won't do anything that's unnecessary."

They stared at each other, both unsure of what to say in the awkward moment.

Adam took a step back. "I should go." He started to say something, thought better of it and walked to the door. Sydney's voice stopped him. He turned and looked at her.

"Adam," she said softly, "was Ethan Reynard the only reason you wanted to be with me this week? You thought he might be watching me?"

He could not deny it. "That was my first thought, yes," Adam answered. She looked away. "But, not my only thought," he said in a husky voice. He was by her side. "Definitely not my only thought. Do you understand?" He breathed rapidly. "It's just that I never dreamed that I would lose control. I can't continue to do that and keep you safe." He sighed heavily. "There's nothing else to say, Sydney." She didn't answer and kept her eyes to the floor. "Except good-bye."

"Good-bye? Does that mean I do breakfast on my own for the next two mornings?" Sydney had followed him to the door.

Adam turned, his heart thumping wildly. What a woman, he thought.

"Eight o'clock?"

"Uh-uh. Nine's good. I have a new place in mind and it's nearby."

" 'Til tomorrow."

"Good night, Adam."

* * *

Adam parked the rented car in the garage in the next block and walked home, a bounce in his step. Even though his thoughts were on a fantastic woman, one who'd admitted she loved him, he was still watchful. The night could be full of nasty surprises and he wasn't about to let this be Reynard's lucky night. What made him more alert was the long period of silence. Since Sunday, there wasn't a peep out of his tormentor. No threatening notes filled with trash. Nothing. Adam was beginning to wonder if the man was backing off, deciding to catch him at another time, another city? Was New York just a tease? Who knew how to figure out evil?

Adam unlocked the door and as was his habit, walked straight to the bedroom in the dark. His hand was on the wall switch when he realized that he was not alone. Too late, his hand was knocked away and he was kneed in the groin and knocked backward. He reached for his assailant, swinging toward the grunts and landed a fist to the chest. He took a sharp punch to the head that rang some bells but he shook it off and swung again. His punch was blocked by the wily attacker and as he raised his arm for another punch, he was jabbed in the side. Adam doubled over and was jabbed again. He grunted and fell to his knees, clutching his waist. He was jabbed again as he fell to the floor, crying out in pain. He'd been stabbed. The thud of unhurried footsteps on the carpet and the click of the door closing were sounds that seemed to be in a faraway place as Adam lay in his spilled blood.

Adam fought against blacking out. He'd bleed to death if he didn't get help. Holding his hand to his side, he dragged himself to the bed. With effort, he pulled himself up and grimaced as he turned on the lamp and picked up the receiver. Gus. Adam swore. Gus had moved from the hotel. He speed-dialed Lucas, then stood. He needed to stem the flow of blood. The movement made him dizzy, but unsteadily, he made it to the bathroom.

"Lucas, here." He frowned at the unexpected grunts in his ear. "Who is this?" he demanded.

"Lucas . . . it's Adam. Hurt . . . need help . . ."

"Adam?" He swore. "Hang on, Adam. Hang on." Immediately after dialing 911, he reached Gus. Lucas said in a rush, "Adam's hurt. That lunatic got Adam."

Sydney eyed the clock. With a sigh she stood up and began clearing the table. Realizing at 10:15 A.M. that Adam was not coming, she bit her lip in hopes of stemming her tears. She promised that she wouldn't go to pieces over this. Her plan to surprise him with breakfast, now seemed so silly. What was she thinking? That by feeding him food that she'd made with her own two hands that he would miraculously fall in love? *Grow up Sydney Cox. You need a crash course fast in gaining some insight on the ways of men. Reva, where are you when I need you so badly?*

Sydney carried the crystal glasses to the china closet, putting them away with care. She loved using her beautiful china and glassware and didn't mind showing them off. In her collection were interesting pieces from the many countries she'd visited, plus her finds from the neighborhood junk dealers. She lovingly folded the French lace tablecloth. Her dinner guests would always exclaim how the lace over the colorful cloth from Kenya dazzled the eye. Linen napkins picked up the brilliant blue and yellow as did the multicolored glass napkin holders.

Her appetite lost, Sydney dumped the batter for cinnamon-apple pancakes, put away the eggs and ham, then poured herself a cup of coffee. She carried the mug to the living room where she sat on the sofa, eyeing the phone. No, she decided, she wasn't going to call again. At ten minutes to ten, she had dialed his number. Who gets a busy signal these days? Obviously he had had second thoughts and just didn't want to talk to her.

Sydney was in the bedroom undressing, thoughtful as she changed from the casual slacks and blouse to a beige conservative work outfit. "Well, Jon Carleton," she mused aloud, "I wonder how you picked yourself up, dusted off your backside and got on with your life?"

* * *

The Restaurant Louise was a hubbub of activity. Dominic, the maître d' and his staff worked nonstop through lunch and were fielding the dinner hour in the same manner—harried.

Sydney was called from one table to another through both sittings and by 9:00 P.M., she was dead on her feet. She disappeared to her office for a quick freshening up. After applying a cold damp cloth to her face, she reapplied her makeup. Smoothing her hair, which was pulled into her usual bun, she left the office but bumped into one of the kitchen staff who carried a tray from Mason. She sent it back instructing the worker to keep it warm, because Sydney knew that she would be leaving late tonight. She returned to the dining room oblivious to the ringing of the phone.

"Whew," Mason exclaimed. He had his long legs propped up on the back of her desk and rolled his head and neck from side to side, shaking out the kinks. It was nearly midnight and he was dressed in street clothes.

"This is just the beginning," he said. "The conference just started."

"Don't I know it," Sydney acknowledged. She grinned. "I'm glad they chose the Hotel Margit though, keeps us working."

"You're right about that." He raised his eyebrows. "What exactly does NOBWSOC stand for anyway? It certainly does tie up the tongue."

"The National Organization of Black Women Saving Our Children," Sydney answered. "I'm glad they chose New York. They haven't been here in nine years. They're a committed group of women of all ages who've put their money where their mouth is, and are all about action, not talking."

"How do you know so much about them?"

"I attended one of their conferences in Sonoma when I was still a student. I believe listening to those dynamic women inspired me to strive to do the best that I could do for myself." She paused. "While it's great to have someone at your back, ready to lend a hand, or catch you should you fall, a big part of making it is the will to want to.''

"And you've done yourself proud," Mason said. He threw her an admiring look. "You're spiffed up especially grand tonight." He checked his watch. "If it wasn't for the time, I'd swear you were headed for a late date." He winked. "How about it? Holding out on me? Besides, how was yesterday, tiptoeing through the North Fork wine cellars?''

Sydney's face clouded. She did give special attention to her dress today, needing the pick-me-up. She'd chosen gold jewelry to complement her tailored beige sheath. Gold grape clusters at her ears and a matching grape cluster dangling from a choker dazzled against her dark caramel-colored skin. She loved the warmth of gold and wore it regally.

Mason saw the frown and in turn his brows furrowed. What a change from yesterday. Something had gone wrong and he had no qualms about asking. If she needed to talk, he would listen.

"Didn't meet with your expectations?''

Sydney looked at him with a sad smile. "It did and then some," she answered.

"So?" Mason inquired, curious.

"It was the no-show without a call this morning that put me in a funk." She shrugged. "I'm over it now, though.''

"Are you?''

Sydney lifted her shoulders in a philosophical shrug. "Got to be." She wagged a finger against any further questions but said, "Life goes on.''

Mason saw the determined glint in her eyes and didn't press. In time, she would speak her mind. She was obviously feeling raw inside. He stood up as she prepared to leave.

"Want a lift?''

"You know I'd appreciate it." Mason lived in the North Bronx and he'd frequently dropped her off on his way uptown.

They were in the car when Mason asked quietly, "Heard from Reva?''

"No." Sydney's lips tightened.

Mason heard the hurt and anger in that one word. "She hasn't called Ferne either?"

"I don't care whether or not she's contacted Ferne," Sydney snapped. "If you're so interested in her whereabouts, why don't you send out the guard for her?"

"Easy there, Sydney," Mason said softly. He kept his eyes on the road.

Sydney closed her eyes and rubbed her forehead wearily. She'd been tense all day trying to act grown up about being dumped, but the strain obviously was getting to her. She had no right carping at Mason. At the rate she was going, he was about the only friend she had left. She felt the car stop and was surprised they'd arrived at her building so swiftly. She looked over at Mason who was staring at her with a thoughtful look.

Sydney rested her hand on his arm, then leaned over and kissed his cheek. "You didn't deserve that. I'm sorry."

"I know." Mason's look was sympathetic as he squeezed her hand. "Get some rest and stay away from that crazy place at least until after one o'clock. It's going to be more of the same for the next four days."

"You're the best. See you tomorrow. No, stay," she said. "Don't get out. Just wait until I get inside. If you turn your back on your car while it's double-parked, it'll be on the hoist, lickety-split. You'll never see it again. At least not until you pick it up from the pound tomorrow." She waved and hurried inside the building.

At her apartment door, she unlocked it and hurried inside. She didn't realize how nervous she'd be in the absence of the secure presence of the doorman. She silently wished that the dispute would come to an end.

The pair of eyes that watched from a dark car were amused as they eyed the scene in the car. Kisses? he thought. Nothing takes these broads long before finding comfort in the arms of another. Her man's not even cold on a slab and she's setting her sights on another victim. His eyes followed her until she disappeared. *Very nice,* he thought. *Wonder how that sexy little body would react under my touch? Might sample some of that before I split town. Not a thing in the world keeping me here now.* A wicked smile split his lips. *Wonder what I would have done if she'd answered the door the other night?* Old Adam trained her well. An amused laugh was lost amidst the sound of the engine starting as he pulled away from the curb and drove off.

By Friday night, Sydney's resolve was strong in refusing to feel sorry for herself. Earlier, when she'd awakened, she had felt she'd returned to her old mien. In short, she was back to her self Before A.S.—Before Adam Stone. She saw in the mirror a confident woman, proud, self-supporting, successful. Yes, she was all there, she told herself, with one little change. She was a tad wiser in the ways of the heart, yet a tad sadder with what she had confirmed, after only three days out of a lifetime. There could be no other to steal her heart because hers would forever belong to Adam Stone.

Sydney had spent a good part of the dinner hours enjoying the casual chitchat with the diners. Many, as from the night before, were members of the Black Women's group. They shared tidbits of their travels to other cities once they learned she was familiar with their activities. She found herself smiling and laughing and was actually feeling good.

At ten-thirty, Sydney was ready to call it a night when she passed by the bar. A tall man left his stool and walked toward her. Trying hard to place his face, just as he called her name, she remembered. How could she forget the man with the engaging smile but whose eyes remained cold and deadly? Mr. Turner!

"Ms. Cox, you may remember me. I was in the group with Adam Stone a few nights ago. My name is Gus Turner."

Sydney stiffened. "I remember, Mr. Turner." She eyed him warily. "How can I help you?"

"I have a message from Adam. Can we talk, Ms. Cox?" He saw that she was ready to take flight. Adam had warned him that she would be hard to pin down for conversation once she heard Adam had sent him.

"I think not, Mr. Turner." Sydney started to walk away, but was stopped by the crack of his voice.

"Ms. Cox!"

Startled, Sydney tilted her head to look into the hard eyes of the man. How like Adam's, she thought, only this man was devoid of a compassionate bone in his body. She looked around the lounge and back at the sharp-eyed man. "Over there." She nodded toward a secluded table. He followed and they sat.

"I'm waiting, Mr. Turner," she said tersely.

"Wednesday night, after he left you, Adam was attacked and left for dead in his apartment." Gus spoke bluntly.

Sydney stared at the man as if he'd just spewed deadly venom into her face and it had rendered her speechless and paralyzed. She clutched at her breasts as if to keep her heart from falling out of its cavity in her chest.

Finally, Sydney felt the intangible poison, feeling almost like crumpled, used cellophane, unwrap itself from her face, and she was able to speak.

"What are you saying?"

Gus' eyes narrowed at her reaction. *She does care.* "He was stabbed in his side. Luckily the killer didn't stick around to admire his handiwork. We got to him in time."

"How bad?" Sydney couldn't ask more.

"Puncture wounds and a bruised rib. He was barely conscious when we found him but he was able to staunch the flow of blood."

"Where is he?"

"Mount Sinai. He's in guarded condition."

"What . . . is his message to me?" she asked with a tremor in her voice.

"That he promised you two more breakfast dates, but would you mind spending one of them with him tomorrow?"

Sydney couldn't stop the tears or the shaking that suddenly overtook her body. She stammered, "Excuse me . . ." and ran from the lounge. Blinded with tears, she stumbled to her office where she sobbed loudly.

Gus followed, ignoring the stares of the curious staff, but stopped briefly to identify himself to the maître d', who deterred him. After assuring himself that Sydney was in no danger, the unsmiling man led Gus to her office.

"Ms. Cox?"

Sydney cried uncontrollably until her body was convulsed with great wracking sobs. She raised her head from the desk and through her tears, cried, "The thoughts I had of him when he . . . he . . . didn't call . . ." Her eyes pleaded with Gus to understand. "He was fighting for his life while I—I . . . had such horrible thoughts."

Gus had seen this kind of emotion before and he knew from experience to wait. Until the first wave of hurt and shock subsided, there was nothing anyone could do. His eyelashes flickered as he stood, his own emotions held immobile. She was not his to take in his arms to console. That was up to his friend. He watched as she excused herself. He heard the running water and she soon reappeared with dry cheeks and tear-swollen eyes.

Composed, Sydney sat down. "It was such a shock," she apologized. "I had no idea . . ."

Gus spoke in a quiet tone. "How could you?" Then with a stoic look, he asked, "Any return message?"

"Yes," she replied. "Breakfast tomorrow."

"Good. He'll be expecting you." He stood firm, then asked, "Can I give you a lift? It won't be a problem. In fact, I was instructed to insist and to ignore the slightest resistance." He never blinked.

A tiny smile tugged at her mouth. "I'm not resisting. Just give me a minute."

As they drove out of the underground garage, Sydney asked the question that plagued her.

"Has he been caught?" Her voice trembled and she held herself stiffly, fearing that she knew the answer.

Gus felt her tension and his hands tightened on the steering wheel. "No."

Sydney nearly shrank away from the hate in his voice. She couldn't help thinking that if he hadn't already, Ethan Reynard should find himself a big boulder and crawl beneath it. Adam, on the heels of his foe, would be enough for any one man to fear. But working along with the man sitting beside her, who shared Adam's deadly thoughts, there would be no safe refuge for that doomed man on this planet.

CHAPTER ELEVEN

It was after midnight, but Gus walked down the quiet hospital corridor to Adam's room, anger in every step. He nodded at the night staff who was used to seeing the presence of the tall grim-faced man.

Gus acknowledged the greeting of the Garrison officer who sat on guard outside Adam's door. They spoke for a while and Gus went inside. He stood by the bed looking down at his friend who was asleep and the sight made his eyes narrow in anger. Adam's dreams were fierce if his rapid eyelid movement was any indication, he thought. Gus could only guess that Adam's thoughts were on his attacker and he was helpless to do anything about it. *We'll get the sucker, buddy. Just get through this.* He took a seat in the shadowed room and watched.

Adam opened his eyes and immediately sensed another presence. Without looking, he knew who was in the room.

"What're you doing back here?" Adam, turning his head to stare at the sleeping man, was careful not to move his aching torso.

Gus opened his eyes and checked his watch. It was nearly 5:00 A.M. He unraveled his long legs and stretched his arms. "Hey, buddy. You must be feeling better. You slept all night."

Gus walked to the bed and ran a critical eye over Adam. "You're looking better, too. What is it that they say? 'Your color's returned'?" He grinned.

"Ugh," grunted Adam. "Don't make me laugh."

"Better do more of it. Your doc looked you over an hour ago. You'll be graduating from this special suite today."

"I felt him. Thought it was a dream," said Adam.

"It was real. If you're good and drink all your milk, you'll be promoted out the door on Sunday." He yawned. "Need anything? I'm ready to split." He hesitated. "I probably won't get back here for a few days, but I'll be in touch." His eyes clouded as he looked away.

Adam saw and he guessed. "Lucas gave you the King case."

Gus nodded. He didn't want to talk about the job, but he knew that Adam wouldn't let up until he was told everything.

"Yeah, Lucas insisted," he answered.

Adam's face reflected his agreement. "I'm not surprised. Mrs. King called me before this happened, and we talked for a while. Her daughter, Kyla, is pretty upset about what could have happened to her." His voice grew rough. "She's going to need a firm but gentle hand, Gus." He looked intently at his friend. "I'm satisfied that they'll both be okay." Concern filled his voice. "Has Mrs. King been informed about the switch? We'd already established a rapport."

"Yeah. I took the file from your place and we've talked. We'll do just fine."

Adam scowled. "That fool's not giving up, is he?"

"Appears so," Gus agreed grimly.

"What'd you do with the note?"

"Lucas. He's filed it along with all the other trash evidence." He lifted a brow. "Only one thing. There was a trace of blood on the note." His voice turned hopeful. "Did you cut him?"

Adam grunted in disgust. "I didn't have a weapon. The blood's got to be mine. I couldn't even get a good hold. My one good punch just slid off whatever slick garment that he was wearing. Real sleek. Wasn't a place I could have cut him if I had the chance."

A cynical smile appeared on Gus' face. "Won't he be surprised. That last note's making a liar out of our boy."

Adiós, BuckWheat. Rot in hell with your buddy.

Adam's eyes darkened, remembering the words Gus had recited to him. "Yeah, he'll be surprised all right."

Gus spoke in an even tone. "You know he'll be back, Adam. Sorry I can't watch your back, buddy, but Lucas has a good man behind you."

"Who?" Adam knew that the best was standing before him.

"Jeremy Gage."

"Jerry? I thought once you and he finished up with Olson's he was off to Madrid?"

Gus shrugged. "Lucas flip-flopped everyone's schedules, since you were attacked." His lips parted in a crooked grin. "Can't go losing his best. He wants you around for a long, long time. He got Lincoln's okay for the guys at the home office to dig into this thing. Wants an end to it."

"Where's Gage now?"

Gus shrugged. "He was finally found. Be here a bit later."

"Found?"

"Yeah. Wednesday night when I got the call from Lucas, he wanted me and Jerry ASAP at your place. But he wasn't answering his beeper. He was off Thursday and was getting some downtime, I suppose. Lucas finally reached him late last night and filled him in."

Adam was curious. "He'd left town?"

"Uh-huh. Visiting overnight in New Jersey."

"Relatives?"

"Could be." Gus didn't expound on his response and prepared to leave.

Curiosity filled Adam's eyes, but he didn't respond. He stared at Gus who was standing in the doorway. Adam realized that he was holding his breath but dared not ask the big man the question that was burning in his brain. His body probably wouldn't be able to withstand any more sharp pains.

Gus saw the war going on in his friend and chuckled to himself. Solemn-voiced and unsmiling, he said, "Don't worry, I'll send somebody on my way out. You need a shave. It's almost time for breakfast.'' He walked away but not before he saw the dirty look he got. As he walked down the corridor, the soft chuckle escaped and he murmured, ''The Iceman has melted.''

Saturday morning, Sydney was awake at dawn. Her eyes felt as though she'd just closed them and she immediately started patting them with cold cloths and then laid down for a while with cool cucumber slices on her eyelids. When she got up, she sat on the edge of her bed, surveying her wardrobe, then immediately realized her stupidity. She wasn't planning on raising the man's temperature while he was struggling to recover!

It was nine o'clock when Sydney walked inside Mount Sinai Hospital. She was dressed casually in a bright yellow cotton short-sleeve sweater, tucked inside ivory-colored slacks. She was flustered at arriving so late. Earlier, when she had taken the elevator to the lobby of her building, she was surprised at the impromptu meeting the residents were having with the building management. The dispute had ended and two new doormen were being introduced to the tenants. Relieved, Sydney introduced herself, welcomed the men and murmured her apologies. She hurried from the building and caught a cab.

Sydney had no idea what kind of diet Adam had been put on and in all likelihood, he had already been poked and prodded and served breakfast hours ago. But she had stopped at the coffee shop a block away and walked out with two hot country-style breakfasts.

Using Gus' information, and following the numbers on the sixth-floor walls to the correct room, Sydney stopped at the doorway, a frown on her face. The one bed in the room was empty. It had been completely stripped. She checked the room number again then saw the name on the small board. *Adam Stone.* Her eyes flew to the nursing station where a lone nurse was busy with a phone call. Sydney's mouth went dry and she sagged against the wall. *Adam!* Her heart pounded wildly and panic filled her eyes when she saw a man coming toward her.

She opened her mouth to speak but no words would come. For some strange reason, she knew that the man was looking for her. She stared at his unsmiling face and a terrible dread came over her. Her eyes filled with tears and she nearly dropped her package because all she wanted to do was to cover her ears against his words.

"Sydney Cox?"

She just stared and could barely shake her head.

"My name is Bob Williams. Mr. Stone's been moved from this unit to the ninth floor. I'll take you to him." He took the package from her shaking hands and gave her a curious stare. As if suddenly realizing, he said, "You must have had a scare. They haven't had a chance to do what they do when they move somebody. He just went upstairs."

Sydney was silent during the ride upstairs and for the first time she wondered what she was going to say. *Hi, Adam. I called you everything but a child of God when I thought you stood me up!* Cut it out, Sydney. Just be yourself. After all, isn't that what attracted him to you in the first place? They stopped outside a doorway where another man sat. She was introduced by Bob Williams and then directed to go inside. She was expected. He handed her the package and then dismissive, began a conversation with his colleague. The door was open and Sydney walked in. Adam was awake. Behind her, she heard the door close.

Almost shy, Sydney walked to the bed and looked down at Adam. He was lying flat and she'd never seen him so still. His eyes never left hers and the look on his face was masked.

"Hello," she said, tremulously. "I'm afraid breakfast is ruined," she managed to murmur. Why was he looking at her like that? What was he thinking? "Adam," she began, until his voice stopped her.

"Maybe not," he finally said, holding out his hand, his eyes still locked with hers. "Let's see what we can salvage."

Sydney's heart felt like it was playing skipping stones inside her chest. She was unprepared for that melodious sound, especially since she thought she'd gotten used to hearing it. She knew now to always expect those delicious shivers.

Surprisingly, the coffee was still hot, the orange juice cold, and the buttermilk biscuits warm. The western omelettes and the home fries had lost their steam, but were edible. Neither of them ate everything and as Adam drank the last of his juice. Sydney cleared away the remnants of their meal.

"It's good seeing you, Sydney. I'm glad you came."

Sydney smiled. "Thanks for giving me another 'first.' You're great for offering the unexpected."

"Am I?"

"Yes," she answered in a soft voice.

A second passed. "When I didn't show up or call you on Thursday morning, you thought the worse of me, didn't you?" A brow was raised in curiosity. "I wonder what you were thinking by Friday."

"Yes, to your first question." Her look was direct when she breathed, "By Friday, I couldn't remember your name. I cured myself of you."

Adam stared at her. "That's not the truth."

Sydney caught her breath as she looked away. *Of course not, Adam. How could it be the truth? It's the granddaddy of all whoppers. I should be made lifetime president of the Liars' Club.*

"Sydney?"

She looked and saw him with an outstretched hand. She put her hand in his and he tugged slightly. She moved closer to him.

Adam reached up and touched her nose, then smiled. "Is it?" He gestured for her to sit on the bed.

"No," she whispered. "I lied."

"I know." Adam had his hand on her neck and he gently pulled her down until her lips touched his. "I want to kiss your sweet mouth," he murmured huskily, pressing her lips hard against his.

Sydney held herself back from leaning on him. "Adam, I don't want to hurt you," she breathed against his mouth.

"You'll hurt me if you stop," he murmured. He thrust his tongue inside her mouth and groaned as he tasted, straining for more of the sweet kiss.

The blood rushed to Sydney's head as she poured her pent-up feelings into her kiss, searching and finding, then suckling his tongue. He in turn sought hers, gently nipping, then tenderly soothing, as he crushed her mouth once again.

Sydney broke away when he flinched. "I've hurt you." She was concerned.

"Yes," he grumbled, "but not in the way you think." He speared her with his smoldering eyes. "I want you, Sydney. I want to love you," he growled.

"Oh, Adam, I want that so much. You don't know . . ." He stopped her with a finger to her lips.

"Yes, I do. You showed me how much and I was a fool to walk away."

"Shh," Sydney whispered, "you only did what you thought best to protect me." She straightened up and moved to the chair, but held his hand tightly.

Adam squeezed her hand. "Don't ever expect that to happen again," he said gruffly.

Her eyes sparkled. "Is that a sure bet?"

"I don't gamble."

Sydney saw the strong look of determination in his eyes and the sensuous message he was sending to her. His eyes never wavered. Unable to bear the raw look of passion, her face grew warm as she bent her head.

Adam felt the warmth coursing through her body, reaching her fingers. He lifted her hand and kissed the pulsing fingertips. "Look at me, Sydney."

The command was filled with the passion that had made her turn away, and Sydney met his gaze.

"I don't know how long it will be before I can keep my promise, but I pray to God that it won't be long. You are one special woman, and I want to make you feel how special you are to me." His eyes still held hers. "I don't want to hold back."

Sydney drew a feathery finger slowly against his palm and smiled when he winced. "I'm sure we'll manage just fine."

"Are you teasing me?" he rasped.

"Yes," she whispered. "I like what happens afterward."

Her heart sang a sweet song and she felt as if she could recite a whole book of love sonnets to express her feelings.

"You don't play fair," he growled.

Sydney laughed. She bent and kissed his mouth quickly then stood up. "I don't want to wear out my welcome. I'd better be going." Her face clouded and she sat back down. "Adam, are you really going to be all right? Mr. Turner told me where you were wounded but I know he downplayed it. How bad is it?"

Adam knew that worried look would remain until he reassured her. Without whitewashing, he explained to her where he'd been injured and the extent. He added that he was told that he was a lucky man. The doctor was satisfied with his rapid recovery and after a full day with a normal temperature, he would be free to leave.

Adam looked at Sydney with remorse. "I guess we can forget today's temperature reading, huh?"

"You're probably right," she said, feathery feelings making her smile with joy.

Adam turned serious. "Are you coming and going without any problems?"

She knew what he meant. "No more disagreements. The men reported for work this morning." She explained about the meeting and the addition of two extra staff members, which was a large part of the doormen's complaint.

"Good." Adam breathed easy but only wished that he could be leaving with her. She wasn't even out of his sight and he was missing her already.

The door opened and a nurse came in with a sinfully cheerful greeting and proceeded to take Adam's temperature.

"Jerry," Adam acknowledged the man who'd followed behind the nurse. "Sorry about Madrid."

Jeremy waved a hand. "I'll get there one day. More important business right here at home." He greeted Sydney with a nod.

After the nurse left, Adam made the introductions.

Jeremy grinned broadly at Sydney and proceeded to vigorously shake her hand. "I remember Ms. Cox from Restaurant

Louise. Great place,'' he said effusively. He added with a glint in his eye, "You sure know your way around a grape."

Not knowing how to respond to that, Sydney said, "I remember. Nice to see you again, Mr. Gage. I'm glad you enjoyed yourself and I'm certain all of us look forward to your returning for another great meal." She turned to Adam, catching him with the inscrutable stare he was giving her and Jeremy.

She pointed to her watch. "Don't want to be late. It's been crazy for the last few days. Call you later?" she murmured, suddenly embarrassed that Jeremy was listening. She hoped that Adam would not personalize his good-bye, and was relieved when he donned his professional mantle.

Adam nodded. "I'll be here. Thank you again for coming." His voice was devoid of any intimate inflections. He turned his attention to the other officer immediately upon her leaving.

"What's your plan?" he asked Gage.

For a second, Jeremy blinked.

"Where I'm concerned," Adam said brusquely.

Jeremy recovered. "The way Lucas wants it played. Distance. You're not to be smothered, otherwise your pal will never surface and, consequently, change up on us. Time is on his side. If not here, then anyplace would probably suit him just fine."

Adam agreed. "Good. That's what I was hoping Lucas would think." He paused. "What about the home office? The boys there on to anything yet?"

Jeremy shook his head. "Too soon. Three years left a cold trail. Even then, it wasn't definite that it was him. He was never seen if I remember correctly." He stared at Adam. "Was he?"

"No. Just the notes, same as always."

"He failed then. What happened?"

"Gus happened." Adam threw him a curious look. "You were there, don't you remember?"

Jeremy shrugged. "I was new back then. I had just arrived on my first assignment. By the time I got settled in, the incident was the talk of the office. Over time, I got sketches of it."

Adam was thoughtful. "Time moves on. Seems like only yesterday that you joined us. But to answer your question, it

An important message from the ARABESQUE Editor

Dear Arabesque Reader,

Because you've chosen to read one of our Arabesque romance novels, we'd like to say "thank you"! And, as a special way to thank you, we've selected two more of the books you love so well to send you absolutely FREE!

Please enjoy them with our compliments, and thank you for continuing to enjoy Arabesque...the soul of romance.

Karen R. Thomas

Karen Thomas
Senior Editor,
Arabesque Romance Novels

SPECIAL OFFER!
2 BOOKS FREE

ARABESQUE
A PRODUCT OF
BET BOOKS

3 QUICK STEPS
TO RECEIVE YOUR FREE "THANK YOU" GIFT
FROM THE EDITOR

Send back this card and you'll receive 2 Arabesque novels—
absolutely free! These books have a combined cover price of
$10.00 or more, but they are yours to keep absolutely free.

There's no catch. You're under no obligation to buy anything.
We charge nothing for the books—ZERO—for your 2 free
books (except $1.50 for shipping and handling). And you
don't have to make any minimum number of purchases—
not even one!

We hope that after receiving your free books you'll want to
remain an Arabesque subscriber. But the choice is yours to
continue or cancel, anytime at all! So why not take us up on
our invitation to receive your free gift, with no risk of any
kind. You'll be glad you did!

Call us
TOLL-FREE
at 1-888-345-BOOK

Accepting the two introductory free books places you under no obligation to buy anything. You may keep the books and return the shipping statement marked "cancel". If you do not cancel, about a month later we will send 4 additional Arabesque novels, and bill you a preferred subscriber's price of just $4.00 per title (plus a small shipping and handling fee). That's $16.00 for all 4 books for a savings of 25% off the publisher's price. You may cancel at any time, but if you choose to continue, every month we'll send you 4 more books, which you may either purchase at the preferred discount price. . .or return to us and cancel your subscription.

THE ARABESQUE ROMANCE CLUB
c/o ZEBRA HOME SUBSCRIPTION SERVICE, INC.
120 BRIGHTON ROAD
P.O. BOX 5214
CLIFTON, NEW JERSEY 07015-5214

AFFIX
STAMP
HERE

BUSINESS REPLY MAIL

FIRST-CLASS MAIL   PERMIT NO. 272   RED OAK, IA

POSTAGE WILL BE PAID BY ADDRESSEE

heart&soul

P O BOX 7423
RED OAK IA 51591-2423

was the same kind of setup. I was alone, it was dark, and he had a knife. Only Gus dropped by unexpectedly and he escaped.''

''Gus is a good man to have around apparently.'' Jeremy asked, ''And Italy eighteen months ago, was that Reynard?''

Adam looked surprised. ''Now you were there for that one. We all knew the attempt on my life was job-related. Our client's enemy, remember?'' He watched his colleague struggle to remember. ''I think the magic of New York City is getting to you, Jerry.'' He paused. ''Or is it being too close to family? Guess it is a temptation to get by as often as you can. No telling when you'll get back this way.''

''Family?'' Jeremy looked blank.

''Yeah, in Newark? Or is it someone special? Well, sorry you had to come from a day off to this.'' He gestured, meaning himself.

''Nah,'' Jeremy replied. ''I'm a Windy City boy. Just looking up some old friends in Jersey.''

Adam listened but his face gave no indication of his thoughts. He lowered the bed. ''I'll catch you later, Jerry. I'm going to get some shut-eye before the crew comes in again.''

When Adam was alone, he lay staring up at the ceiling, his analytical mind straining to bring to the surface some categorized information. He was excellent at placing people in their proper places, mentally cataloging and then placing the data in neat little boxes in his brain. He closed the lids on them until he needed to access the information. His information on Jeremy wasn't computing. Why tell Gus he was a New Jerseyan and reveal to Adam that he was from Chicago?

Adam reached for the phone. After a moment, he said, ''Lucas Parnell, please.''

Sunday at Restaurant Louise was no different from the last few days: hectic. By 9:30, Sydney was ready to call it a night. She was walking to the kitchen to return her dinner tray and to say good night to Mason. Earlier, when she'd arrived from the hospital, and she had popped her head in to say hi, he had

seemed strangely distant. Moods on Mason were rare and she
worried about him.

Her own mood was great. Adam's temperature was normal
and he was being released on Monday. She was ecstatic and
practically walked on air. The kisses they'd shared spoke of
magical things to come when he recovered.

Mason was resting on a stool, watching his assistant, but
Sydney felt that he was miles away. She stood out of the way
of his bustling crew and called him from the doorway. He
turned to her with a distant look in his eyes. He said something
to the worker then walked toward her.

Mason regarded Sydney with a sharp eye. *I'm looking at a
woman in love,* he thought.

"Enjoy your dinner?" he asked.

"Always." Sydney was taken aback by the banal question.
Invariably he would have an original, back-patting comment
about his scrumptious meals.

"What's wrong?" she asked him quietly.

Mason looked at her for a long moment, then said, "Got a
minute?" When she nodded, he left her, gave quiet instructions
to his assistant, then guided Sydney from the kitchen.

Sydney did not speak until they were in her office, both
seated, watching each other.

"How's the patient?" Mason asked.

"Doing okay," Sydney responded in a careful tone. "I'm
accompanying him home from the hospital on Monday."

"Tomorrow?" His eyes flickered. "That's August second."

"Yes, I know."

"Reva's birthday."

"Yes, I know." She shuttered her eyes.

"Have you heard from her?"

"No." Her voice was toneless and then slightly sarcastic.
"Have you?"

"Yes."

Sydney stared at him as if he'd gone mad. "What did you
say?"

"This morning, before I left the house, she called. She flew

in yesterday and was packing, ready to leave again.'' He looked
at his watch. ''They had a 9:08 flight out of J.F.K.''

Stunned, Sydney said, ''They? Mason what are you talking
about?'' She spread her hands in dismay. ''Not a word to me
in weeks and she calls you, when I've been the one worried
sick about what's happened to her and where she'd gone?''
She looked at him. ''Why? You two don't even *like* each
other!'' Her eyes narrowed. ''Or am I wrong about that, too?''

Mason gave her a look that asked her not to go there. When
he spoke, his voice was even but troubled.

''She was in the Virgin Islands with a friend. Someone she
used to date years ago. She called it her standby relationship.''

Joe Walker. Aloud, Sydney said, ''Joe Walker, her onetime
serious love interest. The man she left, to pursue the stage.''
Her initial anger and hurt subsiding, Sydney asked, ''They?''

''I guess it's the same friend. She never mentioned a name.''

''Where are they going?''

Mason hesitated. ''They'll be living in California.''

Sydney's shoulders drooped. *So far away,* she thought.
Ferne, now Reva. We're all so far apart.

''Did she say anything else?'' Her eyes sought Mason's.

''Only that she wants to get away from teaching and acting,
and try something new. She has a job that has nothing to do
with either field, she said.''

''Anything else? Why didn't she call me, Mason?'' The hurt
had returned to her voice.

''Sydney,'' Mason said in a low voice. ''Reva said that she
tried to bring herself to call you after her anger cooled. But
she couldn't face your judgmental looks and lectures on what
she was doing with her life.''

Sydney gasped. ''She said that?''

Mason nodded. ''She sends her apologies for taking out her
frustrations on you.'' His expression changed. ''She thought
that coming from me, you would listen and understand how
ashamed she is.''

Sydney was dazed and felt betrayed. All these years, is that
what their friendship had meant? Was she really thought of as

being the smug, holier-than-thou, know-it-all friend? She stood up.

Mason stood and watched her closely. He knew how much Reva's friendship had meant to Sydney. All three women had been so close. Ferne, Reva and Sydney. Now there was just Sydney, making it alone in New York. He followed her to the door.

"Thanks, Mason. You're a good friend." She raised on her toes and kissed him on the cheek. Tilting her head, she squinted an eye and said, "Tell me something?"

"If I can," he answered, curious.

"You really did like her, didn't you?"

Mason squirmed under her scrutiny. "After a while, she got under my skin," he admitted.

Sydney nodded knowingly. "I thought so."

"It was the acting that I couldn't stand."

They both laughed as Sydney locked her door.

"Mason, you never revealed your feelings to her, did you?"

"No."

"Promise me that you will? She'll be back one day."

"Don't you think it's a little late for that? She's with another guy now." He sent her a rueful look.

"Trust me, that's not forever."

He raised a brow. "You're so sure?"

Sydney was solemn-voiced when she said, "It's my judgmental side. I can feel it."

Mason laughed. "l promise." He grew serious. "I'm going to miss her."

"Me, too," Sydney said, and walked away.

CHAPTER TWELVE

On Monday, Sydney and Adam rode in the back seat of a Garrison International company car, while Jeremy maneuvered through the noonday traffic. She glanced at Adam, who had been very quiet since they left the hospital. Although he never expressed it, she noticed that he moved as if in pain. When he leaned heavily on Jeremy's arm, she knew that she'd assessed correctly. His eyes were closed as he rested his head back and Sydney slipped her hand in his. She felt his answering squeeze though he said nothing.

Adam ran his thumb across the back of her hand. He had no words to express how he felt when she'd agreed to accompany him home. They both knew that the company would be there for him, but her presence personalized his trip home in the absence of family. He was a lucky man and couldn't help wondering how in the world he came to be the one with whom she had fallen in love.

Jeremy stopped the car and turned off the engine. "Last stop," he said and got out of the car.

Gingerly, and with Jeremy's help, Adam eased from the car, but once standing, insisted upon making it on his own to the front door. With Sydney by his side, he followed Jeremy who'd gone ahead and entered the apartment.

"The company took care of everything," Jeremy said cheerfully. "All cleaned up, even emptied the fridge and restocked it." He grinned at Adam. "Nothing for you to do but rest easy until you heal up." He included Sydney in his look. "Someone will be in to do meals and housekeeping this week, so there's no worry of any overexertion. The number for the market is on the fridge. If something is missing, just order, and they'll deliver." While he talked, Jeremy carried Adam's bag to the bedroom, unpacked it and put away the toiletries. He checked the cupboards and the fridge once more, then satisfied, he said, "Well, that's it."

Sydney glimpsed the annoyed look on Adam's face, as he walked to the bedroom. She walked with him and watched as he eased himself down on the bed. She turned to Jeremy, who was standing in the doorway.

"I'm going to the druggist to have his prescriptions filled. I think he would like to get in bed. Would you mind?" The man must be an idiot not to see that Adam was exhausted and needed help getting undressed. Did he expect her to get him into bed?

Sydney looked at Adam and her voice softened. "I won't be long. Is there anything you need?"

Adam held back the tiny smile tugging at his mouth, but his eyes couldn't hide his thoughts. "No," he answered and busied himself with the buttons on his shirt.

Sydney flushed to the roots of her hair as she turned to go, nearly bumping into Jeremy, who still stood in the doorway. "Excuse me," she murmured and hurried from the apartment.

Twenty minutes later, Sydney bumped into Jeremy once again as he was walking to the car. She frowned, wondering why he'd left Adam alone. *The man really is an idiot,* she thought. *And he's a good man, according to Adam.* Her displeasure must have shown because he stopped and threw her one of his boyish grins.

Jeremy left his professionalism in Adam's apartment when he allowed his eyes to stray over Sydney's body. His lashes flickered but all he said was, "He'll be fine now, Ms. Cox. I left the door unlocked for you, so go right on in. See you around." Still grinning, he got in the car and drove off.

Sydney felt like she'd been dipped in oil after that encounter. Was the man really what he seemed? Apparently one of the best officers, but on the other hand, almost bumpkinish. She wondered what his colleagues thought of him. All thoughts of the strange officer disappeared when she closed and locked the door.

The door to the bedroom was open and she could see the foot of the bed. Good, she thought, he's resting. "I'm back, Adam," she called, walking to the compact kitchen. "Be right there." She filled a glass with cold water and carried it to the bedroom.

"Adam?" she called softly. He had fallen asleep and was breathing evenly. Her forehead wrinkled. Should she wake him or let him sleep? He might sleep for hours, and the medication was not doing any good sitting on the table, she decided.

"Adam, wake up," she said in a low voice. She touched his shoulder and he opened his eyes. He looked startled.

"Sydney?" He shook his head, then smiled at her. "For a minute there I was in another world."

"I hated to wake you, but I think you should take these now, rather than later." She handed him the glass and two pills. "I'm almost certain that one of them is an antibiotic to ward off any infection, and that, you definitely don't need."

Adam swallowed then set the glass down on the table. He looked at Sydney who was sitting in a small easy chair, watching him. She looked sad. He'd noticed the wan look on her face the moment she walked into the hospital room this morning. He could also see her concern for him, so he didn't question her. But now he wanted to know what was troubling her. And he wanted to take her in his arms, to taste her, to feel her warm, sweet skin against his.

"I've got another side, you know." His voice was deep and roughly smooth like damask and his eyes darkened with the passion he felt for her.

Sydney, perplexed, went warm inside. "Side?" she asked.

Adam held out his hand to her. "One side of me is as good as new. It can stand as much pressure as I want."

Sydney rose, took his hand and sat down on the bed. "Which side is it?" she whispered, staring at the beautiful shape of his mouth, wanting to taste it.

"You're on it," he said in a hoarse whisper, then groaned as he pulled her down to him. "Sydney, Sydney." His kiss was hungry, demanding, as he sought to claim her tongue. Small sounds of frustration erupted when he couldn't get enough and he thrust his tongue deep into the recesses of her mouth. Satisfied, he reclaimed her lips, melding them to his in a searing kiss.

Sydney hungrily met the onslaught of his kisses as she leaned into him, wanting more. Her head was reeling from the fierceness of his searching tongue and burning lips. She shivered under his touch as he slipped his hand inside her button-front dress. He squeezed her breasts and she felt her nipples strain against the satin fabric of her bra.

"I want you now. Can I love you, Sydney?" he rasped. He struggled to feel her in his mouth.

"Yes, yes," Sydney whispered. "I want you to make love with me."

"Oh, yes," Adam murmured. He suckled one rigid peak, while he caressed her bare thigh. "I want to feel your body," he said against her hot flesh. "Lie with me." He shifted his position toward her, turning his torso to meet hers, when he winced, drawing a sharp breath of pain. He fell on his back, his eyes closed.

"Adam, what's wrong?" Sydney jumped up from the bed, alarmed at his closed eyes and clenched teeth. "Oh, Adam," she cried. "What happened?"

"I may have pulled something," he grunted.

"Oh no, let me see."

She unbuttoned his pajama top and pushed it aside to reveal the large bandage covering one side of his body and held in place with gauze wrapped around his chest. She looked for any staining that may indicate burst stitches. It was still dry and clean. She buttoned the top.

"It looks okay," she said as she straightened her clothes. His expression was one of utter disgust and she could only guess at his frustration. She wasn't doing much better.

She smiled down at him as she adjusted his pillows and smoothed the covers. "I think we'd better wait before we try this again." She winked. "You know what they say about three strikes."

He scowled. "Don't even think it."

"What do you say to getting some rest? When you wake up, I'll have dinner ready. Afraid you blew lunch," she teased.

Adam reached for her hand as she started to leave. "Sydney," his gaze was penetrating. "You know that I appreciate your being with me. This is your day off and . . ."

"Shh, Adam. I'm exactly where I want to be today." Sydney bent and kissed his lips and was thrilled at his warm response.

"What happened to upset you this morning?" He held on to her hand for a bare second.

Surprised, Sydney answered, "You are a detective after all." Her eyes clouded. "Today is Reva's birthday."

Adam remembered what she'd told him about the longtime friendship. "No word?"

"After a fashion," she tried to joke. She sat down in the chair and explained. When she finished, she stood up and said, "Now that's the last word. You must rest."

His voice stopped her at the door. "She'll be back, Sydney."

Adam awoke to delicious smells and he knew he wasn't in the hospital. His kitchen was being put to good use. The bedside clock read five-ten and he realized he'd slept for almost four hours.

"I wanted you to rest but not at the expense of starving you." Sydney appeared in the doorway, looking flushed, but happy when she saw how relaxed he looked. "Ready for some dinner?" Frowning, she walked to him and felt his pajama top. "You're soaking wet."

Adam caught her hand. "No kiss?"

"No," Sydney said firmly, pulling back the covers. "You

have to get changed.'' She turned to the dresser. ''Which drawer?''

''Third from top.'' Adam looked amused at her sudden change of mood. He was learning a lot about this woman. He already knew that she was sweet, loving, smart, determined, and she'd just exposed her protective side. He sat up and swung his legs to the floor.

Sydney was by his side with a dry pair of pajamas, wondering if he was feverish. She felt his forehead, but it was normal to the touch.

''Just checking,'' she said, answering his questioning look.

''Stop worrying, I'm okay.'' He stood up and walked with her out of the bedroom. ''This is my last day as an invalid. Tomorrow, I'll be back to my old self, thanks to you.'' He sniffed. ''Smells great. Keep it warm, I won't be long.'' He walked straight and tall to the bathroom.

Sydney watched him carefully to see if he was acting for her benefit. Satisfied that he wasn't hiding the pain, she began to set the table. Earlier, when she'd checked the food supply, she shook her head at the inadequacy of the so-called stocked fridge and cupboards. Deciding what would be needed for a few meals, she placed the order and the delivery was prompt. She gave kudos because nothing was left off her list. For dinner, she had prepared baked salmon, spinach and mashed potatoes. She'd also ordered a small cake decorated with the words *welcome home*.

Refreshed and in dry pajamas under a short cotton robe, Adam joined Sydney at the small round table in the kitchen area. He looked in amazement. She'd transformed his normally bland-looking table with stuff he didn't know was in the cabinets. Where did she find a lace cloth and crystal candlesticks? He never entertained and he always reached for the same dishes whenever he cooked for himself.

Sydney looked up at him shyly as he stared at the cake. ''Like chocolate?'' she asked.

''Only chocolate,'' he whispered. Though stiff, he bent over and kissed her mouth. ''Sweet chocolate.'' He sat beside her, smiling at her quick flight to the stove.

After their meal, Adam refused to lie back down. "I'll never get my strength if I stay flat on my back," he'd told her.

They were in the living room and he'd just hung up the phone after talking to Gus, who'd called while he was sleeping. Lucas had called also, but Adam decided to wait before getting back to him. The conversation he expected to have was not for Sydney's ears.

The sun had disappeared and the room was bathed in soft lamplight. It was almost eight o'clock.

"You must be worn out," Adam said softly. Sydney was sitting beside him on the sofa, her shoes off, and her feet tucked beneath her.

"Mmm," she murmured as she snuggled against his good side. "It's a wonderful tired," she said sleepily. "I'll go in late and leave early. I'll be fine."

Adam tilted her chin. "Sydney, don't fall asleep. You have to be alert when you leave."

Sydney untucked her legs and sat up. She leaned over and kissed his lips lightly. "I know. But I'm sure I'll be okay. My friendly doormen are back, so not to worry." She checked her watch. "But you're right, I should be going." She frowned. "I thought Jeremy was coming back tonight. You're not going to be alone, are you?"

Adam reassured her. "He's around. He'll be watching as you leave, but you won't see him."

Sydney shivered at the thought. It was like being watched by a thousand eyes that were everywhere.

Fifteen minutes later, Sydney was at the door, insisting that Adam spend the evening in bed, resting. The driver of the car service that Adam had called, had rung the bell, then returned to the car to wait.

"Don't overdo it. You'd be surprised how tired you can get the first day home." She looked about. "Can I do anything for you before I leave?" She started to kiss him good night when she found herself being swung gently into his embrace. "Adam, be careful," she said, concern filling her voice.

"That's just it, I am," he growled, hugging her. "You take

the prize for asking loaded questions.'' He silenced her with a gentle, but firm kiss.

The kiss was long and deeply satisfying and Sydney sighed her pleasure. Since this was all the loving they could do for now, they both were making the best of a distressing situation. Sydney ended it when she felt the extent of his frustration.

''I think now is a great time to scoot out this door,'' she murmured, after giving him one more light kiss on the lips. ''Good night, Adam,'' she whispered.

Adam watched from the window, letting the curtain drop when the car pulled off. Sydney had balked at using the car service, preferring to stretch her legs and walk a few blocks before hopping on the subway for two stops. But he wouldn't hear of the ridiculous suggestion and she had relented. Relieved to see her safely in the car, he sat down and picked up the phone.

''You making out okay now?'' Lucas asked when he heard the familiar voice.

''Yeah, much better,'' Adam answered. ''Thanks for everything, Lucas.'' After a second, he asked, ''Any word from the office yet?''

''Still looking for something up to date. Reynard's last known whereabouts seem to have ended with a location in Idaho. That was almost three years ago.'' There was a pause. ''The time you were attacked. After that, nothing.''

Adam frowned. ''They're still on it?''

''They're staying with this, Adam. Lincoln's orders.'' Lucas remembered the reason for his earlier call. He said, ''Oh, by the way, the info you wanted on Gage's hometown. It's Miami, Florida.''

''Miami?' Adam was puzzled. ''Then what's with Newark and Chicago? The guy doesn't know where he's from?''

Lucas chuckled. ''Nothing's wrong with the man, Adam. He *is* from all those places.''

''What are you talking about?'' Adam was annoyed.

''It's all in his file. Seems he and his sisters were passed around among relatives when they were orphaned suddenly when he was a young man. So he's right. He's got relatives in Newark, Chicago and Miami.''

Adam was silent.

''Don't worry about him, Adam. Whatever you were thinking has no basis. The man had a messed-up childhood but he made it on his own. He's proven himself to be a top officer.'' Lucas paused and gave a self-conscious cough. ''That's probably why he acts the way he does sometimes.''

''You mean humble?''

Lucas cleared his throat. ''Yeah, sort of like he's got to prove he belongs with the group. You know.''

''Yeah,'' Adam said thoughtfully. ''I do see what you mean. I just couldn't understand where he was coming from. He must be about forty, right?''

''Forty-two.''

Adam expelled a relieved breath. ''That explains a lot,'' he said. ''Takes a load off my mind. Thanks for looking out, Lucas.''

''Don't mention it. So you made out okay today? How's the pain?''

Adam hung up after reassuring Lucas that he was fine and would be back to work soon. He added that he'd been knocked off his feet before, but he always came back strong and determined.

Adam turned out the lights and walked to the bedroom. What he'd just told Lucas was the truth. It wouldn't take him long to recover from his wounds, and when he did, there would be no place on earth that Ethan Reynard could hide from him.

When Sydney left the car and entered the building, she walked as if clouds were beneath her feet. And in the elevator riding up, she imagined she was being carried on a giant star. Of course, she mused, what woman wouldn't feel as she did after hours in the company of the man she loved? She locked the apartment door and laughed aloud, filling the silent rooms with a joyous sound at her sudden thought. ''And we never made love,'' she said with wonder. ''Lord only knows how I'll be feeling when *that* time comes!''

In the shower, Sydney hugged herself as she lathered her body with a floral gel. On a day that had started with sadness sitting on her chest because she'd lost a friend, it was ending with a happiness in her heart that she'd never known before. She toweled herself dry and donned a soft cotton granny-style nightshirt bordered with eyelet trim.

Sydney turned out the light, but instead of getting in bed, she walked across the dark room and looked out the window. Bright lights twinkled all over the city trying in vain to match the brilliance of the stars in the sky. She smiled as she looked up at the tiny sparklers that were light-years from earth. She wondered if they could see the sparkle coming from her eyes and wonder if she was one of them, fallen to earth.

Across town in a small Upper West Side furnished apartment, the man sat in the dark, nursing a beer that had grown warm in his hand. His eyes glinted with hatred. Fury ate at his insides that he'd bungled his chance to end this hunt once and for all.

That man was strong and in top form, he fumed, because he should have been dead from those wounds.

Calming himself, he knew that he had to have a clear head. He had to think, plan a way to end Stone's life. Too much time was passing and the longer it took, the better his chance of getting caught.

By the time he finished the warm beer, his eyes glowed like lightbulbs as new ideas pummeled his brain. ''Through the back door,'' he said aloud. ''That's the way.'' He chuckled at his thoughts and then frowned. If his plan backfired, then that meant that he would have to silence more than just Adam Stone.

Wednesday morning, Sydney was up early. By seven o'clock, she'd washed and dried a load of clothes, pressed her outfit for work, eaten breakfast and cleaned the kitchen. She'd packed a light bag with her sandals and a change of casual clothes.

Sydney was only working a half day today, planning to leave immediately after the afternoon meal. She was leaving early to spend the rest of the afternoon and the evening with Adam, promising to prepare a special dinner, especially now that he was feeling so great. Tuesday when she'd spoken to him, he told her that he was feeling fit and that he and Jeremy had walked around four square blocks. The effort hadn't been a strain, he'd told her, and he felt that he was ready to get back to work.

Sydney had also spoken to Jeremy and asked him to order a few items from the market. After quoting the list, she'd hung up after being assured that her foodstuffs would be ready and waiting for her.

At eight o'clock, Sydney was on the train riding the few stops to work, aiming to accomplish a lot in a few, but very busy, hours. The morning sped by quickly as she made calls to vintners, checking on back orders. Carefully studying her inventory had taken up the balance of her morning. Before she knew it, she was in the dining room with Dominic who'd introduced her to some patrons who wanted to meet her. Finally at three forty-five, a little tired after her fast-paced day, she was riding the train to Adam's.

Adam was watching an old western movie when the doorbell rang. He switched the TV off on the way to the door. When he opened it, he could only stare at Sydney who looked more beautiful to him than ever. Was it only a day that had passed when he hadn't seen her?

"Come in," he said in a low voice. Once the door was closed, she was in his arms. He felt her hesitate in pressing against his chest. He murmured against the soft, sweet smell of her shining hair, "I'm okay. No more stitches, no more bandages."

Sydney sighed against his chest. "Thank God," she said. She lifted her head and kissed his mouth. "Thank God," she repeated. Her eyes misted a little as she thought about his near-death encounter. She moved from his embrace and walked into the living room. She was surprised not to see Jeremy.

Adam followed and sat next to her on the sofa. He noticed

her look and said, "He's not joining us for dinner." His voice had turned to its sexiest and his dark eyes captured hers, telling her of mysterious delights to come.

Sydney swallowed the lump in her throat, wondering just how much of his strength had returned. She hadn't expected such a full recovery so fast. He looked as though he'd spent the last few days at a health spa instead of flat on his back in bed. He was dressed casually in white cotton work-out pants and a black short-sleeve baggy cut-off jersey.

Adam looked at her thoughtfully. "Does that bother you?" he asked, softly.

"No, of course not," Sydney answered. She looked at him. "I—I like the idea." Suddenly flustered, she smoothed her skirt. "Well, I think I'd better change ... get ready to fix dinner."

"Change? I like the way you look now." His eyes roamed over her from head to toe with a look that showed his appreciation. The white short-sleeve suit showed her curves to advantage and the short skirt revealed a modest expanse of long leg and thigh. He noticed the pin she wore and remembered it from the night he'd seen her in the restaurant. The ruby-red cluster of grapes picked up the burnished deep brown highlights of her hair. "You're beautiful."

"And you, sir, if you keep looking at me like that, won't get any dinner tonight."

Adam tilted his head to one side. "And that would be a problem?" The thought of what *could* be happening stirred his groin with warmth until he squirmed on the sofa.

Sydney gulped and hastily stood up. "Now's a good time to change," she whispered and left the room with her bag.

Adam watched her go, willing his body to behave. The evening was just starting.

CHAPTER THIRTEEN

When Sydney returned to the living room, she'd changed into tan leather sandals, short denim skirt and bright red V-neck T-shirt. Her hair was caught high, baring her neck.

"Oh," she said, "this is a nice surprise." Adam had set a tray on the coffee table with crystal glasses and a chilled bottle of wine.

"I was hoping you had found this to your liking."

Sydney saw that his selection was the same Riesling that she'd sampled on a night that was now so long ago in her memory. But he'd remembered.

"As a matter of fact, very much. I ordered a supply this morning." She frowned, "But should you be . . ." She stopped, not wanting to be a nag.

"You're right. I'm not imbibing. I've a couple of days left on medication." He lifted a glass full of a sparkling beverage. "Apple cider," he said.

"So, what are we celebrating?" Sydney asked as she sipped her wine.

Adam sat beside her. "You celebrated my homecoming with chocolate cake. I'm celebrating you." He lifted his glass to her. "You're a remarkable woman, Sydney, and I've taken too long to tell you that I'm glad you're here."

"Here?"

"In my life," Adam said gruffly.

Sydney put down her glass and leaned over to kiss him. "I told you that I'm where I want to be." Before he answered back, she got up and hurried to the kitchen. "I want to make the salad first. Did Jeremy get everything on my list?" She began to inspect the bags that were left on the kitchen table.

Adam watched her, amused at her shyness. "He said he did. Don't worry about the salad greens. They were beginning to wilt so I washed them and put them in the fridge. They're in that large covered plastic bowl."

Sydney saw it and closed the door. "That was great, thank you." She looked at him with a smile. "You know your way around the kitchen? Or do you do takeout mostly?" She separated her ingredients for her dishes then turned on the oven.

Adam shrugged. "Mostly out. Irregular hours don't allow much time to expend on preparing decent meals." As if remembering a long time ago, he said, "I can make a mean sweet potato pie."

"You bake?" Sydney looked up in surprise, then continued with her food preparation.

"Yeah, my father taught me everything he knew. He retired after baking for nearly forty years."

Sydney was surprised. Although he'd mentioned having a family, this was the first time that he'd offered so much information. She wondered why neither his brother or father had visited him in the hospital or even accompanied him home. She thought it was a private matter and didn't ask. He had a knack for guessing what she was thinking, so she wasn't surprised at his next words.

"They're away. My brother, his wife and my father. The day before I was attacked, they left on a twenty-one day cruise to Europe."

"How wonderful," Sydney exclaimed. "Special occasion?"

Adam was standing beside her. "It is. My father just got engaged and my sister-in-law hopes she will get pregnant while they're away. Claims Larry is too keyed up when he gets home from work.''

His breath was on her neck, and Sydney flushed when she finally stammered, ''I—I wish them lots of luck.''

Adam nuzzled her neck and whispered, ''I do, too.''

''Adam, I'll never get this dish in the oven.''

He slid his arms around her waist and pulled her against him. ''There's always tomorrow,'' he whispered in her ear.

''Ooh,'' Sydney squirmed, her back pressed against his stomach. ''Don't do that.''

''Don't you like that?'' He blew in her other ear, holding her tight before she squirmed out of his grasp.

''Yes, I do,'' she breathed, her chest thumping wildly.

Abruptly, he let her go. ''That's nice to know,'' he said and sat down at the table. A smile tugged at his mouth. ''Will I be in the way here?'' He had a devilish look in his eyes.

''No, yes,'' she sputtered. She looked at him with pleading eyes. ''Would you select some music to have dinner by?''

He eased himself from the chair. ''I think I can manage that,'' he said smoothly. He crossed the room to the player, searched through some compact discs and put one in. He sat and watched her from the sofa.

Sydney nearly dropped a pan when she heard the first notes. *Their song.* He played the song they'd danced to on the yacht. *He really cares,* she thought. She felt so emotional that she wanted to cry. Then the music stopped. She looked at him.

Adam watched her, the disc still in his hand. ''I'm sorry,'' he said, ''I didn't mean to upset you. Another time?'' he murmured.

Sydney nodded and turned away. Soon she heard the soft instrumental music of Quincy Jones. Adam remained on the sofa.

It was nearly six o'clock when Sydney turned off the oven. She removed the baked tomatoes stuffed with corn and the sour cream biscuits, setting them on the counter. The herbs for the salad greens and the basil for her shrimp were cut and ready for use.

Adam walked in and sniffed the air. "This place has never smelled so good. Can I help?" he asked.

"Almost ready. As soon as the shrimp are done, I just need the salad tossed with these." She pointed to a dish of cut-up herbs, radishes and condiments. "Would you just toss those in the salad while I wash up?"

"No problem," Adam answered. He watched as she emptied the sautéed shrimp and vegetables onto a warming plate and covered it. She set the dish on the beautifully appointed table. "I won't be a minute," she said. "After the salad is tossed, you can use this." She handed him a large colorful blue bowl, then left the room.

Adam was starving. While she worked and he watched the TV news, he had one eye on her. She moved efficiently and swiftly, knowing exactly what she would prepare next. He stayed out of her way in the small kitchen area, which she used with no problem. Now he couldn't wait to taste the goodies she'd cooked. He finished tossing the mixed greens salad, dumped it in the bowl and set it on the table. The stuff he'd poured over them released a flavor that was tantalizing. He heard Sydney open the bathroom door. Just one taste, he said to himself. He couldn't resist picking up a leaf and popping it into his mouth.

Sydney looked down at the table, pleased with her handiwork. She smiled as she looked at the greens. Adam didn't do so bad tossing . . . . Suddenly, she screamed. "Adam," she shouted. "Spit it out! Spit it out! Don't swallow that!" She knocked his hand away from his mouth and tried to pull the leaf from his tongue, but he was already spitting it from his mouth.

"What the . . . ?"

"Adam," Sydney cried. "Did you swallow any of it? Did you?" Tears were welling up in her eyes and her voice trembled. "Please, tell me . . ."

"Sydney," Adam barked. "Stop it. I didn't swallow any of it. It's there in the sink. All of it." He grabbed her by the shoulders and shook her before she went into hysterics. She was frightened to death.

Horrified, she turned her tear-filled eyes to the blue bowl.
"That's poison."

Adam was dumbstruck. "What are you saying?" He let go
of her shoulders and picked up the bowl. "This is a bowl of
spinach mixed with greens. What kind, I don't know, but I've
been eating them for years."

"Adam, please rinse. Please."

Adam went to the bathroom and returned in seconds. She
was ashen and shivering. He went to her.

"Explanation?" His voice was gentle.

Sydney picked out a few dark green pointed leaves. Some
were oval and heart-shaped. "This is Climbing Nightshade."

"What is it?" He could see that she was still shaken.

"It's a common weed that grows in the woods and is occasionally found in some gardens, intertwined around other plants
in thickets. The unripe berries are extremely toxic and can be
fatal."

"Berries?"

"Yes. There are many species of the plant and unless you
are absolutely certain about them, you should never test their
edibility. It's best to leave them alone."

"Then how in the world did something like this get into the
neighborhood farmer's market?"

Sydney's eyes grew wide. "That couldn't be possible. Any
green grocer would know the difference between edible greens
and poison leaves!"

"Who the devil thinks about a thing much less knows about
it?" He stared at her. "How did you recognize it so quickly?"

"Because Ferne and I picked some out of her mother's
vegetable garden and brought them in for dinner. It was the
first summer that I visited. Hannah went into a tirade because
Ferne should have known better. Since then I've made it my
business to study plants and greens. I never wanted anything
like that to happen again."

Sydney emptied the bowl of greens into the trash can. She
washed out the bowl, dazedly wondering if toxins seeped
through plastic. Her hands shook at what could have happened.
Not again, she thought. How could such a thing have happened?

Adam could have died. What if she had stayed in the bathroom a little longer? Her body convulsed with a sob.

"Sydney, don't," Adam said. "Nothing happened. I'm okay. Shh." He held her by the waist and led her to the sofa, but she stopped and twisted herself into his arms.

Sydney looked up into his eyes. "He's never going to stop until you're dead. It was Reynard, wasn't it?" She wrapped her arms around his neck and cried against his chest. "Why can't they find him?" she cried. Her shoulders shook as the tears fell.

Adam's eyes grew hard and cold. The man had gone mad, gotten reckless, sloppy and dangerous, not caring who he killed in trying to get to him. He had to be stopped.

Adam held Sydney close, trying to soothe away her fear. He could only imagine what she felt, blaming herself for placing the order; unable to live with herself if she hadn't caught him in time. Finally the sobs stopped and she was quiet. She unwound her arms from around his neck and hurried to the bathroom.

Adam stared at the kitchen and the dinner that was cold and ruined. Instinct told him that she wouldn't bring herself to touch any of it. He scraped the meal in the garbage, cleared the table and put the dishes in the washer. He found a delivery menu in the drawer and picked up the phone.

Sydney watched Adam from the doorway. He was sitting quietly on the sofa staring into space. Her heart jumped at the fierce look on his face. He looked up at her and held out his hand. She went to him and neither spoke as she sat down beside him and rested her head on his shoulder. Sydney closed her eyes. She was so tired, exhausted from trying to think how such a thing could have happened. So impossible, she thought. So unthinkable. She wrapped her arm around Adam's waist. He was here. He was okay. Her last thought as she gave in to the panacea of sleep, was that he was alive.

Sydney was awakened by voices. She looked around, startled to find herself in Adam's bed. It was after eight o'clock. She realized the voices came from the television, but they stopped abruptly and Adam appeared in the doorway.

"I saw you kicking the covers off." His voice was soft. "You were exhausted. When I half-walked you in here, you protested, but not for long. Feeling better?"

"I'm starved," she blurted.

"No wonder. I'm sure you haven't eaten a thing all day. Come on, I ordered something. I'll zap it for you while you wash your face."

Thirty minutes later, Sydney was stuffed. She'd eaten every bit of the veal scallopine and baked ziti that Adam had ordered. He'd played the requested music to eat dinner by and they talked about things other than what was so prominent in their thoughts. But neither wanted to mar the peace of the evening.

Adam stood up and pulled Sydney with him. She looked at him with a question in her dark eyes.

Adam took her in his arms and murmured, "Remember what you told me that you liked?" He blew a warm breath in her ear. "I didn't forget."

Sydney shivered. "Oh," she breathed.

Adam blew in the other one, this time, whispering, "Like it?"

"Now who's the tease?" she whispered, staring into his intense dark eyes. They were full of the heat that was already beginning to settle in her belly, worming its way to her groin just like a purposeful spiral of red-hot flame.

"Not a tease this time, Sydney." He bent and gently tasted her lips, kissed her neck, and nibbled at her ear. Burying his face in her hair, he murmured, "I want to make love with you." He held her by the shoulders, his gaze intent on hers with a question, which he voiced in a gravelly rasp. "Do you want to love me now, Sydney?"

"Oh, yes. Sweet Adam, yes," Sydney cried.

His mouth crushed hers in a hungry kiss as once again he sought the sweet recesses of her mouth. The feel of her breasts crushed against his chest caused a moan to erupt. "I have to feel you," he whispered as he tugged at her top.

Her hands were under his shirt and she felt him groan when she moved her hand against his chest, parting the bristly hairs away from his nipples and gently squeezing.

"Sydney, Sydney."

Adam pulled away and quickly led her into the bedroom where he pulled off his top and then pulled hers over her head. He slid her bra straps off her shoulders, reached behind her and the lace fell silently to the floor. Adam caught her in his arms once again and the first brush of her soft, warm flesh against his almost made him burst with agony.

"This is what I've wanted for so long, my sweet, so long." He bent his head and tasted one rigid berry-brown nipple and suckled. He took the other into his mouth and allowed his tongue to taste in circular patterns and then playfully fleck the peaked nipple fleetingly. "My God, you taste so good," he uttered in a deep, passion-filled voice.

Sydney was burning up. She didn't know her body could stand so much heat without bursting into flames. What is this hurt that makes her feel so delicious all over? she wondered. His hands were doing things to her at the same time his tongue and his mouth were loving her everywhere. She wanted to feel more of him. All at one time. Sydney tugged at his pants, almost frenzied, pulling at the drawstring. She felt his hands undo it and with a soft moan she pulled at the elastic on his briefs. Seconds later, her hands were on his bare skin.

"Adam," she whimpered. He was standing naked before her but soon she was, too, as she felt the rest of her clothes drop from her body. She cried out at the ugly wound on his side, and tears fell at the marring of such a beautiful, black male body. She gently touched the healing scar, and raised her head to meet his intense gaze. All the love and tenderness she felt for him, she knew was shining in her eyes. "I'm so sorry," she whispered.

Adam caught her hand and brought it to his lips, murmuring, "Shh, it's okay, love. It's okay."

Gently he laid her down and he eased his body onto hers. "Oh God, you're so sweet," he said. Her naked length beneath him sent stars colliding in his head as if he were flying around crazily in another galaxy. His pulsating sex, pressed into her soft, damp mound, was too much to bear. He had to be inside of her to quench the fire that burned his groin. When her soft hands touched his sex, he writhed in sweet agony, which made her legs part for him. He ran his hand down her thigh and when his fingers found the tender inner flesh, he soon found her throbbing womanhood and slipped his finger between the moist velvety lips.

"Adam." Sydney screamed. "Oh, Adam, make it stop," she cried. She grasped his sex and shifted her body to take him inside of her. "What—what . . . are you doing to me? Please . . ."

Suddenly with a soft curse, Adam eased himself away. *Jesus*, he thought, *what am I doing?* He snaked his hand into the nightstand drawer, and after a frustrated grunt, he eased himself once again over her writhing body.

"Adam, please . . ." Sydney moaned. Her hips rose to meet him when she felt his warm length against her.

With a fierce rumbling shout that came up from the bowels of his body, Adam penetrated her with a sharp thrust.

Sydney screamed. "Ad—am . . ." She writhed with the pain that seared her lower insides. A sharp burning pain that was at once, hurtful and unbelievably pleasing. Only a moment did the excruciating hurt last, but her body ached for more. She felt Adam stop and almost leave her, but she held him fast, her hips straining to meet his. Her legs were entwined with his and she wouldn't let go. "Love me, Adam, love me," she whispered.

Momentarily shocked, Adam was lost to the momentum of his passion. His body was following the messages from his brain to give it sweet relief. He was powerless to stop the motion and he gave himself up to the fierce, driving need. His thrusts were deep and fast, matching the turbulent vibrations of her body.

Soon, they both found the rhythm that meshed their bodies into one. The sounds of love drifted all around them but they heard nothing, only the roar of passion that exploded within, sending them hurtling to a place neither had journeyed to before.

Adam lay staring up at the ceiling though the room was dark. He moved his hand across the pillow where she'd lain, feeling the coolness. She'd been in the bathroom far too long, he thought. He sat up and turned on the bedside lamp, then pulled on his pants. Barefoot, he walked to the kitchen to fix himself a drink, then slammed the refrigerator door shut. Now, he wished he smoked, and hungered for one of Gus' cigarettes. Maybe he left a pack around here, Adam hoped. His eyes roamed the room.

Oh God, what happened here? He sat down on the sofa and dropped his head into his hands. Disgusted with himself, he walked back to the kitchen and noisily fixed himself a gin and tonic, medication or no. He swallowed deeply and stalked back to the sofa, a scowl etched into his face.

Was he stupid or what? Couldn't he see the signs? She was so loving and affectionate, but then was so shy when she expressed herself, or when he came on to her so sexily. He looked up when he heard the bathroom door open.

Sydney had donned a knee-length cotton robe she'd found behind the bathroom door. She stared at Adam sitting quietly on the sofa watching her. He swallowed from his glass and continued to stare at her. He's upset, she thought as she noticed the drink. She knew it wasn't water. Why was he so angry? What did she do wrong? Feeling inadequate and miserable, she turned around swiftly and went into the bedroom.

"Damn," Adam swore, putting down the glass. He'd seen the hurt and insecurity on her face. He went to her.

"Sydney?"

CHAPTER FOURTEEN

Sydney was standing by the window, looking through the sheer curtains, but seeing nothing. She hugged her arms around her waist.

"Sydney?" Adam walked to her but didn't touch her. "Please look at me." When she remained with her back turned, he touched her gently on the elbow and led her to the bed, where they both sat. He cupped her chin up to meet his eyes.

"I had no idea I was the first." His voice was gruff as he struggled for the right words. She was so vulnerable right now. "I—I just never dreamed that you were still a virgin. When you spoke of dating in college, I—I thought that you may have had a first love, then." Suddenly he felt inept. There were no words. He dropped his hands and looked away. "I wish you'd told me!" he rasped.

Sydney stiffened. "Why?" she whispered.

"Because I wouldn't have come on so strong and rough," he barked, his voice turning hoarse. He turned to her with a hard stare. "Do you think I enjoyed hearing you scream in agony?" He moved away from her and sat in the chair. He closed his eyes. "Oh, sweet Jesus," he muttered.

The phone rang. "Damn," Adam swore as he jumped up to answer it. "Yeah?" he barked.

Jeremy was startled at the sound of Adam's voice. "Everything quiet? Need me to come around?" He sounded hesitant.

"No," Adam yelled, and slammed down the receiver.

He stared at Sydney, who looked at him with wide-eyed fear. She was almost trembling. "Oh, God," he said and sat down beside her. He put his arms around her and cradled her head on his shoulder. He brushed his lips against her forehead, then softly kissed her mouth.

"Don't be frightened of me, Sydney. I would never do anything to hurt you. Understand? Never." He felt her arm go around his waist and he felt encouraged. He kissed her mouth, then said, "I would have made it sweeter and more pleasurable for you had I known. That's all I wanted to do was to love your sweet self. You're a gorgeous woman and I was so envious that there could have been another to have your love first." His arm tightened around her.

With his words, all the insecure thoughts that she'd had about herself, vanished. That pain she'd experienced was a once-in-a-lifetime feeling. She secretly praised the Lord that the man that had stolen her heart had also taken her virginity.

Moving out of his arms, shifting her body until she was facing him, she said, "You weren't rough with me, Adam." She caressed his cheek and smoothed the hairs of his mustache. "You were responding to my need." She warmed at her frankness, but continued, staunchly overcoming her shyness of the moment to speak her mind. "You made me feel that need to explore and experience the intricate mysteries that were locked up inside of me. I felt a part of myself that I knew existed but had never met." She smiled. "Afterward," she hesitated, "it was pleasurable, indeed. So you see, you did what you set out to do. You loved me sweetly." She leaned over and kissed his mouth.

Adam groaned and caught her close before she moved away. His was a gentle kiss, as he kissed her lips, but was surprised by her aggressive probing, seeking his tongue in the deep recesses of his mouth. His kiss deepened, instinctively, suckling her tongue until she sighed softly at the sudden turn of the chase. He murmured against her lips, answering, "No, I didn't, but I will now."

Breaking away reluctantly to regard him with a saucy smile, Sydney asked, "Can you make me scream again, this time in ecstasy?" She batted her eyelashes theatrically à la Josephine Baker, and suddenly shivered as Adam blew in her ear and slowly started to slide the robe off her shoulders. When he fondled her breasts, she moaned and her body reacted. She felt the moistness between her thighs.

"Let's find out," Adam growled as he pulled off his pants and finished disrobing her. He positioned her naked body on the bed and stood staring down at her. He wanted her again and he could see from her quivering body that she was feeling the excitement and was wanting to experience what was to come. He shut his eyes briefly and prayed for a soft touch, because he wanted to devour her as she lay there, staring at him, trusting him.

His desire for a woman had never been so strong as this. And to know that she loved him, had given her heart to him even before they came together, floored him. That knowledge caused anxiety to fill his eyes. Could he make this second time all that she desired it to be? She reached her arms up to him and with a soft moan, he lay down beside her.

Adam propped himself up on one elbow in order to look at her face as he touched her. He moved his hand slowly in circular patterns on her stomach, then trailing just his fingers, he stroked the valley between her breasts and without fondling them, moved slowly back down to the tender area just beneath her stomach. He bent and kissed her lips but remained where he was as he continued to caress her body in long, soft strokes. His palm was pressed against her stomach and he slid it to her side and down her thighs, then slowly turned it inward and began moving upward.

Stopping the slow ascent, he laid his palm against her mons area and pressed, his fingers stroking the soft, moist hairs. With one finger he titillated the bed of down, then quickly moved it away.

"Adam," Sydney moaned, writhing beneath the tender torture. She sought to catch his hand but it eluded her and she sighed when she felt it on her breast, softly kneading, then flicking the already taut nipples with his thumb.

Adam watched the changing expressions on her face. Her lips went from soft and supple to swollen and pulsating and he couldn't resist bending and tasting them. Her warm, moist tongue tickled his and he groaned his pleasure. He could feel the fire in her body and felt her rising desire to douse the flames. But not yet, he thought. He wanted her to experience her body, to know the power she possessed to make it sing for him. The thought made him surge with a power of his own, realizing that she had given herself to him. He was her first lover. The thought struck him: Could he ever envision her in the arms of another?

Dismissing that thought, he continued his slow descent again to her thighs. He flinched with pleasure as her hands caressed and teased his nipples then moved downward in an exploration of their own as she found his throbbing sex and squeezed.

"No, my love," he whispered as she whimpered at being deprived. "This is for you."

"Oh, Adam, I want you inside of me again. I can feel you want me, too," she whispered in a passion-filled voice.

"You know how much," he answered as he stroked her with his finger. "Soon," the husky response was muffled as he buried his head in her throat, softly nibbling at the tender skin. Then, he thrust his fingers deep inside her.

"Oh," Sydney sighed, as she squirmed and twisted her body, aching to feel more of the exquisite sensation.

Adam felt the tiny nub of her passion and gently massaged. He felt her spasmodic reaction as she closed her thighs tightly and screamed his name. He thrust once more deeply as he smothered the scream on her lips, crushing his mouth against hers.

Sydney writhed wildly against the delicious onslaught of his fingers inside of her. His whispers in her ear brought more screams as her hips rose in a powerful thrust. She dug her heels into the bed and then suddenly, sated, she sank back down, her chest heaving violently. Small sighs escaped her lips as she closed her eyes.

Adam kissed her eyelids, her cheeks, her nose, and finally captured her lips in a gentle kiss. He put his arm beneath her head, cradling her, his hand moving featherlike on her shoulder.

Neither spoke as they sought to control their emotions. Sydney could feel the rise and fall of Adam's chest as she stroked him, and realized the extreme will he had exercised in not giving in to his own pleasure. Her breathing was even now and she eased herself up to look at him.

Adam met her gaze but didn't speak.

"Did my screams frighten you this time?" she asked in a soft voice.

Relieved, Adam didn't trust his voice, but briefly shut his eyes, then pulled her back down beside him. He filled his nostrils with the tantalizing heated musk of her body that mingled with her hyacinth-scented skin. "Are you okay?" he asked in a low voice.

"Ecstatic," she answered.

"I'm glad." His voice was husky and his eyes smoldered.

Sydney smiled and lay down in the crook of his arm. Closing her eyes, she whispered against his heated skin, "I told you, I'm where I want to be."

Adam reached up to turn out the light, then covered them both with the sheet. Sydney had fallen asleep with her arm across his middle. Her manicured fingernails were resting against his wound and he eased her hand up to his chest. It brushed against his nipple and he flinched, feeling his need to have her again.

Taking a deep breath, Adam closed his eyes, contenting himself with the thought that when he opened them in the morning, she would still be in his arms.

Suddenly, as the shock of his next thought jolted his equilibrium with the force of a tidal wave, he opened his eyes to stare at her still form in the dark. He let out an audible breath with the stunning knowledge, never dreaming that after all these years, he would be in such a position. He realized that although in his arms was the place where *she* wanted to be, *he* wanted her there—always. The image of her giving herself to another man because he'd let her go, blew his mind, sending pinpricks of pain to the length of his body.

He squirmed from the stinging sensation and she stirred out of his arms. Gently he cradled her head and closed his eyes, a smile tugging at his mouth. *Now, you are back where you belong.*

The following morning, Adam was reluctant to kiss Sydney good-bye and put her in a cab. When the car pulled off, he went back inside and immediately sifted through the garbage and pulled out the poisonous green leaves. After washing and drying them, he rolled them up in tinfoil, left them on the counter, then picked up the phone.

It was close to nine-thirty when Lucas' secretary put Adam's call through.

"How's the body? Ready to test it out? Got a few new cases I could use you on."

Without preamble, Adam said, "I was nearly poisoned last night. The madman got that close to me with a new bag of tricks."

"Poison?" Lucas frowned. "That's going way out of character. What happened?" he barked.

Anger seething beneath the surface and in every clenched word, Adam explained. Even the verbalizing of it, hearing the words come from his mouth, he could understand the preposterousness of the story. But yet, Sydney had reacted so violently, that he believed her without a doubt in the world.

"Could this be as common as she says it is? Anyone can get hold of this stuff? And how did it get in my grocery bags?" Adam fumed.

"Calm down, Adam. Sydney is right. It's a common weed. Jennifer clued me in on that years ago when we bought our country place in upstate New York. We had to train the kids to keep their hands off any and everything, or else."

"Damn," Adam said with exasperation. "Okay, it's a fact. That still doesn't explain how it got on my dinner table!"

Lucas thought for a second, then asked, "Jeremy personally brought the bags in the house?"

"No. After he placed the order, he stuck around for a while then made himself scarce before Sydney arrived. I tipped the deliverywoman myself, and unpacked the greens. The few I saw looked wilted, so I washed them and put them in the refrigerator."

"What was the packaging like?"

Adam thought. "The spinach was in a cello bag," he recalled with a frown. "So was the iceberg and romaine lettuce heads." Remembering, he said, "The poison greens were in a plain, clear white plastic bag. You know, the kind you get from hundreds of stores? No identifiable advertising."

"So you cleaned them, including the others?"

"Yeah. I just washed them all at the same time."

"Do you have a description of the deliverywoman and the time she was there? At least that'll be a place for us to start."

After giving him the information, Adam asked, "You got a man for this? Jeremy's stretched pretty thin, isn't he?"

"Don't worry, I have a man. He'll be on it pronto. I should have some news by tonight."

Adam rubbed a hand wearily across his forehead. "Guess I'll have to wait until then," he said. "Oh, if you can't reach me, leave a message. I may be out when you call."

"Out?" Lucas sounded curious. "Jeremy's got your back?"

"He'll be around," Adam replied. He could hear the wheels turning around in his boss' head. "I'll be picking Sydney up from work and escorting her home." He paused. "I still don't feel comfortable with her walking around alone."

Lucas was hearing a new voice from his senior officer. *It's about time!* he grinned. "Sure," he answered, "but keep in touch."

"By the way, how's Gus making out with the King case? He could only call once." Adam certainly missed the big guy at his back.

"Mrs. King is getting frustrated that the police haven't got a line on this guy yet. She's got a backup plan."

"What's that?" Adam was curious.

''She'll give it another week and if they haven't caught the guy, she's sending Kyla out of the state to live.''

Adam gave a disgusted snort. ''Like there's no air travel?''

''I know. But she feels that that's the only way she can function on her job. Her folks are high-profile citizens in Idaho. Both judges. The security will be top-notch and she's asked Lincoln to keep a man on the job.''

''Not Gus?''

''That's being debated. I can use you both here. When Mrs. King makes her decision, then Lincoln will make his.''

Adam frowned. ''That'll be hard on the kid, getting used to another officer.''

''If that happens, she'll handle it. Gus said that after the initial scare, she's really turned out to be a gutsy little kid. It's gotten so she even alerts him to strangers who happen to get too close to them.'' Lucas laughed. ''Gus has promised her a job with the company.''

Adam smiled. Sounded like his buddy was getting attached. A problem in some cases, he thought with a sudden frown.

When Lucas hung up, Adam made another phone call. He needed a car. After Adam's attack, Gus had picked up the car from the garage and returned it to the agency. He closed his eyes and rested his head against the sofa, feeling physically and mentally tired. His thoughts were on Sydney constantly since his awakening, and he was troubled by the decision he had to make: be selfish and keep her in his life as he'd vowed last night, or let her go—for her own safety?

Sydney saw Adam come into the dining room and cross to the lounge. Their eyes met, Adam nodded, and continued walking without missing a step. Sydney smiled and her heart did its usual flip-flop whenever he was near. She could swear the feeling worsened since their delicious intimate encounters.

It was 10:45 P.M. when Sydney was finally ready to call it a night. After missing so many hours yesterday and this morning, she played catch-up with her paperwork, answered e-mail and made a few phone calls. It was Thursday night and as usual, the restaurant was busy. Apparently the woman's group from the previous week had spread the word and several patrons asked for her. She spent a good part of the evening chatting with several New Yorkers who were first-time visitors to the establishment. She had even gotten offers to appear as a guest lecturer on the world of fine wines, and someone said she would make a good interview for the popular black woman's publication *Heart and Soul.* She felt that her cup runneth over.

When Sydney left her office to meet Adam in the lounge, she met Mason in the corridor.

"Hi. Calling it quits, too?" Her voice was bright and her eyes sparkled.

Mason stared at her.

"What?" she asked, as they walked.

"You have a song in your voice that wasn't there the last time we spoke." He tilted his head to one side. "And that was only yesterday?"

Sydney flushed. "No, that was Sunday, Mr. Detective." They bypassed the door leading to the garage. "Not driving tonight?"

"Someone's waiting for me in the lounge."

"A date? Mason Wingate, you've been holding out on me?" Sydney flashed him a teasing look.

"Oh?" He raised a questioning brow. "Like you told me there's wedding bells in the air?"

"Mason!" Flushing deeply, she said, "What are you talking about?"

"Nobody walks around like that for long unless they're making a beeline to the altar, my friend." He smiled. "He hasn't asked you yet?"

"I haven't the faintest idea of what you're talking about," she said huffily. But she had a smile on her face when they walked into the lounge.

Adam had seen them coming. He was standing at the bar in a shadowy corner and stepped out when they entered. Sydney caught his eye and walked toward him with a smile.

She held out her hand to Mason, who took it, as he searched the room. Mason frowned when he didn't recognize anyone, then kept step with her.

Sydney noticed and whispered, "You don't see her?"

"No."

"Don't worry, she'll be here," Sydney encouraged. They had reached Adam. She said, "Mason Wingate, Adam Stone. You both may have remembered meeting a few weeks ago."

Both men nodded, sizing each other up as they shook hands.

Surprise filled Mason's eyes. *My girl has worked a miracle with him,* he thought. Gone was the cold, hard mask and Mason could see the softening of the eyes. *I always knew that she was special.* He smiled at Adam, and his grasp became stronger. "Good to see you," he said. His voice was genuine.

Adam was taken aback by the man's friendliness, evident in the familiar handclasp. The tiny tripping of his heart that had started when he'd first spotted them, stopped. He returned the grip and the smile. "How's it going?"

Mason turned at the sound of his name and a woman walked over to them. Introductions were made and after a minute, they all left the lounge, parting at the door as Mason escorted his date in the opposite direction.

Adam held Sydney a little tightly around her waist as they walked to his car.

"You're beautiful," he said.

She was hugging him around the waist, careful of his side. "You know you didn't have to do this," she said, "but I'm glad you did." She felt his answering squeeze on her waist.

When Adam told Sydney that there was no news from Lucas about the greens, she tried to keep the disappointment and fear from her voice as they talked. That only meant that the vigil would have to continue. Her hand tightened in Adam's as he drove.

After Adam parked the car, he rode up on the elevator with her and saw her to the door. He took her in his arms and kissed her with a deep, passionate kiss that was filled with promises.

"Mmm, are you sure you don't want to come in? Coffee? Tea?" she whispered.

"You know we won't be drinking either," he growled as he released her. "We agreed that you should get some rest. You've been going at a pretty hectic pace." He kissed her once more, then said, "Maybe tomorrow night?"

"Must it be maybe?" she asked in a sultry whisper.

"Get inside and lock up," he muttered.

Friday night, Adam repeated his actions and when he was satisfied that Sydney looked fully rested, he whispered to her on Saturday night, "Coffee? Tea?"

"I really don't care for either, sir, but I have some fine sparkling wine that you'll love," she teased.

Sydney locked the door and tossed the keys and her bag on the table. Shrugging out of her suit jacket, she turned to Adam, who was staring at her with an unmistakable message in his eyes. She answered it by walking easily into his arms. "Me, too," she murmured.

"You don't have to ask what I'm thinking?" His voice was velvety smooth as he hugged her close.

"You want to do this and so do I," she said. Standing on her toes, she put her lips to his ear and blew.

Adam convulsed as the warm breath tickled his ear and flew clear to his groin. His arousal was immediate. He caught her mouth in a hard, crushing kiss that was almost bruising. His hand was on her thigh and he bunched the soft cotton of her skirt in his hand and slowly lifted it up until he could feel her soft skin. He uttered in protest when he felt nylon instead, but almost instantly, he felt her warm flesh. She was wearing stockings. He tugged at the lace top until he was able to feel the tender flesh of her inner thigh. He didn't stop until he found the object of his search. He uttered his satisfaction against her swollen lips.

Sydney couldn't let out the gasp that got trapped in her throat when she felt his fingers slip under her panties and feather her already moist center. She strained into him with a soft moan.

Adam muttered, "This is finer than wine, thank you." He unzipped her skirt and it fell to the floor. The matching camisole to her suit was whisked over her head.

Sydney unbuttoned his shirt while he undid his pants, which he kicked away along with his shoes. Then, with a frustrated grunt, not wanting to release her, Adam fumbled for his wallet in his pants' pocket. Finding what he wanted, he tossed his pants away.

Half-clad, they stumbled to the bedroom where later, they didn't know how they'd lost the rest of their clothes.

Sydney slid her hands down his back until she cupped his firm buttocks and pressed him into her belly. His burgeoning erection throbbed against her and she took it into her hands, trying to guide it where she ached with need.

Adam caressed her neck with kisses and nibbled his way down to her breasts, tasting the sweet-scented, salty flesh, searing his mouth in his descent. He wanted to possess her as he never had a woman before. Something about this woman made him want to learn more about her sweet body and try to understand what it was that she did to his. He was experiencing emotions that he had never learned about in school, or at his father's knee, he thought.

Frustration enveloped him as he stopped his ministrations to prepare himself to love her.

"Adam," Sydney whispered, "where are you?" She writhed beneath him as her hands caressed every inch of his naked body. Aching to kiss the nipples that she was massaging with her fingers, she shifted until she satisfied her desire. Her tongue darted around the stiff peaks and she nibbled then nipped until he moaned with pleasure. She answered his gut-wrenching growl with a passion-filled cry of her own when she felt his finger slide deep inside of her. She shuddered, an involuntary spasm so violent that she felt him quiver.

Adam shifted her beneath him once again and as the giant shudder shook his body, he entered her. He felt her rise to meet him and propping himself up with his hands above her shoulders, he thrust, and thrust again. She quickly caught his rhythm, and soon they synchronized the movement of their bodies better than the jewel-like movements of the finest timepieces ever made. Adam sank down on top of her, flesh to flesh, and like time, they moved into oblivion.

Long after Adam and Sydney slipped into a deep, satisfied sleep that lovers knew, a pair of eyes watched the entrance to Sydney's building.

Finally, hours later, starting the engine of the dark car with trembling fingers caused by the anger that seethed within him, he drove off. *A dirty dog and a slut,* he fumed. Almost crying inwardly from rage, he fought against the bile in his stomach rising to his throat. He knew that she had been the cause of him still being alive. It was her fault that now he had to take somebody else's life. *Who the hell studies salads?* He pounded on the steering wheel. It wasn't supposed to go down like this, he raged. All because of her. His eyes glinted. *Well have I got something for you, Ms. Wine Expert. Your Sergeant Stone's going to come running, begging me to end his miserable life.*

CHAPTER FIFTEEN

Monday morning, Sydney lay in bed wide awake and blissfully happy. Saturday and Sunday were two of the most memorable days of her life. What better remembrances to stash away in her memory banks than times spent with one's lover?'' She only wished that she could record the sweet words they whispered; the endearments that brought fierce flushes to warm her body.

Though today she was off, and wished she could spend hours with Adam, she had banking and shopping chores. Adam was meeting with his boss to discuss another priority assignment. But both were looking forward to evening.

Lazily swinging her legs to the floor, she stretched the contented stretch of a pampered feline. Instead of a big breakfast, she would eat light then enjoy high tea at one of the many unique salons that dotted the city. She felt like indulging herself, something her practical-minded self rarely let her do. She might even scour her odd haunts for a grape cluster bracelet to match her ruby-red pin, which she wore almost daily. It took her some time to realize why she automatically pinned it on every day. Indeed, she'd bought it the same day that Adam reappeared in her life.

At ten-thirty, Sydney was dressed and leaving the apartment when the phone rang. She picked the receiver up in the kitchen and was immediately sorry because the Caller ID box was in the bedroom. But she was pleasantly surprised.

"Ferne," she said, barely containing her excitement. "How's the new mom? Are you guys getting used to the new addition?"

Ferne heard the light tone in her friend's voice and was pleased—and curious. "We're all learning something new every day, believe me," she answered happily. "Sometimes I have to practically push Edward out the door to go to work. Sydney, Amalia's just beautiful! I'll be sending pictures soon." She paused. "It's a wonder Hannah hasn't sent you some of hers. She took a bunch while she was here. Edward finally had to put a stop to her snapping away at the baby. Claims it made Amalia fretful."

"You sound just great," Sydney said. "Hannah called when she got back, said you two acted like old-timers at parenting."

"It comes naturally. People always tell you that, but you never believe them. Not until it's for real. Oh, thanks a million for the gift. We used it for the convertible dresser we wanted. Reva's bought the matching lowboy. Oh," she said, realizing the rift still existed between her two dearest friends.

"That's okay," Sydney said. "I'm just happy that she's still in touch with you." She cut the subject short because she had no intention of letting old hurts mar her day. After a few more questions about Amalia, she hung up and left the apartment. She didn't want to take the time to tell Ferne about Adam. She smiled at that. Talking about her love would definitely take at least a day!

Sydney was hurrying upstairs from the Seventy-second Street subway station when she stumbled. Righting herself quickly, she was carried along by the crowd until she reached the street. Taking deep breaths to calm her rapid breathing, she walked at a quick pace to her building. All day it seemed as though there were a million eyes following her. Each time she peered at the people around her, she felt foolish when they stared back and kept on their way. She'd been the most uncomfortable when she was in the tea salon in Soho. The feeling of being watched was strong and her eyes searched the long bar just beyond where she was sitting. No one looked her way or paid her the slightest bit of attention. Except one jerk who thought he was a lothario. All too quickly, she paid her bill and left.

Now unlocking her apartment door, she rushed inside and secured both locks. She threw her purchases on the sofa and hurried to the bedroom where she examined her message box. Thank God. Adam called. She played his message then sighed with relief. He was running late and would call her at six-thirty. He was bringing something in, so she shouldn't bother to cook.

Sydney looked at the time. It was ten past six o'clock. Undressing as she walked to the bathroom, she couldn't help wondering if she were developing an overactive imagination.

Refreshed and dressed in a cool gauze skirt and short-sleeve top, she lay on the bed and closed her eyes. She felt weary and she knew it was only from nerves. She'd never experienced such an intrusive feeling before. Anger made her ball the covers at her sides. *This was her city, why should she fear walking around in it?* At six-forty, the bell rang.

"Mmm," Sydney said as Adam walked quickly past her to the kitchen with his packages. "Smells like The Place."

"You do have a trained sniffer, don't you?" Adam teased, while unpacking the bags. "Chicken and dumplings, fried sweet potatoes, chitlins . . ." He was smiling but when he looked up, he froze. His dark eyes grew almost black as they narrowed, fixing her with an intent stare. "What's wrong?"

"The only thing that could be wrong is the fact that I didn't see you all day," she quipped. She reached for the food and his voice stopped her.

"Don't be flippant. Sydney. It's not you." The steely voice matched the icy eyes. He broke their gaze to sharply survey the area around them and stared at the packages thrown on the sofa. A dangerous look settled on his face as he slowly unbuttoned his jacket and moved quietly around the table and down the hall, motioning her to stay where she was.

Cautiously, he checked the two bedrooms and the bath. Satisfied that she was alone in the apartment, he pulled his jacket shut and walked back to her. He went to her and caught her by the shoulders.

"Tell me what happened to you today. Your face tells stories, Sydney." He led her to the sofa where he transferred her shopping bags to the chair, then sat beside her, holding her hand. He waited.

"It's just a feeling," she began, trying to remember the exact moment it started.

"Go on," Adam persisted.

"Of being watched," she continued, frowning with the memory. "I believe I felt it while still in the neighborhood." Her voice quickened with certainty. "Outside of the bank, stopping to window-shop, walking to the subway . . ." Confidence filled her eyes when she looked at Adam, and straightened her shoulders. "Now I'm certain someone watched my every move in the tea salon," she said with conviction. "You know how you can feel someone staring at you and when you look up, you meet their eyes?"

Adam nodded, but continued to watch her closely.

"Well, that happened in the restaurant. Only the guy didn't avert his eyes. He was standing at the bar, but raised his glass to me, smiling, and showing me his wisdom teeth. He was hitting on me. That's why I dismissed his as the pair of eyes that had followed me all day."

"Black or white?"

"White. Dark eyes. I really couldn't see the exact color from the distance."

"Describe him." Adam was unaware that he sucked in his breath. But from the beginning of her description, his chest deflated. Reynard, at six feet could hardly masquerade at five-six, regardless of how he disguised himself otherwise. "Anything else?"

"Yes," Sydney said, nodding her head. "It happened again, only this time, whoever it was had turned away. The other guy had moved on by that time, so I know it wasn't him."

"What else?"

"I couldn't wait to get home. The subway was the quickest way. Strangest of all was that I felt there was no one intentionally watching me. Although I was jittery, I knew that I was on a train with people just anxious to get home after work."

"Is that all?" *He wasn't on foot.* Adam thought.

"Nearly," she answered in a voice that was suddenly aware. "I felt strange walking home."

He was watching her from a car. Adam raked his hand through his hair, frustrated. He believed that she had been watched, at least part of the day. Finally, he stood and pulled her up with him.

"No sense in starving you to death while we figure this out." They opened the cartons of food and the aroma hit them both, causing hunger pangs to attack their taste buds. They filled plates and sat down at the kitchen table to eat.

The leftovers were in the fridge, the kitchen straightened, and Adam and Sydney were on the sofa, once again trying to solve the puzzle of her mysterious day. It was almost eight-thirty.

Sydney squeezed his hand. "Stop worrying, please," she said for the umpteenth time. She ran a finger across his creased forehead, smoothing out the wrinkles. "These are going to become permanent."

He caught her fingers and kissed them. "Not a problem. As long as you never run from this craggy mug."

"You don't scare me." Her tone was playfully boastful. "Besides," she murmured, "I would never run *from* you, love." She remembered their song.

The unfamiliar endearment always left him with good feelings. He squeezed her hand.

Seeking to take his mind off his stalker, Sydney asked, "So you're certified to work? Good as new?" She patted his side very gently.

"I've felt better than that from you in the past few days," he said, an amused look in his eyes. "Want to try that again?"

Sydney was toying with the buttons on his shirt. "With feeling?" She slipped her hand inside and massaged his chest.

"Always. Never less than your best." He bent to kiss her lips. "Always your best," he muttered, savoring the taste of her lips.

The ringing of the phone interrupted Sydney's answering response to his sweet devouring of her mouth.

"Hello?" she said, trying to use a normal tone. From the kitchen, she smiled at Adam's disgusted look.

"Ms. Cox, this is Lucas Parnell. Adam's not answering his page. Have you seen him?"

Sydney frowned as she beckoned. "He's here, Mr. Parnell. Hold on, please."

He was by her side in an instant. "I'm here," he said, taking the phone. "What's up?"

"He's got to the girl, Adam."

Immediately Adam's thoughts raced to Gus. "Kyla King?" He stoically waited for the answer.

"No," Lucas answered, momentarily forgetting about the nine-year-old. "The delivery girl. The one who brought your groceries. Stabbed."

"What?"

"She's alive. Had unloaded her bike cart and was standing at the outside door waiting to be buzzed in. She was pushed inside and stabbed twice in the back."

"Jesus! Will she make it?"

"Yes, she's stable. She's in Mount Sinai. They'll let us see her but I want you there to identify her. As long as we get there before ten o'clock, we'll get in. You won't be detained too long." He paused. "Since the NYPD is on this, they want a statement from you about the greens. The two attacks are too closely related to be coincidental."

"Are we thinking on the same airwaves?"

"Yeah," Lucas answered. "She can explain how the greens got in the bag and possibly make the person who gave them to her."

"I'll meet you there in half an hour," Adam said, hanging up the receiver.

Sydney listened with her heart in her mouth. Who had gotten hurt?

Adam didn't want to leave her, not now. But he wanted to be of as much help as he could to the police. Maybe, at the expense of that girl getting hurt, the maniac was that much closer to getting caught. *He's going after anybody now. God help anyone else he's used in any way.*

"Sydney, the girl who delivered my groceries was stabbed. But she'll live."

"Oh, my God," Sydney exclaimed and sank back down on the couch.

Adam went to her, and in a calm voice told her everything.

"But I'm coming back tonight," he said when he finished. His jaw jutted out and the slim scar throbbed. "So don't be frightened when you hear the bell. I don't want to leave you alone tonight."

Sydney wrapped her arms around his waist and nodded. She hated for him to leave, but was grateful he was returning. Silently, she prayed for that poor girl—and for Adam.

At the door, he kissed her, whispering, "I'll be back."

Sydney shivered and she hugged her arms as she turned out the lights. She may as well watch TV in bed while she waited for him to return. He could be gone for hours. She walked past the kitchen and wrinkled her nose at a sour smell. "What in the world is that?" she asked out loud. Turning back to investigate, her nose led her to the garbage can. She lifted the lid and winced at the pungent, overripe garbage. She knew she shouldn't have been so lazy about removing her garbage immediately. Bits of chitlins and other stuff lit up the room. "Ugh," she grunted.

The garbage wrapped, Sydney took it to the compactor room and threw it down the chute. "The rodents and those other little creatures are best left outside of *this* apartment," she muttered to herself.

The instant she opened her door, she knew something was wrong. She had turned the lights back on and now they were out. The message got to her brain too late for her to turn and run. She didn't even have time to scream before a hand clamped her mouth shut.

Adam stopped at the desk to sign out. He was pleased that the management had begun to enforce the rule of signing in and out visitors. His initial reaction was to breathe a little easier at the minor deterrent to any deviant behavior. He waited his turn while three visitors who obviously were together, signed the book. Waiting wasn't a problem. Whatever it took to keep his lady safe.

Using his own pen, he signed, and from habit and years of observing, his eyes roamed casually over the page. Under his sign-in signature of a few hours ago and a few names down, a familiar-looking signature leaped out at him. The name wasn't familiar and after a second, he shrugged and turned to go. *Looks like a first-grader's introduction to script,* he mused.

Adam stopped midway out the door. *Or someone writing very badly with his left hand!* He rushed back to the desk and grabbed the book out of the doorman's hands.

"Did this person walk out of here without signing?" he rasped. His eyes bored a hole in the startled man who stammered that he didn't remember.

Adam ran to the elevator, panic drying his mouth. *He's in the building.* He burst out of the elevator and crossed the few feet to Sydney's door in split seconds, calling her name. He knew it was double-locked, so he braced himself to kick it in when to his surprise it flew open. It wasn't locked!

Disbelieving, he blinked in the shadowed room. The only light in the apartment was down the hall, shining dimly from her bedroom. The caution displayed earlier was nonexistent as he pulled his gun and unheeding, ran down the hall.

"Sydney?" he yelled. He could hear her muffled sounds. He ran to the door and the sight that met his eyes filled him with a rage that immobilized him. *He's raping her?!*

Her hands were tied above her head to her four-poster bed and a gag covered her mouth. She was writhing frantically. Her skirt was bunched up to her waist. Sydney stared wild-eyed at Adam, shaking her head furiously from side to side. The masked animal sitting on her thighs, his knees on either side, had both hands on her breasts. When he started rotating his hips, Adam was propelled forward like a rocket, lunging for the imbecile who would dare to hurt her. A gut-wrenching scream tore from his throat as he raised his gun. But Adam's seconds of shocked immobility were his undoing because the man anticipated Adam's move, and at the precision-timed moment, rolled off Sydney with the lightning speed of a martial artist. Adam's momentum landed him on top of Sydney with a sickening thud.

In a flash, the intruder was on his feet and before his prey knew what hit him, crash-landed a blow to the back of Adam's head.

Adam groaned and slumped against Sydney's quivering body.

Sydney's screams were muffled against the cloth in her mouth when she felt Adam's limp form sag in a lifeless heap. Mercifully, she fainted.

"Gotcha," the man said, amused at his night's work.

Adam awoke with fuzz in his eyes, in the dimly lit room. He tried to move and couldn't. He was trussed up in a kitchen chair that had been placed at the foot of the bed. His hands were tied behind his back and each foot was tied to a leg of the chair. His mouth was bound shut with duct tape. Sydney was on the bed, still gagged, but clad only in her underwear. *My God. Has he hurt her?* She was so still. Adam shifted to see her better and was suddenly aware of a dampness on his shirt and knew his wound had opened.

Just then the intruder appeared in his line of vision. He was dressed from head to toe in a black neoprene suit. Black gloves covered his hands. Only the dark irises of his eyes showed through the slits in the mask.

"You're awake at last," the man said to Adam. The whisper was muffled through the thick fabric. He walked to the bed. "Now the fun starts. Did you ever make it in one of these?" He lifted one leg up on the bed and leaned on his knee. He smoothed his sleek suit down by the groin. "Great foreplay.

She'll be begging for it so bad, she'll rip this thing to shreds trying to get to me.'' He laughed. ''Now you can watch.'' His gloved hand touched Sydney's face and skimmed over her breast.

Adam's eyes blazed with red-hot fire.

''Wake up, sister. It's time.'' When Sydney opened her eyes, he slid his hand down her stomach and turned to Adam. ''Keep your eyes open now.''

Get your hands off her! Adam struggled violently against his bonds, inwardly screaming against the pain. ''No,'' he tried to scream, but the word got swallowed up in the dirty tape that gagged his mouth. ''I'll kill you. I'll kill you,'' he mumbled. But only he knew what he was screaming.

With a herculean effort, Adam pulled himself and the chair up from the floor and lunged toward the bed. The chair toppled forward, plunging Adam's head into the iron post, then fell sideways onto the floor. The blow to his head knocked Adam unconscious.

Sydney, daring not to breathe, lay looking at the man as he looked down at Adam. For a long time after Adam fell to the floor, he stood looking at him. Out of nowhere, Sydney saw the knife materialize in his hand. He kicked Adam and the dull thud sent shock waves through her body but Adam remained motionless and never made a sound. The man played with the knife, tossing it from hand to hand like it was a juggling baton. He looked at Adam and then at Sydney. She wished she could see his face, but the only thing that proved he was flesh and blood instead of a mechanical robot was the way his eyes darted back and forth through the slits in that head mask. Maybe he was a cyborg, she thought giddily. Does a cyborg's eyes move like that? She stopped her mindless wandering and looked at him as he turned toward her with the knife. He looked down at her. She could see that he'd made a decision and in the next second, he bent down and slashed the twine that bound one of Sydney's hands to the bed. The weird whisper shattered the silence in the room.

"Tell him I'll be back."

Sydney lay staring up at the ceiling long after she heard the front door close.

He hadn't slammed it shut but she heard the firm click of metal against metal. He had been in no rush to leave. She listened for sounds of him coming back. Suppose he changed his mind? Suddenly, she panicked, and then fought against it. She had to stay calm if hers and Adam's life depended on her acting sanely. With her free hand, she pulled the cloth over her teeth but the harder she pulled, the more it tightened up. The corners of her mouth were cracked and bleeding.

"Adam," she tried to call, but his name was just a low, unintelligible mumble that seared her throat. *Calm down. Think,* she willed herself.

Suddenly, scrunching herself up until she was sitting up straight, she swung her free arm across her body and grabbed hold of the twine that bound her other hand. She pulled on it using it as leverage as she swung her feet and legs over the side of the bed. She reached down and opened her nightstand drawer and searched until she found a pair of manicure scissors.

These had better do the job. She cut, and after several minutes her hand was free. She cut the rag off her mouth and uttered a cry of pain as it scraped against her torn skin. Sydney's legs were stiff and her arms numb, but she hurried as quickly as she could to the kitchen. Adam had to be cut loose.

How long had he been trussed up like that?

She was on her knees, sawing at the rope, tears filling her eyes. "Adam," she called, "wake up." She had his feet loose and she heard him moan. "Oh, Adam. Thank God." Suddenly, sheer terror struck her to the core of her stomach. *She never locked the door!* She scrambled to her feet when suddenly the door was kicked in and it slammed against the wall with a bang.

Sydney cried out in fear, "No-o!"

"Adam?" Lucas called. "Adam? Sydney?"

Sydney fell to the floor, too weak to say anything. The apartment was flooded with light and she stared at Adam's boss. Thank God, she thought, that Lucas came looking when

Adam never showed up at the hospital. Lucas Parnell and Jeremy Gage were the two most gorgeous human beings in the world! Even with guns drawn and looks that would slay dragons.

Lucas was at her side immediately while Jeremy ran to Adam and with one smooth move righted the chair.

"Ms. Cox. Sydney," Lucas said, "are you okay? Are you hurt?" He was picking her up off the floor and had his arm around her as he gently eased her on the bed. He swore when he looked at her face. Her wrists were rope-burned and his sharp eye spied the pieces hanging from the bedposts. He looked around, swung the bedroom door and found what he wanted. He took the silk robe and helped her slide her arms through the sleeves, grimacing in anger as she winced.

"Sydney?" Adam's voice was a hoarse croak.

"I'm here, Adam," she whispered. Her throat was parched. Suddenly the tears fell, coursing down her cheeks like rivulets of silver rain. She went to him and touched his bruised cheek. One side of his face was swollen where he'd fallen on the hardwood floor. She saw the bloodstain that had spread over his shirt. A cry broke through her lips and she turned and fled from the room, slamming the bathroom door. All three men looked after her, helpless to soothe her pain.

Adam was being helped from the chair, Jeremy and Lucas on either side holding him up on rubbery legs.

He leaned heavily on them as they walked him around the room until he could finally stand on his own. Slowly he eased himself out of the room, glancing at the disheveled bed with distaste. He made it to the living room where he sat on the sofa. Lucas and Jeremy followed.

"He raped her." The words came from a hollow place in his chest as he stared bleakly at his colleagues. "I was here and I was helpless."

Lucas' nose flared and his lips tightened. An angry snort burst through his mouth when he said, "She'll need to see a doctor right away."

"You're right, but there won't be any evidence." Jeremy said.

They all looked in the direction of the bathroom, listening to the muted splash of water against hard tiles.

"Damn," Lucas swore. "I didn't guess. Who was it Adam?" he asked in disgust.

"Reynard, of course," Jeremy answered.

Adam looked at them both with dead eyes. "It wasn't Ethan Reynard." His voice was just as cold.

Two pairs of eyes stared at him in disbelief.

"The man was black."

CHAPTER SIXTEEN

Dead silence filled the room, the only sounds in the apartment coming from the bathroom.

Dully, Adam looked toward the door. What could he say to her? he wondered.

"We can talk about this after you're both examined. We'll drive instead of calling for an ambulance," Lucas said in his take-charge manner. A black man? He didn't know how to digest that information. Adam was grimacing in pain. He had to get him to a doctor. Just as he was about to knock on the bathroom door, it opened. But she went into the bedroom and closed the door. Lucas looked helpless. He had to talk to her. But the door opened and Sydney walked into the room. He saw that she had discarded the silk robe for a T-shirt and jeans.

Sydney stood looking at the three sober faces. *Why are they standing there? Can't they see that Adam needs medical help?* She looked at him and her heart jumped into her throat. He had his feet planted squarely on the floor, elbows on his knees and he was rubbing his forehead with his fingers; back and forth, in anguish. She started to go to him when Lucas' voice stopped her.

"Sydney," he said, suddenly feeling awkward. "You know

that, uh, in rape cases, uh, you shouldn't shower the evidence away . . .''

"What?" Sydney was taken aback.

Adam stared at her with a hurt so raw she nearly cried. Lucas and Jeremy had looks of discomfort on their faces and then she understood.

Crossing the room to Adam, she flung her arms around his neck as she sat beside him. "Adam, dear Adam," she whispered, "I should have told you right away instead of running away like that." She kissed his swollen cheek. "He didn't do it!"

The words entered Adam's ears as if they were being telegraphed from a distant planet. He stared at her with a blank look.

"He didn't rape me," she cried.

Audible sounds of surprise came from the two men across the room.

"I wanted to wash the feel of him off me. I couldn't feel him through that rubber, but I still felt so dirty," she whispered. "I'm sorry." She hugged him again.

Adam felt as if he would explode from the relief that washed over his whole body causing a giant shudder. He couldn't speak, but wrapped her in his arms, and as if she were a baby, rocked her to and fro.

Lucas had recovered, but waited a moment to let Adam's head clear. The man had been ready to commit murder. He cleared his throat when the two broke apart. "Adam, you have to see a doctor. No telling what's messed up inside there."

"No," Adam barked. "I'm not leaving her here." His eyes blazed at his boss.

"You both have to be examined, man. Can't you see her wrists?" Lucas tried to remain calm.

Adam couldn't help noticing the angry red marks on Sydney's arms. He noticed her bruised mouth and swollen lips. He had spotted the black and blue bruises on her thighs before Lucas had covered her up. His soul was on fire and he asked forgiveness from his maker for his evil thoughts.

"All right," Adam said wearily. He held Sydney's hands in

his, needing to feel her close to him. "But first, I want to know what happened. How he got in here. I wasn't gone that long." His voice trailed away as he stared bleakly at Sydney. "The door wasn't locked," he said in a hoarse voice. He remembered the shock that had overtaken him. "What happened?"

"I know," Sydney answered, angry with herself for such a stupid move. "I took out the garbage." All three men looked at her. She explained, leaving out nothing and ending at the point she'd heard Lucas and Jeremy burst through the apartment door.

"Damn," Jeremy swore. He looked at Adam, curiosity darkening his eyes. "What made you come back upstairs?"

Adam looked at him. "He signed the book." He explained and when he finished, he look perplexed. "None of this makes any damn sense. He had me. *Had* me right there after all these years. Why didn't he end it instead of playing this damned game?"

"I know why," Sydney said breathlessly. Her voice shook. "He left a message."

The room became still as the men waited for her next words.

"Tell him I'll be back." She looked at the three men who were staring at her expectantly. "That's it. Those were his exact words."

"Back for you, Sydney, or back for Adam?" Jeremy sounded annoyed that she might not have remembered correctly.

Sydney jerked her head to look at him.

"I've repeated his exact words. Now you can read whatever you like into that."

Lucas could see the weariness in her body and hear the waspishness in her voice. They all had to get out of here. Especially Adam. He was stretched as taut as a drum skin. He stood up.

"Let's go. I'll make a call on the way so that we don't have to wait all night in the emergency room."

When they were outside the building, Lucas turned to Jeremy. "Where's your car? Okay," he nodded when Jeremy gestured down the block. "Good thing we got here together. Look, I'll take Adam and Sydney in my car. I want you to get in touch with Gus. Call the office for the number. Tell him to call me with an update on his situation ASAP. I want him. Get on that right away. I expect to hear from him before I leave the hospital.''

''You got it,'' Jeremy said. He looked at Adam and Sydney. ''I'm real sorry about all this, Sydney.'' He eyed Adam and shook his head. ''I couldn't know Adam,'' he apologized.

''Sure,'' Adam said, knowing how he must have felt. ''How could you?''

Hours later, Sydney was back home. She wouldn't hear of staying anyplace else for the night or any other night for that matter. If a person couldn't be safe in one's own home, what was the purpose to anything? Lucas had relented but sent an escort home with her with orders to remain on her floor overnight. He would clear the officer's presence with management, he promised.

Adam was kept overnight. His temperature was a little high and the doctor was taking precaution against a high fever setting in. Sydney had been reluctant to leave him and he her, but neither had any say in the matter. She'd been treated for her rope burns and cut mouth, but otherwise, if she didn't count her mental state, she was fine.

Early Tuesday morning, Sydney called her friend, the only close one she had left in New York. May as well get it over with instead of trying to hide what had happened to her. But how could she, anyway? A sardonic laugh escaped as she waited.

''Hello?'' Mason said sleepily. He squinted with one eye at the clock. It was only a little past seven.

''Sorry, Mason,'' Sydney said. ''I know it's early but can you wake up and talk to me now?''

Mason was instantly alert and his feet hit the floor. Her voice was barely recognizable. ''What happened?'' he roared. ''You want me to come?''

HEART OF STONE   209

"I'm not fine, but I'll live," Sydney said. "No, stay where you are. I just need a friend."

"Where the hell is Stone?" Mason barked.

"In the hospital."

"What?" Disbelief tinged his voice.

"Let me talk, and you'll know everything. Don't interrupt, okay?" She heard him gulp air and knew that he was listening. The swelling had gone down on her lips but the cracked corners of her mouth were still painful, especially if she opened her mouth wide. The result was a sort of low mumble, and she hoped that she was being understood. She explained, beginning with the time she left her house on Monday morning until she went to bed last night.

"Jesus Christ Almighty!" Mason breathed.

"I told you about taking the Lord's name in vain," she scolded.

"He'll forgive me this time, I think." Mason had a hard time digesting her story. It didn't go down too smoothly, the thought of her lying helpless under that maniac, his hands doing what they would. And Stone? Mason had to swallow on that one. He wondered what he would have done in the same situation. Would he have been able to do anything differently? Gotten loose?

"I think I know where your thoughts are. He was helpless to do anything, Mason." Sydney's voice sounded weary. "He's probably doing a whole lot of soul-searching, and doubting himself." She tried to smile and winced at the effort. "You know how you men are."

"Yeah, yeah," Mason said. "I heard about the caveman mentality. But I was thinking more in the lines of Rashomon. That guy was mentally tortured."

Sydney remembered vaguely the story of the Asian nobleman who had watched his wife being raped in a forest by a powerful warlord. How hideous. Mason's voice broke through her thoughts.

"How bad is he?"

"The doctor said that he'd be released today. I expect to hear from him this afternoon."

Mason hesitated, but decided to speak frankly. "You've fallen in love with him, haven't you?"

"Yes, I have."

"Does he know?"

"Yes, he does."

"Then what does he propose to do about it? Are his feelings the same?"

"I don't know, to the first question, and I think so, to the second question," Sydney replied.

"Then why doesn't he say so? I saw the way he looked at you the other night. He was like a cat licking his mouth after he'd feasted on a dish of cream."

Sydney flushed at the accurate description. Had Adam been so transparent? She guessed that men just knew these things about one another.

"Well?" Mason was getting impatient. If Stone walked away from her after putting her through this, he would live to regret his foolish action.

"How can I say?" Sydney answered wearily.

Mason heard the uncertainty in her voice and could have kicked himself for planting seeds of doubt in her brain. "Forget I said any of that." To change the subject, he asked, "Are you taking any time off? Benjamin and Dominic can handle the dining room if necessary. I don't know about your data entry stuff."

"Yes, I'll call Benjamin later. I'm taking the week off. If I walked in there looking like this, I'd probably be offered a movie contract on the spot for the next Halloween flick." She paused. "As far as my orders and stuff, I'm pretty much up to date. I did a lot over the past few days in order to spend time with Adam." Her eyes softened with the memories.

"I don't want to scare you, but are you sure you're doing the right thing staying there alone?"

"Where am I going to go, Mason?"

"The Percivals'?"

"Oh sure, I'm going to do a two-hour commute every day when I could do twenty minutes on the subway?"

He hesitated. "There's always the North Bronx," Mason said softly.

Sydney swallowed a lump. Now she knew how much he valued their friendship. "Thanks," was all she could say.

"Do you need anything?" Mason asked.

"No, nothing I can think of."

"Okay. You take care of yourself. I'll call you later. I may drop by between lunch and dinner one day, so don't be frightened when you hear the bell."

After he hung up, Sydney felt better at having ventilated to someone other than her lover. She knew that with Adam, they would be speaking the words of love.

Tuesday afternoon, Adam was released. The larger of his two stab wounds had split open when he'd been kicked. Seemed like the kicker knew exactly where to aim, the doctor joked; a home run if he ever saw one. With a few stitches holding him together, Adam refused to spend another night in the hospital. And he refused an escort. He could do better on his own he argued. He'd had one to watch his back, and look what happened, he told Lucas.

Adam watched the hands on the clock move from one o'clock to four o'clock. He passed a hand wearily across his forehead and closed his eyes against the last time he'd seen Sydney. Her eyes were haunting him. Her eyes had held the same stark look as that of Curtis Johnson's widow; the very fear that he swore he'd never want to see in them. Her anguish and fear was all for him. Once she'd showered the smell and the feel of that twisted psychotic from her body, she had thought only to ease his fears and anger. And he hadn't the courage to call her. He aroused himself. Sitting here banging his head against a stone wall was not going to make what he had to do any easier. The phone rang as he reached for it.

"Can't leave you alone for a hot minute, can I?"

"Hey, Gus," Adam answered, surprised at the call. "You finished your case?"

"Just about. Mrs. King made her decision to move Kyla to

California with her parents. She's flying out tomorrow. By the time she gets there, Lincoln will have a man in place." He paused. "You okay?" That's all he said but the words spoke volumes.

Adam heard. "Just fine," he answered.

After a while, Gus asked, "How's Sydney? Gonna make it by there tonight? She's got to be doing some heavy thinking about all this. And even if you are all busted up, you've got one good side for her to lean on."

Adam didn't speak for a moment, but then said, "No."

"No, what?" Gus asked, not wanting to believe what he thought Adam meant.

"It's better that I don't see her."

Gus was stupefied. "See her as not in tonight? Or, see her as in not any night?" His mouth was drawn in a grim line as he steeled himself against his friend's answer.

"Back off, Gus. I told you this wouldn't work. Not with any woman." His voice fell. "Not with Sydney."

"What are you talking about?" Gus asked between tight jaws.

"You know what I mean," barked Adam. "I don't need a woman in my life. Ever. So leave it alone!"

Gus lowered his voice because one of them had to act sane. "You mean you're going to throw her away?"

Adam snorted. "If you mean by 'throw away,' am I going to stop seeing her, then you just grabbed the gold ring."

"That's exactly what I mean." Gus was silent for a minute. "Do you mean that?"

"Did it sound like a joke?"

"No, my friend, it did not." In an even tone, he said, "And since I know you to speak the truth, I believe you. And since you are also pigheaded at times, I know you won't be going back on your word, because you believe you're right. Right?"

"What the hell are you getting at?"

"Sydney's a beautiful woman, man. I've never met anyone like her." His voice softened. "You know she must be hurting and feeling vulnerable right now." His voice grew even softer.

Adam stiffened. His eyes narrowed at what he was thinking.

Gus moving in on his lady? *Not yours, my man. You just gave her up. Didn't you?* Adam swore at the voice in his head. His voice was rock-hard when he asked, "I asked you what you're planning to do?"

Gus smiled to himself. Got him thinking now. He said smoothly, "Nothing at all, friend. If anyone should be doing something tonight, it's you." His grin broadened at the low curse in his ear. "By the way, Lucas wants to see me tonight. He told me you fired Jeremy." He gave a short laugh. "Probably wants me at your back so I can save your stubborn hide from getting stuck like a pig."

"For the last time. He'll never get that close again."

Gus became serious. "I hear that it wasn't Reynard. How could you be so sure and what would be the point?"

"It wasn't him. I've tussled with the man before and I know what he feels like. It was someone else."

"That was a long time ago, Adam. People change."

"They don't shrink by half a foot."

"You're certain?" Gus' whole demeanor changed. Somebody had changed the rules of the deadly game.

"I'm certain."

"Then on that note, my friend, regardless of what your feelings may be, I think you should pay someone a visit tonight." His voice was deadly calm. "You owe her. If you're not going to be around anymore, she needs to protect herself. She thinks your enemy is white. Is she going to connect a suspicious-acting brother to you?"

Adam thought, *He's right.* Sydney was out of the room when he made his revelation to Lucas. They hadn't discussed it in her presence.

"Adam?" Gus spoke with a sharp tongue.

"All right. I see your point."

"Catch you at the meeting tomorrow." Gus hung up, a deadly look in his eyes. This thing had gone far enough, he thought.

Adam sat for a long time thinking after Gus hung up. The inner battles he fought with himself resulted in him losing the war. Resolved, he made one phone call to Lucas. Satisfied that his request was granted, he hung up. He should have felt relieved but remorse filled his heart.

It was after six o'clock when Adam finally rang Sydney. He still had no words for what he had to say, but he couldn't keep her in the dark any longer. She had to be frantic at not hearing from him by this time.

Sydney was in the kitchen when the telephone ring made her jump to her feet. She answered it on the second ring, breathless when she spoke. "Adam?" When he answered, she let out a soft cry. "Where are you?" she whispered.

Adam closed his eyes against the pain he heard. He'd worried her to death. *You're an idiot.* "Sydney," he said. *What am I doing?* He hesitated. "Can I come over?"

Puzzled at such a question, she answered, "Yes."

Another pause. "Have you eaten?"

She tried to joke. "I'm just finishing. My mouth is still so sore, I can only handle cold, soft stuff. I just enjoyed a bowl of peaches and a glass of iced tea."

Adam winced, remembering her face. "I won't be long, Sydney," he murmured.

At seven o'clock, Sydney opened the door for Adam. For a second, they stood staring at each other.

Finally stepping inside, he muttered, "I'm to blame for what's happened to you . . ." Her finger on his lips stopped him.

"We went over that last night, remember?" She caressed his cheek and led him to the sofa, where they sat side by side. "How are you feeling? I worried when I couldn't reach you at the hospital, then I thought you may have gone with Lucas somewhere. Are you okay now?"

He was staring at the bedcovers neatly piled up in the chair across from them. They smelled of fresh air and sunshine. His jaw tightened.

Noticing his stare, Sydney got up abruptly and removed the freshly laundered linen to the spare bedroom where she dumped them on the bed. It was a sin to throw them out, but she never wanted to cover her bed with them again. She returned to Adam.

"I'm, uh, getting a package ready for a charity pickup," she said, gesturing at nothing. Suddenly, the memory of the attack made her shudder.

Adam held her gently against his chest, smoothing her bare arm. Her wrists were not bandaged and the darkened ring around them still looked raw and ugly. He kissed the tender part of her sore mouth. He closed his eyes and knew that he was right. Having her in his life would only get her killed.

"Sydney," he said in a low voice. "Sit up and look at me. There's something you have to know."

She sat up, the ominous tone in his voice frightening her. *He's heard from that madman again!*

"It wasn't Ethan Reynard that attacked you last night."

"What? Who then?" She was stunned. "But, the things he said and did to taunt you . . ."

"It was someone else who wanted to make me think that he was Reynard." His eyes narrowed. "He was a black man."

"But . . . but how could you tell? He was all covered in that material . . . that neoprene. You couldn't even see the skin around his eyes with that *Phantom of the Opera* mask he had on. He looked so . . . so alien." Her face was full of doubt.

"Before he woke you, he stretched one foot up on the bed. I saw his skin. The rubberized slip-ons came just to the ankle and so did the pants' legs. The material inched up. I was there at the foot of the bed and I saw it clear as daylight."

There are two killers after him? Sydney thought. "What . . . what does it all mean?" she stammered.

"I don't know." He couldn't lie to her, pretending he was omniscient, when he didn't have the first clue to what was going on. "Long ago while Reynard and Mulhare were incarcerated awaiting the court-martial, they had a couple of goons harass me and Owen. But that was then. What would be the point in involving someone else now?"

Both were silent, reflecting on his words.

Adam stirred, moving away from her, then stood up, raking his hand over his hair. He looked at her and then finally sat down in the chair opposite the sofa.

"Adam?" The minute he moved, Sydney sensed something

was wrong. His whole posture had changed when he sat back down, staring at her with that troubled look covering his face.

"Sydney, remember the funeral I attended? The widow I described to you?" She nodded and his heart turned over at the look that appeared on her face. "I told myself that I would never be the cause of inflicting such pain on a woman. It's not fair to have the lady in your life live with the fear of becoming an instant widow."

Lady in your life? Widow? Why he's never even said "I love you"! "What are you saying?" she whispered. She evaded the question she really wanted to ask.

"You could have been killed last night," Adam said with a rasp in his voice. "I would have been the cause. If not for me, that maniac would have never had a reason to go after you. He did it only to get at me." He shook his head. "And I don't even know why. I don't even know who he is!" He shrugged helplessly. "So how can I even protect you?"

It was Sydney's turn to stand and pace, turning to give him an incredulous look. "You would leave me now? End our relationship, now?" He looked pained at her words, but she didn't care. She had felt fear at his impending words, but now she was angered. How could he leave her after she'd confessed her love and given herself to him? He was cold and heartless! She sat back down and crossed her leg over one knee, swinging her foot. Her eyes blazed with the fury she tried to keep from taking hold of her body, making it tremble.

"Sydney, it's for your safety. It's your life that I want to save." He spoke quietly, trying to select the right words that would do nothing more to heighten her anger.

"It's my life, Adam. I thought it was mine to do with as I please."

His eyes flickered at the sarcasm. "You won't be alone," he said, his voice tightening. "Lucas has arranged for someone to watch you. You won't be annoyed by his presence, because you'll hardly know he's there. The only time he won't be around will be at the restaurant, and after you walk in this building at night."

"Suppose I refuse?"

He shrugged. "It's a done deal. The man will be in place in the morning."

"Isn't that a waste of man power? I'm off this week."

"That's not something you have to worry about," he said flatly.

Sydney stood up and so did Adam. She walked to the door and Adam followed.

"Well then, I guess there's nothing more to say, is there? With Garrison International at my back, why should I complain?" Sydney looked up into his expressionless eyes.

"Don't Sydney," Adam rasped. "I can't ask you to put yourself in the way of danger because of me." His eyes suddenly blazed with the depth of his feelings for her. "Can't you understand that?"

Sydney's lashes flickered with surprise. "You do care!" she blurted. Her voice was filled with surprise.

Astounded, Adam's nostrils flared with anger. "What kind of remark is that? Of course I care. Why do you think I'm doing this? Answer me."

Her whole body softened. "You certainly have an odd way of showing it," she answered in a soft voice. "You're leaving me in someone else's care, when you're the best."

"Obviously not anymore. Apparently, something's happened to my concentration." He stared at her pointedly.

She was enveloped by a wave of confusion. Something was not computing. "Even though we have these . . . feelings, you would still leave me?"

"I have to Sydney," he answered husky-voiced.

She gave him an intense look. "Will you answer a question for me?"

"If I can." His eyes probed hers.

"Even after this is over, when your two killers are caught and put away . . . would you still stay away from me?"

Adam's face was hard and unyielding and his voice just as cold. "With my work, there could be others, Sydney. I will never put your life in danger again."

Her eyes never blinked. Her voice was equally cold when she said, "Good-bye, Adam."

Adam stared at her, but she turned away. He opened the door and closed it softly behind him. He didn't walk away until he heard the click of the second lock.

When Sydney heard the elevator door close, she turned out the light and walked into the bedroom.

Hours later, Sydney rose from the bed and walked to the window. She couldn't sleep. She pulled on a silk kimono and went to stand by the window. It was one o'clock in the morning. Occasional cars and pedestrians broke the silence of the night as she stood and looked up at the ink-black sky. She remembered that she stood here not so long ago and breathed a silent prayer. Now she wondered if anyone had ever heard. Certainly, not the spirit of her old friend.

He stole my heart and my love, La Signora. But he tossed them back to me. Am I destined to live forever with this heart that once more will turn to stone?

CHAPTER SEVENTEEN

When Adam walked into the Empire State Building, the New York headquarters, he raised a brow when he entered Lucas' office. The sober men surrounding the conference table included Lincoln Yates. He took a seat.

"Morning," Adam said nodding at Gus and Lucas. "Good to see you, Lincoln." He was curious at the unexpected appearance of the agency head.

Lincoln looked at Adam. "You, too. How you doing?" His glance adroitly skimmed his officer's body, coming to rest on the bruise above his cheekbone.

"Healing fast," Adam answered, still wondering at the surprise visit. His body took on an alert pose.

Lincoln noticed the ingrained military training. Always the marine, he thought.

"Okay, I won't be mysterious. I'll let you know why I'm here after I'm brought up to date on all that's happened since I left. Seems like fireworks in mid-August." He eyed Lucas. "Suppose you begin, starting with the latest on the grocery girl."

"Her name's Molly. She's fine. Was released from the hospital today. No more leads on her attacker, other than what she told us that first night.''

Lincoln's eyes grew wary. ''And what she told you didn't register until after Adam was attacked.''

''No, given the fact that we were on the watch for Reynard, a black man giving her the greens to deliver never caused a blink of the eye. Now . . .''

''Did he say anything?''

''Only told her that he promised the store manager he would catch up to her and give her the overlooked bag since he was going that way,'' answered Lucas. ''But of course that was a lie. The store manager did no such thing.''

''Any description?'' Lincoln asked.

''Dark brown skin, dark eyes, clean-shaven, natural-style hair, cut close.'' Lucas shrugged. ''General description. Could fit anybody.''

Gus nodded. ''That's what he was hoping.''

''Apparently, he was right,'' Lincoln agreed. ''He can assimilate into the general population.'' He looked at Adam. ''Any ideas about who he could be? Someone you may have had a run-in with in the past? Even in the years since you've been with the agency?''

Adam had spent hours during the last few days asking himself the same questions. He always came up blank and now acknowledged the same to his boss. ''I'm stumped on this, Lincoln.''

''Okay, keep at it, maybe something will pop up.'' He looked at all three men. ''Any word as to where those greens came from? Are they indigenous to places around here?''

Lucas said, ''I checked on that. It's common enough. One of my officers who lives in New Jersey says the stuff grows wild in the wooded area behind her neighbor's house.''

Gus and Adam exchanged looks.

''New Jersey?'' Gus asked.

''Yeah. Why? Know anybody in Jersey?''

''No,'' Gus answered. He looked thoughtfully down at his notepad.

Adam looked at Gus then studied the table.

''You two have anything to add?'' Lincoln asked, aware of

the looks being passed around the table. When they both said no in unison, he added, ''Remember company policy on private investigations.''

Gus and Adam nodded but remained silent. Lucas looked curiously at both men, but asked no questions.

Lincoln reared back in his chair and focused his gaze on Adam. ''Ethan Reynard is dead. Confirmed.''

''What?'' Lucas' jaw dropped.

Gus threw a look of disbelief at his boss.

Adam felt like he was having a slow motion out-of-body experience when he turned his head to look at Lincoln. His ears developed a buzz and somehow he thought that if he were floating above the table looking down at himself, then how could the buzz saw sound so loud in his head? From afar he heard his name and he fell with a bang back into his body.

''Adam? Are you okay?'' Lincoln raised his voice as a look of concern crossed his face. The man had never guessed, he thought.

''What is going on?'' Adam stared at everyone in disbelief.

Gus reached for the stainless-steel pitcher in the middle of the table and poured Adam a glass of ice-cold water. ''Drink,'' he said in a firm voice.

The ice water sliding down his throat and pooling in his stomach felt like nirvana. He was alive and not floating around in someone else's dream. Adam turned his eyes to his friend and nodded his thanks. This wasn't the first time that man had brought him back from the edge of eternity! He turned his questioning eyes to Lincoln.

''Three years ago.'' He waited until the shock waves went around the table before he continued. His eyes stayed on Adam. ''The attempt on your life three years ago happened after Reynard was killed.''

Adam found his voice. ''How?''

''Plane crash. Over mountain country in Nevada. He was traveling under an assumed name belonging to one of his dead marine buddies. Apparently when he left prison, he chose to participate in various nefarious schemes. His favorite was con- ning hardworking Asian immigrants out of their dough.'' Lincoln gave a short laugh. "Ironic isn't it? Served time for his racist actions and when released, still played the racist in the selection of his pigeons."

"He never left those notes." Adam was still jarred.

"No. Couldn't have." A note of curiosity crept into Lincoln's voice. "He probably never gave you a second thought the minute he was set free."

Gus whistled. "That means that . . ."

Lucas finished for him, ". . . someone has a file on you, Adam, and studied it down to what toothpaste you use." He banged the table and reared back in his chair. His sandy brows were raised sky-high. "Well, I'll be!"

Gus looked at Lincoln. "Then this joker was playing the game in Italy and in Adam's apartment."

"That's right."

"Do you have a plan, Lincoln?" Lucas asked.

Lincoln nodded. "Yes, and it begins right here. Adam and Gus will spearhead the investigation." He looked at Lucas. "Sorry. I know you were assigning them both to key cases, but I think you'll agree that we have to end this cat-and-mouse game before it gets any deadlier. Enough innocent people have gotten hurt already."

Adam's eyes grew dark as his thoughts turned elsewhere.

"How is Ms. Cox doing?" Lincoln's voice took on an angry edge and his eyelids masked his rage. "If I get a chance at that bastard for what he did to her, I pray to God, that he sends someone to stop me."

All eyes were on him. Lincoln Yates was not given to emotional outbursts.

Adam masked the surprise in his eyes. So that's the way the wind blows, he thought.

Gus looked at Lincoln with hooded eyes. *Damn,* he thought. *Him, too?*

Lucas looked at the other three men, but kept an expressionless mask on his face. *Sydney Cox. If you only knew; three handsome men are at your feet, ready to do battle for you. If only the other two knew that they have as much chance of winning your heart as the cunning hare has of winning over the steadfast tortoise.* His thoughts turned to Adam. *Don't wait too long son, or you* will *lose the race.*

Adam turned his gaze on the silent Lucas and wondered what the older man was thinking.

By Saturday, Sydney was feeling whole again. Her face was healed and she could eat any and everything. All the bruises on her body had disappeared but her wrists had gone from angry-looking red, to a dirty-looking beige with healing tissue beginning to form. She teased herself that she would have a fine time in the antique shops hunting down a pair of gold wrist cuffs. But when she went out, she substituted her slim gold bracelets for wide beige wood bangles from Kenya.

She found that as each day passed and one more part of her body healed, a little part of her heart closed. This was good, she told herself, because that meant sealing out a little more of Adam Stone.

The past few days at home had provided her with the hours to spend reflecting on where she'd been and what she'd done with her life since college. In the end, she realized that now was no time to second-guess the choices that she'd made. She was solely responsible for who she'd become and she had no regrets. As far as her personal relationships were concerned, she was responsible for them also. She had made the decision not to have sex for sex's sake. Not only because of the health dangers involved but because her body was hers to protect and cherish. It was her right to choose the man who would be fondling and loving it until she chose to end the relationship.

Sydney also realized that although she didn't want Adam to walk out of her life, there was nothing she could do about it, and endless moping and crying was not the answer. She tried looking at her future from a pragmatic point of view.

She wanted children someday and could only envision Adam as their father. But since that was no longer an option, she had to think about the possibility of never becoming a mother. Could she live with that? She wondered if she would be strong enough to deal with that as her birthdays rolled by. Who knows?

Maybe in two or three years, her destiny would be such that
she would meet someone new and fall in love again. Was there
any hard-and-fast law of emotions that there was only one true
love to a customer?

As Sydney showered and dressed, preparing to meet Mason,
she knew that she was a much stronger person as a result of
her soul-searching. She and Mason intended to have a carefree,
mindless day in the country. On Thursday, she'd received a
call from Edward Percival. He had been annoyed that she hadn't
called and that he had to find out about her from Benjamin.
He insisted that she come out to stay at the farm for a few days
but she'd refused. Although Hannah had gone back to New
Mexico to spend more time with her granddaughter, he would
be around. Sydney had agreed to a one-day visit, but that was
all, she'd told him.

Mason had arranged to take the day off and drive her out to
North Fork.

At ten-thirty, Sydney appeared outside of her apartment
building and spotted Mason leaning against his parked car. She
smiled and waved and hurried to him, clutching a jacket and
a blanket.

Mason saw a very different woman than the one he'd seen
when he'd stopped by two days ago. There was pep in her step
and the shadowed eyes had turned into sparkling gems. When
she reached him, he took her by the shoulders and held her at
arm's length.

"My, my, look at you," he said with an all-over admiring
glance. She wore a lime-colored short set with white top and
beige canvas shoes. "You look like a woman who's about to
take on the world." He kissed her cheek.

"And look out world," Sydney flung back. Her eyes twinkled
as she got in the car and buckled up. They were both laughing
as Mason pulled away from the curb.

Adam was sitting in a car parked several lengths from where
Mason stood. He'd arrived on the block early, in between the
shift changes of the surveillance team. The replacement officer
would be late and Adam agreed to fill in. He welcomed the
relief from staring at files and computer screens all day. He

and Gus had spent the last few days poring over five years of case records. All history from Adam's assignments since he'd started with the agency.

He hadn't seen or spoken to Sydney since he left her on Tuesday night. An apprehensive feeling came over him when he drove onto the block, but it soon passed. The chances of seeing her this early in the day were slim to none. When he looked up and had seen Mason towering next to his car, waiting, he was startled.

Adam was contacted by the replacement officer who had pulled onto the block and was parked across the street from Adam. Advising him to wait, Adam hung up the cell phone. Adam waited also, wondering what he would see. His heart pounded in his chest and he swore at himself for the strong reaction. *What did you expect, you fool? She's a young, beautiful and vibrant woman. You walked away. Did you think that no one else was going to step in?*

Adam steeled himself not to jump out of the car and pull Mason's hands off her. The kiss to the cheek blew his mind and he broke out in a cold sweat. "She's mine!" he swore out loud. Then he shook his head as if to clear it. No, he thought, not anymore. He watched as they pulled off and soon the operative across the street followed.

He could see the blanket slung over her arm and the happy smile she wore. They were going for a day of fun, he surmised, and couldn't help wondering if they were headed for Brooklyn and a secluded spot in the Japanese Gardens. He closed his eyes against the thought. Wearily, he rubbed his forehead thinking deep down that Mason would take care of her. He was certain that if anyone came threatening close to her, they would soon back off from the imposing figure of the chef.

Adam called the officer and advised him to return to the block. Maintain surveillance of the building he ordered, and hung up.

Traffic was normal for a Saturday morning and Mason drove at a leisurely pace. He was glad he'd taken Sydney's suggestion to spend the day in the sun doing absolutely nothing. It had been some time since he'd been out this way with her.

"You look quite contented, sitting over there, mister," Sydney said. "No regrets, huh?"

Mason grinned. "None at all. I was just trying to remember the last time we all came out here with Ferne. I know we had two carloads of folks."

"Yeah, that was just before Ferne and Edward moved away. Besides them, there was Reva and her date and some of Ferne's friends from the shop."

Mason flicked a quick glance her way but she didn't notice and kept on talking. Reva's name on her lips sounded odd but apparently only to him. He made no comment.

"Have Ferne and her father patched up their differences? A new baby should make some kind of dent in the old man's iron hide."

Sydney sighed. "No. The rift has gone on too long now. Ferne's been married almost two and a half years."

"Stubborn guy." He gestured with one hand off the wheel. "What in the world does he see wrong with Edward Marsh's occupation for Pete's sake?"

Sydney shrugged. "Just the old way of thinking he has, I guess. He's a strong-minded individual, independent, successful, and has a strong sense of family. When he sent Ferne to Sonoma to school and at the same time learn the business from their cousins out there, he was grooming her to follow in his footsteps. Things were going along fine until the day Edward Marsh walked into Amalia's. The vineyard and the wine business went out of her head. She would have followed Edward anywhere his teaching job took him."

Mason looked thoughtful. "But Percival is right though. An archeologist can end up just about anywhere. Suppose he was sent to Egypt? Or Greece? It would be a mighty long time before Percival saw his daughter or any little grandkids."

"That's why he should be grateful she's still in the States," Sydney remarked dryly. "But he's not," she added. "He still can't envision a son-in-law of his not out there trying to become a mogul. At least, enough of one to support his daughter in the style he would like to see her living.''

In just more than two hours, they reached Francesca Vineyards and were greeted heartily by Edward Percival.

"Edward," Mason said, as his hand was gripped.

"Let me look at you," he said to Sydney, surveying her with a critical eye. He frowned, "Besides being too thin, not a thing wrong. Is there?" he added.

"No, Edward, I'm fine. No aftereffects from my ordeal." *Only a broken heart,* she thought.

Edward hugged her and sighed with relief, then led them into the house. "You two hurry and freshen up. We have a big barbecue spread cooked up for you."

Sydney could smell Edward's special sauce wafting over the farm when she got out of the car. She realized how hungry she was and couldn't wait to dive in. She looked closely at the beaming Edward. She hadn't seen him this happy in more than two years.

Before she left the room she said, "Now what are you so happy about? It hasn't been that long since I've been out here."

Edward couldn't help but grin sheepishly. "I spoke to Ferne last night." At Sydney's surprised look, he added, "She'll be here for the summer's-end bash on Labor Day."

"What?" Sydney was flabbergasted and happy at the same time. "When is she coming? Is Edward coming with her?"

"Whoa," Edward said, beaming like a lightbulb. "They'll all be here the Friday before. Hannah's staying down there until then and will help with Amalia on the return trip." He sucked in his breath.

Sydney could see the emotion on his face and she nearly burst inside. *They're a family again.* She could only say, "I'm glad, Edward."

Edward cleared his throat and said brusquely, "Now I expect to see you both out here that weekend. Come prepared to stay over. And don't forget to bring the actress with you." He turned away, calling over his shoulder, "Hurry out here before this crew eats up all the ribs."

Neither Mason nor Sydney said a word to each other about Reva Fairchild.

Sydney woke up feeling lazy and lounged in the bed until almost nine o'clock. It was the last Monday in August and she would miss these lazy days. But, she was anxious to get back to work, feeling rejuvenated after her short recuperative period. She was also excited about a new product Edward's winemaker was producing. A soft, supple merlot, full of plum, it was sure to be a future winner. For those who wanted a change from the full-bodied cabernet sauvignon and still wanted a fine red, the merlot was the way to go.

She was sitting on the edge of the bed, contemplating whether to fix breakfast or scoot down to the corner coffee shop. "Boy, are you ever getting lazy," she said aloud. With one last stretch and yawn, she stood up, but sat back down when the phone rang. Her eyes narrowed and her mouth grew dry. The ID was blocked. Hesitant, she picked up.

"Hello?" She held her breath.

"Good morning, Sydney."

That voice. Would she ever forget it?

"Hello, Adam." If she'd forgotten about him, why did her limbs go weak? The bed felt good under her.

"How are you?"

"I'm well, and you?" Sydney's ears were ringing. *Why all this small talk?*

"Okay." He paused. "Sydney, the officer who has been watching you has been removed. I wanted you to know that." God, how he's missed her, he thought. Why was he doing this? Anyone could have made this call.

Sydney didn't answer. What was she supposed to say to that? Thank you?

"Sydney?"

"Is that the only reason you called me, Adam?"

"Yes."

"Your call is appreciated. Good-bye, Adam." She placed the

receiver in the cradle very softly and walked to the bathroom, slipping out of her gown on the way.

Gus threw down his pen and reared back in his chair. His dark eyes were amazed and disgust filled his voice when he said, "That's it?"

"I told you it was a bad idea." Adam looked darkly at his friend. "My voice was the last thing she wanted to hear."

"Well do you blame her for hanging up?" He repeated Adam's words verbatim. "You didn't *say* any thing!"

"What the hell was I supposed to say? I was the one who walked away."

"And it's been killing you ever since."

Adam didn't answer and turned back to his computer. For the last two weeks, he and Gus were office-bound. Both were accessing the files in the mainframe at the Washington headquarters. Some records had been express mailed to them. They had come up with nothing so far and they were now working on the third year. Adam was frustrated and Gus was angry. Both needed a break and some physical activity.

Gus got up and refilled his coffee mug. "If this is what it's like being stationary, I think it'll be a long time before I come in from the cold."

Adam nodded in agreement. He was used to moving, interacting with his client and his colleagues and breathing fresh air. Staring at screen and other data was driving him crazy. Especially since he couldn't see an iota of progress.

Gus sat back down. "Adam, I've been thinking."

"About what?" He was flipping through a case that he'd looked at more than once. Something about it was bothering him but he couldn't identify it.

"Sydney."

Adam's head snapped up. "What about her?"

"I've been thinking that the woman has been through a lot and she probably could use a friend."

"You?" Adam's eyes grew cold.

Gus shrugged. "Look, it's quite evident from that plastic

call you just made, that you don't want the woman. If not you, why not somebody like me?'' He stared at Adam with a hard look. ''You know I wouldn't make a move otherwise.'' He shrugged again. ''I can't see the harm in asking her out to breakfast, given her work hours. Might be a different kind of date.''

Breakfast! The word pierced Adam's ears and visions of breakfasts past danced in his head. Toy soldiers marched in front of his eyes and they all wore name tags. *Lincoln. Mason. Gus.* All making a beeline to the Restaurant Louise. He shook his head to clear away the horror show as he looked at Gus.

''Well,'' Gus was asking. ''What do you think?''

''You can do what you damn well please.''

''Is that right?'' Gus said smoothly. After a second, he stood up, and shrugged into his suit jacket. As if the idea just hit him, he said as he walked to the door. ''I guess you're right about that.''

''Where the hell do you think you're going?''

''To breakfast.'' Gus said and walked out the door.

Adam was dumbstruck.

After showering, Sydney made a pot of coffee. She sipped a cup while she took her time dressing and when she finished, rinsed the cup and prepared to go to breakfast. Her lazy spell had won, she chuckled to herself. She was dressed in casual white cotton slacks and a navy T-shirt, and decided she looked decent enough if she wanted to go downtown shopping.

The doorbell rang as she picked up her bag and her keys. Startled, she stood stock-still. Who could that be this time of morning? she thought. Her eyes flew to her watch. It was only ten-thirty! The bell rang again and this time her visitor spoke.

''Ms. Cox? Sydney? It's Gus Turner from Garrison International.''

Gus Turner? Her mind raced. Adam's friend. What could be wrong? Panic settled in her stomach and threatened to well up into her throat.

''Ms. Cox?''

Sydney went to the door and pushed aside the door viewer. It was him. No one else had eyes like that. She opened the door but didn't undo the second lock. "Yes, what is it?"

Her caution was highly approved and Gus silently commended his friend. This woman was not going to be taken by surprise ever again.

"Have you had breakfast?"

"What?" Was she hearing him correctly? Was the whole world going crazy? First Adam, now him.

"I don't want to come in. Would you come downstairs? I want to talk to you." He waited.

Sydney closed the door, hardly breathing. She had thought the worst and it had affected her in the way she would never have believed. She was over him.

She heard the elevator come and go. When she felt her pulse slow down, she opened the door and left the apartment.

Gus was waiting outside the building when she appeared not five minutes after he left her. He removed his dark glasses and put them in his jacket pocket. He wanted her to see his face and read his eyes.

"The place on the corner all right?"

Sydney nodded. "I was just on my way there."

"Good. Shall we go?"

Sydney's stomach felt like it was tied up in a thousand granny knots. *What more is going to happen today?* she wondered, on her serene, do-nothing Monday.

"You thought I came with bad news about Adam, Ms. Cox." Gus spoke bluntly.

They were seated and refused menus, ordering the standard ham, eggs, toast and coffee.

"Please, call me Sydney. After all that's happened, I feel that we're all kin. Just Sydney, please." She drank some of the hot coffee that was set before her and stared frankly at this handsome man. "And to answer your question, yes, I did." She raised a brow over her cup then asked, "Did you?"

"No."

Her coffee sloshed when she set the cup down. She dabbed it up. "You didn't?"

"I wanted to see you and hoped you would have breakfast with me." He lifted a shoulder. "We're here."

The muscles bulged beneath his jacket and Sydney could envision all the rippling that must have been going on under that shirt. "Excuse me?" She swallowed again.

"I don't think I have to repeat myself."

"Mr. Turner . . ."

"Gus."

"Gus, are you hitting on me?"

He lifted the other shoulder and stared at her "What do you think?" His voice was smooth.

Sydney blinked. *Yes, the whole world is going crazy,* she thought. "I say you are and I wish you wouldn't."

"Why?"

"Because I don't know you and I'm not interested in knowing you." she said with a touch of annoyance. She was not amused and she wondered why he was suddenly looking like she was a big joke.

"Is that your only reason?" Gus asked, spearing her with a probing look.

"No, yes, that's my only reason," she sputtered. "Why are you interested if there were others?"

"Could Mason Wingate be one of them?" he asked.

"What?" Sydney jumped up from the table. "You take your suspicious . . ." She was stopped by his hand on her wrist. When she winced, he let go.

He was standing, towering over her. He spoke softly, and he no longer had a face of ice. "I'm sorry. I didn't mean to hurt you. Would you please sit down? Hear me out?"

Sydney sat, angry and bewildered, but she believed he was not a threat to her, even with his bizarre question.

"You are a beautiful, intelligent woman, Sydney. You shouldn't ever blame a man for trying." He sat back and stared at her thoughtfully. "Adam is a stubborn man. And Adam is a fool."

"Adam is stubborn, I agree. But that is no concern of mine, Gus."

"You still love him."

Her lashes hid her eyes and she remained silent.

"Sydney?"

"Did he send you?"

"No."

She believed him. "Then why are you here? To make your own move?"

He shrugged. "That's what he would think."

Her look was incredulous as her eyes opened wide. "He knows you're here?"

"There's a good chance that he's guessed by now. I didn't leave much room for doubt in his mind."

Suddenly, Sydney laughed, and her eyes crinkled shut with mirth. Trying to hold the laughter down, she whispered, "You didn't!"

"I did." Her laughter was good to hear and he wished his hardheaded buddy could hear the same. It would be balm for his soul.

Sydney held out her hand. "Nice to meet you Gus. I think I like you." She smiled at the firm, sure feel of his grip. And for the first time, she could see beyond the dark of his eyes to the tiny light that hinted at a smile.

CHAPTER EIGHTEEN

Adam stared at the closed door for what seemed like an eternity before he roused himself from his awestricken state. He couldn't believe that he had practically given his permission for Gus to make a move on his lady. *Yes mine,* he fumed to himself. *She's mine and I love her!* He blinked at his inner admission. *Love her?* After all these weeks, he could finally confess it to himself. Then why had he been so afraid to admit the same? Because he did love her and wanted to keep her safe—and alive. The only way he knew how was to keep her as far away from him as possible.

He stood up and paced the room, finally walking to the window and staring out at a sea of glass and brick buildings, rooftops and blue sky. From the forty-second floor he had a bird's-eye view of the panorama of the city, and with the same isolation, he questioned his actions. Was he being selfish and stubborn as Gus suggests? As his friend pointed out, who really was safe and could be protected from the maniacs in the world? One could do only what was humanly possible. The rest was left in the hands of God.

Lucas had made the decision to pull the man from Sydney. There had been no sign of the attacker and no indication that he was following either Adam or Sydney. The man power was needed elsewhere given Adam's and Gus' present assignment.

Adam returned to his desk, straightening his shoulders with a new resolve. He had to trust in himself that he was doing the right thing and pray that the Lord was on his side. He was going to reclaim the love of his lady and prayed that she would be forgiving. He knew that it wouldn't be easy and he didn't expect it to be. He had hurt her badly and he wondered if he had wounded her to the point of being embittered for a lifetime. He closed his eyes on that thought. He had the rest of his life to repair the damage that he'd done. He could be relentless in his professional career he knew; if it took that much effort and concentration to win her back, then that was his personal mission in life.

A deep sigh of relief escaped and settled in the air. The peace that suddenly invaded his mind spread like a blanket of warmth throughout his body. There was an inner calm that he hadn't experienced in years. Not since before Owen had died. A faint smile touched his lips as he picked up the case folder on his desk and settled back to read it for the umpteenth time. He murmured, "Hope you enjoyed breakfast, my friend." The smile spread to his eyes as he started to read.

At 12:45 P.M., Gus walked into the office, shrugged out of his jacket and hung it up on the clothes tree. He sat at his desk and looked at Adam who appeared engrossed in what he was reading.

Adam looked up, tossed aside the folder and stood up. He put on his jacket and walked to the door.

"Where're you going?" asked Gus. He stared at his friend with disappointment, wondering at the silent treatment. His little scheme didn't work. *Don't know what else to do with this man,* he thought. Adam's voice interrupted his self-chastisement.

"To lunch," Adam answered. He gestured to his desk. "Take a look at that case, would you? One of my first when I joined the agency. A young woman was killed. See what you think." He turned to leave, then asked, "How was breakfast?" Adam's voice was low and smooth.

Gus looked wary. "Great. I enjoyed it a lot."

"Good," Adam said with a crooked smile, "because you'll never have another like it. Catch you later." He left, closing the door very softly.

"Well I'll be," Gus muttered. "It worked!"

Gus was studying the case file that Adam had indicated. At first glance, nothing caught the eye unless one was looking for a specific incident that may have involved Adam. This one did. It was the first year of Adam's employment with Garrison and his fourth assignment. He was sent to Athens, Georgia, to protect a businessman and his daughter who were being threatened by a former female employee, who was a drug addict.

The small home-appliance store was being robbed of merchandise. The store owner suspected the fired woman of giving keys to her accomplices. When the man's daughter confronted the employee, she was attacked and her life threatened. The employee was arrested and released because of lack of evidence. She went to the shop in broad daylight, apparently drug-crazed, and threatened to kill everyone in the store. She pulled a gun on Adam. He drew his and she dropped hers, apparently scared. She put her hands up over her head and started to walk toward Adam, when suddenly someone shouted that she had a gun. Adam didn't see it but she pulled a small handgun from behind her neck.

Too late to stop her, Adam ducked and she fired, the bullet striking a kid who was crouched on the floor. The woman fired again, walking right toward Adam and he returned the fire. He shot to maim but she lunged and the bullet struck her in the chest, killing her instantly. She was nineteen years old.

Gus stared at the file in disgust, then rubbed his forehead wearily. So many deaths. So many youngsters dying needlessly from that nastiness they kept putting into their bodies. Why? Who had answers to that ageless question? He riffled through the pages again, lingering on pertinent points. It was a concisely written report, just the facts. One thing bothered him: her name. GeeGee. A nickname? *Who saddles a kid with a name like that to carry into the corporate boardrooms? People just don't think,* he mused. Didn't anyone take the time to find out whether that was just her street name? It was even on the front cover in big block letters, the way the office manager dictated procedure. He closed the file and stared solemnly at the name on the cover. GeeGee Graves. On the inside cover was an attached sheet, listing a dossier, including rudimentary information such as address, age, birth city and the like.

Gus perused the page and his eyes lingered on the check mark next to married. Married so young. Dead so young. He wondered if she had been a mother, and his eyes clouded. His glance caught the space for name and his eyes narrowed. *GeeGee Gage-Graves.* In parentheses next to the "First Name" space and beside her nickname was the name, *Gemma.*

So that was the reason. She was probably always called by her initials. Even after marriage her initials stayed the same. Her closest friends probably never even knew her first name. She was just GeeGee Gage and later GeeGee Graves, another lost teenager.

Gus had spotted the reason for Adam's interest in the old case. Gemma Gage-Graves was from Georgia; the one state Jeremy Gage never claimed.

A big fishing expedition you're on, Adam, Gus thought. But nothing gets overlooked or tossed aside. He was still looking at the file in deep thought when Jeremy Gage knocked and then walked in.

Gus looked up in surprise. "You're back?" Jeremy was the lead officer on a case in Philly for the past week and a half.

Plopping down in a chair and loosening his tie, Jeremy said with an exhausted sigh, "Yeah, just got in this morning. Lucas wanted a report ASAP. We just finished."

"Sounds like a rough one."

"More nerve-racking than anything else. Waiting days for the jewels to arrive, checking the building and employees for security risks . . . and then just waiting." He looked around. "Where's Adam?"

"Lunch."

Jeremy threw a glance at the folder on Gus' desk. "You guys come up with anything yet?" He gestured, then grinned broadly. "Could that be the one?" He frowned then walked to the desk and looked down at the folder that Gus picked up and waved airily.

"Just something Adam wanted me to look over," Gus said, the folder now lying facedown, with his hand over it. He kept the expression from his eyes but he was suddenly alert. "Not much to it."

Adam walked in, surprised to see Gage. "Finished up, huh?" He hung up his jacket and sat down at his desk, wondering at the tension in the room. Gus wore an expressionless look so there was no help there.

"Yeah," Jeremy answered, looking from Adam to Gus. Then, nonchalantly waving, including both men, he sauntered to the door. "Just stopped to give a shout. I'm going to get some sleep." His hand on the doorknob, he asked Adam, "How's Ms. Cox?"

Adam eyed the man thoughtfully. "Since I haven't seen her lately, I really can't say." His tone was as blank as Gus' face.

Jeremy's eyelashes flickered. "Just wondered about her. Some ordeal." He clucked in sympathy and then closed the door.

Both men looked at the closed door for several seconds before speaking.

Adam nodded at the folder still lying facedown on Gus' desk. "You found it?"

"Yeah." His voice sounded as if he didn't want to jump to conclusions but yet he knew the coincidence was too great.

"Did he get a look at it?"

Gus nodded. "I believe he did."

"So what do you think?" Adam asked, keeping his own opinion out of his voice.

"The same as you," Gus answered. "I think Gemma Gage-Graves and Jeremy Gage may have something in common."

Adam said, "Like, is he Graves, going by Gage, or is he Gage and she was a close relative? Sister? Cousin? Sister-in-law?"

"Forget the first suggestion," Gus said, shaking his head. "A quick calculation would make him seventeen years her senior."

Adam shrugged. "So, a nineteen-year-old and a thirty-six-year-old can't fall in love and get married? It happens."

"He's forty-two now, though it's hard to believe with that angelic-looking baby face of his."

Adam agreed, then said, "Okay, let's go with the second suggestion. Sister. He's got family all over, so we've discovered, why couldn't some still be living in Athens?" He paused. "Suppose we pull up . . ." Gus stopped him with a wave.

"Already got it," he said. "Come take a look." He whistled. "Well, I'll be. Who can afford to raise fourteen children in these times? Who the devil would want to?"

"The rich and famous and the mentally well-adjusted," Adam answered dryly. He whistled, too. He had scooted his chair over to Gus' desk and was staring at the computer screen. The detailed background of Jeremy Martin Gage was in full view. He was the second oldest and the only son living. His older brother died of leukemia at the age of twenty-two.

By the time Adam and Gus finished reading the essay, they knew as much as anyone would want to know about another person. The agency required the pertinent information both to protect its clients and the lives of its officers.

Apparently, very early on, Jeremy took on the role of older brother, mother and father to his twelve younger sisters. As they became of age, they moved to various states, marrying and pursuing different careers.

Adam rolled back to his desk with the folder. He opened it and scanned the pages, a frown marring his forehead.

Gus said, "I know what you're wondering."

Adam looked up. "What Jeremy left out of the dossier was the fact of Gemma's drug addiction and her death. He had listed her as if she were still alive."

"Right." Gus looked at his friend. "Now I wonder why he would do that, while applying for a new job?"

"Concealing information that could easily be ferreted out?" Adam's frown deepened. "It's obvious he didn't want the information known, but why?

"Unless when he joined the agency, the less anyone knew

about that part of his life the better for his plan to work,'' Gus answered.

"His plan to kill Adam Stone because in his mind, the man was guilty of murdering his sister?"

"Right."

Adam shook his head. "Far-fetched."

"Is it? He had two years to study your every habit and monitor your movement. How hard could that be?" Gus gestured toward the screen. "He was a former police officer. When he caught up with you in Boston, as a Garrison officer, he knew all about you. Your past history was locked into his brain. Somehow, he got his hands on one of those old notes left by Ethan Reynard. He learned to imitate and duplicate them."

Adam looked at Gus with a question in his dark eyes. "That case was on the up and up. Everything was reported exactly as it happened."

"You don't have to defend yourself or that report to me," Gus said in a low voice.

"She had a gun," Adam said almost as if speaking to himself. "People were yelling that she had a gun, but she had already dropped it. She was so petite and cute, she couldn't have been so devious." He looked at Gus. "That's what I was thinking."

"You weren't thinking right, man. You'd forgotten your training. In Vietnam, who would think a kid would walk up to you and shake your hand, only to release a live grenade? Or that a pretty, petite woman was a kamikaze who would detonate herself in the middle of a camp?"

Adam nodded, a bleak look filling his eyes. "I'd forgotten for a moment."

"Well, thank God you recovered in time."

"Yes, thank God," Adam said. The bleak look remained.

Silence ensued in the room, neither man ready to take the next step, which meant accusing a colleague of being a killer.

It was close to four-thirty when Gus noticed the weary look on Adam's face. The man had been through a ton of different emotions in the last few days, he thought. He needed to break away for a bit.

"As far as I'm concerned, we're not ready to bring this to Lucas. How about you?"

"It's still a bit raggedy," Adam answered, frowning. "I'd hate to give a report with so many loose ends. But still, the man is here and if he even suspects . . ."

"He won't do a thing. Not now. He hasn't got a plan. Just remember he wants to get away with this. *He's* not the one playing kamikaze."

"You're probably right," Adam said.

"I feel that I am. Look, why don't you knock off now? I want to access the mainframe in DC again. There's a few cases I want to look over, see if I can tie them into an idea I have."

Adam cocked a brow.

"Go on. If I'm right, you'll know soon enough."

Adam reared back in his chair. "You're sure?"

"Yeah, go on."

Adam stood and got his jacket and shrugged into it. He glanced at his watch and a sudden look of determination settled on his face. When he looked at Gus he caught the slight smile that his friend tried to conceal by staring at the screen.

"What's that smile for?" Adam muttered.

Gus broke out into a grin. "Just that I know that look, friend." He busied himself with the screen again. "Enjoy yourself." He didn't look up and seconds later he heard the door close.

Gus sat back in his chair after Adam left, still smiling at the astuteness of his friend. *Friend!* He could remember a time years ago that that word wasn't part of his vocabulary if it applied to him. Not until five years ago when he had first met Adam, a man who reminded him so much of himself. Quiet, rock-hard stare, cold eyes and a serious no-nonsense demeanor. With similar military backgrounds, his was Army, they recognized in each other a kinship.

He mused over the "friendships" that he had in the service, which were very casual. In that world, you couldn't be a loner or, as the saying goes, "your ass is grass." Gus knew that there had to be some sort of trust and camaraderie or else there was no "back" protection when the time came. After eleven years in the service, Gus quit, tiring of his special-forces duty.

He was restless and wondered if he was longing to find a woman and settle down; to marry again.

Abruptly, Gus left the office and returned with a Pepsi from the vending machine outside the door. He sat and resumed his thumbnail sketch of his life, wondering why the sudden need for nostalgia. He knew the answer to that when he thought of Sydney and Adam together. He had had a love once: his high school sweetheart in Detroit, Michigan.

They were both young, she in college and he in the Army. He insisted that their long-distance marriage would work; there would be his leaves and her semester breaks. They'd been married a year when she got pregnant. Ecstatic, she traveled from Michigan to South Carolina to tell him the news. Many plans were made for their future and baby names were discussed.

Gus grimaced and then smiled. She'd told him that his selections were outlandish and would cripple their child for life.

Gus rubbed his eyes, remembering that time. God, how he had loved her. He'd made love to her that weekend so gingerly, that she had protested. "I'm no porcelain doll," she'd said. "Love me, husband!" And he had.

Gus inhaled deeply, thinking about the next time he saw her: in Michigan, in the hospital morgue. His sweet wife looked like a stranger and he had cried. The beating she must have endured to try to save her life and that of the baby. But that wasn't the plan of the man who had raped her as she entered their apartment building. He intended to eliminate all possibilities of being identified. The same exact spot where he'd violated her, was where he had strangled the life out of her, killing her fetus.

Gus knew that after his wife's murder, he had changed into the hard, cold-eyed man that other men feared, and some women watched warily. All but Adam. They were two of a kind and had formed a genuine friendship almost from Day One. They understood each other and that's why Gus knew without a doubt in this world that when Adam walked out that door, he was on his way to pursue his woman.

With a soft chuckle, Gus gave his full attention to the data on the screen. It wasn't long before his expression changed to the hard, professional mask, the one that led passersby on the street to hurry on their way.

Jeremy Gage left the two men in the office with their stoic faces and noncommittal responses to him. *You weren't quick enough, Turner. I saw the case file you tried to hide.* "GeeGee," he muttered. For God's sake, couldn't they use her given name in one of the last official documents about her life and death?

He stopped in the men's room, doused his face with cold water to clear his head, and stood still for a moment. He was bone-tired and had to think. They weren't languishing over a five-year-old case for no good reason, he thought. Just an insignificant case of the killing of a black nineteen-year-old. He had to think.

He left the building, opting to leave the company car, in preference to traveling on the subway. It was the fastest mode of transportation to his apartment on One hundred thirty-eighth Street in Manhattan. He rented the upstairs of a fairly new home in the historic Strivers Row section of the famed Harlem community. He was dead tired and he decided he needed sleep before he could even think about making any plans. He had to be as sharp and alert as Stone and Turner. The two of them together were lethal and he could ill afford any more mess ups.

When Jeremy left the subway and walked the few blocks home, he had already formulated the skeleton of a plan that would finally set him free. But he would need the cooperation of his prey, and that of his pigeon, Ms. Sydney Cox. This time Sydney, he thought, it will not be a tease. When he reached his apartment and went inside, he was chuckling with glee.

His baby-looking face in the creases and wrinkles of a forty-ish male, seemed ludicrous and almost demonic.

CHAPTER NINETEEN

On Tuesday evening, Sydney was sitting in her office wiping the mist from her eyes, while trying to tidy up at the same time. She picked up napkins and bits of crackers and tossed them in the trash and wiped off her desk with a damp paper towel. The crew had already carried the crystal flutes back to the kitchen.

Earlier, when she'd arrived at work at eleven forty-five, she was met by her boss, Benjamin. With him were Mason, Dominic and the rest of the staff, all welcoming her with a huge bouquet of flowers.

Her heart was overflowing with good feelings. She hadn't realized how they'd felt about her. After all, she thought, she really hadn't been on board for long. Then, just before the start of the dinner hour, she had returned to her office only to be surprised by a sumptuous spread. Mason and his cooks had prepared some of their specialties, each trying to outdo the other with their presentations. The pastry chef had made a to-die-for chocolate torte with a deep dark decadent frosting. Dominic popped the cork on his special cache: Roederer's Cristal, 1988 vintage Champagne. The full-bodied wine brought oohs and ahs from everyone and tears to Sydney's eyes as she

xpressed her thanks to Dominic. The top-of-the-line bubbly
was a rare treat.

Sydney had felt truly loved in the room of special people.
Without knowing it, she had been working with casual acquain-
ances who thought of her as a friend. She felt slightly embarrassed as she looked at her coworkers in a new light. She
wondered if they had ever thought of her as "Miss Thang,"
going about her business with a vengeance while bestowing
upon them plastic smiles as she rushed about.

The world is a mysterious place, she thought as she sat down,
pleasantly pooped. Here, to replace one lost friend were a host
of others, waiting to be cultivated. It was up to her to take the
next step in extending her hand in friendship, especially to
Mason's assistant who had in the past, extended the olive
branch. Sydney had never reached out to take it.

With all the good vibes, she felt that new friends were just
what she needed, especially after last night.

Then, at five o'clock in the evening, she had been preparing
a light meal of salad and salmon croquettes when the phone
rang. It was Adam. Flustered, she quickly refused his offer to
take her out to dinner and hung up. When the phone rang again,
she refused him a second time. He didn't call a third time and
she didn't know whether to be sad or glad. She didn't want
him to walk back into her life only to realize he'd made a
mistake and walk out again. She wouldn't know how to handle
such monumental rejection.

Sydney was about to leave her office when the phone rang.
"Hello?"

"It's Adam, Sydney. Are you feeling better tonight? I'd like
to take you out to dinner."

"What?" Sydney plopped back down in the chair, flabbergasted. "I—I . . . told you that I don't want to see you again,
Adam. I . . . just can't do that to myself." She tried to quiet
the thumping against the wall of her chest. She was certain
that he could hear it. "Please don't call me anymore."

"I can't promise you that, Sydney. I want to see you." His
voice lowered to a husky whisper. "I must talk to you."

Sydney groaned inwardly. *He knows what his voice does to*

me and he's working it! She shuddered as her ears tingled from that deep vibration. She calmed herself before she spoke again. "I don't think we have anything more to say to each other. Good-bye Adam." Firmly, she hung up the phone. Calming herself by taking deep breaths, she smoothed the skirt of her cranberry-colored sheath, fingered the ruby-red grape cluster at her shoulder, and left the office.

Standing in the softly lit entrance to the dining room, she surveyed the room with a practiced eye, and nodded in satisfaction. It was going to be a busy night, of which she was grateful. She would have less time to think about that magical voice that still resonated in her ears.

Adam watched Sydney from the shadowed, glassed-in area of the lounge. He was seated at a small table, his fingers drumming lightly over the chilled wineglass. When he spotted her, the heat in his eyes sped rapidly to his belly causing a conflagration that fired up his groin. Suppressing an audible groan, he sipped the fine red wine and waited.

After she had refused to have dinner with him, he spoke quietly to Dominic. After making his request, the slim-hipped man with the congenial face, smiled, his eyes lighting with glee. A short time later, Mason appeared and they spoke quietly and with frankness.

"Adam," Mason said.

Without preamble, Adam said, "I messed up."

Mason nodded, "I know." He looked Adam squarely in the eye. "You aiming to fix it up right? If not, I think the best thing you can do is leave it alone."

Adam shook his head. "I'm not leaving it alone and yes, I aim to make things right. If not tonight then tomorrow or the next night. If not then . . ."

"Okay, okay, I get the picture." Mason grinned. "Now what do you want me to do?"

Now Adam sat and waited for his plan to be executed. The appearance of Sydney in the dining room meant that things were already in the works. His heart pounded in his chest as he saw Sydney walk toward the lounge. She stopped to speak

o the bartender. When she turned and saw Adam, the smile
lied on her lips.

"Adam?" Sydney's eyes widened in surprise. "Why ... I
lidn't know that you were ..." She was at a loss for words.
He must have been right here when he called me, she realized.

"Hello, Sydney." He gestured toward the dining room. "I
aave reservations for dinner." He eyed her intently. He knew
hat his love for her was evident in his eyes. He wanted her to
see and know that he had been a fool.

"That's, uh, wonderful," Sydney stammered. "I had no
dea." *Why is he staring at me like that?* she wondered. *Oh
Adam, why did you do this to us?* Why had she lied to herself,
pretending that she could ever forget this man? Seeing him,
standing like that, his eyes smoldering with heat, brought back
such memories that her body began to warm. His strong, mascu-
ine body that she knew so well, bulging with firm, huge muscles, made her eyes begin to mist. She turned to go before she
made a fool of herself. "Well," she managed to say, "enjoy
your dinner. I have to get to work." She lifted a hand in a
small meaningless wave and tried to walk out of the lounge
with dignity.

Before she rushed to her office, she was stopped by Dominic
who needed her opinion. She coughed, cleared her throat and
brushed her damp eyelids. She only hoped that she wouldn't
stumble over her feet when Adam was seated. That would be
one two-hour period that she wished would zoom on by. So
much for being so grateful for a busy night, she thought, as
she followed behind Dominic.

Adam stood up when a gentle-voiced woman spoke to him,
asking him to follow her. He was led around the dining room
to a side corridor and eventually was guided to Sydney's office.
When he entered, Mason was there, looking mighty pleased
with himself. And well he should, Adam thought. The room
had been transformed into a miniature dining alcove for two.
Flowers, chilled Champagne, candlelight and the food aromas
tickled the palate.

Adam turned to Mason and held out his hand. "Thanks,
man." He couldn't say anything else.

Mason was standing with his arms akimbo. watching the reaction of the other man. *This is a serious brother in love,* he was thinking, when Adam offered his hand. Mason took it.

"No thanks necessary. Just treat my girl right." Mason gave a small salute and quietly closed the door behind him.

Adam sat down and waited, praying that his plan was not going to become the biggest mistake of his life. *No, you idiot,* he thought, *you already made that one when you walked out of her life. Just pray that she still feels the same as she did before you made the most colossal of all wrongs.*

Frowning, Sydney wondered why Dominic wanted a hard copy of her changes that she'd made on next week's wine list. She'd already put it into the system for his perusal. As she walked down the deserted corridor, she wondered why Adam had left. He wasn't in the dining room and he wasn't where she'd last seen him, in the lounge. Suddenly, feeling down at his absence, she realized how much she was going to miss that man. She opened the door to her office and stood mesmerized.

Adam stood. He walked over to her and gently pushed the door shut. He then looked at her.

"Would you do me the honor of dining with me tonight. Sydney?"

Sagging against the door, she held her hand to her breasts to keep her heart from jumping out of her chest. She looked from Adam to the beautifully appointed table and back to the man she was still in love with.

"Adam . . . I . . ." she was breathless.

"Is that a yes?" he murmured, staying where he was. If he moved any closer to her, he couldn't take responsibility for his actions.

Sydney nodded her head. "Yes, Adam."

"Thank you," he whispered. He seated her then sat down across from her.

Sydney was stunned. The staff had done this all in a matter of twenty minutes since she'd left the office. They'd brought in a small table and covered it with mauve linen. She looked over at Adam who had moved the flowers to her desk where she'd placed the beautiful bouquet earlier.

"This is so lovely," she whispered, "and so unexpected." She could hardly find her voice.

Adam opened the Champagne then poured for them both. He sat and held the flute up. "A toast?" He looked at her intently, and when she nodded, he spoke.

"Sydney, to you. You've made me a happy man tonight. You'll never guess what this means to me." He took a sip and sat down the crystal.

Sydney sipped the Champagne, and for the first time in her professional career, did not mentally "taste" the beverage. She was overwhelmed.

"Adam, I don't know what this all means. If it's just for tonight that you want to wine and dine me . . ." she gestured hopelessly. "I can say with all honesty, that I am flattered. Any woman I suppose would be ecstatic over all the attention and what you must have done to pull this off. But, I don't want to give you any false impressions by my accepting your unique dinner invitation."

Adam listened to her words carefully. He breathed easy, when he realized she'd said *"If it's just for tonight."* He had a chance. *Thank you, dear God.*

"Sydney, if you'd turned around and walked out that door, I would have understood. But, that wouldn't have stopped me from coming back tomorrow." He stared at her. "And no, it's not only tonight. I have something to tell you and I'm hoping that you will listen." He lifted the stainless-steel warming covers off their plates and put them aside. "I think we'd better eat. Mason may get attitudinal if these go back untouched."

Sydney smiled. "How is it that you've come to know my friend so well?"

The small table had been discreetly cleared, and now at eight-thirty, Adam sat across from Sydney, watching her toy with the flute of Champagne. Although they'd made small talk during dinner, he could see that she was still curious at why he was there.

"I was a fool," he said quietly.

"Excuse me?" His voice startled her, as they had been

comfortably silent for the last few seconds. She regarded him curiously.

"That night that I left you, it was the hardest thing that I've ever done in my life. If you don't listen to another thing I say tonight, believe that." His eyes bored into hers and his voice was low but distinct. "I'd never met anyone like you before and I know that I never will again. You're not 'any woman,' but a most unique individual." His voice was controlled and unrelenting as he continued. "So unique that I won't know what to do if I can't have you in my life."

What is he saying? That he wants me, now? Sydney listened, determined not to fall for sweet words that might mean absolutely nothing in the morning.

"I can see that you find it hard to believe what you've just heard. I can't say that I don't blame you, but that's the truth." Adam wanted to hold her, to erase the doubt from her eyes and kiss the cry of surprise from her lips. He wanted to love her.

"I love you." The words were a husky whisper on his lips.

Sydney could only look at him, stunned, at the words he'd uttered so softly.

"I love you and I'm asking you to let me back into your life. I want to show you how much you mean to me."

"Adam, don't," Sydney whispered. "Please don't ask me that." She looked at him with pleading eyes. "I've got myself back and I don't want to lose me again," she murmured. "Can you understand that?"

Her words wrenched his heart. Her hands were clenched into small fists on the table. He took them in his hand and held on tightly. "I do understand that, Sydney, and God forgive me for not thinking before acting. I was doing what I thought was best without giving any thought to what I would be putting you through." He released the tight grasp he had and turned her hands so that her palms were held faceup. He leaned over and kissed her fingertips.

"I took a lot from you. You gave yourself to me because you loved me." He took a deep breath. "Right now, I want to hold you, to ease your fears. But I can't because I want you to come to me on your own. I want your trust again. If not now, at this moment," he lifted a shoulder, "then I can wait for that for as long as it will take you." He released her hands and sat back, watching her with pain-filled eyes.

A lump had formed in Sydney's throat and she tried hard to swallow it before it choked her to death. Now was not the time for him to perform CPR on her when all she wanted was to feel and taste his passionate kisses. *Oh, what should I do?* Sydney cried to herself. She'd already covered her heart and what price must she pay to reveal it to him once more?

Adam was as still as an unmovable mountain as he watched and waited. He could almost feel her inner turmoil because his own insides were churning like a threshing machine. He knew the exact moment when she made her decision and his shoulders slumped.

A ragged breath escaped at the same time Adam stood. Sadness settled in his chest like a lump of coal. He couldn't help feeling like the monster who had gotten caught and was now paying for his evil deeds.

"I told you that I can wait, Sydney." He walked to the door. "Call me. Anytime." The door was ajar when he turned and asked, "Will you be getting a ride home tonight?"

"I don't think so, but I can manage with a cab, Adam."

Adam shut the door. "Can you find out before I leave, please?"

"That won't be necessary." She was standing and she put her hands behind her back and pulled on her fingers. *Why doesn't he leave?* she agonized. *I can't stand his being so close. Oh, what's wrong with me? I want him to go, yet I want him to hold me in his arms.*

With a glint in his eyes, Adam walked to her desk and stared down at the phone, reading the names and the extension numbers. Satisfied, he picked up the receiver and punched in a number.

"Mason Wingate, please." He nodded and waited.

Sydney looked astonished. Finding her voice, she said. "Don't you dare."

"Yeah, this is Adam Stone, Mason. Yes, everything was

just great. Thanks again.'' He paused. ''Did you have plans on dropping Sydney off tonight?'' He listened, then nodded. ''Okay, thanks. Yeah, good night.'' He placed the receiver in the cradle and looked at Sydney. ''He's meeting someone after work tonight. He said to tell you that he'll see you tomorrow and to have a good night.'' His face was expressionless.

''You had no right to do that,'' exclaimed Sydney. ''He's not my keeper or my chauffeur.''

''Half of what you just said is true,'' Adam agreed with a bland voice. He shook his head. ''The other half? Not true. I am making it my right to protect you whenever and however I can.'' His face softened toward her as she looked at him with such bewilderment. He certainly had made a mess of her life.

''Sydney. Please don't fight me on this.'' He checked his watch. ''You know you don't have to stay any longer. Can I drop you home? If you insist upon a cab, I'll wait with you.''

Sydney felt such confusion in her jumbled thoughts. She fingered the pin on her dress, finding comfort in the feel of the smooth clumps beneath her fingers. Why couldn't she just say yes? She wanted to be near him so badly. But was she being weak to acquiesce?

''Sydney?''

She decided. ''Yes, I'll ride with you, Adam. Give me a minute, will you?''

He nodded. ''I'll be in the lounge,'' he said, and left.

Adam had parked in the underground garage and after their silent walk to the car, he opened the door for Sydney and she slid into the passenger's seat.

''Oh,'' said Sydney. She had sat on something and raising slightly, she pulled a small brown paper bag from beneath her, the object slid out and fell to the floor. She bent to pick it up.

Adam had started the engine when he saw what she held in her hand. He didn't pull off but instead, sat back and watched her.

Sydney was fondling the bracelet. ''Would you turn on the

light, please?'' When he complied, she whispered, "How beautiful!'' She looked at him with a question.

"It's yours, if you will have it,'' he said gruffly. "I didn't want to give it to you before. I wanted to eliminate the possibility of your thinking I was trying to buy your affections.'' He stared straight ahead.

Sydney gasped at the ruby-red grape clusters that were an exact match for her pin. The tiny gold clasp shone brightly against the twinkling facets in the cut stones. "It's a perfect match,'' she murmured as she held the bracelet up close to the pin on her shoulder. She stared at him. "When did you . . . how did you find this? I've looked all over town.''

"I know.'' A smile tugged at his lips. "At Garrison, we're a bunch of nosy investigators.''

Sydney smiled. Then, slipping the bauble back into the plain bag, she said, "Under the circumstances, I can't accept this, Adam.'' She handed it to him, but instead of taking it, he released the brake and headed for the exit.

"I can't either, Sydney,'' he said, once they were out on the street. "It's yours for whatever you want to do with it.'' There was finality in his voice and a grimness to his expression as they continued the drive in silence.

It was after eleven-thirty when Sydney sat up in bed, a frown marring her features. Not able to sleep, she turned on the light and stared at nothing. The same confusion that had enveloped her earlier was drumming in her head. Something was clamoring for her attention.

After Adam dropped her off, she had showered and immediately dressed for bed, exhausted after her first day back on the job. She had reflected on the day's events that left her feeling good about her new friends and herself. The only thing that disturbed her was Adam Stone and her feelings about him. Try as she would, she couldn't find a reason to hate or dislike him. The man had apologized for his error in poor judgment. He told her that he loved her. *I love you.* Those words spoken so simply had completely gone over her head. Wasn't that what she had yearned to hear? Yet she hadn't believed him; hadn't trusted herself enough to bare her heart to him once again. But when she refused him, had he stalked away mad, like the injured lover? No, she thought. He was willing to stick around to endure her coldness, because he wanted to protect. Protect her because he loved her!

And the bracelet? Sydney picked it up from the nightstand and slid it across the palm of her hand. It was his token of love for her.

Suddenly, tears welled up in her eyes. *Why am I being so hard-hearted about this?* she asked herself. *I love him and he's admitted he loves me.* What more should she ask for? she thought. An agreement written in his blood? Sydney got up and opened her closet door and pulled a picture album from the shelf. She got back on the bed and flipped through the pages until she found what she was searching for.

She stared at the features of Maddelina Torreano. La Signora. It had been so hot in Florence that summer, yet she had always dressed in exquisite black lace and cotton. Each costume, elaborate in fine detail with excellent tatting.

Sydney studied the wizened dark eyes in a face withered by many years. The picture was taken in the beautiful gardens and the slender figure was seated on a bench with a background of a profusion of colorful flowers and olive trees. Sydney could almost smell the sweet garden smells wafting delicately through the warm breeze while faraway string serenades caressed the ears.

Sydney reflected on the conversation on that last night she was ever to see the old woman alive. Words came back to haunt her. *He had married another.* Those were the words that had bothered Sydney. The old woman was sad when she had uttered those words. She had discovered that her true love didn't wait for her but had married another. La Signora had lost her love forever; Sydney thought. The young Maddelina couldn't believe that love was at her doorstep and she had traveled far and wide seeking it only to find that it had been lost to her forever. *Is that what is in store for me?* Sydney asked herself. She closed the album and put it on her dresser.

Married another, married another—the words were a song in her head. Is that what he would do if she kept her heart closed to him? The thought sent a blinding flash of pain to her temples. The vision of him ever loving another like he loved her was a vision she closed her eyes against. *No.* The inner cry tore through her throat. "No!" That could never happen. She was being a fool.

Sydney got up and hurried to the bathroom and closed the door. When she emerged, she was freshened and spritzed with her favorite scent of heather. She hardly ever indulged in the use of heavy perfumes when she was working. Perfume and smoke were anathema to the nasal passages when professionally tasting and sniffing fine wines. But she knew that she was guilty at sometimes spritzing herself with a delicate scent while at work. She recalled wearing her favorite heather scent the night Adam appeared at Restaurant Louise.

Dressed casually in jeans and T-shirt, she called a car service and in seconds was locking her apartment door.

Adam looked warily toward the door. Who was making a social call at almost 1:00 A.M.? He had not gone to bed since dropping Sydney off, his head filled with thoughts of her and what he must do to convince her of his love. He was dressed in white cargo shorts, was shirtless and barefoot. He walked to the door and looked through the viewer, his body steeled against what might come. Adam stepped back and swore, flinging open the door.

"What are you doing here?" His eyes blazed with fury. "You came out of your apartment alone? Traveled here by yourself?" His heart was thumping at the risk she'd taken.

Sydney stepped back, startled at his outburst. She realized that he was perfectly right. She had given no thought to the danger she had put herself in, especially after he had seen her safely inside for the night. Before she could speak, he pulled her inside and shut the door.

Adam saw that he had frightened the life out of her with his outburst. *Oh God, what have I done?* She had to have a good reason for coming there this time of morning.

"Sydney," he said. "As usual lately, I didn't think. Come inside." He led her to the sofa and sat down next to her. "Tell me what's wrong," he said in a calmed voice.

After Sydney recovered, she reached into her jeans' pocket. She held up the bracelet. "This is the kind of clasp that requires another pair of hands," she said softly. "It will have to be changed to something I can put on by myself." She gave him a shy smile. "After all, when you're off in Kalamazoo on a job, how else will I ever be able to wear it?"

Adam was speechless as he stared at the facets catching the light. He looked at her in awe. "Does this mean that you haven't changed your mind? You still love me?" He held his breath.

"It does," Sydney answered. "I realized that your mouth can utter many untruths, but what's in your heart remains true and steadfast." She touched his cheek in a soft caress. "I've never stopped loving you, Adam." She laid the bracelet on her arm and held it out to him. "Please," she whispered.

He fastened it on her slender wrist and watched as she twisted and fingered it. "Just as I imagined it would look against your lovely skin." He took her hand in his and kissed her palm. When he raised his head, he was seducing her with his eyes. "I love you more each time I see you," he said husky-voiced. He leaned toward her and kissed her cheek, blew softly in her ear, then smiled at the shudder that rippled her body. "Still like that?" he whispered in her other ear.

Sydney groaned after the shiver rocked her body down to her bare toes. She wriggled her feet out of her sandals. "Can't you see you knocked me right out of my shoes?"

Adam laughed, the low rumble rolling around in his chest. He pulled her into his arms and kissed her with a hungry passion. He rained tiny kisses on her eyelids, tickled her long lashes with his tongue, kissed her nose and nibbled her neck. Each of her tiny sighs encouraged his explorations of her body. Her hands caressing his naked chest and the tiny squeezes to his rigid nipples were driving him insane. "Sydney," he murmured, "I want you."

Sydney gasped. Her hands were on his bare chest and she felt as though she were in heaven again, a place she dreamed of whenever he took her into his arms. "No more than I, you, my love," she whispered.

CHAPTER TWENTY

The heat in his loins made it quite evident that he wanted her and when she struggled to feel him, he heard her frustration. With his help, he freed himself, twisting to kick away his shorts. Dressed in briefs, he stifled the yell, holding it in his throat when she slipped her hand inside and touched him.

"Oh," Sydney gasped. The throbbing manhood in her hand nearly seared her fingers. "Adam . . . oh, God," she whispered. Suddenly, her clothes were on fire and she needed to shed them before they burned into her skin. She jumped up and fumbled with the zipper on her jeans. Vaguely, she sensed Adam disappearing but her attention was held by ridding herself of her clothing. Shackles, she thought, giddily. She wanted her naked body next to his. Then, she felt his hands on her back removing her T-shirt, then unhooking her bra. She turned to him and threw her fevered body against his. Her breasts against his hard chest and his firm belly moving against her drew a whimper. "Adam. Adam."

"I'm here, my love," he whispered against her sweet-smelling hair. He thought of heather and remembered the first time he'd loved her. When she had given her sweet self for the first time to a man. To him. The tiny envelope he held in his hand was laid on the table as he gently eased her down on the wide sofa.

"I can't feel you," Sydney murmured as she writhed beneath him. In seconds, he removed his briefs and she shimmied out of her wispy underpants.

"I feel you now, sweet Sydney." Her moist feminine mound was pulsating against his sex and he felt as if he would burst if he couldn't have her now. "Sydney?" His voice was a low growl. "I have to have you." He explored her silky womanhood, inserting one teasing finger inside. At his touch, she exploded.

"Adam," she screamed, "what are you doing? O-h-h-h . . . can't wait . . . A-dam . . ."

Too late for protection, he didn't stop her, but moved his finger to catch her rhythm. Her hips moved involuntarily, arching to meet him, straining, until she screamed again.

Sydney's blood was racing through her veins until she saw red behind her closed lids. She lay spent, her breasts heaving against his chest. She felt relieved but her body still ached for him. She opened her eyes to catch his intent stare. He was poised over her, easing his full weight to the edge of the sofa. She could feel his sex against her thigh. She wanted him inside of her.

"Adam?"

He kissed her nose and smiled. "I'm here."

"You made me feel good," she whispered shyly.

Adam grinned. He kissed her lips, pushing his tongue inside to taste hers. "That was my intent, sweetie."

"I didn't make you feel good." She kissed him back, chasing his tongue now.

"I felt good, giving you pleasure," he murmured against her throat.

"But," she whispered, letting her tongue dart against the hollow of his throat, "I want to pleasure you now," she said huskily. Her tongue darted into his ear.

Adam groaned as he squirmed against her. "Is that so?" he murmured as he tasted her lips. His hand toyed with her swollen breasts until the nipples were once again brought to firm peaks.

"Yes," Sydney moaned against the new onslaught of desire wrought by his magical hands.

"How do you propose to do that?"

"Well, we have to change positions," she said, suddenly feeling shy.

Adam's eyes twinkled as he propped himself on one elbow, his thumb flecking her nipples. "We do?" he asked in mild surprise.

"Yes," she whispered. "You have to get up a second." She shifted from beneath him when he moved. He was lying on his back, watching her. Sydney was perplexed and felt a little embarrassed. The movie that she saw with lovers on a couch looked so easy, she thought. *There's no place for my knees,* she groaned inwardly.

Adam saw her consternation and smiled, guessing what she wanted to do. He reached up and eased her down on his body. "Here, let me help you," he whispered. He adjusted his muscled physique so that she fit perfectly, her knees comfortably on either side of him and her mound fitted snugly against his manhood. When she sank down on him, he groaned. "Is this what you wanted?" he asked through clenched teeth.

"Uh-huh," Sydney breathed as she concentrated on rotating her hips in a slow rhythmic motion. Her hands were on his stomach, then his nipples, where she kneaded them into nut-hard stiffness. She adjusted her body, moving up so that he could taste her breasts. When he suckled them, she groaned and her hand caressed his body, moving slowly down his thigh until she found his sex. Slowly she moved her hand up and down and squeezed, then released. She smiled at his sudden yell as if he were in excruciating pain.

"Sydney," Adam gasped. "you lied to me."

"Hmm," she said almost distractedly. She loved the feel of him beneath her. "What?" she murmured.

"You're not giving me pleasure, you're killing me!"

"Oh," Sydney said, "you don't like it?"

"In Jesus' name, yes!" he exploded. "It's a slow, sweet death!"

Sydney smiled and sat up, sinking down once more on him.

'Then in that case, I have to stop,'' she said, her eyes sparkling. 'I want you alive, my love.'' She tilted her head to one side. 'Then this is the end of our sex life together?''

Adam groaned as he swiftly slid from beneath her. "My God,'' he growled, "I've created a teasing vixen.'' He stood and pulled her with him, reached for the packet on the table and hurried her to the bedroom. He pushed her gently on the bed and after putting on his protection, he lay atop her once again. Her body was hot and she waited for him with excitement shining in her eyes.

"I love you, my sweet.'' There were no more words as he plunged into her, her feminine lips enveloping him tightly. He screamed her name as he sank deeper inside with each thrust of his hips. Her legs wound around his as she gave herself to him. He could feel her love and he knew nothing else as he was lost to all reason.

Sydney rode with him letting him take her on his journey. She was feeling every desirous shudder that emanated from his body to hers. When they finally met, they continued together, until both traveled as one.

A long while after Sydney and Adam lay quiet from their tumultuous lovemaking, neither could sleep. Before they were sated, Adam had to reach in his nightstand drawer once more. The second time brought new, deeper feelings of love. Feelings they talked about.

Sydney lay in the valley of Adam's long arm. She adjusted herself so that his arm was comfortable. Earlier, he teased her that it had gone numb. She pleased him by kissing it back to life.

"Adam,'' she whispered, "are you asleep?'' She felt his belly shaking. "Yes,'' he whispered back. Sydney pulled his mustache. "Tease,'' she said with a tiny giggle.

"Ouch.'' Adam kissed her forehead. "What, love?''

"How long would you have waited?''

He understood immediately. "I told you.''

"Suppose I remained aggrieved and cold-hearted?''

Adam didn't have a ready answer and he was silent. Thoughtfully, he answered, "I would have died a little each time I saw

you, knowing that I was the cause.'' As if the thought pained
him, he said, ''I believe then I would have left you so that you
could open up and live again. There would be no sense in two
of us dying slow deaths.''

''You would have left me alone?''

''Yes, so that you could have a life.''

''There would be no life without you, Adam. I know that
now.'' She paused. ''Do you?''

''Yes,'' he agreed. ''I know that now.''

''What are we going to do?'' Sydney was fearful of her joy
ending all too soon because of one lone madman.

Adam didn't want to think beyond this moment, but he knew
he had to. Softly he caressed the outline of her jaw with his
knuckles. He didn't know how, but that madman would never
get another chance at her—or him, Adam thought. He felt the
gentle rise of Sydney's breasts against him and knew she'd
fallen asleep. He kissed her brow and covered her nakedness.

Earlier, when he'd spoken to Gus, he was told that it was
time to meet with Lucas. The cold trail of Ethan Reynard led
to the mysterious paths taken by one Jeremy Gage, since the
death of Gemma Gage-Graves, five years ago.

Jeremy Gage lay down on his double-size bed, staring up at
the ceiling. The room was dark and little light slipped past the
room-darkener shades even though it was past dawn. He'd
never undressed for bed the night before. After eating Chinese
takeout, he'd sat for hours reflecting on his mistakes that
resulted in Adam Stone remaining alive. He chastised himself
for the biggest mistake of all. That stupid teasing scene in the
bedroom of that woman!

God, he had felt so in control. He had been pumped and he
knew it . . . But the great almighty Stone was helpless; probably
for the first time in his career. Big, bad Sergeant Stone. A soft
chuckle escaped as Jeremy played the scene over in his mind
when Stone had lunged for him and nearly cracked his skull
open. Trying to save his woman from violation. He laughed
out loud.

Jeremy's eyes narrowed. Save his woman would he? Who the hell was there to save his sister from being shot down like a dirty dog? Not a damn soul tried to save her.

He rubbed his eyes wearily. GeeGee was only nineteen. He tried to save her from the streets. Lord knows he tried, but she was so weak. She'd married that no-good man to hold on to her supplier. What better way than to sleep with the dealer?

He thought of years of trying to be mother, father and older brother to his twelve sisters. He'd been successful in seeing seven of them make something of themselves. Out of the other five, two of them were drug addicts lost to him years ago. They didn't want to be found and he'd given up searching for them. One was in prison for murder and wouldn't see the light of day until she passed her fiftieth birthday. The next to the youngest accepted his offer of help to go through a drug rehab program. After a year, she was back on the streets and finally had moved away from under his watchful eye.

Jeremy agonized over his failure. He had failed to care for his siblings in the way his parents would have wanted. It was with a vengeance that he tried to save his baby sister. He was successful in getting her into program after program, each time thinking that it would be the last. He'd been thankful that at last she was free from drugs. She'd left her husband, got a job in that store and was planning a future for herself that didn't involve getting high. She'd changed neighborhoods and friends. She was doing so well and he was feeling so proud of himself for hanging in there with her.

At last he could hold his head up, walk proudly into the station house and not worry that he had to go out on a call only to have to arrest his own sister.

A dark cloud passed over his face. But it happened. Just the way he had envisioned. Only there was no arrest. He'd got the word in the station house as he was going off duty. A smart-ass white officer, who in the past, had arrested GeeGee, joked that there was no sense in going home. Jeremy didn't have to worry about GeeGee anymore, because she was resting in the morgue. Jeremy saw red, and decked the man, knocking him cold. That same day, he quit the force.

For two years, working for a firm as a private investigator
he tracked down the man who had murdered his sister. She
was only a teenager who was on her way to making something
good happen in her life. And Adam Stone had taken that away
from her—and once again reminded Jeremy that he'd failed
losing one more sibling to the streets.

Now angry with himself for his stupid actions, he knew that
he should have taken Stone down when he'd had the chance.
That simpering woman would never have been able to identify
him as the murderer. Now he had to strike and disappear. There
was no doubt that his career with Garrison International was
gone. Before the day was over, he knew that his two colleagues
would call a meeting with Lucas. A report would be given
containing their suspicions about the GeeGee Graves case.

Jeremy's lips split in a crooked smile. The tall sly fox had
done his best to keep him from spying the case name, but he
had been too quick for Gus Turner. The smile disappeared.
When unable to contact him, he knew they'd send one team
out to search and others would be ordered to be on the alert
for his appearance on the street. That meant he had to leave
these quarters in a few hours.

Jeremy got up, undressing as he walked to the bathroom.
His forehead was creased with frowns as he tried to think of
a safe house for himself. He had to be settled by nightfall.

As the water broke over his head, a kernel of an idea grew
to the size of an acorn. The more he thought, the more it grew
until he opened his mouth and laughed, ignoring the soapy
bubbles that slid into his mouth. His kernel was now a giant
walnut and his eyes glinted with malice as his brain raced to
fine-tune his plan.

Late Wednesday morning about eleven-thirty, Adam was
finishing up his last personal phone call.

"Yeah, thanks, again, Vic. Appreciate the favor, man." He
listened for a second. "Yeah, straight to my place, tonight. I'm
working late, but I should be there by the time you drop he

off." He paused. "And Vic, remember, to the door?" Satisfied, he hung up.

Gus was busying himself with fine-tuning the report, but he unabashedly listened to every word of Adam's end of the conversation. He raised his head and cocked an eyebrow. "To the door? *Your* door? Tonight?"

Mildly amused because he knew that Gus caught every word, Adam raised a brow. "You heard right."

"Then I must be missing something here or is this too private?" A rare smile reached his eyes. Assuming a crestfallen look, he said, "Definitely no more breakfasts for me? Or anyone else?"

"Affirmative."

After a few minutes, Gus asked, "Calling in some markers?" Vic was a PI that they all called on occasionally.

Adam nodded. "Uh-huh. A few of the guys'll be helping out. I know Lucas can't spare any more men, so this is the next best thing so that she can carry on a normal life. Until . . ." He paused. "Anyway, Vic will relieve Frank who's seeing her to work and who will hang around all day." He shrugged. "It'll have to be this way for as long as it takes. I'm not taking any more chances with her life." He looked hard at his friend.

"I hear that," Gus said in a low voice. "Love can make you do the darnedest things." He shook his head to clear the faraway look in his eyes. "You *are* in love with her?" At his friend's nod, he said, "I'm in your corner." His eyes were hooded briefly before he said, "Second chances are almost nonexistent for some of us."

Adam knew about Gus' wife. He knew the reason for the cold and deadly look in the man's eyes. His jaw grew tight thinking about what he'd do if Sydney were harmed in the slightest way. He thanked God for her and wished that there was some way that Gus could find some inner peace.

"Maybe," he responded. "But life is a mysterious walk. You never know what's going to hit you when you round the next corner."

Gus gathered some papers together and put them in a folder, then stood. "Time to see Lucas."

Without a word, Adam stood and followed Gus out the door.

Lucas was on the phone. Adam and Gus listened, both wearing expressionless masks, but one's thoughts mirrored the other's as occasionally they exchanged glances.

Lucas hung up the phone and reared back in his chair, a sober look on his face as he looked at his officers. After he'd read their report, he had it faxed to Lincoln Yates who read it personally and who had called Lucas immediately upon finishing.

"No bones about it, Lincoln's got a bug up his butt for that sloppy oversight on Gage's application. He's really kicking himself because he gave the guy high marks after interviewing him."

Adam shrugged. "Some things fly. He should know that."

"Yeah," Lucas grunted. "Anyway, he put a priority one code on this. Everything else takes a backseat. As safely as we can manage. No one is to ignore potentially life-threatening situations in whatever case they may be working on. You two will continue to work on this." He eyed Adam. "Even though you're the primary target, you're still the better judge at the way this man is going to go."

"Are we so sure of that?" Gus spoke frankly.

"Why not?" Lucas' tone was sharp.

Adam looked at Gus knowing exactly what he meant. He answered Lucas. "Because if we are looking for Gage, he knows that by now. Nobody knows what his next move will be. He has to change his game plan and get out fast. When he left this office, he knew that my partner here," he nodded toward Gus, "was on to him." He paused. "Lincoln may have messed up on not fine-tooth-combing Jeremy's essay on the application, but he never hired any dummies." He paused again. "It would do all of us good if we remembered that when we begin the hunt. None of us was the wiser all these years, thinking that Reynard was alive and well and after me."

Lucas nodded in agreement. "Good point." He frowned. "But who in the hell would've thought that that was what was going on." He grunted in frustration. "Okay, so do you two want to waste the time checking out his digs? Or do you want another team to work that while you and Gus take a different tack?" He stared at Adam.

Adam thought, then said, "No. We'll take that. Never know what the landlord might offer." He acknowledged Gus' nod of agreement.

"Okay, get the ball rolling and keep me up to date." His voice halted the two men at the door.

"Gus, Lincoln sent a message."

Gus turned, looking curious.

"Mrs. King wants to get in touch with you. Wants to thank you personally, she said." Lucas saw the guarded look quickly enter Gus' eyes and he held on to an impending smile. What was it about these two deadly looking guys that attract the women? he thought. With a straight face and bland voice, he added, "Both suspects have been apprehended and are being held under arrest. Kyla positively identified the one who took her away from the camp."

Gus looked relieved. "That's good news."

Adam was watching his friend closely.

Lucas tore a page off his notepad and extended it to Gus. "Here. Lincoln was firm on policy in not giving out private numbers. She left hers *and* her private number at the bank." Lucas still hid the smile as Gus pocketed the note and walked back to the door.

"Thanks," Gus said and walked out.

Adam, lifting a shoulder at Lucas, a you-got-me look on his face, closed the door softly behind him.

At the elevator, Gus was silent, staring at the floor numbers zooming by.

"Private number?" Adam asked.

"Ah-huh," Gus answered. He stepped inside the elevator.

"It was like that?" Adam asked.

Gus turned a sharp look on his friend. "You know better than that. I was on assignment."

Adam stared straight ahead. He thought of a time when he was on assignment and had gotten sucker-punched by big dark brown eyes. He glanced at the silent Gus. Mrs. King must be a special kind of woman to have seen beyond the rock-hard exterior to glimpse the real Augustus Turner. Adam hoped his friend wasn't having an "age" thing regarding a relationship. Although Carrie King, at forty-one, was only three years his senior, she obviously didn't have a problem with that.

"Go for it, man," Adam said softly. "Take that walk around the corner. Second chances?"

Gus' face showed no emotion at Adam's words, and his eyelids shuttered his thoughts as he remembered thinking about her—fleetingly—in the past few weeks. And now? Maybe there was something to second chances. He threw Adam a look. "Just might be something to that, Adam." He stared straight ahead. "Just might be."

Sydney was ending her day at 9:30. She had spent the day checking her stock and conferring with Mason on any special dishes that he was planning. Her eyes were tired and so were her feet. She could hardly wait to take a hot bath. A devilish thought entered her mind when she envisioned strong brown hands lathering her body with scented gel. She flushed as the memory caused her nipples to tingle against the lace of her bra.

Anxious to get to Adam's apartment where she would stay the night, she reached in her purse for her escort's cell-phone number. At first she'd been embarrassed at taking up their time, but soon realized that Adam was doing what he thought best to protect her. She let him have his way, knowing he was acting out of his love for her. She agreed to staying at his place tonight simply because she wanted to fall asleep in his arms. She'd heard his small sigh of relief when she'd accepted his invitation.

Sydney was dialing Vic's number when the door opened. Mason was standing there with a stricken look on his face. She hung up the phone.

"Mason?" Her throat went dry. "What is it?"

He closed the door and crossed the room to sit down. "Do you remember a Joe Walker?"

"That's Reva's friend." Sydney's eyes widened. "Why?" she breathed.

"He just called me." Mason jerked his head toward the kitchen. "He left a message for you this morning. When you didn't return his call, he thought you wanted nothing to do with him or Reva, so he called me." He stared at Sydney. "He wanted to know if you've seen Reva."

"What?"

"She left him a week ago, saying she needed to think about her life. She felt as if she was running in place." His voice was strained when he asked, "You haven't heard from her?"

"Mason, you know as sure as you're sitting there, half scared to death, that I would have told you something like that! What kind of question is that?" A worried look filled her eyes. "What's happened to her?" she asked in a shaky voice. Then her eyes lit up. "Ferne. She must have gone to Ferne's."

Mason looked skeptical. "Ferne would have called you."

"Maybe. Maybe not." She picked up the phone and dialed Ferne's number."

"Ferne? Have you heard from Reva?" Sydney asked in a rush.

"Sydney?" Ferne frowned, the happy smile dying on her lips when she first heard her friend's voice. "What are you talking about? She's not there yet?"

"What are *you* talking about?" asked a surprised Sydney. "Yet?" She looked at Mason, shaking her head in puzzlement.

Ferne took a deep breath. "She called me two days ago. She didn't say where she was, but she was heading home to New York. She realized that she'd been a fool to toss away a valued friendship. She's done a lot of thinking about it and wants to see you and apologize." Ferne hesitated. "She wanted to surprise you and swore me to zipped lips." Her voice shook a little. "She should have been there."

After asking about Edward and Amalia, Sydney hung up, promising to keep Ferne informed. She turned worried eyes to Mason and quickly repeated all that Ferne had told her. "What happened to her?'' She shivered as her imagination went over-board, envisioning everything from a car wreck to an abduction. But where?

Mason wearily rubbed his forehead. He wished he had an answer and he also wished that the flutter that had started in his gut would disappear.

''She's probably somewhere close by taking deep breaths. You'll hear something tonight.'' He wished he felt as convinced as he sounded. He stood up. ''I've gotta get back.'' At the door, he turned and said, ''Call me when you hear anything.''

Sydney looked at him. ''You do the same?''

''You know it.'' He closed the door softly behind him.

Troubled, Sydney picked up the phone and dialed her num-ber, hoping that there would be a message from Reva. She listened. Besides Joe's message, there were no other calls. Sydney hung up the phone, refusing to think the worst again. Surely her friend was okay. Suddenly, her eyes glittered. Of course! *She's at her old apartment. What a dummy, you are, Sydney Cox,* she chastised herself. Her excitement died. She was no longer a contributing roommate so why would she go there? *Reva Fairchild, what's happened to you?* Sydney wondered, the tiny nuggets of fear entering her mind once again.

Sydney dialed her escort's number. She needed Adam and she prayed that his late night was ended by the time she arrived at his apartment. Only the warmth of his arms around her, shooting those delicious rivulets of heat waves into her body, would warm her through and through tonight.

CHAPTER
TWENTY-ONE

Jeremy had a sardonic smile on his face as he watched from the shadows deep into the lounge room of the Restaurant Louise. Dressed in black, he was an unobtrusive figure among similarly clothed men. He'd ensconced himself earlier in the darkened corner where he had an unobstructed view of the entrance to the dining room—and the movements of Sydney. He knew when she left the room completely, could see her when she and the maître d' conferred and could see when she left the restaurant for the night, taking the down escalator.

Earlier, after he had showered, changed and packed his luggage, he'd taken the train, rather than a cab, downtown. He didn't want the two big men to trace his cab ride to the Hotel Margit where he'd checked in under an assumed name. Once settled in, he'd made several discreet phone calls. When finished, he knew exactly where Adam and his buddy were and he knew what they knew about Jeremy and GeeGee Gage-Graves. What had surprised him and made him chuckle with glee was the strong-arms that Stone had acquired to guard his lover. Calling in markers, was he? Jeremy was hidden from view when Sydney entered the hotel lobby alongside a private investigator whom he recognized. He was familiar with some of the PIs from the local investigative agency. Common sense told him that a different body would be picking her up late tonight and Jeremy made it a point that he would be around when her new escort arrived. It was too late to risk making more phone calls. He was on his own from now until the end of his business in New York City.

As Jeremy watched from the lounge, he was not disappointed in his long vigil. He immediately recognized the investigator who stepped off the escalator and walked toward the entrance to the dining room. Vic Muncie. Jeremy's eyes crinkled. Adam was as crafty as his reputation. Vic was no lightweight and was as shrewd as they come, he thought. He saw Sydney tentatively approach the big man. After he pulled something from his pocket and spoke to her, he saw her smile with relief, say something in answer, then walk by his side as they headed for the down escalator.

Jeremy left the lounge, but instead of following the couple, headed for the hotel garage. The car he rented in yet another assumed name was necessary to facilitate his movement around the city, and provide a crucial means to a quick exodus.

Expertly and adroitly maneuvering the dark vehicle through the crowded streets, Jeremy parked around the corner on Second Avenue. It was 10:30 when he signed a third assumed name in the guest book and took the elevator to the eighth floor. Riding alone, there was no one to see the evil glint in his eyes. This time, there would be no more games with the smart sophisticate that Stone fancied. Jeremy's lips parted. The only regret that he would have was that Stone would never have time to mourn. Just before the man took his last breath in a few hours, Jeremy would let Adam know that his lover was already waiting for him in the great beyond. His smirk widened. Just one last twist of the knife in revenge for GeeGee.

Jeremy stepped off the elevator, watchful, listening, then entered Sydney's apartment the same way he had before. He smirked after closing the door, locking it, and in the dark, waited, suddenly experiencing déjà vu.

* * *

Reva Fairchild sat in the corner restaurant on East Seventy-second Street, toying with a second cup of coffee, letting it grow cold, as she did the first. Running her hand across her face, then resting her elbow on the table, she cupped her chin while she thought. She grimaced, muttering under her breath, "How much more time do you need, dummy?" For the last two days, she'd been holed up in her motel room out at LaGuardia Airport, thinking. She had refused to come into the city just in case she chickened out and wanted to take flight again. When she'd called Ferne from the airport on her layover flight from California to Arizona, she'd thought then of returning to Joe. But she nixed that idea. She'd taken advantage of Joe's good nature long enough, playing with his infatuation with her. She no longer wanted to string him along, letting him think that he had a chance with her, eventually claiming her as his wife.

Reva signaled the waitress for another cup of coffee. When it arrived, she sipped the hot, strong, brew. Here she was just past her thirty-second birthday, lonely, no man, no job and one less friend in her life. A friend that she'd embarrassed, yelled at and wronged with her wild and thoughtless accusations. If Sydney never spoke to her again, she wouldn't be surprised.

Reva's eyes clouded as she sipped from her cup. How long has it been? Twelve? Thirteen years since they first met? And inseparable? How foolish to treat a valued friendship so shabbily. How foolish of her not to have acknowledged her friend's forgive-and-forget request. Reva stood. It was time to stop playing the great procrastinator and imitating Rodin's famous sculpture, *The Thinker*. It was now or never. *She should be home by now,* Reva thought as she walked out the door. An anonymous call made to the restaurant informed her that Sydney had left for the night. Pushing her long hair off her face and straightening her shoulders, Reva walked resolutely to Sydney's apartment building.

* * *

"Yeah, there'll be a change in plans for tomorrow, Vic. I'll call you." Adam closed the door, then went and sat down beside Sydney on the sofa. He gave her a thoughtful look. "What's wrong?"

Sydney clutched his hand in hers, nervously, rubbing her thumb across his knuckles. She raised worried eyes to his questioning ones. Sydney smiled, then quickly kissed his inviting lips. "Can't put anything over on you, can I?" she asked playfully.

"Do you want to?" He wondered where that came from, and waited.

"No, love. That was a poor attempt at a little humor. Especially when I'm not really feeling so jovial."

"Want to talk about it?" Must be a job problem, he thought. Neither Frank nor Vic had reported anything negative happening today.

"Joe Walker called Mason tonight."

Adam's lightning memory pulled up the name. Joe Walker, Reva's friend in California. "Why?" He already guessed that it had to be about Reva Fairchild. A pair of dark, bewildered eyes, was also dredged up from his memory banks.

"Reva's missing."

Adam's lashes flickered, but he remained silent.

Sydney explained, telling him all that she'd learned from Mason and from Ferne. Her voice broke on a note of hopelessness and she splayed her hands indicating her helpless feeling. "What can anyone do to help her if she doesn't reach out?" Sydney asked in a frustrated voice.

Adam kissed her brow and pressed her hand. "Not a thing. She has to want your help. Until then, you wait and do nothing."

"That's so cold, Adam," Sydney said.

"But the practical truth," Adam replied, quietly.

"She must be so confused. I wonder what's going on in her mind." Sydney smiled at Adam. "You've never met her, but I think the two of you would get on well. I wish things could have been different these past two months, when you and I became . . . lovers." She flushed when Adam gave her a lingering kiss.

"Why?" Adam kissed her again on her cheek.

"Oh, I don't know," sighed Sydney. "Just to experience the feeling of completeness in my life. Loving you. Having my old friend Mason, and my new friends at work, Ferne Marsh, although she's so far away . . . Reva coming back would complete the circle."

"Could happen sooner than you think. Didn't Ferne say she was headed back to New York?"

"Uh-huh," Sydney answered, nodding her head. "But that was two days ago. No telling what went through her head at the last minute. Who knows where she could be now."

Adam stood. "Don't think the worst. She'll be okay. You would have heard something by now if she wasn't." He was standing by the refrigerator. "How about a drink? Wine? Or would coffee do it for you?"

"Wine, thanks," Sydney replied.

Adam selected a Pinot Grigio, a crisp, dry white that he knew Sydney liked.

When he was seated again, after tasting the chilled beverage, Adam set his glass on the table. Waiting until Sydney savored the first sip, he took her glass from her hands and set it on the table.

"Sydney," he said, as she looked at him, "I have to tell you something." His voice was as somber as the look in his eyes.

Sydney stared at him, suddenly fearful. She'd never seen his eyes look so troubled. Cold and hard, yes, but now he was apparently struggling with something personal. "Yes?" she whispered, almost wanting to hug him against her chest.

Suddenly, Adam stood and paced the room, raking his hand over his hair. Finally, he stopped, settling himself on the arm of the easy chair. He crossed his arms across his chest and stared down at her.

"What is it, Adam?" Sydney murmured.

"I have to leave the country." He winced at the expression of abandonment that appeared in her eyes.

"What?" She could hardly catch her breath and she had to stop herself from clutching at her heart. What was he saying?

"I'm not leaving until after this—after my case is wrappe
up. When my would-be killer is caught and put away, then I'
have to leave for another assignment."

"Where?" Sydney asked.

"Madrid."

"Spain?"

"Yes," Adam answered quietly. He stayed where he wa
until she sorted her thoughts.

Sydney looked away, staring at nothing. She couldn't thin
about him being so far away from her. What was it people sai
about long-distance relationships? Forget about it! She turne
her gaze to him as he watched her so intensely.

"There's no way that you can be reassigned?" Her voic
sounded bleak.

Adam shook his head. "Lincoln mapped everything out i
a conference call with us tonight. Gus and I are needed for thi
job." He hesitated. "Originally, Jeremy Gage and Gus wer
the team, but now," he shrugged, "I'm the replacement fo
Gage."

Sydney wondered what had happened that Gage was nov
on another assignment. She voiced her thought and Adan
answered.

"Gage is our suspect, Sydney." He slipped into the chair
steepling his fingers as he rested his elbows on the arms. "W
believe he's been pretending to be Ethan Reynard all thes
years. Somehow he found out that Reynard was dead. We thin
he's the man that attacked us in your apartment." He explaine
all that they had dug up on Gage and his reason for hunting
down Adam.

Sydney's eyes grew wide at the incredible story. Jeremy, the
killer? Right under their noses all this time? She shuddered t
think that she'd been alone with the man, and trusting that he
was protecting Adam. "Does he know?" she asked in a steady
voice.

"Yes, he knows we're looking for him."

"My God." She looked toward the window. "Do you think
that he'll try coming here again? Wouldn't that be pretty risky?"

"He knows that." Adam was quiet and after a moment, he

said, "Don't worry about Gage right now." His look was intense when he added, "I want to talk about us."

"Us?"

"I don't want to leave you."

"But you must," Sydney added, flatly. *A man's got to do his job, right?* she asked herself. She was immediately sorry for her selfish and self-pitying thought.

"I must. It's what I do, Sydney," Adam said in a firm tone. She nodded, suddenly feeling miserable.

Adam wanted to go to her, and hold her tight. But he wanted her answer to be uninfluenced by soft kisses and caresses and sweet murmurs in her ear. He'd thought long and hard about his decision and he had to steel himself against her answer.

"Sydney," he said, raspy-voiced, "I want you to go with me."

"Madrid?" Sydney was dumbfounded.

Adam nodded. "As my wife." He took a deep breath as he heard her surprised gasp. "Will you marry me, Sydney?"

"Marry?" Sydney stood, her mouth suddenly dry. She walked to the kitchen and soon cold water was soothing her throat. She walked back and sat down on the sofa. *Marry him and leave the country?* "But you won't be staying there, will you?"

"I've committed to two years." Adam watched the panoply of emotions on her face. He was staunch in keeping his own emotions hidden, because if she refused him, he wouldn't know how to keep the demons inside of him quiet and scare her half to death.

Sydney's eyes teared. Why was she taking so long in answering this man that she loved? When she knew that he'd been wounded, each minute she had died a little until she knew that he would live. She answered the question that had been orbiting inside her head like a potter's wheel gone crazy. Could she really live here while he was there? A definitive *no* resounded against her eardrums. She looked at Adam who was wearing his professional look of indifference and she smiled. She went to him.

Adam watched her come to him as if she were unreal. He

imagined reaching for her and watching her disappear as if she'd never existed. He waited, with closed hands.

Sydney sat down on Adam's lap and wrapped her arms around his neck. She bent and whispered in his ear. "Some of the best vineyards in the world exist in Spain." She cocked her head and added, "Of course I'll marry you."

Adam let out a breath and buried his head in the softness of her neck. "Jesus," he breathed. After a minute, he looked into her eyes. "You'll marry me only to trample through vineyards?" He saw the twinkle in her eye. He hugged her waist, squeezing the tender flesh around her middle.

"Is that the only reason?" Adam whispered in her ear. The expected shudder that coursed through her body brought a smile to his lips. God, how he loved this woman! His own insides warmed at her touch and the feel of her soft curves pressing against his belly. He held on tightly unless he began to think that it was all a dream.

Sydney cupped Adam's chin, forcing him to look at her. "No, love. Who was it that said he's created the world's greatest tease?" She smiled and kissed his lips. "I love you, Adam Stone. You've stolen my heart, you know. What will I do with you leaving me here and traveling across the world with my heart in your pocket? I'd just die."

Adam closed his eyes. What in the world had he done right to attract the eye and capture the love of this beautiful creature? Whatever it was, he prayed that it would always remain a part of him. He held her head against his chest, smoothing the wispy curls from her face. He kissed the top of her head, inhaling the soft scent that he loved. He would forever associate the clean smell of heather with her hair and soft skin.

"I love you, Sydney," he murmured. "Don't worry about your heart. It will always be safe with me." He kissed her forehead.

Adam and Sydney sat for a long time holding on, neither wanting to stir from the warm comfort of the other's arms. Finally, desire and the natural need to express their passion led them to the darkened bedroom where behind the firmly closed door, and amid the dancing shadows, they loved.

CHAPTER TWENTY-TWO

Reva entered the building, surprised at the new sign-in setup. 'And long overdue,'' she said to the stern-faced man at the door. ''And a welcome change,'' she flung over her shoulder as she walked to the elevator.

Reva dug in her bag and found her ring of keys. She'd never given Sydney her spare key and now she hoped that her friend hadn't changed the locks. Reva had decided if Sydney hadn't arrived, there was no turning back. She wasn't leaving. If she left, she didn't know whether she would have the courage to return. So she would just let herself in and surprise Sydney—and prayed that it wouldn't be the biggest mistake that she'd ever make.

Everytime Jeremy heard the elevator come and go, he was alert for the muffled sound of footsteps coming his way. He frowned when there was no sound for seconds after he heard the faint whine of the car motor fade, and wondered what she was waiting for. He heard the soft tingle of keys jingling together and he relaxed his body, ready to strike and get out. *What was taking her so long? Doesn't she know her own door*

key? Instead of standing behind the door, he stood flattene
against the wall by the light switch. When she reached out, h
would grab her arm. Then it would be over and he would b
out the door and on the way to his main prey. She would neve
know who or what hit her. He held the sharp-edged knif
tightly, the gleam of the blade glinting softly in the dark roon

Reva had the key at the lock but had inserted it wrong. Sh
removed it and tried again. This time the lock turned and sh
twisted the doorknob to enter. Just before she pushed the doc
open, she heard the elevator motor start. Hurriedly she pushe
in the door, not knowing if the car would stop with her still i
the hallway. She didn't relish the idea of running into a strange
She knew that that was the one thing that Sydney feared. Sh
reached for the light switch and was stunned when she wa
immediately grabbed by the wrist. She screamed, dropping he
shoulder bag and nylon duffel bag. The metal luggage cart fe
in the doorway. She tried to back away, stumbling over th
fallen bags and the cart wheels, at the same time a strong arr
tried to pull her inside the dark apartment. Instinctively, Rev
grabbed the door frame and dug her heels in the floor.

"Help!" Reva screamed at the same time she heard th
muffled curse coming from her attacker. The powerful ma
now had her by her long hair, finding it hard to lift her ove
the fallen bags, his feet getting tangled up in the cart. He trie
to kick them out of his way, swearing all the time, calling he
vile names. She caught the look of stunned surprise on his face
vaguely thinking that she'd never seen him before and stupidly
what was he doing in her friend's apartment?

She saw the flash of the knife as he bodily lifted her, strug
gling with her height and the hold she had on the door frame
refusing to be pulled inside the apartment. He slashed at he
arm, then suddenly, her back was against his chest and his arr
was around her neck. Just as the cold steel of the knife touche
her throat, the elevator door opened exposing the attack to tw
astonished women.

All Reva remembered was the stinging warmth on her necl
as she was released and violently pushed toward the strangers
As her eyes closed on black and muted red floating fog, th

sound of high-pitched screams rent the air like the furious cry of a thousand angered bats.

Adam sat up immediately, the green digital numbers shining eerily in the dark, but turning to normal when he turned on the light. It was 2:33 A.M. when he picked up the telephone receiver. He felt Sydney stir and awaken.

"Hello?" he said cautiously. All senses were primed and ready for anything.

"Adam, this is Mason Wingate." He paused. "If Sydney is there, I must talk to her." Hesitating, he added in a calmer voice. "Reva's been found."

Adam stiffened. *What's that supposed to mean? Is she alive or dead?* he questioned himself. Without replying, he handed the phone to a scared Sydney, who watched him with fearful eyes. "It's Mason." He took her hand in his and watched her closely.

"Mason?" Sydney held her breath. "What's wrong?"

"Reva is in Lenox Hill Hospital. She was attacked entering your apartment," Mason said quickly. *Might as well tell her everything,* he thought. "Her throat was cut and she's in surgery now."

"Oh my God!" Sydney yelled. Tears sprang to her eyes and she dropped the phone. She threw off the covers and stumbled to the bathroom.

Adam picked up the phone. "Tell me what you told her," he demanded. As he listened, Adam's eyes grew cold and dark. Had not Sydney been in his bed, she would have been the one in surgery right now, or worse. He watched as she climbed back in bed. He handed her the phone.

"Mason," Sydney said, her voice trembling. "Is she . . . she going to . . ."

"I don't know anything. No one's come to tell me a thing."

"I'm coming to be with you, Mason. Wait for me." She got the floor location and then hung up.

Adam was already in the bathroom. When he returned he was half-dressed. "You okay?" he asked gruffly. He still had a hard time dealing with the other alternative had she gone home.

Sydney was dressing. She passed by Adam, and stood on her toes to kiss his mouth. She nodded. "I'm okay," she murmured. She didn't have to ask him to accompany her. He probably would have been insulted had she voiced the question.

Before they left the apartment, Adam pulled her close in a tight embrace. "I'm glad you're here." His voice broke as he just rocked her in his arms.

Even through his lightweight jacket, Sydney could feel the quiver in his chest. She realized that she had been the intended victim and he was scared to death at what could have happened. She hugged him tightly around his waist, grateful to be alive. But her eyes clouded at the beautiful woman who had been mistaken for her. What could she ever say or do if Reva Fairchild died in her place?

"Who called you?" Sydney asked Mason. They'd arrived fifteen minutes earlier, and he had led them to chairs in the corridor. She and Adam listened as he explained.

Mason looked weary. He rubbed his forehead now as he talked. "Through the most unlikely roundabout way of my job. Since it was Sydney's apartment, the building management contacted her emergency person. Only, one of them was the victim. I was listed next, but they only had my work number. After a slew of calls, they reached me." He looked at Adam. "The scenario was the same when I tried to find you." He slid down in the chair and crossed one ankle over the other. "It took some doing as you know to get your number." He shrugged. "That's it." He stared down the long corridor. "We just wait."

Sydney held Adam's hand. She felt a twinge in her chest as she looked at her friend. He was hurting for Reva. One thought sped through her mind and that was she hoped that Mason would speak his mind to Reva if she survived. The look on his face gave away how deeply he cared.

"She was coming to stay with me," Sydney said softly. "She'd forgiven me."

"Apparently," Mason replied. He'd explained how the superintendent had found her before the ambulance arrived. The two frightened women had stayed with Reva while other floor residents called 911 at hearing the commotion. The would-be killer, after pushing Reva into the startled women, had raced to the exit door leading to the stairs and disappeared. The super had put the luggage in the apartment and secured the door. "She obviously has no place else to go, Sydney." He stared pointedly at his friend.

Sydney looked helplessly at Mason. "I just don't understand." Her voice sounded puzzled. "She's so intelligent, a talented teacher, business smart and so savvy in many ways. How could she let her life fall into such shambles?" She lifted a shoulder and spread her hand in a gesture of futility.

Mason stared at Sydney, remembering a time when she had gone to pieces. But she'd bounced back on her own. For some people it was easier. Soon afterward, the protective man beside her had walked into her life. He answered in a matter-of-fact tone. "Things happen to us that are least expected." He looked expectantly toward the sound of muffled footsteps on the polished floor. "She'll be okay." He stood. He knew that she would be, from the look on the doctor's face as she approached.

All three wore concerned expressions as the doctor explained the extent of Reva's injuries.

"She was deeply slashed on her arm, requiring twenty stitches and it is not life-threatening," explained Dr. Davis. "The cut on her throat required many more and will leave a permanent scar. But she's a lucky woman and she'll be grateful that she's still with us when she awakens. The blade of the knife had not plunged deeply enough and was at the wrong angle to do severe damage. Had the attacker had a good hold on her, nothing could have prevented major damage from being deadly. Appears she was really struggling to live."

"Can we see her?" Sydney asked.

The doctor nodded. "Just to look. After she awakes, one at a time for short periods."

Adam and Mason watched through the glass wall as Sydney stood by Reva's bedside. After a long while, she bent and kissed her cheek, then turned away.

"You all right?" Adam asked. She was holding back her tears.

Sydney nodded. "Okay," she murmured. She turned to Mason. "Will you stay?" When he nodded, she turned to Adam. "I want to stay, too," she said.

Adam checked his watch. It was almost three-twenty. He didn't want to leave her alone, but he guessed this was the safest place for her right now.

"Okay," he answered. "I'll be back for you. Don't leave until Gus and I get here."

Sydney knew that he'd called his partner and his boss. Whatever they planned, he hadn't discussed it with her. She said, "I'll be here." She put her arms around his neck and kissed him tenderly. "Be careful, love," she whispered.

Adam whispered back, "Why wouldn't I be? We have a date, don't we?" He winked at her, waved to Mason and walked hurriedly down the corridor.

Gus was waiting for him in the hospital lobby. "Anything?" Adam asked when he reached him.

"*Nada.* Nothing," Gus answered in disgust. "You'd think with all the witnesses who described the same guy, we'd have something more concrete . . . like what color car he jumped into." He scratched behind his ear. "A black man running through these streets like demons were after him, hardly disappears without somebody seeing how he escaped. Car, subway, helicopter!" He snorted in disgust. "So where do you want to take it from here?"

"Like we discussed," Adam replied, "it's me he's coming after. After missing Sydney, he's probably enraged at the double cross. She was going to be his last little dig in my side. Failing that, he doesn't have the time to try again. For now Sydney is safe."

They walked outside the building. It was quiet except for a few workers coming and going.

"Like Lucas suggested, I should go it alone, without you

guys at my back. It's the only way to draw him out. He's mad
enough to do something stupid.''

Gus gave a short laugh. ''Yeah, like walking up to us right
now and asking, 'How y'all doing?' ''

Adam didn't smile. ''That's not so far-fetched.''

Gus grew serious. ''All too true.'' Grimly, he thought of just
such instances where they'd been taken by surprise by crafty
suspects. As they stood there, two Garrison officers arrived.
They spoke briefly to Adam and then disappeared into the
hospital.

''Okay, let's go to my car,'' Gus said. ''In case he's watching,
he'll wonder why you're leaving Sydney alone.''

''He'll realize that she's not alone and that there're too many
ways he could get trapped in there,'' Adam added.

''Right.'' Gus unlocked the doors and they both slid inside
the car. ''He'll decide to follow us.''

Adam nodded and they drove in silence to his apartment—
and to whatever fate awaited him at the hands of Jeremy Gage.

Who the hell was that? Furious, Jeremy raced down the exit
stairs, past the doorman and out the building, only minutes
after he slashed her throat. Running toward Second Avenue
instead of heading toward his car, he raced for two blocks
before he slowed to a walk. Although it was midnight, the
streets were crowded with sleepless New Yorkers, looking for
God only knew what this time of morning. He looked out of
place, dressed all in black, amongst the summery-clad crowd.
He ducked into the shadowy recess of a deserted storefront and
sat down, head on his drawn-up knees, assuming the posture
of a sleepy street person. Out of one cocked eye, he saw people
pass without giving him a backward glance.

Finally, after all seemed quiet and he didn't notice any cruis-
ing company cars, he unfolded himself and walked to his car
at the same pace as the other night people. Once inside, he was
as anonymous as anyone else driving an American-made dark-
colored car. Jeremy even boldly slowed down as he passed
Seventy-second Street, taking a very deep interest in the Lenox

Hill Hospital ambulance that was just careening out of the block. He drove past the commotion-filled block, noting that they had gotten there quick. They'd come and did what they had to do in thirty minutes.

Deciding that he was safe for now, with all the officers concerned with that strange woman, Sydney Cox and Adam, he had an unexpected breather. He returned to the Hotel Margit where he could think uninterrupted. The restaurant was closed, so there was no chance of running into anyone who would be looking for him.

Hours later, Jeremy checked out of the hotel. He was dressed for travel in an unassuming dark navy nylon warm-up suit. It was just after 3:00 A.M. when he drove the quiet streets uptown to the hospital. The Seventy-seventh Street entrances were brightly lit as he expected and the street itself offered no shadowy space to remain incognito. He made a right on Park Avenue.

Jeremy had long ago reasoned that the strange woman had to be a good friend of the Cox woman. Who else would have her own key? He surmised that by now, Sydney must know about the attack. Or killing? And she would definitely head for the hospital. And where Sydney was, Adam would be. All Jeremy needed was a glimpse of either of them and then he would know how to move.

Not long after Jeremy parked himself in the shrubbery on the corner of Park Avenue, his uncomfortable vigil paid off. There was no mistaking the two figures who stood outside the main hospital entrance. They were joined by two Garrison officers who then went inside, leaving Adam and Gus standing on the sidewalk. He watched the scene, thoughtfully, finally ascertaining the meaning behind the actions. When they walked to Gus' car, Jeremy swore. Which way would they go? If they went straight ahead and turned on Fifth Avenue, he would lose them. On the other hand if they made a right on Park, he had them covered. But why head uptown if they were headed for Adam's?

Jeremy was crouched low on the passenger's side of his car, barely able to see out. He waited until several changes of the light, when he saw Gus drive by. Jeremy slid behind the wheel and started the engine. After several turns, he was headed downtown for Adam's apartment. He was there when he saw Gus drop Adam off and drive away before his colleague was inside the front door. He watched as Adam looked up and down the street, waited for a minute and then go inside.

Jeremy saw the lights go on in the bedroom. He grinned. The man was a creature of habit; walking through the dark room until he reached the bedroom to give himself light. Bad habits died hard.

Gus was driving downtown on Park, when he frowned. He didn't like Lucas' and Adam's plan. Jeremy Gage was like an enraged bull now and liable to go berserk. If he did, how many innocents would get hurt? Leaving Adam completely unprotected, in his opinion was stupid, but he had been out-voted. He shook his head. "This doesn't feel right," he muttered. He glanced at his watch: four-ten. Lucas would still be awake he surmised. Picking up his cell phone, he pressed Lucas' number.

"Lucas, Gus here," he said when his boss answered. "My gut tells me something's wrong." He hesitated. "Are you certain you pulled everyone from Adam?"

Lucas heard the concern in the big man's voice. He quickly thought back to a time when he was a field operative and he'd had those same feelings. He said, "Yeah. Everyone's gone They all checked in." He paused. "What do you think's going on?"

"I don't know," Gus said slowly. "I was just thinking that since he's got to make a swift move on Adam and then hightail it out of here, he's hardly going to spend days waiting for the opportune moment. He's got to make that moment happen for him at his discretion, not ours." He added, "And, like yesterday!"

Lucas pondered the man's words. Everything he said, rang true. But as crafty as Gage was, he would spot a Garrison man

in a heartbeat and the whole idea was to give him enough rope
to get careless.

"I don't know, Gus. The way we planned it is the best way
to smoke Gage out."

Gus grunted in frustration.

"But," Lucas said, "what you're saying has a whole lot of
merit." He thought. "Okay, suppose we make it a one-man
surveillance. You. Provided," he added with emphasis, "you
play it close."

Exactly what he wanted, Gus breathed to himself. "Thanks,
Lucas. I'm on my way."

"Gus," Lucas said quickly, "take it slow out there."

"Gotcha," Gus said and ended the connection. He'd been
driving as slowly as he could and he was now in lower Manhattan. He had more than thirty blocks to cover back uptown. In
seconds he was headed back to Sixty-first Street, talking out
loud. "Like old times, Adam. I got your back. Let's hope I'm
right on the money."

Adam turned on the bedroom light. He sat down on the
rumpled covers, then fell back against the pillows and closed
his eyes, remembering how his covers had gotten so messed
up. *What a fine woman I fell for,* he thought. Soon to be
mine forever. He knew that whatever happened now—and he
believed without a doubt that Gage was on his way—that he
would fight to the death to keep himself safe for her. Just the
thought of in years to come, another man holding her, loving
her, because he was dead, was agony to envision. No, he knew
that in the wee hours of this morning, that it was over for
Jeremy Gage; the end coming in whatever manner Gage's
actions dictated. In custody—or dead.

Adam turned out the bedroom light and walked the short
distance to the bathroom. Soon, water was pelting the shower
curtain with the force of a building storm.

Jeremy was in the narrow alleyway making his way stealthily
to the back of the house, curious as to why the bedroom light

went out. He stopped, listening, his eyes adjusting to the black space. The backyard was as dark as a cavern.

From memory, Jeremy felt his way around the small patio and garden chairs, listening for sounds coming from inside the apartment. Feeling his way, he stopped at the back door. He could hear the sounds of running water. He frowned. There was no light visible inside the kitchen. It had to be from the bathroom, he thought. A bathroom without a window! Go figure. Jeremy stood still, cocking his ear to the door. His eyes widened in disbelief. Humming? Startled, he stepped back, bumping into a small table. The scrape on the cement sounded voluminous to his ears. Damn, he swore silently.

Jeremy couldn't believe the man was taking a shower! And singing? A snort of incredulity escaped. Did they think they were dealing with an amateur? His look turned sardonic. Leave it to Lucas and his archaic way of thinking, he thought. Bet old Adam and Gus are fuming at the way the old man is handling this. Jeremy could just hear the man telling his crew to back off—to wait until Jeremy Gage made a new plan.

"Well, old man," Jeremy muttered under his breath, "looks like you blew." Quickly he reached into his pocket and seconds later, the back door lock clicked open with hardly a sound. He pushed in the door and quickly stepped inside, ready to adjust his eyes to the dark. Suddenly, he screamed in pain as something hard came crashing down on his arm. Before he could recover, the door was flung wide open and a fist landed on his jaw, another to his stomach and another to his chin as he tried to recover against the surprise attack. He raised his hand ready to bring down the knife on the flailing body, when another crashing blow knocked the weapon from his hand. Jeremy swore and lunged at Adam, who karate-kicked him in the groin. Jeremy yelled and doubled over. He could barely see among the darkened shadows but he could make out Adam's muscular form as Jeremy dodged another kick and landed one of his own to Adam's midsection.

Adam grunted from the blow but remained on his feet as he body-tackled the man and they both crashed to the floor, slamming against the open door with a resounding bang. Adam shook his head after a swift kick dizzied him, but managed to get in one of his own to the man's broad chest. He could feel the man searching for his dropped knife in between kicks and punches. "Not a chance," he muttered, and catapulted to his feet in a catlike move as his assailant landed another blow to his stomach. Jeremy was on his feet now, swearing his rage. As he reached for Adam again, Adam backed off, pulling his gun. In the dark, he released the safety and Jeremy froze at the tiny sound.

"Give it up, Gage," Adam breathed heavily, while maneuvering toward the light switch. "Just give me the reason to kill you right now," he rasped.

"It'll never happen, Stone." Jeremy's foot lashed out, kicking Adam's hand. He turned and ran out the door, disappearing in the backyard, jumping the low wooden fence. Jeremy raced through the unlocked back door of a tall apartment building.

"Damn you," shouted Adam as he turned on the light, found his gun and gave chase over the fence. He was in time to see the door slowly closing. He raced after Jeremy, rage filling his soul. *You're not getting away from me again. Not again.*

Gus was walking toward Adam's apartment, shaking his head at how the man could fall asleep so fast. He *was* acting the part of a zombie though, Gus mused. He stopped as he heard noise coming from the back of the house. Pulling his gun, he raced to the back only to see the silhouette of Adam jumping over the fence and disappearing.

"Adam," he shouted, and took after him. By the time Gus jumped the fence, he looked quickly down the alley and then at the dim light over the slowly closing door. He headed for the building and slipped inside. He heard racing feet on the cement stairs and running steps on the landings. "Adam," Gus shouted. "Stop, for God's sake." Gus knew that Jeremy had shown up and cursed the minute he'd agreed with Lucas. In his gut he knew that Lucas had made a mistake. Why did he agree to his plan? He raced behind the two men, because he heard two sets of running feet. If Adam caught that man, he would kill him. Gus raced for all he was worth.

Jeremy tried each landing door. "No Entry" was posted on

two floors. He tried the fourth floor, but let the door go as he heard Adam gaining on him. He raced another two floors and at the seventh, he heard Turner's shout. He couldn't help thinking that the man was good! Jeremy now had to get both of them off his back. Forgetting about hiding on one of the floors and making it back down the other side, his best bet was to make it to the roof. There, it would be easy to use the fire escape ladders down to safety. He didn't know how many floors he had to go, but this building wasn't as tall as some of its neighbors, he'd noticed. He was right. There were only twelve floors. He only had to worry about the roof door being locked.

Adam thought that by now Jeremy would have tried to exit on one of the Re-entry floors. He stayed with the sound of running footsteps and wondered at what the man was planning. When he heard Gus calling, he didn't answer, not wanting to give his position away. Jeremy couldn't have known how close Adam was. He raced until he reached the roof stairs. He looked up to see the door ajar.

Adam flattened himself against the wall and took great gulps of air. He bent over, letting the blood rush to his head. He wondered what had happened to his partner. Cautiously, Adam reached the door and slipped outside. The rooftop was illumined by lights from taller neighboring buildings. The city was stirring as people awoke and prepared for work.

Adam's quick gaze searched the corners and he knew Jeremy was hiding behind the chimney stacks or had already escaped down the safety ladder. Suddenly he saw him moving toward the building edge. Adam left his crouched position.

"Stop, Jeremy," he shouted. "Move away from there." He pointed his gun and started to walk toward the man, who kept edging for the ladder. "Don't do it!"

Jeremy was so close to freedom. He would get away this time, same as he did in the past. He was going to see Adam Stone dead if it was his last act on Earth. He turned the rock in his hand into a flying missile as he lifted one leg over the roof edge, grabbing the steel rope ladder.

Adam fired at the thing whizzing toward his face, swiftly wondering if Gage had had another knife. He ducked and the rock slammed against the brick wall. Gage was going over the side and Adam fired again, running toward him.

Gus heard the shots. "Adam, no!" he shouted as he burst through the door.

Jeremy quickly hoisted himself over the side, but miscalculated. "Damn," he swore. He was on the other side of the ladder holding on with one hand while his arm dangled helplessly at his side. He tried to swing his body over to grasp the other steel cable. He looked up to see Adam standing at the edge, his gun aimed at his head. He stared at the man he'd hated for so many years.

Adam stared impassively at the man, who'd made his life hell. Had tortured the woman he loved. Hate burned in his eyes as he watched his hunter swing like a rag doll in the slight breeze of the early morning. Vaguely he sensed Gus at his side but he never moved his position.

"Adam," Gus said softly. "You've got him. Put away your gun."

Jeremy tried swinging again, but missed. His hand was cutting into the cable and he was slipping. Suddenly he closed his eyes and banged his head against the wall. He screamed, his eyes a blaze of hate as he stared toward the sky. "Why are you making me fail again? Why? You made me nothing but a failure!" he yelled. He turned his hate-filled eyes on Adam. "You lose, you damned arrogant, coldhearted killer. You know you murdered my sister . . . shot her down like a dirty dog! Go rot in hell!" With a maniacal laugh, Jeremy suddenly pulled himself up, planted his feet on the brick wall, then pushed away from the building, releasing the cable. He yelled, "GeeG-e-e-e!" He sailed downward, slicing through the rushing air like a black-winged bird. In seconds the morning was still again, and it appeared that the eerie scream and vanished echoes had only been a dream.

Adam lowered his gun and holstered it. He looked down, but barely made out the form of the man below. Only the dull thud of flesh against stone resounded in his ear. He felt a hand on his arm and turned. Gus pulled him away from the edge.

"Come on, buddy, let's go. It's over."

CHAPTER
TWENTY-THREE

Sydney sat in the room by Reva's bed waiting for her to finish dressing. It had been almost two weeks to the day since Reva had nearly been killed. Her wounds were healing and she was fit in every other way. Her disposition and outlook were upbeat. She was fast becoming the old sassy Reva.

The bathroom door opened and Reva appeared, dressed for travel. Her hair hung loose, brushed back off her face.

"You look great," Sydney said.

"Liar," Reva said.

Sydney raised a brow. "Me?"

That brought a wan smile to Reva's lips, and her eyes glistened.

Sydney saw and said, "Don't start," in a watery voice.

"Okay," Reva said and sat down on the bed. She waved a hand. "Well, this is it. Just waiting for my cousin."

The two women looked at each other. They had spent many hours the last few days talking about the hurtful past and their futures. Futures that would find them parted once again.

"You're sure you won't change your mind?" Sydney asked softly. "You're certainly welcome."

Reva shook her head. "No. Staying with my cousins in

Brooklyn is the best thing for me right now. But thanks for the offer. When you leave for Spain in a few weeks, then I'll take over your place. Not before,'' she said firmly. She tilted her head. "Why, you're still courtin'. Picture me trying to cramp Adam's style when he wants to sleep over.''

Sydney smiled. "Light stuff for him. I told you that he was very resourceful.''

Reva laughed. "So you did.'' Then, very softly, she said, "God, I'm going to miss you. So far away!''

"There's always e-mail,'' teased Sydney, a lump forming in her throat.

"Look, Sydney, why don't you go. I'll be fine until Theresa gets here. Next thing you know, I'll be bawling again. Besides, that fine brown man is probably catching a fit downstairs. After all, you've only been up here for an hour.''

Both women laughed.

Sydney stood up and hugged her friend, who responded with a tight hold around her shoulders. "Call me when you get settled,'' she whispered, and left.

Adam stood when he saw her. She had tears in her eyes. He took her hand and they walked outside.

"How is she?'' he asked softly.

Sydney looked at him and smiled. "We're going to be just fine.'' She hugged him around the waist as they walked to his car.

It was two weeks and two days after Labor Day and Sydney couldn't believe that she had been gone that long from Restaurant Louise. The days had passed like a whirlwind as she prepared for her wedding. Tomorrow, she was to be married and the day after, she was flying to Spain with her husband. Benjamin had insisted on throwing a small reception for them. Ferne and Reva would be with her. Edward Percival would give her away and Gus Turner would stand with Adam.

Sydney had just spent some of the happiest days of her life. She and Adam hated to part, even to say good night. Soon, she sighed, there would be no more good-byes.

It was just past nine o'clock. She had showered and slipped into a satin gown when the phone rang.

"Is this really necessary?" Adam growled, when she answered.

Sydney couldn't suppress the soft laugh that escaped. "But we're getting married in the morning, love. Isn't it bad luck to see the bride before the ceremony?"

Adam swore under his breath. "Whoever proved that crazy nonsense?" he said, husky-voiced. "I want you to sleep in my arms tonight," he whispered.

Sydney shivered as that deep-velvet voice did crazy things to her insides. Why she had even suggested this silliness to him was beyond her. Tradition! She wanted to feel him beside her as she dreamed about their future together. Who cared whether they walked into the chapel arm in arm after sleeping breast to chest? Not a soul on this Earth!

"Adam. That was the worst suggestion I've ever made in my life," she commiserated. She sighed. "But I guess I'll just have to live with it." She whispered. "I love you."

"Love you, too," Adam whispered back. After a pause, he asked, "Do you mean that?"

"Of course, I mean it," she said indignantly.

"No, not that," he said, impatiently. "I mean about your suggestion being the worst?"

"Yes," she sighed. "May I bite my tongue if I ever utter such nonsense again."

"Can I be a witness to that?" Adam asked lightly.

"Sadist," Sydney said. "Good night, love. See you in the morning."

"That you will, my sweet," Adam whispered. He hung up his cell phone and got out of the car, then walked from the garage. "Very early in the morning," he said aloud. He was ringing her bell in five minutes flat.

"Adam!?" Sydney said when she heard his voice at her door. She unlocked it and he stood there staring at her with that crooked smile that made her heart jump.

Adam stood with his back to the door. He pulled her in his arms and blew in her ear. "Like that?" He smiled felt her quiver and the tips of her breasts grow rigid against his chest.

He murmured in her ear. "Didn't I tell you that I'd see you in the morning?" He held her by the waist and walked toward the bedroom. "Come, my sweet. It's time to start a new tradition."

And they did.

EPILOGUE

" 'Bye," Sydney called to Gus as he slammed down the trunk then slid behind the wheel. He waved to them and with a broad smile, he pulled off for the airport. The woman beside him and the little girl in the backseat waved until the car disappeared.

Sydney turned to her husband who held her close around the waist. She rested her head on his chest. "I like Carrie King," Sydney said. "And Kyla is just too precious."

Adam was staring thoughtfully after the car. "She's right for him," he said quietly. They turned to go inside the spacious villa they'd rented.

"I'm glad she decided to vacation here. I think Gus was getting a little homesick. Do you think they'll get married?"

Adam shrugged. "Hard to say. But from the looks of him these past three weeks, I wouldn't take a bet on that."

Sydney smiled. It was nearly sunset and she and Adam sat outside watching the sun fade over the horizon in a blaze of red and golden-yellow hues.

It was just more than a year since they'd arrived in Spain last September. Her husband loved his job, recruiting and training special officers for the new office. He looked forward to the next year to be just as rewarding. Sydney was happy in Spain and had loved working at her job, assistant to the sommelier at a fine restaurant.

Adam looked at the smile on his wife's face. "Happy?" he asked, caressing her hand with his thumb.

"Mmm," she murmured, kissing him with her eyes. "Does it show that much?"

He threw her a look. "Is it me, or the coming of some more Americans?" he teased.

Now Sydney did lean over and kiss his delectable lips. "No one can ever make me happier than you can, my love," she whispered. She snuggled against him. "Even though I'm ecstatic that Mason and Reva are coming."

Adam kissed her back. "It's working out between them," he stated.

"Yes. Reva opened up her eyes and saw something that she'd never seen before. A man who was in love with her. Right under her own eyes. She's deliriously happy with her new job as assistant curator with the Brooklyn Museum. History was always her thing." She squeezed his hand. "I'll be happy to see everyone when they arrive for our special event."

Just then they heard the faint sounds coming from inside and they both jumped up. Sydney smiled as Adam beat her to the bedroom. When she reached the doorway, she stood and looked at her family and tears sprang to her eyes.

Adam cradled his three-month-old daughter in his arms, crooning and rocking her back to sleep. He looked down at his wife who rested her head on his shoulder.

He kissed both his ladies on the forehead. His daughter, Dacey, had beautiful dark brown eyes like her mother and was going to be a heart-stealer. Just as her mother had stolen his. He laid his sleeping daughter down then turned to his wife and hugged her close.

"And you're my special event, my love," he murmured in her ear. "For always." He smiled when she quivered.

Dear Reader,

I hope you enjoyed this story of finding love and keeping friendships.

Sydney and Adam were standoffish and unapproachable, each thinking that they were immune to that alien emotion—love. *That* only happens to other folks. Of course they were wrong.

In writing their story, my aim was to convey that a deep and lasting love between two people, can, and does happen—especially to those so unaware of the mysteries of the heart.

A special thanks to all of you who responded so positively and warmly to WHITE LIES, FATHER AT HEART, NIGHT AND DAY and NIGHT SECRETS. Many of you have asked for Dieter Howard and Mari Kincaid's story from NIGHT SECRETS. Thank you, and I certainly will inform you if indeed they begin to take on a life of their own.

As always, I welcome your comments. Please include a self-addressed stamped envelope for a reply.

Thanks for sharing,
Doris Johnson
P.O. Box 130370
Springfield Gardens, NY 11413

About the Author

Doris Johnson lives in Queens, New York with her husband. She is a multipublished author who has written other books. She enjoys lazing on beaches, poking around in flea markets and collecting gemstones. Frequently the lore of gemstones is incorporated into her stories.

COMING IN AUGUST . . .

UNTIL THERE WAS YOU   (1-58314-028-X, $4.99/$6.50)
by Francis Ray

Best-selling author Catherine Stewart, renowned for helping troubled children, retreated to a friend's mountain cabin in Santa Fe after a traumatic assault. Once there, she couldn't resist helping others. She never thought they'd come to her aid, and she never dreamed that her roommate, Luke Grayson, would help her overcome her past and lead her to love.

A TASTE OF LOVE   (1-58314-029-8, $4.99/$6.50)
by Louré Bussey

Nia Lashon took a position as a maid at Roland Davenport's chain of Caribbean resorts in St. Croix. Roland's never believed that he could run his business and have a serious relationship. Until Nia. Now Roland is determined to give Nia the inspiration to reach her goals and the passion she's always yearned for.

FANTASY   (1-58314-030-1, $4.99/$6.50)
by Raynetta Mañees

Struggling singer Sameerah Clark landed a job on the Fantasy cruise liner, but she hadn't realized it was as back-up vocalist for singing idol Tony Harmon. She blurts out her frustration, but the fiery beauty with the melodious voice only intrigues Tony. After his invitation to sing a duet ends with a bold kiss, desire courses through Sameerah's blood.

WHEN LOVE CALLS   (1-58314-031-X, $4.99/$6.50)
by Gail A. McFarland

Thirty-something Marcus Benton had forsaken all for his career. Then, when phone lines accidentally crossed in a vicious storm, fate brought him to Davida Lawrence, a forty-year-old widowed mother. The possibility of becoming a husband and father challenged everything Marcus struggled for. Their age difference made Davida doubtful of a future together. Only by trusting in each other can two uncertain people find a forever kind of love.

SPICE UP YOUR LIFE
WITH ARABESQUE ROMANCES

AFTER HOURS, by Anna Larence   (0-7860-0277-8, $4.99/$6.50)
Vice president of a Fort Worth company, Nachelle Oliver was used to things her own way. Until she got a new boss. Steven DuCloux was ruthless—and the most exciting man she had ever known. He knew that she was the perfect VP, and that she would be the perfect wife. She tried to keep things strictly professional, but the passion between them was too strong.

CHOICES, by Maria Corley   (0-7860-0245-X, $4.95/$6.50)
Chaney just ended with Taurique when she met Lawrence. The rising young singer swept her off her feet. After nine years of marriage, with Lawrence away for months on end, Chaney feels lonely and vulnerable. Purely by chance, she meets Taurique again, and has to decide if she wants to risk it all for love.

DECEPTION, by Donna Hill   (0-7860-0287-5, $4.99/$6.50)
An unhappy marriage taught successful New York advertising agency, Terri Powers, never to trust in love again. Then she meets businessman Clinton Steele. She can't fight the attraction between them—or the sensual hunger that fires her deepest passions.

DEVOTED, by Francine Craft   (0-7860-0094-5, $4.99/$6.50)
When Valerie Thomas and Delano Carter were young lovers each knew it wouldn't last. Val, now a photojournalist, meets Del at a high-society wedding. Del takes her to Alaska for the assignment of her career. In the icy wilderness he warms her with a passion too long denied. This time not even Del's desperate secret will keep them from reclaiming their lost love.

FOR THE LOVE OF YOU, by Felicia Mason   (0-7860-0071-6, $4.99/$6.50)
Seven years ago, Kendra Edwards found herself pregnant and alone. Now she has a secure life for her twins and a chance to finish her college education. A long unhappy marriage had taught attorney Malcolm Hightower the danger of passion. But Kendra taught him the sensual magic of love. Now they must each give true love a chance.

ALL THE RIGHT REASONS, by Janice Sims   (0-7860-0405-3, $4.99/$6.50)
Public defender, Georgie Shaw, returns to New Orleans and meets reporter Clay Knight. He's determined to uncover secrets between Georgie and her celebrity twin, and protect Georgie from someone who wants both sisters dead. Dangerous secrets are found in a secluded mansion, leaving Georgie with no one to trust but the man who stirs her desires.

Available wherever paperbacks are sold, or order direct from the Publisher. Send cover price plus 50¢ per copy for mailing and handling to Kensington Publishing Corp., Consumer Orders, or call (toll free) 888-345-BOOK, to place your order using Mastercard or Visa. Residents of New York and Tennessee must include sales tax. DO NOT SEND CASH.

LOOK FOR THESE ARABESQUE ROMANCES

AFTER ALL, by Lynn Emery (0-7860-0325-1, $4.99/$6.50)
News reporter Michelle Toussaint only focused on her dream of becoming an anchorwoman. Then contractor Anthony Hilliard returned. For five years, Michelle had reminsced about the passions they shared. But happiness turned to heartbreak when Anthony's cruel betrayal led to her father's financial ruin. He returned for one reason only: to win Michelle back.

THE ART OF LOVE, by Crystal Wilson-Harris (0-7860-0418-5, $4.99/$6.50)
Dakota Bennington's heritage is apparent from her African clothing to her sculptures. To her, attorney Pierce Ellis is just another uptight professional stuck in the American mainstream. Pierce worked hard and is proud of his success. An art purchase by his firm has made Dakota a major part of his life. And love bridges their different worlds.

CHANGE OF HEART (0-7860-0103-8, $4.99/$6.50)
by Adrienne Ellis Reeves
Not one to take risks or stray far from her South Carolina hometown, Emily Brooks, a recently widowed mother, felt it was time for a change. On a business venture she meets author David Walker who is conducting research for his new book. But when he finds undying passion, he wants Emily for keeps. Wary of her newfound passion, all Emily has to do is follow her heart.

ECSTACY, by Gwynne Forster (0-7860-0416-9, $4.99/$6.50)
Schoolteacher Jeannetta Rollins had a tumor that was about to cost her her eyesight. Her persistence led her to follow Mason Fenwick, the only surgeon talented enough to perform the surgery, on a trip around the world. After getting to know her, Mason wants her whole . . . body and soul. Now he must put behind a tragedy in his career and trust himself and his heart.

KEEPING SECRETS, by Carmen Green (0-7860-0494-0, $4.99/$6.50)
Jade Houston worked alone. But a dear deceased friend left clues to a two-year-old mystery and Jade had to accept working alongside Marine Captain Nick Crawford. As they enter a relationship that runs deeper than business, each must learn how to trust each other in all aspects.

MOST OF ALL, by Louré Bussey (0-7860-0456-8, $4.99/$6.50)
After another heartbreak, New York secretary Elandra Lloyd is off to the Bahamas to visit her sister. Her sister is nowhere to be found. Instead she runs into Nassau's richest, self-made millionaire Bradley Davenport. She is lucky to have made the acquaintance with this sexy islander as she searches for her sister and her trust in the opposite sex.

Available wherever paperbacks are sold, or order direct from the Publisher. Send cover price plus 50¢ per copy for mailing and handling to Kensington Publishing Corp., Consumer Orders, or call (toll free) 888-345-BOOK, to place your order using Mastercard or Visa. Residents of New York and Tennessee must include sales tax. DO NOT SEND CASH.

ROMANCES THAT SIZZLE
FROM ARABESQUE

AFTER DARK, by Bette Ford   (0-7860-0442-8, $4.99/$6.5
Taylor Hendricks' brother is the top NBA draft choice. She wants to prote
him from the lure of fame and wealth, but meets basketball superstar Dona
Williams in an exclusive Detroit restaurant. Donald is determined to pro
that she is wrong about him. In this game all is at stake . . . including Taylo
heart.

BEGUILED, by Eboni Snoe   (0-7860-0046-5, $4.99/$6.5
When Raquel Mason agrees to impersonate a missing heiress for just o
night and plans go awry, a daring abduction makes her the captive of seducti
Nate Bowman. Together on a journey across exotic Caribbean seas to t
perilous wilds of Central America, desire looms in their hearts. But when t
masquerade is over, will their love end?

CONSPIRACY, by Margie Walker   (0-7860-0385-5, $4.99/$6.5
Pauline Sinclair and Marcellus Cavanaugh had the love of a lifetime. Ur
Pauline had to leave everything behind. Now she's back and their love is
strong as ever. But when the President of Marcellus's company turns up de
and Pauline is the prime suspect, they must risk all to their love.

FIRE AND ICE, by Carla Fredd   (0-7860-0190-9, $4.99/$6.5
Years of being in the spotlight and a recent scandal regarding her ex-fianc
and a supermodel, the daughter of a Georgia politician, Holly Aimes has turn
cold. But when work takes her to the home of late-night talk show host M
chael Williams, his relentless determination melts her cool.

HIDDEN AGENDA, by Rochelle Alers   (0-7860-0384-7, $4.99/$6.5
To regain her son from a vengeful father, Eve Blackwell places her trust
dangerous and irresistible Matt Sterling to rescue her abducted son. He accep
this last job before he turns a new leaf and becomes an honest rancher. A
they journey from Virginia to Mexico they must enter a charade of marriag
But temptation is too strong for this to remain a sham.

INTIMATE BETRAYAL, by Donna Hill   (0-7860-0396-0, $4.99/$6.5
Investigative reporter, Reese Delaware, and millionaire computer wizard, Ma
well Knight are both running from their pasts. When Reese is assigned
profile Maxwell, they enter a steamy love affair. But when Reese begins
piece her memory, she stumbles upon secrets that link her and Maxwell, a
threaten to destroy their newfound love.

*Available wherever paperbacks are sold, or order direct from th
Publisher. Send cover price plus 50¢ per copy for mailing an
handling to Kensington Publishing Corp., Consumer Order
or call (toll free) 888-345-BOOK, to place your order usin
Mastercard or Visa. Residents of New York and Tennesse
must include sales tax. DO NOT SEND CASH.*